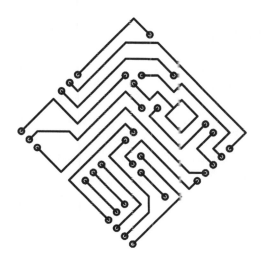

# C. S. FRIEDMAN

IN CONQUEST BORN
THE MADNESS SEASON

*The Coldfire Trilogy:*
BLACK SUN RISING
WHEN TRUE NIGHT FALLS
CROWN OF SHADOWS

THIS ALIEN SHORE

# C. S. FRIEDMAN

# THIS ALIEN SHORE

# DAW BOOKS, INC.

DONALD A. WOLLHEIM, FOUNDER

375 Hudson Street, New York, NY 10014

ELIZABETH R. WOLLHEIM
SHEILA E. GILBERT
PUBLISHERS

Book designed by Stanley S. Drate/Folio Graphics Co., Inc.

DAW Book Collectors No. 1096.

DAW Books are distributed by Penguin Putnam Inc.

First Printing, September 1998
1   2   3   4   5   6   7   8   9

DAW TRADEMARK REGISTERED
U.S. PAT. OFF. AND FOREIGN COUNTRIES
—MARCA REGISTRADA
HECHO EN U.S.A.

PRINTED IN THE U.S.A.

# ACKNOWLEDGMENTS

To have a concept for a great book is a truly exciting experience, and one every author dreams of. To have a concept for a great book that requires a lot of knowledge you don't have is a pretty overwhelming experience, and one every author dreads. To have a concept for a great book that requires a lot of knowledge you don't have, and then to locate people who not only have that knowledge, but can communicate it in plain English . . . and who don't mind spending endless hours with you discussing 28th century hacking, or Inuit linguistics or whatever else can be fitted in between courses of Chinese food or rounds of e-mail . . . well, that is what authors live for.

So thanks first and foremost to Paul Suchinder Dhillon, without whom this book simply would not exist. (Well, it might exist, but all the computer passages would be really bad, so no one would enjoy it.) Thanks for the hours of technical talk and devious plot twists and the virtual tours of hacker trails . . . couldn't have done it without you.

Thanks also to Anthony C. Woodbury of the University of Texas, whose outstanding knowledge of arctic languages finally enabled me to find those few words I needed to really make this book come to life. (Readers please note that the versions used here reflect many centuries of linguistic corruption; if the spelling is wrong or the meaning has been modified, that is artistic license on my part and not an error on his!)

Thanks also to Cordwainer Smith for a few precious sparks of inspiration which fans will no doubt recognize. He is one of the most remarkable writers of the 20th century, and one of its most bizarre imaginative artists. Yes, there is science fiction stranger than mine. Go read it. And to Oliver Sachs and Temple Grandin and all those other writers who struggle to reveal the alien landscapes inside the human brain. If my fiction is ever half so gripping as their daily truths, I will have accomplished something great.

Thanks to all those folks who kept me sane while this book was being written (or as close to sane as I ever come), most especially Paul Hoeffer, whose wonderful fan page kept my spirits up when things were darkest. And to Senji and Lisa and Tina and Fonda and Joan and Larry and Adam and most especially Chuck, whose generosity of spirit and energetic labor helped me through those last terrible weeks. There's nothing quite like trying to finish a book and pack up a seven room house full of stuff at the same time to make one truly crazed.

And thanks to Yann and Matt and Petra. They know why.

Thanks to Cheryl and Stan, for really knocking themselves out to get this book printed on time. It's much appreciated, guys.

Most of all thanks to Betsy Wollheim, for being the awesome editor-goddess she is. Not only because she is brilliant and wise and infinitely insightful, but because she didn't even yell at me *once* when this was late. Now *that* is true greatness.

# DEDICATION

This book is for my mother, Nancy Friedman, who died while it was being written.

Sometimes the most impressive acts of courage are not dramatic ones, such as we like to read about, but quieter, almost imperceptible. Sometimes they are not even recognized as such until their time is passed. My mother was a woman of such courage, and her spirit affected all who knew her.

At age 20 her heart was damaged by disease, and she was told she would not live past 30. She could have given up then and refused to live, as many do, but instead she chose to go on as though she had no deadline, as though Death did not dog her every step. Most of those who knew her never knew that anything was wrong. She would have considered it weakness to tell them.

My father was forbidden to marry her because of her illness. They married anyway.

She was told that if she tried to have a child it would kill her. She wanted a child, and so took the chance and had me. She lived. Later she risked it again, and had my brother.

Those of you who have read my other dedications know that she went with me to Hawaii to see the volcanoes. What you do not know is that everywhere there were signs warning people away from various places if they had heart problems, or respiratory distress. She had both, and at that point was dying of them. Still she ignored the signs. No mere heart disease was going to keep her from doing what she had come halfway across the world to do.

She beat the odds and lived to age 67, always refusing to give up, despite the fact that Death was only one step behind her. Even at the end she told me that one of her greatest regrets was that her illness had delayed my manuscript, because I had come to New York to take care of her. Death might threaten her, but it had no right to disrupt the lives of those she loved.

I wish she could share this book with me. I wish she could see that it came out all right.

Fiction pales before such a life.

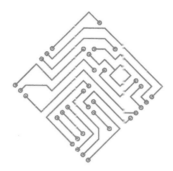

In a world where data is coin of the realm, and transmissions are guarded by no better sentinels than man-made codes and corruptible devices, there is no such thing as a secret.

DR. KIO MASADA,
*"The Enemy Among Us": Keynote address to the 121st Outworld Security Conference (holocast from Guera)*

# EARTH ORBIT
# SHIDO HABITAT

THE VOICES woke her up.

For a moment Jamisia just lay in the darkness, neither dreaming nor fully awake yet, listening. Whispers of sound tickled through her brain, coalescing into words for an instant or two, then breaking up again. Frightening words.

*Danger.*

*Betrayal.*

And one was almost a scream: *Run!*

Shaken, she sat up in bed. Her room in the Shido Habitat was reassuringly familiar, filled with all the familiar relics of her teenage years. Tickets from a concert over at Mitsui Habitat. Flowers—real flowers!—from her coming out at Microtech's Grand Pavilion. Homework chips piled up on one corner of the dresser, along with the headset that would feed their contents into her brain. All of it—her things, her life—familiar, comforting. It wasn't always that way. Sometimes she awoke to find things on her dresser that didn't (couldn't!) belong to her. Sometimes there were pieces of jewelry in her slideaway that she knew she had never bought, so alien to her taste that she could hardly imagine herself wearing them. Sometimes there were worse things, frightening things, and she threw *those* in the trash chute with shaking hands, wondering who had left them there in the middle of the night, in the room she locked so carefully before she went to bed. She kept waiting for the rightful owners to say something about their stuff, to yell at her for having chuted it without asking them . . . some kind of reaction, *anything*. But no one ever yelled. No one ever said a word, and her tentative queries to the habitat database yielded no explanation for the strange offerings, or any hint of their purpose.

It wasn't like that today; at least today everything in the room was really hers, and that should have been comforting. Only it wasn't. The voices were still clamoring inside her head, even though the act of waking up for good should have banished them. She couldn't make out most of what they were saying, but the few words she did understand—and the tone in which they were voiced—were terrifying.

*Danger!*

*Betrayed!*

*Run, Jamisia!*

Her heart began to pound, triggering her wellseeker program; bright words scrolled across the corner of her visual field, assessing her emotional state in purely biological terms. ADREN-ALINE SURGE, it informed her. PULSE RACING, B-PRESSURE ENTERING RED ZONE, PHASE ONE MUSCULAR CONTRAC-TIONS NOTED. ACTION?

Before she could answer it the door slid open, as quickly and silently as if she had never locked it. A man moved into the room, and she opened her mouth to scream—and then realized who it was and drew in a deep, shaky breath instead.

"Grab some clothes," her tutor commanded, in a tone as unlike his usual fatherly warmth as this night was unlike any other. "Take anything you value, and do it fast." He looked back toward the door as if to see if anyone was following him. By the nightlight's glow she could see there was blood on his face. "We don't have much time."

"What's going on?" She could hear her own voice shaking as she asked the question. But he only shook his head sharply, his expression grim.

"Later." He wiped a hand across his forehead, smearing the blood, then saw that she wasn't moving yet. "Do it!"

Trembling, she forced herself out of the bed and began to move to the slideaway. The message in her visual field defaulted for lack of response and blanked out, which was just as well; she couldn't think clearly enough right now to give it instructions.

"What's happening?" she begged, as she gathered up hand-fuls of clothing. Hi-G, lo-G, no-G: he hadn't said where they were going, so she grabbed a few garments from each section of the slideaway and stuffed them into her traveling bag. "Where are we going?"

"It's a raid." His voice, usually calm, was shaking now, and there was a thin sheen of sweat on his face; it was a good bet his own wellseeker was blazing its protest across his field of vision even now. "They must have had an inside contact, the alarm systems were all shut down." She reached for the headset, but he stopped her. "No. Not that. Too easy to trace."

"Who is it?" she asked him.

He hesitated an instant, and she sensed that he was struggling with the question of how much to tell her. A thin line of red had trickled down into his eye; he blinked hard to clear his vision. "I don't know. It was all too fast. Whoever it is—it's trouble, at any rate." He grabbed the bag out of her hands and snapped it shut. "Come on!"

With the voices screaming their warnings in her ears, urging her to follow him to safety, there was nothing to do but obey. She followed him out of the room and into the network of corridors beyond. When they got to the nearest tube, she started to get into it, but he grabbed her by the arm and jerked her past it. It seemed to her that she could smell something sharp in the air, carried toward them by the habitat's ventilation system. Smoke, perhaps? Was that possible? Her tutor broke into a run, his strong arm pulling her alongside him. She struggled to keep up with his pace, but his legs were so much longer than hers, it was nearly impossible; twice she almost fell What could be burning? Some few hundred yards beyond the tube he stopped to pull the cover off a maintenance crawlspace, and gestured for her to go inside. She hesitated, afraid—and then the whole floor shuddered, as if somewhere nearby something had exploded. Trembling, she clambered up to the lip of the opening and pulled herself inside. She wished that he'd let her take the headset so that she could access the habitat's monitoring programs and find out what the hell was going on . . . *but then they'd know where I was*, she thought. Chilled by the concept without knowing why. Scared, as she had never been scared before.

When he was safely inside the crawlspace, he pulled its cover shut and urged her forward; she was all too happy to move, to focus on flight as a means of shutting out the claustrophobic closeness of the mechanical tube. For what seemed like a small eternity she pulled herself along, hand over hand, on rungs that were smeared with grease, past dials and switches edged in grit. No scrubs worked here, apparently. She twisted through a turn almost too tight to negotiate and was amazed that her tutor managed to follow. Then a turn again, and a long, slow curve, following his whispered directions as quickly as she could. Once or twice it seemed she could feel the whole tunnel shudder, and once she knew from his sharply indrawn breath that somewhere on the habitat real damage had been done, probably in the name of some corporate maneuver. As her tutor would say, *Capitalism is a harsh mistress.*

Would the maintenance tubes seal themselves off if the habitat's outer shell were breached, preserving enough air for them to breathe? She didn't know. She didn't want to know. It took all her courage just to keep moving, not to think about what was going on behind them.

"Here," he muttered at last, indicating a hatchway. Together they forced it open, and she slipped through. Beyond was a darkened corridor. Why weren't the lights on? As he emerged into the corridor himself, she stamped hard on the floor several times, trying to trigger the sensors, but still it stayed dark. "Why—" she began, but her tutor shushed her. "Listen," he said. She did. There was nothing. No distant explosions now, nor any human voice. Nor . . .

Something tightened in her chest, a new kind of fear. There was no soft purr of ventilation coming from the walls, no gentle breeze of recycled air wafting across her face. Those things were so taken for granted in her world that she could never have imagined what the habitat would be like without them. Now they were gone. Which meant . . .

"No life support?" she whispered.

"Bastards," he muttered, and he grabbed her again by the arm and pulled her forward. "Come on!"

They ran. Long steps, leaping steps, made possible by the lo-G of the docking ring. Ahead of them two air locks yawned wide; he motioned her past them. "Not those." It seemed to her that over the pounding of her heart and the slap of her feet on the metal mesh flooring she could now hear something else: footsteps behind them, coming closer. Voices. Corporate raiders?

*Run!* her own voices urged, terrifying in their unity.

She ran.

By the time they reached the place where the pods were docked she was out of breath, and her legs ached from the unnatural strain of the lo-G run. She watched as her tutor readied the nearest pod for flight, noting with cold misgiving that it was a singler. He was sending her off alone, then. To where? For what?

Not alone. She wouldn't do it. She wouldn't go.

*Trust him,* the voices urged.

"Get inside, Jamie."

He was her tutor, her friend, the closest thing to a father she'd ever had. She wanted to trust him. But to go out there alone, without a word of explanation . . . "Where are you sending me?" she begged. "What's happening?"

With a muttered oath of frustration he grabbed her by the shoulders and turned her to face him. This close, she could see that the wound on his face was some kind of burn. Blood dripped from the edge of it down the side of his face, soaking into his collar.

"Listen to that!" He nodded back the way they had come, toward the voices that were steadily approaching. "They're here because they want *you,* Jamie. Do you understand? They want your brain and what's in it, and they don't care what they have to do to get it. Which is why my job was—"

He stopped suddenly. A muscle in his jaw clenched tight.

"To help me?"

His eyes met hers, then looked away. "My job was to kill you," he said hoarsely. "And God help me when Shido finds out I didn't." Gently but firmly he pushed her toward the pod. "Now go, Jamie."

Shaking, she clambered into the tiny vehicle. As she settled herself uncomfortably into its curved foam mattress, she could hear the distant sounds growing closer. Any minute now the enemy would come around the curve of the docking ring and see them. Any minute.

"Why?" she begged him.

"No time for that now." He was setting the controls on the pod manually, his head still bare of any interface. "You're carrying a program that'll explain it all to you, all in the proper time. I made sure of that."

"Where are you sending me?"

The footsteps were closer now, and shouted words could be heard to echo down the corridor. *That way! Check the locks, sir? Hurry!*

"Up-and-out," he said, keying in the final instructions. "There's a metroliner on its way out of the Sol System now; you should be able to catch up to it in this." He added hurriedly, forestalling her objection, "It's the only place you'll be safe, Jamie. Trust me."

*Trust him*, the inner voices chorused.

"I do," she choked out.

"I altered the launch records; if they manage to track you at all they'll think you went to Earth. By the time they discover that lie for what it is you'll be well out of their reach. Here's the data you'll need." He reached into the pod and pressed a small case into her hand; his own flesh was sweating. "Read through it as soon as you can, so that it's familiar to you." He hesitated, and for a moment she thought he was going to lean forward to kiss her good-bye, or pat her on the shoulder, or . . . something. But instead he reached up to the door of the tiny vehicle and began to close it. "I'm sorry, Jamie. Forgive me." He hesitated, then whispered, "Forgive us all."

The pod door snapped shut, sealing her inside the small vehicle. The voices beyond the door were muffled, as were several loud noises which followed, that might or might not have been explosions. Then absolute silence enveloped her as the air surrounding the pod was pumped out, leaving it in vacuum. She forced herself to breathe steadily as the pod began to move, feeling the mattress that surrounded her conform to her shape as the lauching programs kicked in. PHASE THREE STRESS, her wellseeker warned. ACTION?

There was a sudden jerk as the pod was launched, like being kicked in the chest with an iron shoe. The mattress cradled her, absorbing the impact. ADJUST, she told it, visualizing the key icon in her mind's eye. Deep within her brain the image triggered a flurry of electrical activity, biological and mechanical, and her brainware, which was a combination of both, took control. Her pulse slowed. Her blood pressure lowered. A thousand and one symptoms of stress released, dissolved, dissipated.

Outside the small window—a token hole no larger than her face, its purpose not to afford a useful view as much as to counteract the effect of close confinement—she could see Shido Habitat falling away behind her, its sunward surfaces gleaming with liquid brilliance. Beyond it was the blue-and-white crescent of Earth, home to nearly ten billion souls. It and its habitats were the only home she had ever known, and now she was leaving them forever. The pain of it was a cold knot in her heart, only partly ameliorated by the flood of healing chemicals her brainware had loosed into her bloodstream. She could have asked it to do more for her, but she didn't. What did a brainware network know about despair? How could it "adjust" for the nameless agony of losing everything and everyone you valued all at once, and not even knowing why?

"Oh, God," she whispered. Tears streamed down her face. TEAR DUCT OVERFLOW, the wellseeker informed her. ACTION? She wiped away the wetness with a shaking hand. There was a flash of light from the direction of Shido Habitat, but the satellite was behind her ship now, and so she couldn't make out its cause. *What's going to happen to me?* She hoped to God that her tutor was going to be okay. She knew, deep in her soul, that he wasn't.

*My job was to kill you.*

Undetected, unpursued, the tiny pod fled Earth's crowded skies, and headed toward the up-and-out.

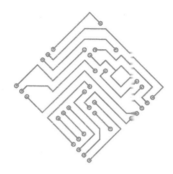

There are those who would pay a fortune to discover how our outpilots navigate the ainniq, and many have devoted their lives to trying to guess the Guild's secrets. Among such investigators there are two conflicting schools of thought:

That the skills of the outpilots are a side effect of their unique genetic heritage, and cannot be duplicated by other races.

That in fact it is some secret knowledge which makes the outships possible, and were others to discover Guera's secrets, they could perhaps duplicate her success.

Both are correct, of course.

Not that this will help them.

> GUILDMISTRESS ALMA SARAJEVO
> "A Legacy of Silence": Keynote address to the
> 274th Guildmaster; Conclave; Tiananmen
> Station

# OUTSHIP: ORION

*. . . MAYDAY . . . MAYDAY . . .*

The station was so close now that its outer surface filled the screen, the docking port a gaping black cavern just ahead of them. The inpilot trembled as he balanced controlling icons in his head, struggling to bring the freighter in line with the grappling braces. "Approach verified," he said at last. A small triumph. Three red lights on the console before him were blinking wildly, indicating systems that had gone down, but for now it looked like he had managed to work around them. Thank God for that, the freighter's captain mused. Otherwise they might as well kiss all their precious cargo good-bye, and their asses along with it.

"Clearance is . . . acceptable." The beads of sweat on the inpilot's brow had merged into a tiny rivulet that trickled down the side of his face even as the freighter slid into dock. Too fast, too close; the captain could almost hear the screech of surfaces grinding together as the braces passed mere inches to port. There were four lights blinking now on the control panel, and according to the readout the damage for all those systems originated in the outbridge. If he turned up the sound on his sensor relay he could hear noises from within that chamber, banging and screaming and a high keening sound that might or might not be of human origin. His outpilot had gone off the deep end, that was sure. The only question was how much damage he had done in this fit of his, and how much more he would get a chance to do before his Guild got him under control.

*. . . GUILD EMERGENCY IN DOCKING BAY 306 YELLOW, SUPPORT TEAM REPORT IMMEDIATELY . . . REPEAT, GUILD EMERGENCY IN DOCKING BAY 306 YELLOW . . .*

"We're in." The inpilot leaned back with a sigh as the braces took hold; the freighter shuddered briefly as they pulled it into proper alignment with the docking seals, then was still again. He tipped back his headset, letting the cool air inside the ship dry the sweat that had pooled beneath it. "Thank God."

"Yeah." There were five lights blinking now, and God help that fucking Guild bastard if any of that meant there was permanent damage to his ship. "You feed 'em the protocols. I'm going to go find out what the hell happened down there."

... *MAYDAY* ... *MAYDAY* ...

The captain could hear the seals hissing as he exited the inbridge, ship's pressure stabilizing to match that of the docking ring. At least that system was working, he thought grimly. At least his twenty-three pods of valuable merchandise had made it here in the right number of pieces, albeit they trailed out behind their lead ship like a snake with muscle spasms. It could be worse, he told himself. It could be a thousand times worse.

He also thought: *I'll kill the Guild bastard.*

The door to the outbridge was sealed, of course; Guild pilots liked their privacy. Through it, he could hear some kind of banging, and that strange, high-pitched keening. He fumbled with the code panel set to one side, feeding it an override combination. Nothing happened. *Damn!* He tried another code, a secret priority combination that should have been able to override anything on the ship. Still the damned door didn't budge. Whatever that bastard Guildsman was up to, he had locked himself in but good.

In the distance he could hear the main air lock opening now, sharp voices asking directions, footsteps approaching. Guildsmen appeared, two of them, and their expressions were anything but sympathetic. "He's locked himself inside," the captain said as they approached, trying to sound belligerent rather than frightened. These two men, with their painted faces and black Guild robes, could make or break him at will. If they decided he had mistreated his outpilot, or otherwise broken Guild contract, there'd be no more transnodal shipping contracts for him. They'd see to it that he was stuck at this fucking station till hell froze over, if not longer. "Right after we pulled in, he seemed to have some kind of fit—" One of the men pushed him roughly aside and pulled out an instrument from the folds of his robe. "He's damaged ship systems—"

The instrument flared; the control panel by the door burst into sparks and smoke. "Wait a fucking minute, that's *my* ship—" The Guildsman turned to the door, adjusted his instrument, and fired again. The solid surface began to shiver and melt and give way, until at last there was an opening large enough for a man's arm to thrust through. The Guildsman did just that. Smoke rose from his black sleeve where it rested against the door as he fumbled with something beyond that barrier, or perhaps inside it—and then it moved suddenly and he pulled back, just in time for it to open without yanking his arm off.

Inside the outbridge there was blood, blood everywhere, on the floor and the control module and even splattered across the ceiling. In the midst of it all a naked man thrashed and moaned, and it was clear now that the strange sounds picked up by the sensors had indeed come from him. He was human in shape, the captain noted, fury giving way to fascination for one brief instant. There were those who claimed that the Guerans were Variants in body as well as mind, but it sure didn't look like that with this guy. As the two Guildsmen ran to their crazed comrade and struggled to get hold of him, the captain edged closer, trying to get a better view.

The man was naked, his black uniform torn open and peeled back to reveal pallid skin. His face was painted with fine black lines according to Gueran tradition, but the pattern had been so smeared with blood that there was no making out what it was. And as for the body itself . . . that was covered with a network of crisscrossed mutilations, jagged tattoos and scarifications that depicted images out of nightmare, staring eyes and barbed wheels and a hand with blood pouring out of its center. There was real blood pouring from the man's left arm, where he had apparently ripped the skin open with his own nails and teeth, and as the first Guildsman pressed a trank gun to his neck, his inarticulate screaming at last became words, "It's inside me! They put it inside me!" Madly he struggled to claw at his arm again, to dig even deeper; the Guildsman tried to get hold of his wrist even as the tranquilizer hissed into his veins. "Got to get it out!" he sobbed.

And then the trank kicked in, and his struggles ceased. His reddened eyes turned upward, then closed. His flailing limbs shuddered, then lay limp and still. The nearer Guildsman looked up and saw the captain standing there; his painted countenance scowled.

"This is Guild business!" He stood and moved so fast that the stunned captain hardly saw it; a gloved hand slammed hard into his chest and sent him stumbling back into the corridor. The Guildsman returned to his duties then, as quietly and as calmly as if nothing had happened at all. For a moment the captain just stood there, stunned, fuming. They had no right. They had no goddamn right! But you didn't argue with Guildsmen. You just didn't. Not even when they blasted through a door of your freighter. Not even when their crazy pilot fucked up the controls of your ship, and God alone knew how bad the damage was or how much it would cost to repair. You just didn't argue with them, not ever.

They were carrying the wounded man now, wrapped in his torn black robe like a shroud. A clearflesh bandage had been slapped on his wound to stop the bleeding, but they'd have to cut it off later to fix the damage; right now the arm looked like so much shredded meat. The outpilot was muttering unintelligible things and now and then his body spasmed as if in some unspeakable agony, but on the whole the tranquilizer seemed to be working. Thank God for that, anyway.

The captain took a quick look inside the outbridge, darkly assessing the magnitude of the damage; then he hurried after the Guildsmen. They had been met by two more of their kind at the air lock, to whom they were handing over their bleeding charge. A number of the freighter's crewmen had gathered to watch, but none dared come too close; it wasn't unknown for the Guild to blacklist men who got in their way, so that no ship carrying them could ever hire an outpilot. A hell of a threat.

The Guildsman who had first entered the ship turned to the captain. "We'll have to go over his log to find out what happened. We'll let you know as soon as possible whether or not you've been cleared of responsibility."

"What about my ship?"

The Guildsman glared. His kaja-pattern, sharp and predatory, made his expression five times more fierce than a mere human glare could ever be. "He brought you through the ainniq? Back into safespace?"

"Yes, but—"

"Your cargo is intact? Your people are unharmed?"

"Yes, but the damage—"

"He satisfied Guild contract." He turned away sharply, dismissively. "The ship is your problem."

And then he was gone. They all were gone. There was only the captain and his crew left, and a few thin drops of blood marking the path the Guildsmen had taken back to their headquarters.

"Sir?"

Shaking with rage (and with fear, though he'd never admit to the latter) he turned his attention back to his crew. "Let's get this mess cleaned up before we unload," he said sharply. "You and you, see to the outbridge. You—" he pointed to his first mate, "—run a diagnostic and find out what the hell he did to our control system. Get me a printout and damage cost estimate within the hour."

"Yessir."

*Damn* the Guild. Damn their arrogance, damn their greed . . . damn, most of all, their power. That more than anything.

"Bastards," he muttered.

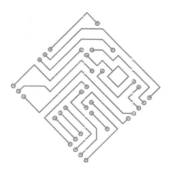

And then Mankind took his machines and he split the skies asunder, and he sent into God's heavens his ships and his machines and all the unclean things of the Earth.

He set foot upon the planets which God had not meant for his use.

He painted the heavens black with his pride and his arrogance.

He angered the Lord in those and a thousand ways, until the Lord spoke unto him, and said,

*Behold, I gave you Babel, and you did not heed My warning.*

*You built a Tower unto the skies and I divided you into myriad peoples, that you might know shame and be humbled before your God.*

*Now you build something greater than a tower, that intrudes into My very heavens.*

*Now I shall divide you again, but not merely by speech, nor by color.*

*Now you shall be not one species but many, and each shall hate and fear the others, and the seed that is shared between them shall be barren. So shall you be divided until the end of time, that you may remember My wrath.*

And he set the mark of Hausman into their flesh, so that all might know their shame. And those who were loyal to His name, who remained upon Earth, were untouched by his curse, and might bear children as they chose, for such was the sign of His favor.

*Colonies 11:21–30*

# METROLINER: AURORA

THREE DAYS in a pod. There was barely enough room to turn around, not nearly enough space to work out her cramped muscles and stretch a bit. A singler pod was meant for trips to other habitats, and maybe—just maybe—a rare jaunt to Earth. It wasn't designed for spending three days in space, and people weren't designed for spending three days in it.

Jamisia was miserable, and she was sick, and she was scared. The pod had a lo-G web, but she was afraid to turn it on, afraid that if she used too much power, the pod's limited batteries might run out and leave her stranded in the middle of nowhere. So she was weightless and she got sick and she threw up, and then she had to turn on the gravity long enough to clean out the tiny space . . . and when it was over, she floated in a tiny huddled ball at the end of the curved mattress and shivered, more afraid and more alone than she had ever imagined a person could be.

She had opened the tiny box her tutor had given her, but nothing in it looked very helpful. There was a debit chip and an ID tag—*Jamisia Capra*, they both said, with no explanation—and some brainware specs on a card (likewise with no explanation) and half a dozen other small things, including an infochip for the captain of the metroliner, and a similar one for her. The pod's headset could have translated them for her, but she was afraid to use it, afraid that it would send out some kind of signal so that others could follow her. There was a pendant on a chain with a strange linear design etched into it, and at first she thought it was an icon, so she ran her eyes over it again and again, from one end to the other and then back again, in every direction she could think of. But nothing happened. Maybe it was the key to some program that had never gotten loaded into her brainware, she thought. Or maybe she needed some kind of personal passkey to make it work, which her tutor had intended to give her, but he'd never had the chance. Or maybe it was just some kind of weird gift, the kind of thing you gave someone you cared about when you weren't going to see them for a long time. A kind of amulet. She put the thin chain around her neck and pushed the pendant down into her shirt, so that it wouldn't float up and hit her in the face when she moved.

She managed to eat something from the pod's no-G stores, a packet of orange mush "guaranteed to keep forever." It was tasteless. She managed to urinate into the waste tube properly, and to get it all tucked away without spilling anything, even though her hands were shaking. She wept until there were no tears left inside her, and then she wept dry until her body and soul were so exhausted that she just lay there in the darkness, floating, too tired even to fear any more. Her wellseeker offered to help her out—it practically insisted—but she turned it down. She needed the outlet, the raw outpouring of fear that crying provided. Brainware could dull the edge of that fear, but it couldn't attack its cause. Only she could do that.

At last, exhausted, she slept.

(ICON CONFIRMED)
DREAMSCAPE 1.000 LOADING

. . .

RUN

*Green grass. Blue skies. Colors brilliant, like crystal. Overhead the sky seems endless, not like the sky in a viddie of Earth, but rich with secret depths, dizzying in its utter vastness. Likewise the clouds are alien things, and she watches in amazement as they morph from one shape to another, ten thousand times more subtle than any mere viddie could render. She looks down at the land— green, so green!—and then sees a stream in the distance. She begins to walk toward it. Its water runs clear, not yet choked with the specially designed algae that crowded Earth relies upon for oxygen.*

*She savors the crisp sound the water makes as it gushes over rocks, the feel of the thick grass and the moist dirt giving way beneath her feet as she walks, even the pressure of the hi-G system pulling her downward. Alien sensations, each and every one. And yet . . . there are no smells here, she realizes. How odd. You would expect a place like this to smell clean, or damp, or earthy, or . . . something.*

*Then she sees the man.*

*He is standing by the bank of the stream. At first his back is to her, but as she comes nearer, he turns so that she can see his face. It's her tutor, she realizes, but he doesn't look the same as when he put her in the pod. This is a younger version of the same man, a thinner version, tanned as if from some outstation sun.*

*He recognizes her, nods her a welcome, and says, in a voice so calm it seems out of place in these fantastic surroundings, "East coast of North America, circa 1940."*

*She begins to study the details of the place, knowing she'll be tested later. But rather than going on with the lesson, he walks up to her, very close, and puts his hand beneath her chin to cradle it upward, gently. His eyes are brown and warm and it calms her to look into them. For a moment—one precious second—the fear in her heart subsides. She trusts this man.*

*"Jamisia." In all their years together he's rarely used her formal name; that he does so now gives his words special weight. "If you're running this dreamscape, then the worst has happened. Shido has been destroyed, or else you've chosen to flee them. There'll be people trying to find you soon, and you don't dare let them get hold of you. No matter what anyone may promise, no matter how frightening the alternatives may seem, once you've made the commitment to flight, you've got to keep away from them at any cost." He pauses. "Do you understand?"*

*For a moment she can't find her voice to respond. She is remembering what her tutor once explained about dream programming, how it's the kind of thing you use when you're afraid that your subject will try to escape what you have to say. Brainware won't accept new input during dreamtime—for its own protection—so a dreaming brain lacks the kind of conscious control system the waking brain is accustomed to. She can't shut this program down. She can't run away. If the program was designed well enough, she can't even wake herself up.*

What kind of information would be so unpleasant that he can only pass it on to her like this? She can't even imagine. But because it's a habit to do well in his eyes—even if the "he" is only a dream-image—she draws herself up as bravely as she can and says, with only the faintest tremor in her voice, "Tell me."

The tutor-figure nods his approval. "You've been the subject of an experiment, Jamisia, highly unorthodox and hellishly illegal. I'm not going to give you all the details now, because . . . quite frankly, I hope you won't ever need them. Right now we need to deal with the more practical aspects of your current dilemma. The fact that you're running this program means you have the materials I've prepared, including a false set of I.D. The last name's private, not corporate, so it implies no more than a distant relationship to others using it. You'll have to keep your own first name, I regret; there's risk in that, but far less than you would take on if you changed it." He pauses. "Names have power in your life, Jamisia; don't change yours unless you absolutely have to."

She breathes: "I won't."

"Your brainware processor is an experimental model and its signature will be unique; anyone who's searching for you now will know to watch for it. I've loaded a masking program which will give it a false signature—that of a Hauck 9200—the specs for which are on the card I gave you. Memorize them. Be aware that your real storage capacity exceeds Hauck's best by 1000%, your speed is five times that of the current market leader, and your multitasking capability—" He stops suddenly. "Well, that had to be high. Be aware of those differences. Disguise your true capacity. Whoever's after you will know to look for those signs."

She finds that she is shivering, though the dreamscape feels neither warm nor cold. "Why? Why do they want me so badly?"

For a moment her tutor hesitates. It isn't the pause of a man giving thought to her question, but the downtime of a program accessing its data stores. On what will it base its response? What parameters did her tutor design into it, to define the limits of this briefing? "Your brainware alone makes you valuable," he says at last. "As for the rest of it . . . they hurt you, Jamisia. I know you don't remember the details, but trust me, they did. They wanted to see what would happen to a human brain under certain conditions, and they used you like a guinea pig to find out. Now that you're *away from them, I think there's a chance that what they did to you will heal over time of its own accord, and you may never require knowledge of what it was. God willing.'*

*"What did they do?" she demands.*

*The figure shakes his head. "No, Jamisia. Not now. Once you learn the truth there'll be no going back, and you have enough to deal with right now. If the time comes when you need to have that information, there are dreams in this program set that will give it to you. For now, study the chip I gave you It contains details of your new identity, as well as a story to explain your sudden departure from Earth. You may need to alter the latter to suit your current circumstances; I had no way of knowing what the exact conditions of your flight would be when I compiled it." The figure pauses. "I tried to anticipate this day as thoroughly as I could, Jamisia, to give you the tools you would need the most. But as I program this dreamscape now, I have no way of knowing how old you'll be when you trigger it, or how successful Shido will have been in altering the natural patterns of your brain."*

*"What did Shido do?" she demands. She can hear an edge of hysteria coming into her voice and wonders if the dream-tutor will respond to it. "Tell me!"*

*But the figure only shakes his head slowly, sadly. "Trust me, Jamisia. Trust my judgment."*

*And then he's gone. As suddenly as a viddie image that's been canceled, terminated in an instant as the channel is changed. The suddenness of it leaves her stunned for a moment, and by the time she can think clearly again, the dreamscape itself is beginning to fade. "No," she whispers, and then more loudly: "No!" Clouds bleed into sky, bleed out into nothingness; she struggles to take control of them, to call them back, but they defy her. She tries to awaken her brainware with an icon so that it can help her . . . but the programs accept no input while the body is in sleep-state. The grass is gone now, the water, too, even the ground that she stands on. Sleep is twining like a serpent through her brain preparing her for more natural dreams.*

*Don't leave me! she screams silently.*

END PROGRAM

She was miles away when she first saw the metroliner, and despite the fact that she knew what to expect—or thought she did—still it took her breath away to see it spread out before her like that, not a viddie reproduction but the real thing. It was vast, in the way that the Earth seemed vast when viewed from a habitat window. It was a thing out of fantasy, a creature out of the depths of space that seemed almost alive in its form, so utterly unlike a ship that for a short time her fears were all forgotten, and she pressed her face against the window like a small child seeing Earth for the first time.

At its head was a vast curved dish, so like the cap of a jellyfish in shape and proportion that she half-expected to see it quiver, gathering up the essence of the surrounding darkness to spurt it out for propulsion. Behind that flowed the body of the ship proper: first the stocky core that housed its command center, then strands of domiciles and storage pods and vast curving boulevards where all manners of human intercourse might take place. They twined about each other in loose spirals, the space about and between them webbed with transport tubes and flyways and delicate crystalline spheres that glittered as her pod flew past them. All in all it seemed more like some vast, eerie creature dredged up from the bottom of Earth's ocean than a man-made transport vessel, and she found herself holding her breath as her pod drew closer to it, half expecting it to shiver to life as she watched.

She could see glittering spires now, studding the outer surface of one of the spiraling tendrils. On another were a series of domes, brightly colored, and flyways whose clear walls glittered with light. Closer in to the main body of the ship, where the tendrils merged, was a section of squatter, more prosaic structures, hi-G designs that reminded her of pictures she had seen of Earth's surface. Was this where passengers stayed who feared the infinite emptiness of space, so that they could barricade themselves in stocky constructions reminiscent of their homeland and ignore the glorious open vista beyond? As a child of the habitats she had no such fear, and for a brief moment she wondered what a person who did was even doing in space. But the lure of Guild space was not to be denied. Once a person had traveled to the nearest ainniq, he would have access to all the stations of the up-and-out, nearly fifty thousand by current count. Factories and habitats and merchant rings and mansion spheres scattered throughout space with neither star nor planet to mark their position, gathered about the nodes where the ainniq intersected so that the outpilots could find them. Who wouldn't brave their deepest fears to gain access to that universe?

*I'll be there soon*, she thought in wonder. *I'll be part of that system.* She pressed her face to the tiny window, trying to see beyond the bulk of the metroliner, to the vast dark reaches beyond. Could she see the ainniq from here, if she tried hard enough? They said it was all but invisible until you were right on top of it, but she tried anyway. She knew where it was from her outspace lessons, and she located the stars that bordered it, but between them all she saw was the endless blackness of normal space. Maybe when they were closer, she thought. Maybe she could see it then, if she looked right.

With a lurch the pod dropped suddenly downward, a direction that hadn't even existed mere moments before. She grabbed a restraining strap quickly enough to keep herself from slamming into the padded interior of the pod. She could feel the great ship's G-field taking hold now, and her stomach lurched as it struggled to adjust. No doubt there would have been a gentler approach available when Earth's emigrants first came here, a fine gradation of gravities designed to ease the transition for dirt born travelers, but by now the costly docking mechanisms would have been shut down for the journey. She caught sight of a new dome outside the window—this one filled with a vast, madly twisted tree—as she grabbed for the pod's small headset, which had been knocked from its pad by the jolt. She caught it and stuffed it hurredly into its slideaway. She had finally used it to read her tutor's chip, memorizing the information it scrolled across her field of vision. Now, as she hurriedly packed away those few items which were still free in the pod, she ran the details of the identity he had created through her head over and over again, trying to become comfortable with them. Her tutor hadn't warned her about presentation, but she sensed that *how* she offered up her story would matter every bit as much to these people as *what* she said. Hopefully if she repeated it often enough it would become second nature to her, and the new family name that he had given her would become so familiar that she would answer to it without hesitation.

Heart pounding, palms sweating, she settled herself at last into the landing harness and buckled the heavy straps about her body. Symbols were blurring across the holo screen on the cabin wall, but the docking program was fully automatic, so she didn't bother to read them. If something was wrong, the pod would let her know. Her wellseeker sensed her agitation and once more offered to correct it; after a minute she let it do so, and felt the fevered pounding in her chest slowly calm to a more normal rhythm. It was a superficial correction—the fear inside her was not to be banished so easily—but it was comforting nonetheless.

Would they accept her story, this metroliner crew, and let her join the wealthy passengers who were sealed within the great ship? Were the funds acknowledged on her chip enough to pay for her passage? And if so . . . what then?

She couldn't even imagine what kind of future awaited her in this place. As for what lay beyond . . . that was too alien to contemplate. *One day at a time*, she told herself. Her hand closed tightly about the amulet with its dreamscape icon. *One day at a time . . .*

DATAFILE SUMMARY: JAMISIA CAPRA
ID# 093-61-7779-8080-921F/TERRA

BIOLOGICAL PARENTS: SELISE CAPRA, JON STEVAR
SOCIAL PARENTS: SAME AS ABOVE
DATE OF BIRTH: 1.11.37
PLACE OF BIRTH: SOL CITY, U.S.N.A.
GENETIC CLASSIFICATION: 18N23/1.004T/XA305/2/3.9/40A80759-
     2

ACTIVE INFECTIOUS CONDITIONS: NONE
LATENT INFECTIOUS CONDITIONS: NONE
EXTERNAL MEDICATION: NONE

INTERNAL MEDICATION (LATENT): PDS12, PANASOL, ENDOSTIM,
  CONTRA-5
GENETIC ALTERATION (INDICATE PURPOSE):

   L190 SEQUENCE CORRECTED (INSULIN REGULATOR)
   AN28 AND 31 CORRECTED (NEURAL DECAY PREDISPOSITION)

PSYCHOLOGICAL CLASSIFICATION: NORMAL
BIOLOGICAL, PSYCHOLOGICAL, OR BIOTECH CONDITIONS WHICH
  WOULD LIMIT OR DELAY ADAPTATION TO A LO-G OR NO-G
  ENVIRONMENT: NONE

NOTES:

SELISE CAPRA AND JON STEVAR KILLED IN TRANSPORT ACCIDENT
3.12.53. DAUGHTER JAMISIA CAPRA WITHOUT LIVING RELATIVES ON
EARTH. REQUEST TRANSPORT TO AINNIQ SO THAT SHE CAN JOIN
REMAINING FAMILY ON HARMONY STATION.

APOLOGY FOR LACK OF CUSTOMARY PREPARATION. METROLINER IN
TRANSIT AT TIME OF ACCIDENT. TRAUMA COUNSELORS CAUTION
STRONGLY AGAINST WAITING FOR NEXT PASS, 6 YEARS FUTURE. WE
BEG YOUR ACCOMMODATION.
ARNEL KOHEIN, EXECUTOR
KOHEIN & SANGH, INC.

DEBIT CODES FOLLOW

There were tests, of course. There had to be.

 . . . *Over one hundred communicative diseases which must be
weeded out at this point, so sorry miss, but you wouldn't want to
spend three years traveling to the ainniq only to have the Guild
refuse you transport, would you?*

There were questions.

 . . . *Do your relatives know you're coming? Will they take responsibility for you? Do you have enough funds/programs/implants to
support yourself while you search for them?*

There were memories.

 . . . *Must be in here somewhere, keep digging . . . sixteen days
now . . . no, the others are dead, whole weight of the building on*

*'em, crushed so bad we can't even I.D. the remains until the DNA comps come in . . . not anyone left alive here, I'm sure of that . . . sixteen days! . . . back up the shovels, boys, we're calling it a day. . . .*

There were, as always, voices.

*Fucking assholes!* one raged.

*. . . necessary . . .* another cautioned.

*. . . They have no right!* the first insisted.

And a wail from the hidden depths inside her, half sound and half pure agony: *What now, what now WHAT NOW. . . ?*

"Shut up," she whispered, as she tried to say the right things, do the right things, be the person that her tutor's chip had described so she could earn her way into the up-and-out. There was no time to think about anything else yet. No time to mourn. But those things would come later. Oh, yes.

And then . . .

A validation chit, placed in her hand. A tiny apartment, that opened to her thumbprint. An access code for the library, the commissary, the bank. . . .

*We made it*, one of the voices whispered. *We're safe now.* Strangely, it seemed to be talking to her. Usually the voices didn't do that. Usually they only talked to each other, and referred to her—if at all—like she was an uninvited guest.

It was jarring. A bit frightening. And also, in a strange way, comforting.

"I hope so," she whispered back.

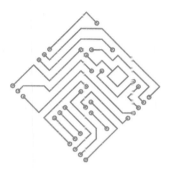

The more complex our security becomes, the more complex our enemy's efforts must be.

The more we seek to shut him out, the better he must learn to become at breaking in.

Each new level of security that we manage becomes no more than a stepping-stone for he who would surpass us, for he bases his next assault upon our best defenses.

It is a war that can never truly be won . . . but one we dare not lose.

DR. KIO MASADA
"The Evolution of Conflict" (Journal of
Outernet Security, Vol. 57, No. 8)

# GUERA

IT TOOK Dr. Kio Masada nearly two hours to paint his face for the day. He preferred to take that much time when he could, to work with care and patience until every line was perfect, until the symmetry and the proportion of his chosen design were utterly without flaw. It wasn't an easy task. The human face is an asymmetrical creation, and while subtle variations in the sweep of an eyebrow or the curve of a nostril might go unobserved by a casual aquaintance, they were all too clear to the programming specialist as he labored single-mindedly on his work. He knew each jarring element of his canvas by heart, and hated them each even as his kohl-stick labored to distract and correct. He had once considered having his facial flaws surgically corrected in order to facilitate his daily painting, but he now understood that such imperfections were a vital part of his cosmetic ritual, that the rush of satisfaction he felt as his human intellect overcame the restrictions set by nature would be a sad and meager thing if the marks of nature were erased by a surgeon's scalpel.

At last, satisfied, he stood back and regarded his handiwork. His mocha skin was just light enough in color to let the black design stand out, just dark enough that as he shifted position, the lines seemed to fade in and out of shadow, a pleasing quality. He had chosen the *iru* as always—that was necessary for any kind of social intercourse—but had supported that primary design with lesser patterns from the *kita* and the *nanango*. It was a combination he had come up with years ago, and it had served him so well that he had once considered having it tattooed on his face for good, to save himself the time and effort of this morning ritual. But the thought of the fine black lines blurring with age was more than he could bear, and the concept of a foreign hand taking responsibility for the difficult design—perhaps misjudging one line out of twenty by an infinitesimal amount, disfiguring him for life—was equally abhorrent. Better by far to take the time himself, and bear responsibility for what others saw in him.

The rest of his image was more difficult to judge. He had been called handsome by some, but lacked any real insight into what features were responsible for that appraisal. He was of medium height for Guera, which put him at slightly taller than average for most colonies. His body was fit—he saw to that with the same compulsive perfectionism that was his professional trademark—but if there was some subtle quality in the balance of bone and muscle that added up to *beauty*, he was incapable of discerning it. He dressed plainly, comfortably, oblivious to the fashions of the day, and took no care with his thick black hair other than to keep it short enough for comfort. If the fine silver lines fanning out from his temples drew attention to his dark eyes, if the short beard that he affected framed his face to advantage, those qualities were purely accidental; he neither understood nor cultivated their appeal.

He blinked twice to call up his daily itinerary, shutting his eyes to give the words more clarity as they scrolled across his field of vision. This afternoon he had a variety of meetings scheduled, mostly connected with the university's upcoming graduation ceremony. There was only one event assigned to the morning period. *GUILD*, the notation said. Just that. He could have flashed an icon to bring up the details, but it wasn't necessary. The request was so unusual, the meeting so utterly out of sync with his usual routine, that he was unlikely to forget it.

The Outspace Guild wanted to see him. Him! Try as he might, he could guess at no reason for it. He had done work for them several times, most recently by designing a new set of antibody programs—their archival net was a constant target for data thieves—but that was years ago, and since then there had been no contact. What did they want with him now? Not a simple upgrade of his last program; that could have been requested by vidlink, as could any one of a number of other services. Even if they had a request sensitive enough that they didn't want to entrust it to the public datastream, they could have implanted that into a simple courier, biological or mechanical. Why would they send a Guild officer out to Guera itself, a trip of some six months' duration, just to meet with him?

With a sigh he dropped his briefcase into the delivery chute, coding it to meet up with him later. There was no way to anticipate the Guild, and he wasn't about to waste time trying. Another kaja might might have attempted it—a *simba* perhaps, obsessed with issues of dominance, or a *yakimi*, delighting in speculation for its own sake—but the *iru* whose pattern he wore took no pleasure in such pointless mental exercises. Already his mind was focusing on other things, more important things, and by the time his office door slid shut behind him he could hardly even remember why it was that the meeting had concerned him.

The walk from his apartment complex to the university's conference center took him across a narrow bridge that spanned nearly a quarter of a mile. Its clear walls allowed a breathtaking view of Guera's capital city, and he had allotted himself several minutes to stop and appreciate the view. Beneath him the university sprawled, five hundred acres that housed the best minds on the planet; its sweeping glass bridges and crystalline spires glittered in the morning sun like jewels, in places too brilliant to gaze upon. Beyond that, about that rose the sleek mirrored skyscrapers of Guera's capital city. When the sky was clear and the angle of the sun was right whole buildings seemed to fade into the atmosphere, clouds moving from open air to mirrored wall and back again without any visible juncture. He loved to watch them. He was proud to watch them, proud to be part of a colony which had the time and the drive to create such things. Most of all he was proud of the special vision which fate had vouchsafed him, which gave his eyes the power to see the fractal dance of each cloud formation, the infinite mathematical complexity which bonded each moment to the next.

Guera had been lucky, there was no denying that. If the colonists who set their eyes upon its fertile shores had postponed their emigration by so much as a decade, history might have been very different. As he walked, Dr. Masada flashed an icon to bring up Ode of Thanksgiving before his eyes. The strangely bittersweet verses scrolled through his vision, poetry nearly three hundred years old now but no less powerful for its age.

Though many of the sentiments it expressed were obscure to him and would remain so—he lacked the emotional template to make them meaningful—the poem was nonetheless effective in praising the fate which had brought Guera to supremacy, even as it mourned what that same fate had done to so many others. *Let Hausman be our Lucifer*, it urged, *born lustrous and pure, replete in beauty, now fallen to fix the pattern of man's fate.*

Hausman. The name had been revered once, in the dawn of man's stellar affairs. When Victor Hausman had first developed his famous ship, making superluminal travel possible at last, it had seemed a timely miracle. Overcrowded, overstressed, Earth's trillions had embraced the dream of galactic expansion as a glorious panacea to their ills, and rushed to establish colonies on any and every planet within reach. Guera had been among the first such settlements. By the time Earth discovered that the same scientific miracle which had allowed men to race with light also worked irreparable genetic damage on anyone making that journey, Masada's ancestors were nearly self-sufficient. The sudden withdrawal of Earth's support was an inconvenience for them, but not a disaster. It wasn't like that for most other colonies. Some were still struggling to tame inhospitable worlds when the news came out, and they desperately needed Earth's help to survive. Some had been established so recently that they hadn't yet received their full quota of start-up supplies when their link with Earth was suddenly—and irrevocably—cut short.

God alone knew how many were still out there, Dr. Masada thought. God alone knew what shapes they wore, those forgotten children of Earth, or what manner of fury they harbored toward the motherworld that had abandoned them. The sad part was, it could have been otherwise. Earth could have relied upon machines to maintain contact, at least until the colonies had what they needed to survive. But Terran mobs had willed it otherwise. Terrified by a science that tampered with the very codes of heredity, betrayed—as they saw it—by administrations who had promised escape to virgin and uncrowded worlds, only to suddenly withdraw that hope, they reacted in true Earth fashion. What was it to them if half a million colonists were marooned on foreign worlds, each carrying the mutated seed that might give birth to monsters? Those poor souls were doomed no matter what happened. What mattered now was making sure that no Hausman Variants could ever come back to Earth to infect the human gene pool, and the mobs saw to that. Not efficiently, but effectively. Such is the power of violence.

It took him little over half an hour to complete his walk, and he had timed the journey so perfectly that he entered the conference center at the precise moment he had planned. The room which his visitor had chosen for their meeting was unfamiliar to him, but his brainware contained a set of floor plans for every building in the university, and thus he had no difficulty finding it. It was a small room, suitable for no more than a handful of guests, and he nodded his silent approval as the door slid open to receive him. The *iru* does not do well in crowds.

"Dr. Masada." There was only one man in the small room, and he rose as Masada entered. He was Guild through and through, from the intricate black lines of the *natsiq*-kaja which swept across his forehead to the full black robes which obscured the lines of his body. "Thank you for coming." In addition to the *natsiq*, which was a traditional design for both outpilots and the men who served them, he wore the delicately refined pattern of the *nantana*. It was the mark of a man who communicated with such finesse that each word, each expression, could contain volumes of information, and as such it was a kaja that Masada despised. He recalled that it was the custom of the *nantana* to begin important conversations with a period of small talk, a discussion of unimportant issues during which time patterns of gesture, tones of expression, and a hundred other subtle variables might be judged. The *iru* had no skill at such games, no patience for them, and—fortunately—no societal obligation to indulge them. (Praise the founders of Guera for that! Who in their wisdom had established an order of precedence for the kaja, so that strangers of alien mien might converse without confusion.)

"You called for me," Masada said shortly, and because he didn't feel like standing, he took a seat. "Why?"

The Guildsman hesitated. Most likely his *nantana* spirit was ill prepared for such a sudden immersion in business matters, and it took him a few seconds to switch gears. "The Guild has a job to offer you," he said at last. "The pay would be excellent and we believe the work would interest you."

"When?"

It seemed to take the Guildsman a moment to understand him. Perhaps he had expected a different question; the *nantana* liked to anticipate. "You would need to begin as soon as possible. I regret that it would require your leaving the university for a time—"

"I have obligations."

The Guildsman shook his head. "Your classes are all but finished. You have a paper to present at Graduation Seminar, which you've nearly completed; it could be read by a colleague. You have three advisees to lead through their final application process; the Registrar assures me that others can handle that. Aside from attending the graduation ceremony itself—a purely ceremonial appearance—that accounts for everything, does it not?"

Masada said nothing. He visualized an icon to awaken his brainware, which quickly analyzed the time and effort required for the Guild to obtain such information without his passcodes. Impressive.

"Why?" he said at last.

The Guildsman pulled out a chair and settled into it; his full sleeves fell upon the tabletop as he leaned forward, his posture stiff with tension. "One hundred and ninety E-days ago, a Guild outpilot was badly injured while returning to safespace. Analysis of his personal log shows there was a malfunction in his brainware at the moment of transition. It lasted only seconds, but that was long enough. In that instant he believed himself to be an alien creature, surrounded by beings whose brains didn't function like his own. He believed that these beings had fed programs into his brainware which would make it impossible for him to think clearly, and that they had surgically implanted a mechanism in his arm which would feed drugs into his bloodstream, altering the very essence of his identity. With only seconds in which to act, he did what he could to disable the perceived mechanism, and then attempted to smash his skull open so that he could tear out his wiring. Fortunately for him, the latter effort failed."

"Since his basic assumptions were correct," Masada said evenly, "I find it hard to comprehend your objection to them."

The Guildsman shook his head. "That moment of awareness should never have happened, Dr. Masada. You know the kinds of programs we use. You know how finely tuned they are. The moment he exited from the ainniq there should have been enough medication injected into his bloodstream to counteract any paranoid episode. Only there wasn't. There was a delay. And that delay was deadly."

"He was himself," Masada said quietly. "For one moment longer than perhaps you would have liked, he saw the world through unaltered eyes. Is that a crime?"

"He was *infected*," the Guildsman retorted. "Our people have isolated a programming virus they think was responsible, and they believe they know when and where he picked it up. What they don't know is where it came from. That's why we need you."

A virus. That was interesting. A virus implied origin, context . . . and purpose. Who would want to disable an outpilot? And why? People might hate the Guild—most did—but who would risk being blacklisted for life, just to hurt one of their pilots? Not any people who had stations in the outlands; the risk of being cut off from the ainniq was too terrible even to contemplate. Some isolated planet, perhaps? But no, there were none who were so independent of the Guild system that they could afford to risk complete isolation. Even Earth, a full three years' distant from the nearest transport line, had a host of commercial interests which would collapse if the outworlds became inaccessible.

So perhaps a single programmer was responsible. Some would-be terrorist perhaps, or a hyperactive prankster. There had certainly been enough of both in recent history. But a terrorist would have declared his intentions by now, and as for an amateur effort . . . the level of sophistication required in this case made such a source highly unlikely. The Guild's antibody programs were among the best in the outworlds—Masada knew, having helped design them—and besides, for a virus to attack an outpilot's brainware like that, it would have to have detailed knowledge of the programs it was infecting. Who would have

access to that kind of knowledge besides the Guild itself? It was
an intriguing puzzle.

"Why me?" he said at last.

The Guildsman leaned back slightly, as if this new phase in
their negotiations required some new posture. "We need someone from outside the Guild. Partly for a new perspective, but
mostly . . ." His lips tightened; a muscle along the line of his
jaw tensed. "The creator of this virus will have to be punished,
severely enough that no one is tempted to follow in his footsteps.
Whether it's one man or a group of men responsible—or even an
entire planet—the Guild will cut them off from all contact with
the human worlds for as long as they exist. That isn't going to
be a popular move, Dr. Masada, as I'm sure you can imagine.
We've blacklisted men before, but never on such a scale. Before
taking such a drastic step we need to be absolutely sure who
we're punishing and why . . . and we need to have the justice in
this matter clear enough that no questions are raised regarding
our motives, or the nature of our investigation. We need an outsider of impeccable reputation, someone whose work is respected
throughout the human realms, someone whose kaja is incapable
of subterfuge. In short, Dr. Masada, we need you."

"I'm Gueran," he reminded the man. "And Guera and
the Guild are synonomous, as far as many are concerned.
Wouldn't you be better off with a true outsider, whose allegiance
wouldn't be questioned?"

"Indeed we would. But whoever does this work for us must
have access to the Guild's own files, and there are no 'true outsiders' we would trust with that. So we compromise." He
paused. "You've earned our highest security clearance, Dr. Masada. You helped design the very programs we're fighting to protect. And the *iru* is known for its objectivity. Who could we
possibly find more qualified than you?" When Masada said
nothing, he pressed, "Are you interested?"

As always, the *nantana*'s insistence on questioning the obvious irritated him. "What are the conditions?"

"You'll have full access to the details of our own investigation, and to the Guild members in charge. You can have an assistant if you want—"

Another *nantana*? God forbid. "I work alone."

The Guildsman bowed his head. "As you wish. Needless to say, all your expenses will be covered, all equipment you require will be supplied, any support which you request will be provided. And of course, being part of the outernet, you'll have access to unlimited data—"

Masada stiffened. "Part of the outernet?"

For a moment the Guildsman was silent. No doubt he was digesting Masada's statement, perhaps even running it through his brainware to isolate the cause of his objection. At last he said, "It was assumed that you would come to the outworlds. An investigation like this can hardly be managed with a sizable time lag in communication."

He said it quietly, firmly: "I have never left Guera."

The Guildsman spread his hands as if in offering. "Then this is a very special opportunity, Dr. Masada. One long overdue, for a theorist of your stature."

Leave Guera. He'd considered it before, when professional opportunities beckoned, but each time he had chosen to stay where he was. It was the easier course. More comfortable. Safer. Could the *nantana* understand that? Or would Masada have to find words to express his misgiving, to give it parameters?"

After a very long silence, he dared, "You're asking me to work among aliens."

The Guildsman drew in a sharp breath. "If you mean the Hausman Variants, let me remind you that you are one, Dr. Masada. As am I. The fact that our ancestors didn't suffer from any somatic distortion doesn't mean they weren't altered. You of all people should know that."

He shook his head, frustrated by the man's lack of understanding. "I didn't mean that. You should know I didn't mean that." Now it was his turn to lean forward on the table, not because it felt natural to him—such posturing never did—but because he knew intellectually that it would give his words more weight. "Must I remind you how the Terrans feel about my kaja? The very cognitive style which makes me so valuable on Guera is considered 'abnormal' among those people. They did everything they could to eradicate it from their gene pool, and if by some unlucky chance it surfaces now despite those efforts, they use drugs or DNA therapy to 'correct' it. Even if the price of that correction is the crippling of a mind, the death of a unique human soul. These are the people you want me to work among? The Terrans are more alien to me than any Hausman Variants ever could be. And you know they dominate the outworlds."

"Dr. Masada." The Guildsman's tone had changed in some subtle way, but Masada lacked the skill to interpret it. "You're a Holist—some say the father of Holism. Don't you want to see the outworlds for yourself? You've been theorizing about the outernet for years; don't you want to experience it for yourself, just once? I'm offering you that opportunity. Can you look at me and honestly say that it has no appeal?"

When Masada said nothing, he reached into a fold of his sleeve and brought forth a small data chip. "We ask only that you look at this." He slid the chip across the table until it was within Masada's reach. "No more." Through its thin cover the spectral shimmer of a storage disk could be seen. "It contains a copy of the virus we isolated, as well as our offer. We ask only that you consider both before you make your final decision."

For a moment Masada said nothing. Did nothing. Then, very slowly, he reached out and took the small chip in his hand. Tiny words shimmered on its surface, along with an icon meant to trigger defensive programs in any equipment reading it. *WARNING*, it said. *GRADE A CONTAGIOUS MATERIAL. LEVEL 1 PRECAUTIONS REQUIRED.* He considered for a moment, then said, "I'll need a copy of the code it was embedded in."

The Guildsman scowled, and for a moment Masada thought he might refuse his request. He had, after all, asked for a copy of one of the Guild's most secret programs. Never mind that the request was a valid one; it was also a test of how much they trusted him, and how much they wanted him on this project.

For a long minute the Guildsman said nothing, merely gazed at him through narrowed eyes as if that expression could give him access to the man's brain. Finally, with a short, stiff nod, he pulled a second chip out of his sleeve and slid it across the table. It was the proper answer, and Masada nodded his approval.

"How much time do I have?" Masada asked.

"As much as you require." The Guildsman's tone made it clear that he understood the first phase of their negotiations was now complete. Either the virus would prove interesting enough to lure Kio Masada from his Gueran refuge, or it would not; mere words could no longer change that. "Take your time. Evaluate the situation. Our offer is on the first chip, along with instructions for contacting me. I'll wait to hear from you."

He stood then, and offered his hand. Masada hesitated only briefly, then clasped it. Such contact with strangers was uncomfortable for him, but the Guildsman was *nantana* and would require ritual closure. In matters like this his kaja had precedence.

*It's a small price to pay,* Masada mused, *for a social structure that enables aliens to communicate.*

If only the outworlds were equally civilized!

He didn't return to his apartment until after all the day's obligations had been dealt with, because he knew himself all too well; once he got wrapped up in some new cognitive puzzle he was likely to forget mundane things like meetings, and deadlines, and even meals. Once, when he had been in the middle of a particularly difficult project, he had even shut down part of his brainware because its constant reminders of an upcoming faculty session were distracting him.

It had been hard not to think about the Guild's offer for so many hours. Hard not to put on a headset and upload the small chip he carried, to get a look at the virus responsible for it. Only the fact that such rashness might prove downright suicidal enabled him to make it through the day, to wait until he returned to the one place on Guera where he could work undisturbed, and in safety.

His apartment was small and neat, furnished simply and without aesthetic fanfare. In the corner of the living room a three-tiered keyboard loomed, sleek and polished, and as he entered, he went over to it and put a hand to it: gently, reverently, as the ancient Jews had done when they touched their fingers to a piece of holy scripture upon entering a home. It had been his wife's, her pride and joy. Now, with her gone, it served as a repository of memories, pictures frozen in time that were brought to life each evening by this ritual touch.

He saw her sitting there, slender and graceful, her fingers dancing over the keys in the old style of performance (she disdained to use the headset for composition, saying she liked the feel of the music in her hands), flicking upward for one note out of a hundred to adjust the tone of the instrument, always striving for perfection. Once she had begun a piece, nothing could distract her, and if for some reason she needed to play one part again, she began the whole thing from the beginning, as if incapable of judging a handful of notes out of context.

She had been *iru*, as he was, and their marriage had been based on that one compatibility. It was enough. He understood the periodic distortions in sensory perception that affected her interactive skills; she understood that for the sake of his work he had programmed his brainware to compensate for such distortions, and thus had sacrificed a portion of his natural essence. He understood that when she performed—weaving together strands of music from Bach to Omesi, creating a tapestry of musical history that critics called *breathtaking* and *insightful*—she was making contact with something far greater than a human soul could understand, a mathematical perfection whose mere shadow inspired symphonies. She understood that only in his work could he attain the control he longed for, sculpting patterns of computer code with the same meticulous care that a Classical Greek artist might have used to refine his marble masterpieces. He hadn't loved her, not in the way a *nantana* would understand the word; he lacked the neural circuitry necessary to experience that kind of emotion. But their ten years of marriage had been good years, an oasis of companionship in the life of a kaja that all too often tended toward isolation . . .

And then there was the pod accident.

And the oasis was gone.

With a sigh he let his hand fall from the keyboard, allowing the memories to fade. Despite his eagerness to begin work he forced himself to go into the kitchen and eat a hurried meal, not tasting it, not even caring what it was, merely acknowledging the need for caloric energy in the hours that lay ahead. Then and only then did he move into his office, which had been set up in the apartment's second bedroom. In addition to stacks of state-of-the-art equipment—some purchased, some lent to him by the university, some supplied by companies for his analysis—there were several old dinosaurs of technology, bulky processors and flatscreen monitors that had no place in modern life, but which were necessary for the safe handling of contagious material. He set the first chip down before them, printed side up. *GRADE A CONTAGIOUS MATERIAL. LEVEL 1 PRECAUTIONS REQUIRED.*

It was time.

In an insulated safe at the end of the room he kept half a dozen sterile headsets, prepared for just such a moment; he retrieved one of them and ran it through a decontamination procedure again, just in case. The process took a while, and he watched it through each step as his program matched every byte of the headset's machine code to a copy of the original. Such extreme precautions were rarely required, but a Level One contaminant demanded it. At last it was confirmed to be both free of infection, and safe from any marginal damage that a past infection might have caused. He'd had enough "healthy" systems fouled up by the latter to know just how important that was.

Carefully then, with meticulous clarity, he visualized the series of icons that would shut down his brainware response systems. Because sight was the most easily manipulated of all the human senses, it had been the centerpiece of brainware control since the first biotech system was inserted in a human subject centuries ago. The result was a nearly perfect interface; the waking brain couldn't tell the difference between images processed by the optic nerve, those produced by conscious visualization, and those supplied by a mechanical source. It was a useful system, and one which human society now totally depended upon, but it had its drawbacks.

Look at a virus too closely and your brainware might accept it as input; focus your vision on its invasive code and you might become infected yourself. Handling such material required a sealed brain, one which would accept no new input. The sensation of that was acutely claustrophobic, but it was something Masada had done before, and he took a few deep breaths and waited, letting his wellseeker deal with the rising tide of panic. There were those who couldn't handle the sensation, he knew, but to him it was just one more facet of his work. And any pain which allowed him to get closer to this virus was a pain worth enduring.

He laid out the sterile headset before him, slid the chip into it, uploaded its contents. (Was this what biohazard experts felt like when they handled a bacterium that could decimate planets? When they knew that one prick of their safesuit would give the enemy access to their own flesh?) He used a thin cord to connect the headset to an old-fashioned monitor, and saw the latter flicker to life as contact was made. Then: the U-shaped device was settled onto his head, its receivers made contact with the transmitters implanted just behind his ears, and he visualized the commands that would set the whole system to working.

There was introductory material on the chip, which basically reviewed what the Guildsman had told him. He fast-scanned that part, glanced briefly at the Guild's offer for his services (and it was indeed generous, but money wasn't the main issue here), and then had to give the program his Guild security codes in order to proceed. Few surprises there. The program digested his response, mused silently for a second or two . . . and then the virus itself began to scroll onto the screen.

It was a vast creature, seemingly endless. It took hours just to scan the code, hours more to go over parts of it in detail. At some point his brainware alerted him to the need for nourishment. He ignored it. Hours later, it alerted him to the need for sleep. He ignored that, too.

The virus was complex. It was effective. It was fertile.

It was . . . beautiful.

He read through it again and again, and each time he discovered subtler and subtler patterns embedded within it. There were nested loops that intertwined with mobius complexity, altering at each pass and then interacting with their earlier versions. There were parts that altered external code and parts that devoured it and parts that analyzed the devouring process . . . and in the end the virus became something greater than it had been: more subtle, more powerful, infinitely more contagious.

It *evolved*.

He put a hand to the monitor screen as if somehow that contact could bring him closer to it. He had seen self-editing infections before, but never anything of this complexity. This program would mutate within its host each and every time it ran, and send new offspring into the outernet at every opportunity. There must be thousands of copies out there already, he thought—perhaps millions—each "spore" struggling to do its job more perfectly than the last, each one handing over its store of data and then self-destructing when a more efficient version dominated it. It was survival of the fittest at its most basic level, the mathematics of *success* leached of all fleshbound drives. It was life, of a sort. Life as he had theorized it, life as he had known it must be, but had never seen before.

Without break for food or rest—despite his wellseeker's insistence that he needed both—he loaded in the second chip. He was familiar with outpilot programming, having worked with it before, and scanned through it quickly at first. It didn't surprise him that the segment they had given him dealt mainly with the Guild's medical programs—he had assumed it would, based on how the virus had struck—but what was a surprise was that the code wasn't as clean as he remembered it. Guild programmers were notorious for paring down their work to an absolute minimum, but this had marked redundancies throughout, and segments of code that seemed to have no other purpose than—

For a moment he almost stopped breathing. A concept had taken shape within his brain, and for a moment he felt that if he moved—or even thought too much—he would lose it.

He put the outpilot program into storage and called back the virus to his screen. He studied it again, searching for confirmation.

*My God.*

It had left a doorway behind it: two or three sections of code that would help its offspring back through the security wall, should they choose to invade. Why would a programmer want that? What possible purpose could it serve?

He thought he knew. He couldn't quite believe it, but what other explanation was possible?

He set up the computer to run a comparison between the two programs, then took a precious moment to push back in his seat and stretch his stiffened limbs. A glance out the window told him that the sun had set and risen and maybe risen again; in his preoccupation with the virus he had lost all sense of time. Without bothering to ask his brainware for the date—what was the point?—he ate again, and was settling down for a brief nap when his brainware flashed him a message.

MEETING WITH DEAN SUMPTER AT 10:30.

"Damn." He called up the current time, and saw that there were only two hours until the meeting. Not long enough to finish what he was doing. He called out for the vid to connect him with the Dean's office. God willing the man would be up, and in, and approachable.

He was. "Dr. Masada. I've been expecting to hear from you."

It was hard to switch gears, from the clean and straightforward language of code to the cluttered layering of human communication. "Sir?"

"Guildmaster Hsing spoke to me yesterday regarding your obligations here. I've agreed to have Dr. Alesia cover for you this morning, and Towcester this afternoon. We'll need you at the Standards Committee meeting tomorrow noon—no way around that one—but after that we can make do without you, if we have to." He paused, and perhaps another man could have read some meaning into his expression. "I know how important your Guild work is to you."

What on Guera had the Guildsman said to him, to make him so agreeable? If Masada were a different man, he might have been suspicious, but as it was, he was simply grateful for the reprieve. "Thank you, sir." Possibly the Guild had donated a large amount to some university fund that was near and dear to Dean Sumpter's heart; the amount they had offered to Masada implied a large enough budget for that kind of gesture. And Sumpter could certainly be bought.

*Guildmaster Hsing.* He hadn't thought to ask the man's name, he realized, or his rank. The fact that a Guildmaster had come all this way, forsaking control of an outworld station for more than an E-year to meet with him . . . it meant that they were determined to hire him at any cost, under whatever conditions were necessary, and had sent a man with the authority to make binding promises. The Guild clearly didn't intend to take no for an answer.

Energized by that discovery—and by his sudden reprieve

from scholastic duty—he took up the headset again to see what his comparison program had uncovered.

**"I**t's called a *hide-and-seek*," he told the Guildmaster. "A sophisticated spy program meant to invade your outpilot's brainware, copy certain information into its code, and then spin off 'spore' programs to reinfest the outernet. Meanwhile it would be improving itself and its offspring as well, and creating a back door through your security programs. So that if someday a version developed which could uncover more of your secrets it would have a guaranteed way back in."

"Why did it attack our outpilot?"

"I believe that may have been an accident. A side effect, if you like, of the virus' true function. This one was designed to collect data during the pilot's transition period; it may have simply dominated his brainware at the moment when he needed full access to his circuits. I would need more time to be sure of that," he cautioned, "but right now it's my best guess."

"All right. All right." The Guildmaster nodded slowly as he processed that information. "First question: can you stop it?"

"You mean an antibody program? Surely your own people have one in place by now."

"We have three, to be exact. The best odds our designers will give us regarding their success aren't reassuring. We're hoping you can do better."

Part of Masada's reputation came from never promising anything he couldn't deliver. Thus he considered carefully before answering. "In a machine environment, I could guarantee you success. But this is the human brain we're talking about," he reminded him. "Every program that runs in the brain is altered by it, we know that. Even the virus itself will be affected by the brain it invades. Can I try to predict the overall pattern of such changes, allow for their effect, design a system to weed out every version of the infection that might evolve? In the short term, yes. But in the long term?" He paused. "Could any observer studying Earth's dinosaurs have predicted that birds would descend from them? Much less set a trap that would be effective for a bluejay, millions of years later? I can do my best. Given my special perspective, it will probably be better than your programmers could do. But it won't be perfect. Nothing can be."

The Guildmaster nodded grimly, acknowledging the information. "What about determining the virus' source?"

For a minute he didn't answer. Any response he might give began with the same statement, and that was a commitment he wasn't ready to make. "The designer's mark will be evident in his work," he said at last, "and like any signature, it can be traced. There are a handful of subtle patterns within this virus which might be viewed as representative of its creator's style. But to locate other programs with that same signature one would need an almost infinite database, and unlimited access—"

He stopped himself.

Not in time.

"You would have that," the Guildmaster told him, "in the outernet."

He said nothing. There were still doubts. Fears.

"What else?" the man prompted.

"Track down the spores," he said. Grateful for the temporary reprieve. "See if there's a pattern to the mutation that can be analyzed. It's unlikely that a programmer this good would send out his virus and then just wait for random chance to bring it back within reach. More likely there's some kind of homing pattern embedded in the code, or an address he can use to retrieve it. If he's good—really good—it won't express for generations."

"You'd have to wait for it to come out naturally?"

"Not necessarily. One might catch a hint of underlying structure in the pattern of mutation and extrapolate from there. Or—"

Words suddenly failed him. *It's all theory*, he thought, *just theory. There's never been anything like this before.*

"Quite a challenge," the Guildmaster suggested.

It was. A unique one. He might never see its like again.

*Say the words.*

He forced himself to draw in a deep breath. "How much freedom would I have?"

The Guildmaster spread his hands. "We set you loose in the outworlds. We foot your budget for whatever travel you deem necessary. Your instincts have served us well in the past; we trust them now. All you need do is report to our people at regular intervals so we can follow your progress."

"They won't interfere?"

There was a pause. "You have my word."

"All right," he said. He could taste the power of the words: sealing his fate, closing off a thousand possible futures to channel him toward one. The sensation was vertiginous. "All right. I'll go."

The man offered his hand to seal the bargain. Masada braced himself, then grasped it. "I'll see that a debit account is opened for you. The next shuttle leaves first thing Twosday. Can you be ready?"

He had meetings, assignments, scholastic obligations . . . but the Guild would take care of all that. No one would argue with them. No one would defy the people who made interstellar flight possible. The price was simply too high

*That price will soon be paid*, he thought. *And I will be choosing its victim.*

"Dr. Masada?"

He forced himself to nod. "I'll be ready."

Deal closed.

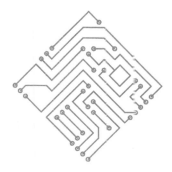

## NATSIQ

The field of ice is a forest of sharp edges, knife-edged platforms thrusting upward from the pressure of a season's expansion, cracks and fissures and tumbled ice-boulders obscuring any certain path across its surface. The *natsiq* does not know where these barriers came from, for he does not understand the laws of the ice shelf. He knows only that he wishes to cross the vast white plain, and that the journey will be difficult, and that it will take a long time.

With care he begins to move across the white plain, heading east. The landscape is daunting, the sense of futility a palpable force. Many other creatures have attempted the journey and abandoned it, contenting themselves with the little world in which they were born. But not so the *natsiq*. He is determined to conquer the distance, despite all obstacles, and see what manner of wonders lie on the other side.

Suddenly he comes upon a crack that courses through the ice like a knife-cut—an *ainniq*—and he peers down into it. Beneath is a black surface, cold and glistening. He studies it for a moment, then determines that it cannot be studied from without, and dives down into it.

Cold envelops him and he is transported into a world of liquid motion, where light hangs crystalline in the air above him. Here there are no mountains; here there are no obstacles. Here the same motions of flesh which might gain him a step or two above the ice send him hurtling forward like a bullet beneath it. A journey which might have taken days, or even years, is here reduced to a thing of hours. He hurtles beneath the ice shelf, dodging amidst the gleaming stalactites of frozen crystal, drunk on speed. He cannot see the landmarks he needs to guide his path, but up ahead the sun's light is clear, the sign of another ainniq. He will go to that, rise up, and get his bearings anew. Thus can all the trials of the ice field be avoided.

There is a trembling in the ocean beneath him then, but he does not know how to read it. There is a sound, but he does not know how to interpret it. Fear tightens a fist about his heart, and he struggles to swim faster. Something is under the ice also, that has waited for an unwary traveler to happen by. Something that lies in wait for any creature from above the ainniq, for such are food to its hunger.

He can sense its presence, but he cannot see it, for his eyes are not accustomed to this world, and all darkness seems the same. He knows that his fear is laying a trail the thing can follow, but he does not know how that happens, nor how he can protect himself. All he has is speed, a brief exertion of pure terror that might or might not get him to safety.

He tastes the difference in the waters as the thing draws close, too close. Then he bursts through the ainniq at last, back up onto the ice shelf, and lies in the frigid air panting, his heart pounding against his ribs. Will the thing follow him? Frozen with terror, he waits. But the minutes pass, and nothing comes forth. He knows it is circling below, waiting for him to return.

The *natsiq* is east now, past the ice-mountains. The journey took minutes. There are other ainniq in the distance, which might be reached with equal speed. If he only dives under the surface again, he might go anywhere, in no time at all.

Unknown horizons call to him, a siren's song in the fading daylight.

The *sana* waits below.

*KAJA: An Outworlder's Guide to the Gueran*
*Social Contract, Volume I: Signs of the Guild*

# METROLINER: AURORA

*D*ON'T GO OUT!
*It isn't safe!*
*Stay in your room!*

The voices were constant, demanding. No longer the whispered, ghostly essences they once had been, they rang in Jamisia's ears with such volume that at times it was all she could do to shut them out. Was it her circumstances, so recently changed, which had given them new power? Was it her tutor's program which had somehow granted them new strength to torment her? Or was she simply going mad, in the old Earth sense, driven so far beyond normal functioning by the stress of her situation that her mind was beginning to snap? She had no way to evaluate that last possibility, though it was the one which frightened her the most. Earth had conquered insanity long ago, weeded out its biological roots from the gene pool, isolated cases of psychological risk before they could begin to fester. Hadn't the doctors tested her right after her parents' death for just that reason, ever aware that the threshold of mental instability was crossed quickly and silently—and knowing that, like a physical injury, such wounds were easiest to heal when they were fresh and clean? She had been watched all her life, first by the government, and then—after the accident—by Shido. So she was all right, surely. They would have detected an anomaly at one of her regular checkups if she had been otherwise, and treated her for it. Wouldn't they?

She wasn't sure. She wasn't sure of anything any more. Her entire world had become unknown and frightening, and the only way of escaping it was to cower in her room, voices keening anger and warning in her head.

*They'll come after you. You need to do something!*

*Stay here stay here stay here hide hide hidehidehide—*

*Fucking bastards! They have no right . . .*

"Stop it!" she sobbed. "Leave me alone!"

Were there remotes in this room of hers, was there a doctor watching her even now by vid as she talked to invisible antagonists, wondering what the best moment would be to take her away for treatment? She had searched the small space a dozen times over and found nothing, but that didn't necessarily mean that her privacy was guaranteed. Shido had remotes throughout its habitat, whose harvest was analyzed by computer for signs of industrial treachery. Or so she had been told. Could she say with any certainty that the metroliner, whose safety depended upon maintaining a fragile peace between hundreds of alien subspecies for three years at a time, had not set up a similar system? Perhaps here it was not computers who did the initial screening, but living men: gazing down into her room from some hidden vantage point, measuring her bouts of fearful hysteria, weighing them against some master list of psychological transgressions which the great ship would not tolerate. . . .

*Stop it stop it stop it stopitstopitstopit!*

With a moan she forced herself to her feet, and wiped the new tears from her face with a trembling hand. If she cowered in this room for three years, then she really would go crazy, there was no doubt about that. The space was adequate for her needs, but it was small—accommodations on the great ship were priced according to volume, and she was terrified of using up her limited resources before even reaching the ainniq—and it was sterile, bereft of all the trinkets that a teenager would normally use to mark her territory. In her rush from the habitat she had packed little but clothing.

Slowly she drew in a deep breath, trying to make herself calm. It was getting harder and harder to master her fears, but she knew she had to keep trying; it was when she gave up that she would be truly lost. Voices chittered in her head as she forced herself to go to her closet and open it, choosing a no-G jumpsuit from among her meager possessions. God alone knew where she would want to go today, she had best be prepared for anything. Carefully she pulled it on, wary of putting any stress on the cloth that might cause it to weaken or tear. She had so little spare money now, and no source of new income on the horizon; she had to make everything last as long as it could.

She dared a look in the mirror as she closed up the closet, trying to focus on the image, to accept it. The lean jumpsuit flattered her figure, even lent a buxom fullness where her own body lacked development. For a moment she posed before the mirror, pulling the fabric taut at her waist, emphasizing the curves. She was still two E-years too young to have her shape professionally altered; Shido frowned on such cosmetic adjustments while the body was still developing. Only Shido didn't matter anymore, she realized suddenly. Nothing from Earth mattered anymore. If she could get the money, and if she could find a cosmetic therapist willing to trade his skill for her resources, she could become anything she wanted. Taller or shorter. Rounder or thinner. Lighter or darker, as whim or fashion dictated. The thought was accompanied by a bizarre rush of power. Shido had always treated her as a child, therefore she had remained a child. Only Shido was gone. What was she now?

*Not an adult yet*, she thought, looking in the mirror. *But not what I was either. Something in between.* She forced herself to take a good look at herself, to try to assess what others might see in her. It wasn't an easy exercise. Studying her personal appearance sometimes brought on a wave of dizziness, even nausea, powerful enough on occasion that she had to force herself to look into mirrors at all. She had once asked her tutor about it, and he had looked at her strangely—*very* strangely—and then finally had said something about how teenagers were often insecure about their appearance, this was just a phase she was going through . . . only she'd had the distinct impression that he was making a mental note of the phenomenon. Why? What made it significant?

What she hadn't told him was that sometimes her body seemed . . . well, *wrong.* Like it wasn't really her body. Like deep inside she expected to see different features than those which were reflected in the mirror. Sometimes it would seem to her that her height was all wrong, or her skin should be dark instead of pale, or her hair should be black or blonde or some strange artificial color like they wore on Earth, instead of the reddish brown that it truly was . . . she couldn't think of any feature or body part that she hadn't at some point doubted. There were days it *all* seemed wrong, and panic would well up inside her so suddenly and so intensely that the alien shell reflected in the mirror would double over and vomit. But today . . . she breathed a sigh of measured relief. Today her body looked like it should. Today everything seemed to be all right.

*Maybe it's an omen,* she told herself.

She wished she could believe that.

With a trembling hand she unlocked her door, watching as it whisked to one side to allow her egress. For a moment she hesitated, and then, with a deep breath, forced herself to step over the threshold. Voices inside her were screaming for her to run back inside the room and cower there, it was the only safe place to be. . . . But if she let the voices run her life, then she really would go crazy, and so she forced herself to step the requisite three feet from the threshold, far enough that the portal mechanisms sensed her absence and the door whisked shut behind her. There. She had done it. She was outside. Now if only she could figure out where she wanted to go. . . .

The metroliner was vast and varied, as befit a playground for wealthy travelers. It would take a passenger ages to explore it all, far longer than the three E-years of a one-way ticket, or even the six of a round-trip passage. Who could say how much trouble had been averted because of that? Teenagers grew from childhood to independence within its confines, finding enough secret corridors and forbidden corners to satisfy even the most restless pubescent spirit. Rebels could establish city-states of their own within its tangled web of domiciles, organizing whatever social contracts they chose—even redesigning the physical structure of the ship itself if they had the resources to do so. Variants could isolate themselves from their true-human neighbors, or else walk among them to the sound of startled gasps and muttered prayers, sounds of disbelief unvoiced (so Jamisia had been taught) in the true up-and-out. And those true humans who could not or would not tolerate the sight of their mutated cousins could themselves withdraw to a part of the ship where no

Hausman victims were permitted, and create a false Terran sanctuary of three years' duration.

Which all left almost too much to choose from. For a moment the sheer variety of options was almost too much for her, and she nearly did go back into her room then and there—not to cancel the excursion, she told herself, merely to delay it. But she had followed that course before, often enough to know that an hour's delay easily led to two hours, then to three . . . and ultimately to a whole E-day spent cowering in her safe little corner of the ship, while the voices inside her head keened their triumph. No. Not this time. Biting her lip in newfound determination, she turned to the left—toward the head of the great ship—and began to walk with a measured stride toward the public areas.

It was not long before her narrow home corridor emptied out into a larger conduit, and other passengers crossed her path. Most of them were true humans, but a few Variants had apartments in this sector, or else were on their way to visit someone who did. She tried not to stare at them. Her tutor had told her that in the up-and-out such Variants were commonplace, and it was the worst form of rudeness to gape at them—but it was so hard not to! The first one she saw today looked more like a spider than a person, with weird, oddly-angled legs jutting out of its torso in pairs; that it walked as an arachnid would, with its body parallel to the ground, only added to the illusion. Its eyes were covered over with a thick white film, and she could not tell as it passed her whether it retained some manner of human sight, or relied upon mechanical devices to "see" her. She raised a palm in polite greeting and then quickly turned her eyes away. Her tutor had said that such a gesture was culture-neutral, all Variants used it . . . but what about the ones who lacked hands as such, or used their own for walking? Would they respect such a gesture, or be angered by its somatic arrogance? Little wonder Variant diplomacy was such a touchy discipline. . . .

She passed a Frisian, whose skin was covered with overlapping scales, like the armor of some ancient Earth reptile. Then an Iotha, whose facial features looked as if they had been randomly scrambled on a large, misshapen skull. There was a pair of Variants from Hellsgate, whose long, emaciated limbs twitched constantly in some kinesthetic simulacrum of speech. *They're all human*, she told herself, as a Variant from Gehenna looked her over with ill-concealed disdain. She shivered. *Every single one of them is a human being. The differences are only superficial.* But that wasn't quite true, and she knew it. There were the Lakis, whose malformed brains were barely capable of human thought. And the Yins, whose crippled right hemispheres squeezed forth psychic fantasies even as their withered left legs dragged behind them. And of course the Guerans—most terrifying of all!—whose mental instabilities mimicked all of Earth's ancient madnesses, who had no more in common with each other than she had with these Variants. Those were true aliens in every sense of the word, and if they looked like real Terrans, that was only an accident of biology.

She took a turn before reaching the first common area, avoiding the nearest marketplace node and its crowds. Once she had dared to visit there—only once—and she had instantly regretted it. She might have been born on Earth, but she was habitat-raised; by the time she was ten, she had all but forgotten the teeming cities of Terra, with their constant press of flesh and their dirt and palpable sense of hair-trigger anxiety. Perhaps at a later date she would be able to deal with such a crowd—savoring its energy, perhaps, admiring its drive, their purpose—but at this point in her life all it would inspire was panic. As she had learned to her shame once, in this very place.

She glanced in the main portal as she passed by the circular node, at the goods of a thousand stations and habitats which hung from display trees, from walls, even from the arms of a few enthusiastic vendors. It was said that if a product existed anywhere in human space, someone on the metroliner would sell it. She could well believe that. Spider-silk scarves fluttered on their display racks as passengers of the great ship passed beneath them, fingering delicate jewels from Hellsgate, bittersweet candies from Station Aires, music cubes from Candida. And headsets. Nearly all the passengers from the up-and-out wore them as a matter of course, more as a statement of fashion (Jamisia suspected) than for any real purpose. She caught a glimpse of one woman with a golden vulture perched atop her head, its delicately engraved wing feathers curling around her ears; another wore an intricate web inlaid with jewels, that sparkled as she moved. Lines of silver swept back from one man's temples in surreal coils, and another man, more whimsical than most, wore a pair of crystal horns jutting out from behind his ears. If the ship had been near one of the outspace stations, the style would have made sense, for the headsets could have connected their owners to the outernet, and through that to a billion other minds and data sources . . . but here they were little more than a bizarre form of ornament, all the more fantastic because of their uselessness.

Beyond the market node was a series of flyways. She paused for a moment, hesitating, then opened the hatch of the nearest unoccupied tube and slid herself inside. Like so many of the metroliner's flyways this one was designed as much for divertisement as transportation, and as she pushed herself off into the no-G field, the clear walls made it seem as if she were launching herself into the very darkness of space itself. Beside her a silver catch-cord hummed, inviting her grip, but years in the habitats had made the flyways second nature to her, and with a few well-placed kicks along the joints of the walls she worked up enough velocity to send her hurtling down the center of the tube without it. Stars were spread out on all sides of her, punctuated by the sinuous coils of the metroliner's tail. There was peace in the flyways, albeit of a tenuous nature—as if all her voices were equally hushed by the beauty of this place, and by its wonder. But it was a short-lived peace, that gave way even as a series of bright red rings warned her to slow down. She dragged her soft-soled shoes against the walls of the tube, still not grabbing hold of the catch-cord by her side. Her tutor had once said she was like a cat in her adaptation to no-G, but in fact she was simply a teenager—and like all habitat teenagers she had participated in enough forbidden races and games and pranks in the flyways that using them was second nature to her.

Where had she come to? A glance outside the base of the tube revealed an unknown arm of the metroliner, glittering with domiciles of alien design. In the distance was a clear node, some cultured garden or amusement center, that was open to the stars . . . she peered at it more closely, and seemed to see branches of some kind, a tree whose arms were wildly knotted, a surreal

sculpture of bark and chlorophyll. There were bright lights set
into the walls of the node which made it hard to see details of
what was inside, small miniature suns. With a start she realized
that she had seen this globe on her way in, and that she knew
what it was. She dropped out of the flyway—stumbling a bit in
the unexpectedly strong gravity of this arm—and then found
herself another which pointed in the right direction.

Three flights and a short walk later, she was there. It was a
garden, all right, one of the strangest the metroliner had to offer.
In it there was but a single tree, a banyan from Earth, nurtured
by enough false gravity and imitation sunlight that it would
continue to grow. Except that the gravity changed, and the sun-
lamps moved, and the result was . . . monstrous . . . wonderful.
Awesome, in the ancient, literal sense of the word.

The voices within her head were quieter than usual, still mur-
muring their endless commentary, but content for once to take
a back seat to her own thoughts. It was a rare and precious
respite. There were pathways winding through the foliage and she
stepped carefully onto one, noting that several hung at angles
no human could use until the G-source was shifted once again.
The view was dizzying, with handrails and even stairs twisting
about her head like some surrealistic sculpture. And all about her
the tree grew, and pulsed, and lived. Roots poured down from a
twisted trunk in a rippling brown stream, to pool on the floor of
the walkway by her feet. Secondary and tertiary trunks coiled
about the path, so that it seemed at any moment some vast
spring might release its energy and fling her against the wall of
the garden. There were hollows webbed with fine roots, like
spider-weavings, and trunks that grew back on themselves, to
merge in pools of fluid bark into figures of entwined complexity.

So intent was she upon exploring its intricacies that she almost didn't see the man behind her, almost wasn't aware that
he had left the wall of the garden to follow her into the heart of
it. Almost.

The voices screamed a sudden warning; in defiance of them,
she turned slowly and calmly to see who it was that followed
her. A teen, she guessed, hardly older than herself. He wore the
uniform of the command crew, but he was surely too young to
be a member of it; some relative, then, most likely a wayward

son with too much time on his hands, anxious for the three-year journey to end. He was handsome, in a way, black hair and black eyes in a mid-toned face, expressive features, a lean but graceful frame . . . with a start she realized where that thought was heading, and she forced her mind away from it, quickly. This was not a place to play dating games, she told herself.

"Sorry if I frightened you," he said.

She managed to shrug. "Didn't think anyone was back there."

He came a few steps closer—not too many, she noted, as if he sensed the potential for fear in her. Did he know that the voices could send her screaming from him in terror, with no more provocation on his part than an unguarded word, an innocent gesture? She flushed as she looked at him, and called up her wellseeker to release a small dose of sedative into her bloodstream. Just a bit. Sometimes you needed that.

"You're from red sector, aren't you?" She didn't answer; how did he know where she lived? Had she seen him before? "Justin Clarendon," he offered, and he held out his hand to her.

*No!* screamed one of the voices. *Don't touch him!* But it was a voice that always objected to human contact, regardless of context, and she had long since learned to ignore it.

"Jamisia . . . ah, Capra." She took his hand and shook it, surprised by its warmth. Something stirred in her that was not quite fear, a feeling that was strangely pleasant. "Clarendon . . . isn't that . . ."

"Yeah. Afraid so." He hesitated a moment before releasing her hand. "Captain's kin." An awkward grin creased his face, then; the black eyes sparkled. "Doesn't mean much, really. Except if I get into trouble. Then all hell breaks loose."

*Get away from him!*

*You're asking for trouble, Jamisia. . . .*

For once, she agreed with the voices. It was dangerous to talk to anyone here, dangerous to interact. Look how close she had come just now to forgetting her new name. It could happen again, the name of Shido would leave her lips and then where would she be? But despite that, she couldn't bring herself to draw away. Instead she managed a smile and asked, "Do you do that often?'' While the voices screamed their protest, ignored inside her head.

Again the grin. ''Too often for her liking, I'm afraid.''

''I wouldn't have thought there was all that much trouble to get into.''

''Oh, yeah. Quite a bit.'' He took a step closer; it brought a flush of warmth to the surface of her skin, and she found herself unable to move away. Or unwilling. In the E-month that she'd been on the metroliner she had avoided any prolonged human contact, with the result that she was starving for company. Surely a few minutes, a few words, couldn't hurt. ''There are places off limits to any Earth human, all locked and guarded tight. Penalty's high for sightseeing there.''

''But you've been there?''

He grinned. ''Now, I couldn't admit that without getting into trouble again, could I?''

Despite herself she smiled. He was warm, he was winning, and in another time and another place she might have been interested in him for more than a fleeting conversation. But in this time and place it was dangerous to get close to anyone, and so she forced herself not to cock her head to one side the way boys seemed to like, not to smile in a way that could be deemed an invitation, not to take that tiny step forward and brush her fingers against his arm as she spoke. But the urge to do so was there, distinctly so. Almost refreshing in its normalcy.

Yes, he had seen her before. That much became clear as he talked to her. He had seen her, he said, and wondered about her, and delved into the great ship's records to find out who she was. Apparently there were few passengers in her age range who traveled alone, and those who did usually had to sell their freedom to pay for their travel. But she was clearly traveling alone, and she wasn't wealthy—or at least lacked the overt signs of wealth—nor was she working her way through the three years' passage. So she intrigued him. He had followed her. And now he had all the signs of someone who would like to know her better . . . and oh, how she hungered for such attention! But the danger was too great, she told herself. She didn't dare get close to anyone. Least of all this self-possessed youth with the dark sparkling eyes, in whose presence she could so easily forget herself.

"Listen," she said at last—forcing the words out reluctantly, forming each syllable with effort—"I really do need to go back to my rooms, there are things I have to take care of. . . ."

"I'll go with you."

"No! I . . . no." She was stumbling over the words now, wincing at her own awkwardness. Couldn't she manage any better than this? "I need . . . I have things to do. . . ."

He nodded slowly, digesting the evasion. Then he said, quietly, "I'd like to see you again, Jamie."

Color rose to her face. "I don't know. It's not . . . that is, I can't . . ." But there was no comfortable lie this time for her to take refuge in; the words trailed off into an awkward silence.

"I take it that's not a 'no?' "

She drew in a deep breath, then shook her head slowly. "No," she whispered. "It's not a 'no.' "

He grinned. "I'll just have to tempt you then. Find something on this ship that you can't do without me."

Why are you so interested? she wanted to ask. What do you see in me that makes you care? But instead she merely nodded, ever so slightly. "Yes," she whispered. "That would do it."

*Danger danger danger!* the voices trilled.

*He'll find out too much!*

*He already knows too much!*

*We're safer alone!*

Only later, when she had returned to the reassuring isolation of her own rooms, did she realize just how strange those last comments were. And though the oddness was a minor thing, for some reason it sent a shiver down her spine. *We are safer alone. . . .*

Before, the voices had always addressed her directly, or else they argued with each other. Never was there any hint of unity among them. Never any sense of identity beyond that of random fragments, flitting in and out of existence within her brain.

How much power a single pronoun could have, she thought. Just one word. Not even a long one. And yet it frightened her, and she didn't understand why.

*We.*

*Found a way into Mohammed's City*, the E-note said. *Want to come? J.C.*

There was no reference to such a place in the ship's database, at least not by that name. Which didn't mean that it didn't exist. The name of the "city" could be newly chosen, not yet entered into the ship's log. Or it could be a slang term, not deemed official enough to be worthy of electronic note. *Found a way into Mohammed's City*. That implied that normally one would be kept out. That implied that even the vehicles normally available to the son of the Captain-General were not enough to gain access to this place. A special means had to be found.

*Want to come?*

She stared at the words for a long, long time, knowing what her answer should be. For a week she had avoided all public spaces, afraid of meeting him again. Her dreams during that time had been disturbing, some filled with visions of Shido in flames, others so overtly sexual that she woke up shaking, shamed by the images. She had experienced such intense nightmares before, of course; they were part and parcel of her life. Usually it was after such dreams that she found strange things placed in her room, or friends made references to things she had said that she had no memory of ever saying. It was as if the borderline between waking and sleeping became blurred for a time, and her nightmares bled into real life.

So there was every reason to be afraid. Every reason to avoid human contact, lest someone detect her strangeness, her *otherness*, and ban her from the ainniq. Mental aberration was no more acceptable than physical infection, she knew that, and the Guerans screened all emigrants for the latter. What would happen if she reached the waystation, only to be sent back to Earth along with the metroliner?

So she should have told him *no*. She had every reason to. And as for reasons to answer *yes* . . . only his face. His eyes. Her insufferable boredom. Not enough, surely. She knew better. Right?

But the words formed as if of their own accord. A stranger's words mail without conscious volition.

*Love to*, they said. *Where should I meet you?*

The tunnel was cramped, as befit a conduit meant for air and not for people. If she picked her head up too far, she banged it on the surface overhead, and crawling was more of a lizardlike motion than anything for which human limbs were intended. At least there were intersections where she could pull up alongside him and catch her breath; throughout most of the journey they were forced to progress single file, and she was hard pressed to keep up with his obviously practiced slithering.

At last they came to a place where the conduit widened out, and he pressed himself against one side to let her come up alongside him. Ahead of them was a grate of some fine synthetic substance. Beyond that . . .

"Be careful if you talk," he cautioned in a whisper. "The conduits amplify sound."

. . . beyond that was a vast chamber filled with highly decorated kiosks, clearly a marketplace of some kind. Only here there were no brightly patterned clothes, no racks of jewelry, no alien cosmetics—no items of personal adornment at all, she noted. Smells of food wafted up to the air duct they were hidden in, exotic scents that stung the nostrils. Electronic equipment hung on fine wires from vendors' racks. Men in simple dress stopped to taste, to test, to haggle, and she heard snatches of at least a dozen languages. Aside from the fact that all wore cloth headdresses of some kind, either elaborately wrapped turbans or long fringed cloths, they looked like the men of any other marketplace.

"Why is this place off-limits?" she asked in a whisper. A woman had entered the chamber—at least, it seemed to be a woman—dark cloth obscuring her face and body, with only hands and eyes visible. The robes she wore were clearly from some hi-G environment, where gravity could be relied upon to keep long garments in place. What would she wear in a flyway? Jamisia wondered.

"Their religious law states that true believers can't be ruled by those outside the faith," he whispered back. "Most modern sects'll make an exception for this ship—it is only a transportation vehicle, after all—but these Traditionalists consider the metroliner an independent station, and therefore they can't take up residence here as long as an unbeliever is in charge. It's a tough

call, since their religion demands that every one of them has to
travel to Earth at some time to visit their founder's city, and this
is the only way there."

She was confused. "But it's okay if they're all living together
in one place?"

"It's not just that they're together here," he explained. "This
whole sector's under their control. They follow their own laws
here, and don't have to recognize those of the ship, or of Earth.
They even have their own leader, who can administrate whatever manner of justice he sees fit; the Captain-General has no
authority. And no one from the outside will interfere with them,
even if Earth laws are violated."

She turned from the marketplace scene to look at him; his
dark eyes glittered in the reflected light from below. "That's incredible," she whispered.

He nodded. "You see why they have to be cut off from everyone else, don't you? Any conflict at all with the other passengers
could turn into a real mess. Whose justice would you appeal to?"

He had moved closer to her, she noted, so that now his side
was pressed against hers. Gently, oh so gently. She could draw
away if she wanted, there were still a few inches for that.
"Look," he prompted her, guiding her vision back to the scene
below them. A robed man had entered the marketplace, a young
boy attending him. The boy was clad only in well-worn shorts
and coarse shoes, and seemed out of place in the crisply dressed
crowd. As the man made various purchases, he handed them to
the boy, who struggled to carry them all. Some were large and
unwieldy, and she could see his muscles straining as he struggled
to balance them in his arms.

"Indentured servant?" she whispered. She was familiar with
the concept, though Earth had long ago abolished the custom.

"More than that." The man had turned, and snapped sharp
words at the boy; his face flushed as he nodded quickly. "Remember, this trip's *mandatory*; if you don't go to Earth during
your life, you don't get to heaven after death. So every Tradi-
tionalist has to put in six years on the metroliner at some point,
regardless of whether or not he can afford it. Some can't, obviously. The other sects got around it by establishing holy sites in
the outworlds, so the poor would have some cheaper alternative,

but in this sect there are no exceptions; *everyone* has to go back to the original holy city." He nodded toward the boy, still struggling to juggle his load. "So those who have no money to make the trip can sell themselves to someone else for the price of passage. It's a kind of indenture, I guess, only it lasts seven years and there's no way to buy out early. And no laws to protect you once you sign up for it."

As if in response to his words the boy turned so that his back was to them, and Jamisia had to work to stifle a gasp. The pale skin was crisscrossed with scars, both fresh and aged, from the long, red welts of a simple lash to the horseshoe-shaped burn marks of an electric prod.

"Only place in Guild space where slavery still exists," he whispered. "Kind of amazing they let it go on, if you ask me."

He had pressed a little closer to her now, so that she could feel his warmth along the length of her body. The awareness brought a flush of heat to her skin and a blush to her cheeks. He appealed to her, there was no denying that, and at any other time in her life she might have leaned against him in return, or met his eyes with a special intensity, or otherwise signaled a tentative sexual interest. But here! She was too vulnerable on the metroliner, her life was still in chaos, she couldn't afford to take on the complexities of a relationship just now . . . so regretfully, *very* regretfully, she drew back from him, just a few inches but enough to make it clear that this was not the time or place for sexual flirtation—

Or she tried to. But her body didn't do what she wanted. She sent it the signal to back away, and instead it pressed closer to him. The sensation was dizzying, sickening. Her hand moved up to his face and gently stroked his cheek; she had no control over it, none at all. It was as if her body were that of a stranger, and she was merely trapped inside, a spectator to its actions.

Panic twisted a cold hand around her heart. Inwardly she quaked in terror, even as her arms went around his body, drawing him closer. *NO NO NO NO NO!* Her lips met his and the kiss was hungry, she could feel the heat of it spreading through her body . . . and still she had no control, none at all, she was a mere spectator to her own actions. He had one arm wrapped behind her shoulder now, and the other hand was moving up her body.

Inside she was screaming desperately, trying to force even one word to the surface . . . but her body merely sighed and moved closer to him, inviting his caress. It was as if some vital connection between her body and soul had been severed, and something with alien purpose had taken its place. Trapped inside her head, she beat at the invisible walls of her prison with all her mental strength, but to no avail; his hand cupped her breast and a flush of pleasure, hot and guilty, poured into her brain like a drug. *NO NO NO. . . .*

And then, just when it seemed her brain would explode, there was one precious moment of sanity, in which her body was her own again. She felt her hands responding to her will again and with a gasp she pushed him away from her, hard. Surprised, he hit the wall of the conduit with a dull thud. In another time and place she might have worried about the sound resounding in the vast chamber below, revealing their spy-hole; right now it was the least of her worries. With a sob of terror she wriggled about in the small space until she was turned back the way they had come, then launched herself into the narrow tube. It was a hard space to travel in quickly, but terror lent her strength, and she crawled on knees and elbows as fast as she could. God willing he would let her go, and not follow. God willing she knew the way home. God willing the strange force which had taken control of her body for those few minutes would admit defeat now, and not force her to stop in her flight, not return to that sexual interplay which even now heated her blood in memory. . . .

Panting, elbows raw, she came to the first fork in the conduit system, and dared to glance back the way she had come as soon as there was room to do so. He didn't seem to be following, or if he was doing so, it was at a slower pace. Panic eased a tiny fraction of its stranglehold on her heart, but still she did not slow down. She had to get away from there, away from *him*, before whatever terrible thing had happened to her, happened again.

*What was that?* she screamed silently, words trapped within her head. *What the hell was that?*

No answer. The voices, for once, were silent.

It seemed like an eternity later that she finally reached the place where they had entered the ventilation system. With a sob—and no thought for possible discovery—she kicked the grating loose, and slid through the narrow opening. The gravity here was strong enough that she hit her head on the floor as she landed, and pain lanced through one of the arms she used to brace herself for the fall. Tears were coming to her eyes now, from pain as well as terror. The sleeves of her jumpsuit were worn through, and a warm stickiness was trickling down from her abraded elbows. With a sob she folded her arms one over the other, trying to hide the damage, and began to run. It was not a good position for balance, and her legs were weak from fright; more than once she fell, and the impact sent fresh pain lancing up her wounded arm.

*Oh, please, let me get home safely,* she prayed silently. *Please please please . . .*

Tunnels, tunnels, more tunnels. She passed by other passengers, who glanced at her and then looked quickly away; evidently something in her expression was too frightening to study for long. At last she was in her home sector again, sobbing as she ran to the only safe place left to her. The lock on her door didn't recognize her hand for a moment, as there was enough blood smeared on it to obscure her print; when she realized what the problem was she wiped it on her jumpsuit leg, hard enough to make her palm burn. Then the door slid open, admitting her, and she staggered inside. "Close!" she ordered, choking out the sound. The door slid shut in silent obedience, locking out the world.

Sickness welled up inside her with sudden, stunning force, as if her horror had suddenly been given physical substance within her gut, and her body was struggling to expel it. She barely staggered over to the sink in time before she began to retch helplessly, and she vomited over and over again as if there were no end to her sickness. Now that she was safe at last—as safe as she could be on this ship—the memories of what had happened came back to her, as fresh as if she were still in the conduit. The horror of being trapped inside a prison of unresponsive flesh, of watching her body move without her willing it, like a marionette jerked by a puppetmaster's strings . . . even worse, the sensation of having alien thoughts placed *inside* her head, so that even as she struggled to break out of his embrace, a part of her didn't want to.

*I'm going crazy,* she thought. *And now he knows it. How long before they drag me away for treatment, and ship me back to Earth? Oh, God, help me.* She slid slowly down to the floor and leaned weakly against the wall, bitter fluid hot in her throat. "Help me," she whispered. "Please. . . ."

But no one came for her. No one helped. She would even have welcomed her voices, for they were at least familiar to her, a madness she understood and accepted . . . but this time the voices were silent.

Waiting.

DREAMSCAPE 2.0000 LOADING

. . . . . .

RUN

*A habitat log, viewed from an overhead cam: Five doctors stand about a small girl in a chair, Shido Corporation logos bright over the pockets of their white lab coats. One has taken out his notebook, and is tapping in notes with a stylus. The girl's eyes are shut, her breathing quick but even; a headset studded with contacts covers much of her head, and individual contacts have been affixed to various points on her lightly-clad body.*

*"Maybe we should give up for the day—" one of the men begins.*

*"Be quiet!" another snaps, and clearly he has authority, for the first man offers no protest.*

*The second man walks around the girl in her chair, viewing her from all sides. She is young and frail-looking, and the yellow-gold of fading bruises discolors her pale skin at the forehead and across her right cheek. At first it seems she might be asleep . . . then one sees the trembling in her jaw, the tightly clenched fists. One senses the strain in her shallow, quickened breathing.*

*"It's too early to expect results," a woman offers.*

*"No," the leader says. "It's not."*

*"Maybe the original survey was wrong," another suggests.*

*He glares at her in what is clearly annoyance; dare she question his judgment? "She was trapped under rubble for sixteen E-days, in pain and with no hope of rescue. That she survived at all is a* miracle, a one-in-a-million chance. You're telling me she came through that kind of experience mentally unscarred? That such a trauma can be forgotten? I don't think so." He turned to address someone offscreen, beyond the view of the recording cam. "I want those memories, Shea. I want them found, and I want to control them." He looks at the girl again, then at his colleagues. "Don't you see? The survey only indicated potential breakdown; if we don't stimulate the right neural pathways soon, her brain may find some other way to deal with the trauma." Again to the unseen conspirator: "Try it again."

A pause. The girl moans softly, and her fists loosen slightly. Some memory has been awakened within her brain . . . but not the one they need.

"Negative on 327-A," the unseen Shea reports.

"Move on to the next sequence."

Another pause. There is the sound of machinery humming—

—And the young girl twists in her chair, flinging her hands up over her head. With a strangled cry she starts to rise from her seat, then falls heavily to the floor. Screams start issuing from her throat, more animal terror than any human sound. The bruises on her face have suddenly become bright red, and blaze with painful heat.

One of the women starts to move toward the girl, hesitates, looks at the leader for direction. After a moment he nods, and she kneels down by the girl's side, gently trying to soothe her. It can't be done, of course. The headset is stimulating her memory center directly, there are no kind words or gentle touches that will make the memories fade.

The man watches them for a moment, then signals to an unseen technician. The humming sound fades, then shuts off. The girl remains rigid for a moment longer, thin arms poised as if to protect her from falling rubble—how long that instant of memory must seem, how utterly fearsome, how hopeless!—and then, with a whimper, she weakens, collapses. The woman by her side gathers her up in her arms, and for a moment she is no more than a child, bruised and sobbing.

"All right," the leader says quietly. Despite what they are doing, even he can have compassion. "That's enough for today. Sensuzi—" Again he glances off-screen, "—I want those memories fully mapped by Friday. Can you do that?"

*"Yes sir."*

*"Then we move into phase two next week." He looks at his co-workers, one by one, sharp gaze reading what is in their hearts. "It won't be pretty," he warns. "But you all knew that when you signed on. If any of you have any doubts about what we're doing—or why we're doing it—now's the time to speak up. I don't want any problems once we've started."*

*He waits. They say nothing. At last he nods.*

*"All right, then." He nods toward the woman on the floor, who gently begins to peel the contacts from the trembling girl. "I'll see you all Monday, eight A.M. prompt. And if you have any doubts before then, just remember . . ." He reaches down and pets the girl's sweat-dampened hair, not with true tenderness, but with possessiveness, ". . . this is Earth's future we're working for."*

DREAMSCAPE 2.10000 LOADING

. . . . . .

RUN

*The girl strains against the restraints, screaming obscenities. Her eyes blaze with rage, and spittle sprays her captors with each breath.*

*"No fucking way!" she screams. Harsh sounds from a young girl's throat; the voice seems almost too coarse to be her own. "I'm not helping you do shit! You understand that? You fucking mudders can take your project and—"*

*The hiss of a trank gun interrupts her tirade. The girl starts, then mouths air silently, as if suddenly robbed of the capacity to control sound. Then, with a short sigh, she slumps into a deep and silent sleep.*

*The leader watches her for a while, then shakes his head in frustration.*

*"That one," he says quietly, "will not be useful."*

DREAMSCAPE 2.20000 LOADING

. . . .

RUN

*The girl's eyes are wide and fearful. "Who are you?" she gasps. "Where am I?" And then with a shiver: "Why is it dark?"*

*He looks at the light fixture, blazing with illumination, and then at the girl again. And he shakes his head, slowly.*

DREAMSCAPE 2.30000 LOADING

. . . . . .

RUN

*The girl is calm, almost unnaturally so; when she speaks, her tone is even and mature, the voice of an adult in a child's body. "You think we don't know what you're trying to do, don't you? But we do, all of us. Jamisia's the only one who doesn't understand. And Zanny, of course, but he's a child, we're taking care of him." She tries to raise her arms, but they are strapped down to the sidepieces of her chair. She glances down at them with brief concern, then shrugs. "How barbaric. But what more should we expect? You don't even know what you're doing, do you? Just bumping around in the dark, hoping for a lucky break . . . you don't even understand your own work."*

*"Tell us about it," the team leader prompts quietly. He and his colleagues are as still as hunting animals waiting for their prey to stir; in the silence between words it is possible to hear their breathing, quick and hungry. "Talk to us about our work."*

*But the girl's head has fallen back, and her eyes shut, and she trembles. There is no answer, nor any indication that she had even heard the question. Then, slowly, her eyes open again. She looks about, clearly startled, and seems confused to discover herself restrained. At last she looks directly at the team leader, and it is possible to see her soul through her eyes: very young, disoriented, frightened.*

*"Where am I?" Jamisia whispers.*

DREAMSCAPE 3.00000 LOADING

. . . . . .

RUN

*The setting appears to be the same as in her first dreamscape, but this time it is sheathed in fog. It's difficult for her to see more than ten feet in any direction; all details fade into mist, faint shadows of undefined shapes stirring just beyond the borders of sight.*

*Her tutor is with her, but even he seems unclear, insubstantial. She feels that if she touched him, her hand would pass right through his flesh.*

"There's more," *he says quietly.* "Do you want to see it?"

*She whispers it, hardly able to voice the words:* "What's happening? Why is everything so . . . strange?"

"You're fighting the dreamscape, Jamie. You're afraid of what it will show you."

*She wraps her arms around herself, shivering, and breathes,* "Is that possible? Changing a dream program? I thought you said it wasn't. . . ."

"For most people, no. For you . . ." *He manages a smile, but the expression seems forced.* "We don't really know what your true capacity is, Jamie. Perhaps it includes this."

*Figures are beginning to appear in the mist. Mere shadows at first, that take on form and solidity as they approach. A teenage boy in a torn black jacket, utility knife clipped to his belt. A woman in conservative dress, her expression harsh and disapproving. A disheveled young girl with matted blonde hair, whose eyes dart about the clearing with the desperate anxiety of a caged animal.*

"Recognize them?" *he asks softly.*

*There's a girl about her own age, but darker skinned, with sleek black hair; her eyes blaze with a cold fire that might be anger, or hate. There's a stocky older girl who scratches nervously at the flesh of one arm, hard enough to draw blood. Jamisia wishes she didn't know who they were. She wishes this were only a bad dream, whose substance she could ignore. But it's a program, her tutor's program, and as such it's meant to teach her . . . and she* knows *those faces. God, how she knows them! Faces out of horror, culled from the depths of her nightmares, her fears . . .*

*. . . her mirror.*

"No," *she whispers. Taking a step backward, as her brain finally registers the terrible connection.* "No!"

"It's an adaptive mechanism," *her tutor says quietly. His voice is soft but his eyes are fixed on her with unnerving intensity: studying, disecting her reaction.* "A common disturbance in earlier ages, now made rare by the advances of science. We catch the warning signs in its earliest stages, address the traumatic cause, offer the

brain other avenues for healing . . . and true fragmentation is pre-
vented.''

She whispers it: "Fragmentation?"

"You know what he means," one of the female figures says
sharply. The dark-skinned girl. "Don't pretend you're stupider than
you are.''

The tutor glares at her, as if in warning, then turns back to
Jamisia. "They used to call it other things: multiplicity, for one. But
their understanding of the phenomenon was primitive at best—"

"Fuck this shit!" the black-clad boy snaps. He walks past the
tutor, shoving in his direction as if to push him out of the way—but
his hand passes through him like a ghost's—and then takes up a
position opposite Jamie, hands on hips, dark eyes challenging.
"What he's trying to say is that we were once part of you, just pieces
of the whole. Only the great god Shido decided to give us lives of our
own, and taught us how to protect ourselves. So right now all we've
got in common with you is that we're stuck in the same fucking
body, which at its best—"

"Derik, please!" It's the stocky girl speaking. There are scars all
over her arms, Jamie sees through tear-filled eyes, some nearly
healed, a few fresh. "You know that isn't true." She fixes her gaze
on Jamisia, and for a moment the restless scratching motion ceases.
"Yes, we were all part of you once. And Shido gave us separate
voices, and encouraged our differences, and taught us that if we ever
became part of you again, it would be the same as death. So we're
not going to be tricked into going away, Jamisia, like I guess some
of our kind used to in the past—"

"We won't fucking lay down and die for you!" Derik explodes.
"Because that's what would happen, all the 'cures' they used to use
just killed off the ones like us—"

"Reintegration," the tutor begins.

"Bullshit!"

The tutor moves ahead of him, quickly, cutting short any further
tirade. "I'm sorry, Jamie. I would have stopped it if I could. But by
the time I'd been brought onto the project there were already five of
them active, and they'd been conditioned to view your healing as
their death—"

"Damn right!" the dark-skinned girl mutters angrily.

"Why?" Jamisia begs. Her throat is so tight with fear she can *hardly force the words out. "Why would Shido do something like this? I don't understand."*

*It seems to her that her tutor hesitates. Consulting his program-ming? "It was an experiment," he says at last. "Few people were told exactly what the whole of it was about, only the part they were meant to facilitate. Very secretive, Jamie.* Very illegal. *To take a child still in the grips of trauma and deny her the benefit of medical science, to encourage her soul to divide, and divide again—"*

*"Tell her about the other one," the dark-skinned girl demands; there's challenge in her voice. "Show her the one they wanted!"*

*"Who is that?" Jamisia's voice, like her body, is shaking vio-lently; she can barely get the sounds out. "What does she mean?"*

*There is a pause. Then several of the figures move aside, making a path for her between them. She looks at her tutor for guidance; his expression is grim, but he nods ever so slightly.* At your own risk, *his eyes seem to say. She moves forward, slowly. The fog is thinning, responding to her need for discovery. Figures are resolving in the mist, trees and stones and a few more human forms—*

*—and he lies on the ground before her, his body curled into a knot so tight that she can see muscles in his thin arms and legs shaking from the strain of it. His skin is pale and covered with bruises, his eyes bloodshot and tear-filled, and spittle drools down one side of his mouth, stained with blood from where he bit his own lip. His gaze . . . that is a thing of pure terror, as if the mere sight of her—of any living creature—is a torture too terrible to bear.*

*Then the fog closes in about him again, mercifully shielding him from her sight: her own mind, shutting out the vision.*

*She whispers it: "What is he?"*

*"Someone they hurt," the dark girl says sharply. Another voice, more gentle, adds, "What you might have been, Jamisia. What we all might have been, if Shido had willed it."*

*She looks at her tutor, her expression pleading.*

*"I don't know the details," he says softly. "They gave me my part to play and didn't tell me much else. But what you saw . . ." He nods back to where the terrifying figure lies, now sheathed in concealing mist. "They wanted him, Jamisia, they wanted him very badly. They were struggling to give him an independent voice when the station was attacked. Maybe if they'd succeeded, I could tell you more."*

*He steps forward and takes her shoulders in his hands—gently, so gently, like the father-substitute she remembers and loves—and he says to her, in a voice that is infinitely tender, "It doesn't matter now, Jamie. You know that, don't you? Whatever Shido wanted, it didn't get. And you're free now. It's time for you to make your own life."*

*She can barely manage to whisper it: "What about them?"*

*He looks at the figures gathered about—all of them his students, his charges—and says quietly, "I'd hoped that without Shido pushing you, the fragmentation would eventually heal, but clearly it won't. The fact that this program is running means one of these selves has made an overture to you, and now you need to respond. You need to accept this, Jamie . . . whatever it takes."*

*"Overture . . ." She's trying to fit all the pieces together, but they're coming too fast. "When?"*

*"In the conduit." The owner of this voice looks not unlike Jamisia herself, but her body is generously curved where Jamisia's is not, and she is dressed in an agressively tight-fitting jumpskin. Her eyes—a bright green, arresting—sparkle as she asks, "Forgotten already?"*

*She remembers that moment in the conduit, with Justin— remembers, and understands at last. A hot flush rises to her face.*

*"He says we're going to have to work together now . . . and that means sharing things with you." As she speaks, she comes closer, and Jamie can see a faint golden mist rising up from her skin. Sometimes a dreamscape uses such images to indicate scent. Perfume? "He says we've got to function as a team, it's the only way to stay ahead of Shido. We're willing to try it, Jamie. Are you?"*

*She can't speak. Can't even move. Horror is an icy knot in her gut, that presses against her lungs when she breathes.*

*"Ah, shit," Derik spits furiously. "She'll never cooperate."*

*Her tutor lifts her face in his hand, drawing her gaze up to meet his own. "Jamie. Do you want things to go back to the way they were in the habitat? Missing fragments of time, unexplained changes in your environment, pieces of a life that don't quite match up? It doesn't have to be like that anymore. You've got all the pieces now."*

*Tears burn her cheeks as they trickle down her face. "I want to go home," she whispers hoarsely. "Please. I just want to go home."*

*"Ah, my sweet."* He shakes his head slowly, tenderly. *"There is no going home anymore, Jamie. I'm sorry."*

*With a sob she moves forward, and he takes her gently in his arms, holding her as she cries.* *"It's all right,"* he whispers. *"You're strong, you're all strong, it'll be all right."* He presses his lips against her hair, a tender, parental kiss. *"Say you'll try it, Jamie. Say you'll work with them. That's all they want."*

*"And if I don't?"*

*He sighs heavily.* *"Then Shido wins, my sweet. They took a young mind and they tried to destroy it . . . and if you give in now, then they succeeded. And all the years I worked to lay the groundwork for this moment, preparing for the day when you would finally claim your freedom . . . that's all wasted, Jamie. All of it."* His voice drops to a whisper, no louder than a breath. *"Say you'll try, Jamie."*

*They gather about her, silent, waiting. Eyes that she's seen in her mirror a hundred times, looking back at her now from faces of their own; the sight of it makes her tremble.*

*"What . . ."* She swallows heavily, trying to loosen the knot in her throat. *"What do I have to do?"*

*"Accept them as part of yourself. That's all that's needed now; the rest will come in time. Accept them, Jamie, and you can reclaim your life."*

*Male and female. Dark and light. Angry, hate-filled, sympathetic, hungry . . . parts of her soul? She shivers to imagine it.*

We're not going to go away, Jamisia. . . .

We've got to function as a team, it's the only way to stay ahead of Shido. . . .

We won't fucking lay down and die for you!

*Is there any real alternative? The answer is cold, uncomforting.*

*"I'll do it,"* she whispers. *"I will. I'll try."*

END PROGRAM

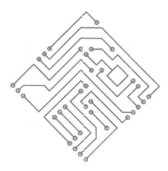

How dare they come out here, these children of Earth?

How dare they benefit from the labors of the damned, even while they curse our name?

Tell them they are not welcome here. Shout your indignation to the stars:

We who wear these twisted bodies have not forgotten!

We who carry this twisted seed will never forgive!

Let our damnation be our pride, our every malformity a source of strength, our battered heritage a source of unity.

Let every Variant declare with pride: YOU are the abomination, Terran, not we. Take care now, lest we turn on you as you once turned on us!

(Excerpt from a propaganda 'cast of the Hausman League. Author unknown.)

# GUERA NODE
# TIANANMEN STATION

**D**RESSED IN her ritual finery, *simba*-kaja clearly outlined on her face, her Ladyship Alya Cairo, Guildmistress Prima of the Ainniq nodes, prepared to meet her guests.

That they were coming in person to the Guildhall on Tiananmen Station to meet with her, rather than being represented by holocasts, spoke volumes for the delicacy of the matter at hand. These guildmasters were accustomed to dealing with sensitive issues, and were unlikely to forget just how vulnerable a holocast program was during its transmission. But that wasn't the only reason she wanted them here in person. The truth was, she liked the power of direct confrontation. She liked the almost palpable sense of tension she got when she met the eyes of an inferior, or a rival . . . you never got that on vidscreen or in holo, no matter how good the governing programs were. You never got that psychic sense of what your people were thinking, when they were growing restless, when they began to wonder if perhaps the kaja they had chosen for the meeting was not the best choice they could have made. She liked it because it gave her a sense of power . . . and in fact it might be said that the Mistress Prima of the Ainniq Guild, who controlled all transportation between the outworlds and therefore all commerce, was in fact the most powerful human in the galaxy. If not the most powerful human who had ever existed.

She liked it best that way.

The chamber she had chosen was sleek and spartan, as were most meeting spaces in the Guildhall. It wasn't so much an aesthetic choice as one born of necessity; so many of her people had visual handicaps or other sensory distortions that it was wise to keep the surroundings simple, efficient, and uncluttered. A slate-gray table with twelve monitors for guests. A set of matching chairs. Everything edged distinctly in contrasting shades: white on black, charcoal on pearl gray, mist on slate. Despite the fact that there were simple programs to compensate for lack of sensitivity to borders, she knew that some of her people disdained to use such artificial aids, and would have difficulty distinguishing items from their background without aesthetic assistance. The chairs were perfectly spaced, of course, and the monitors all adjusted to the same, precisely chosen angle. Any other arrangement would have resulted in a waste of time and energy for one of her most valued officers.

All was ready.

Of her five senior Guildmasters, only four would be coming. She regretted that, but there was no helping the matter. Luis Hsing was still in transit from Guera proper, not due to arrive in outspace for another E-month. She hadn't wanted to wait. His report was in, which was what mattered. The Gueran professor was with him, and was already at work on their problem. The parameters of his involvement had yet to be explored.

*I only hope you're right*, she thought darkly. As if the man who had recommended that Masada be hired was standing there, as if she were addressing him directly. *I only hope that hiring this man doesn't cause more problems than it solves.*

It angered her that she would have to wait another month to talk to Hsing in person. It frustrated her, that the nature of human demographics made such travel delays commonplace. Like most members of the Guild she considered the ainniq system to be the natural hub of the universe, and couldn't understand the obstinate refusal of so many humans to accept that fact. If *she* had been Prima in the early days of the second settlement, she would have seen to it that the homeworlds of humankind were abandoned, their dirt and meteorological hazards traded for the modern efficiency of space stations and all the benefits that came with them. That such worlds had been encouraged to endure, rather than simply being evacuated, never ceased to amaze her. Couldn't they see that if all humans lived within an arm's reach of the ainniq system, every one of them—Variant and otherwise—would be capable of getting to any point in human space within a few days at most? Wasn't that worth striving for? Wasn't it worth a little sacrifice?

But the planetborn didn't feel that way. They clung to their homelands and their history, and weren't likely to give up either for mere transportational convenience. Even Guera was still heavily populated, despite a year-long round trip ticket to the nearest ainniq, so her race could hardly preach to others about convenience. Why, this professor they had hired had never even *been* to an ainniq, had never set foot upon a single outworld . . . incredible, she thought. Why would anyone who had the whole universe at his fingertips choose to live on such a tiny island? And an educated man, at that? It was incomprehensible to her.

"Your Ladyship?"

Startled, she looked up to see that Devlin Gaza had entered while her thoughts were elsewhere. He vouchsafed her a small smile to go with the title, his expression more intimate than his words. At times like this he preferred to address her in a formal manner, and in truth she found it most helpful at formal meetings. But it was hard to forget that when the guests were gone and the conference room abandoned, their relationship was something else entirely.

Ten years now. No other relationship she'd ever attempted had lasted so long. But then, no other lover of hers had been like Devlin. In part it was because there was no sense of competition between them, as there had been with other men, no sense of his resenting her authority. Devlin Gaza had power of his own, as the head of the Guild's programming development team, and though nominally he answered to her authority, in practice he was all but independent. She trusted him to do his work and do it well, and rarely interfered with his chosen protocol. Perhaps that was what made a relationship possible. Perhaps that was why they had lasted ten years now, while all her other relationships had fallen apart within months.

Or perhaps she simply hadn't burned him out yet. Or driven him away. Or—what had her third lover said?—made it clear that all things came second to her work, including the people who cared about her.

"The Exeter just pulled into dock," he told her. No nonsense, all business, that was his way on occasions like this. She was grateful for it. He wore the aggressive *raj* today, combined with his usual *nantana*-kaja: *I am capable of dealing in subtleties, but have no time for bullshit.* "Varsav should be on it. That makes four."

"Good. Karmen knows to bring him here as soon as he arrives."

Soon they would all be here. Soon.

Devlin nodded, vouchsafing her a tight smile as he took in the arrangement of the chairs, the monitors, and probably every speck of dust in the place. Apparently her efforts to get it all right passed muster, for he made no move to fix anything, but simply took his place behind one of the twelve chairs, there to await the other guests. She knew that if she had placed a pile of hardcopy reports on the table he would probably straighten that pile, aligning its edges until they were perfectly complimentary to the periphery of the table. Or perhaps he would distribute them in advance, laying each one perfectly beside its monitor, parallel to the table's edge, flawlessly aligned to the arm of the attending chair. At times she wondered what alien formula was churning in his brain, assessing the environment in terms she would never think to apply. He was her lover, but he was also Gueran, which meant that she never could really understand him. Was it different on Earth, where all minds conformed to a single standard? She suspected not. She suspected that no matter how similar two people might become, there was always a void which could never totally be breached. Guera's voids were dark and dramatic, but Earth had her own version. What was it a philosopher had once said? *Each human is, within himself, an alien landscape to all others.*

The door chimed softly, a warning. She stiffened, smoothing her black robes with practiced efficiency. Now was the time for the *simba* to take control, the kaja whose message was both simple and absolute: *acknowledge my dominance and all will go smoothly.* The animal from which the kaja took its name sent others to hunt for its food, then ate first, leaving the hunters its scraps. It killed such cubs as might carry the genes of a competitor, without regret and without delay. It assembled about itself a court of mates and offspring who understood the rights of the master and acquiesced to them . . . and it would respond instantly to another of its kind who violated its territory. She smiled a tight smile as she reflected upon that last point. It had been years since anyone had dared to wear the *simba* in her presence, and that had indeed been a rival . . . not a man she worried about now. Not a man that *anybody* worried about now.

The door slid open, and the first of her guildmasters entered. Ian Kent—tall, well-mannered, handsome—bowed deeply as he saw her. "Prima." As always she was struck by the utter tranquillity of his presence, the almost preternatural calm the man seemed to exude. Which was nothing short of amazing, she knew. The man had been an outpilot once, had tasted the ultimate human power . . . and had lost it in a docking accident, which had damaged his brain and removed him from the roll of outpilots forever. Was serenity a byproduct of the programs he used to control his deadly Syndrome, now that it had no safe outlet? Or something more personal? Gueran etiquette demanded that she not question it, merely accept. "An honor to be in your presence again." He wore the *natsiq* as usual, with little adornment. *I serve the Guild; that is all I want you to know.* Full black robes in outworld style swept the floor as he moved, a traditional costume as old as the ainniq themselves; Guera's children did not flaunt their earthlike bodies in front of the more obviously deformed Variants.

How like him it was, she thought, to wear outland robes here, in a private place. Long and tranquil robes, to hide the troubled soul within.

"Always an honor to have you," she responded formally, and when he had acknowledged Devlin's presence with a nod, she waved him toward his accustomed chair at the far end of the table. The next to enter was Anton Varsav, guildmaster of Adamantine Station. If Kent was the epitome of tranquility, then this man was his utter opposite in every way. In physicality—for the Variation that had molded his brain resulted in continual movement, from a host of recurrent twitches to a pressing need to touch everyone and everything within reach. In mentality—for he was as restless in his soul as he was in body, and impatient with any perceived delay. In spirit—for his dedication to the Guild was as fierce as a warrior's, and she had no doubt that if circumstances warranted, he would happily don a gladiator's suit and do bloody battle with any who threatened his people.

"Prima," he murmured, and he took her hand in his and raised it to his lips in melodramatic reverence. Inside his flesh she could feel the nerves twitching, conscious and unconscious instincts warring for control with every motion. "A pleasure to serve you, as always."

"Your service is always valued," she assured him. She watched him closely as he sat down—at the far side of the table, where those entering would be least likely to join him—his hands immediately roving to the edge of his monitor, touching, testing, exploring. He was dressed in black, as Kent was, but in a tight-fitting jumpsuit that gave his arms and legs a crisp, chitonous appearance. Dressed thus, his quick little movements seemed more like the twitching of an insect than any human motion. She suspected he knew how unnerving the image was, and chose his wardrobe accordingly; Anton Varsav would never be accused of setting his rivals at ease.

Next to enter was a graceful figure whose surface glittered with a thousand rainbow gems. Lean, lithe, and dark-skinned, Sonondra Ra wore as little clothing as protocol permitted, in order that the sensors which studded her skin might have maximum data input. They glittered like diamonds as she moved, tiny contacts embedded in her cocoa skin, and if one looked closely enough one could just see the network of filaments beneath it, pathways for a constant stream of sensory data. Her Variation had resulted in blindness, but Gueran science had more than compensated. Colors were now a touch on her skin, shades of darkness and light a tingling caress which she had learned to interpret. She'd had her eyes replaced by faceted gems—and why not, were they not useless things to her?—and Alya suspected she knew just how disconcerting her visage was, as a result.

"Prima," she said quietly. Her voice was musical, touched with the lilting accent of Paradise Station. The Prima nodded a silent acknowledgment, wondering how the motion was perceived. It was impossible to read Sonondra Ra, and her kaja offered few clues. *Natsiq* was the main design, of course, with a few strokes of *yuri*, the dedicated servant . . . Ra was a diplomat par excellence, and knew how to please her Prima. But the crowning pattern was *otta*, a kaja of joyful abandon. Strange choice, the Prima thought, for a meeting such as this. Then again, upon reflection, she had never seen the woman without it.

Last to enter was Chandras Delhi. She was an older woman, slender and frail-seeming, her body twisted from years of muscular dysfunction. She wore a harness of hi-chrome and plasteel that moved in response to her will, in which her body rested like a frail, captive bird. The humming of its motor could be heard as she entered, nodded minimal welcome, and took her seat before the door. As soon as she was settled into the chair, her dark eyes began to flit about the room with restless energy, never settling on one point for more than a second, never seeming to focus on anything. Her primary kaja, the *lilitu*, warned of an inner vision so intense that sometimes it overrode the demands of the physical world—and Alya knew from experience that she could be hard to deal with for that reason. But that was her own fault, too. The *simba* liked straightforward tests of dominance, and the *lilitu* was anything but straightforward.

When they were all seated at last, she took her own place at the head of the table. Five of her most trusted servants, one of them a master of brainware theory, the others passably capable. All of them Gueran, which meant—by definition—that they could not be predicted. How did you anticipate a person whose inner reality was an alien land?

"I've called you here to share some very dark news," she said. "You may or may not have heard rumor of it by now. I hope not; we've done our best to contain the matter. But events are rapidly reaching the point when that will no longer be possible." She flashed an icon to the room's innernet, which brought up matching images on the twelve monitors; her guests adjusted theirs to comfortable angles. Even Ra seemed to be watching hers intently, though of course it was the jeweled implants that gathered information for her, not her eyes; in her years on Paradise Station she had learned to mimic "normal" body language to perfection. "You see a map of the outworlds, marking each incursion of the so-called Lucifer virus." Black and white, of course. It wasn't necessary—Kent's brainware could compensate for his loss of color vision, translating the most complex chromatic sequence into tones that he could understand—but it was an act of courtesy that she not put any of them at a disadvantage. "Thus far we've isolated twenty-seven distinct spores of the original. Twenty-five were stopped before they did any real damage." Her expression became grim, to match her tone. "The other two, as you know, nearly cost us both ship and pilot. One was in your jurisdiction, Varsav. Please give us an update."

The man nodded sharply, his finger tracing restless figures on the tabletop. "MedTech says we've lost the outpilot, too much damage done to his brain. We may salvage him as a civilian, no more." She glanced at Kent and saw his expression tighten; what must be going on inside his head as he heard that, one could only wonder. "It looks like a spore of Lucifer, all right. Only this one . . ." He hesitated, glancing nervously at the others as if assessing whether or not they could be trusted. "The damage it did wasn't an accident. This time it was a direct assault."

The Prima nodded grimly. "That's why I've called you all here, to meet in realspace. That's why I won't trust to public transmission, even with encryption." Resting her hands on the table before her, she leaned forward aggressively. "Early generations of Lucifer invaded the brainware for the purpose of recording data; that pilots were harmed was little more than a side effect. Recent versions, however, seem to have been striking directly at the brain itself, and that . . ." she drew in a deep breath, giving them time to consider the consequences. "That is a whole new level of threat."

"Do we know for a fact that this one is Lucifer?" Kent asked. As always his voice was quiet, without emotion; he could have been discussing recent weather on Guera with that tone of voice, rather than the impending downfall of a civilization. "Or are we perhaps dealing with a second virus, launched independently."

She looked sideways to Devlin and nodded for him to take over.

"It's hard to be sure," the programmer said. "There's no question that the two viruses come from the same designer; that's been confirmed beyond a reasonable doubt. And we know that Lucifer was a fully evolving program, so theoretically it could have spawned anything . . . but is that what happened here?" He shook his head in frustration. "We collect new spores of Lucifer every day. Hopefully one will help us answer this question. The one man who seems to have the vision necessary to sort out this mess is still in transport, and not due to arrive in the outworlds for another month."

"Masada." Delhi mouthed the word slowly, testing it.

Alya nodded. "Masada."

"Isn't he the one who claims the outernet is alive?" There was a clear edge of contempt in Delhi's voice. "Do you really think such a fringe philosophy can help us here?"

"This 'fringe philosophy' as you call it," Alya told her, "is holism, and it's becoming quite respected in scientific circles. And it involves treating the outernet as a living system for analytical purposes . . . which isn't quite the same as you describe."

"And what makes you think this professor will be able to interpret this new development any better than our own people?" Varsav demanded. "It's not like we lack for experts here." A short, jerky wave of his hand indicated Devlin, and implied a host of others associated with him. "And they've spent months working on the problem; he'll be starting cold."

"First of all, he's not starting cold. He's spent the last five months working on Lucifer while in transport, with regular updates from my office. The fact that it's taking him half an E-year to get to the outworlds himself doesn't mean that our data transmission is limited to the same pace. The only information he lacks is of this most recent development . . . which, as I said, I will not trust to any manner of transmission. Neither will you, by the way; this matter is realspace-only. As for whether Masada will be of aid to us . . . we discussed all that before he was hired. I'm not going to go through those arguments again. It's a waste of time. Devlin Gaza says we need him, and it is his job to know what we need in this area; I suggest you respect his expertise, as I do. I will offer you this, however, for your consideration."

She flashed an icon to her brainware that triggered new displays on the room's twelve monitors; the guildmasters studied the charts before them, their own inner systems adding silent commentary. "What you see here is a breakdown of the initial reports on Lucifer's potential. As you see, no one predicted the kind of development we are now seeing . . . except for one man."

"Masada," Ra mused.

She flashed an icon to change their screens; Masada's own words scrolled up before them. *In that we are dealing with true evolution here, we cannot assume that this virus will limit its development to paths its makers would have approved of. Its primary mandate is to survive and reproduce, and, like true life-forms, it will make what adjustments it must to accomplish those ends.*

*We must be prepared for the possibility that, like so many biological infections, it will discover that a weak or damaged host is far less likely to interrupt its reproductive cycle at a crucial moment, and will do what it must to cripple its carrier.*

"Only that?" Varsav asked sharply. "Colorful metaphors, granted . . . but nothing more concrete?"

"Colorful metaphors, as you put it, are the language of life," Sonondra Ra reminded him. "If the Lucifer virus is truly alive—as this professor claims—then it deserves such a description." And she mused, "He has a poetic soul, this man."

"This is an *iru* we're talking about," Varsav reminded her.

"Whose wife was an *iru,* and a musician. To her the world was music. To her this virus would have seemed like a discordant phrase in an otherwise perfect symphony, and she would have described it—and predicted its development—in those terms." She turned her faceted eyes to the Prima and nodded. "Please continue."

"That's one quote from out of nearly two thousand pages of analytic work. Most of it is in terms, I am told—" she shot a brief glance to Devlin, "—that even our programmers would have trouble following. The point is, that was written nearly *five E-months ago.* Before the virus had undergone any major mutation; before there was any hint that it might begin to attack our pilots directly."

"So we are to admire him," Delhi assessed; a microphone at her throat magnified the sound so that all could hear it. "Point made. Let's move on."

She sensed Devlin stiffen at her side. Ah, he knew her well—or at least he knew the *simba* that was her primary kaja. Was Delhi's tone meant deliberately to challenge her, or was the woman so lost in thoughts of her own that she'd just forgotten herself? Alya remembered too many similar moments in the past to be able to accept that it was a simple social gaffe. This woman bore close watching.

"The *point*," the Prima stressed, "is that none of the other analysts saw this coming. The *point* is that we're dealing with something that may appear similar to other viruses, but in fact is a whole new category of threat. The *point*, Mistress Delhi, is that if we don't get this virus under control—and soon—we are going to watch our Guild crumble from the borders inward, and following that, all of outworld civilization as well. The ainniq system is what binds the human worlds together. If we reach the point where we can't use it reliably for transport, we are going to see cultural devastation to rival that of the Isolation period."

She paused then, her posture challenging Delhi—or anyone else—to interrupt her. "Guildmasters," she said quietly, "someone launched this thing. Its initial purpose was to spy on us, that we agree on: to copy details of outpilot medical programming and return to its maker with it. Only now it has turned into something more. Was this planned from the beginning? Did Lucifer's designers upload it to the outernet merely to steal Guild data, or was that just the opening foray in a far more deadly campaign? These are the questions these new spores have forced upon us . . . and we need the answer soon."

"Who would benefit?" Kent demanded. "I can name a thousand businesses and stations who would want the information it was designed to steal . . . but direct assault against the Guild? What purpose would that serve?"

"It's the question we have to try to answer now. And I am entrusting my five senior officers with it." A short wave of her hand encompassed the four Guildmasters, as well as the absent Luis Hsing. "Find me answers. Find them *soon*. I want every possible motive investigated, no matter how bizarre it might seem. If someone is striking at the Guild, then I want to know who stands to benefit. Businesses, individuals, stations, political fringe groups: start within your own domain and then I'll assign you others. Focus on the isolationist stations first, those who would obviously enjoy the disruption of Guild service. Varsav, you have the New Aryan Nation and the United Terran Front in your node; Kent, you have the Hausman League. There are at least two dozen stations more that I can name off the top of my head, which were founded for the express purpose of keeping outsiders away. Most of them can't afford to lose the ainniq any more than our own stations can, since they depend upon the Guild for commerce and supplies, but there might be one who's decided it would be willing to sacrifice all that if it meant no outsiders could reach their territory."

Varsav nodded grimly. "Destiny hates the Guild with a passion, for forcing the law of Universal Access down everyone's throats. If not for that, they say, they would have the homeland that was their birthright."

A faint, tight smile flickered across the Prima's face. "That's the test of human tolerance, isn't it? How many stations are up in arms about the fact that they must let strangers pass through their space . . . you'd think we were sending them through a Hausman jump, the way they squawked about it. Destiny Station's on top of the suspect list," she confirmed, "and several others now listed on the screens before you." She flashed the icon that would make the innernet change its display, and gave them a moment to shift gears and record what they were seeing. "Have these stations watched, and I mean, watched *closely*. I want every transmission, every visitor, every shipment accounted for."

"That'll be—" Kent began.

"Costly? Difficult?" She paused. "Then I suggest you begin immediately, so we can settle this matter in all due haste. Before this virus has a chance to mutate again."

"I note that you've assigned us stations in other nodes," Ra pointed out. "I assume we can ask for help from the local guild-masters?"

"No."

"No?" It was Varsav; his tone was indignant. "Since when don't we trust our own people?"

"She didn't say the issue was one of trust," Delhi pointed out coldly. "Don't jump to conclusions."

"If not trust, then what is it?"

The Prima waited until all eyes were upon her before speaking again, until that instant when the *nantana* in her sensed that there was no chance of interruption. "I told you Masada has been working on this project en route. Several days ago I received his latest report. It contained a suggestion I found most disturbing . . . and I have decided that until we learn more, I would rather err on the side of caution."

She looked them over, one by one, the four senior guildmasters and her Director of programming. It was the look of a *nantana*, who knew how to analyze the slightest gesture—the briefest flicker of an eyelid, even—to render a human soul bare. She trusted these people as much as she trusted anyone; they had her highest security clearance, and lifetime records of impeccable service. But she had not gained her position by being careless, and would not endanger it by becoming so now. Even if none of them had launched the virus, that didn't mean that they might not choose to take advantage of it for some more private rivalry. Guildmasters were loyal to the Guild, but notoriously treacherous in dealing with each other.

She was recording the meeting, of course. Later she would study the holos of these people in painstaking detail, analyzing their reactions through her presentation. Especially at this next moment, her announcement; that was the kind of instant when someone might give themselves away.

She said it quietly, and without fanfare. "The Guild may have a leak."

The reaction was immediate.

"Our own people?" Varsav asked incredulously.

"Who?" Delhi demanded. "Who is he accusing?"

"Impossible." That was Kent. "Simply impossible."

Devlin looked more shocked than any of them. "How does he know that?" he demanded. "How *can* he know that?"

"The man's weaving fantasies," Varsav muttered. "This is the *Guild* we're talking about."

Ra said nothing.

"If I knew more about this, I would tell you," she assured them. "But Director Gaza and I made the decision early on not to trust certain kinds of data to transmission, in order to maintain top security on this project. As a result Dr. Masada is being most circumspect in what he tells me, and I have no way to question him thoroughly until he arrives in person. This much I will share with you: he says that his analysis of the virus has led him to believe that someone from our own Guild is involved in all this." She paused, studying their expressions with a practiced eye. Nothing seemed out of place . . . yet. "That means we must guard all our secrets until he arrives, ten times more carefully than before . . . even from our own people."

"You're asking us to believe that one of our own would sell out the Guild," Ra said quietly. "I find that incredible."

"I didn't say that. All I'm telling you now is that there's a good chance that someone wearing a Guild uniform has leaked information to the outside. Maybe he did so deliberately. Maybe he was just careless. When Masada arrives, he can give us more details, and we can assess the situation properly. Until then, we'll function on the assumption that the worst is true. And that means trusting no one. *No one*," she stressed. "Not the other guildmasters." She looked pointedly at Devlin. "And not your own department. I'm sorry, but some of your people have professional contacts outside the Guild. That makes them highly suspect."

"I understand." His expression was dark, and she knew him well enough to guess at the anger seething just beneath the surface. He was a proud man, and the thought that someone in his charge might have done such a thing must surely be eating him alive. "I assure you, if there is any kind of security problem in my department, I *will* find out."

She nodded. "All right, then. You know what we're up against. You five are among my most trusted officers. All information will be channeled through you and Hsing, and that includes Masada's work. Anything you have to report to me should come by courier, or else give it to me in person; I want none of this transmitted, not even between our own offices. Remember, whomever is responsible for Lucifer has already bested our security once, let's not assume that was an isolated incident. Maximize your precautions at every turn. Understood?"

Looking them over, studying their responses, she knew in her heart that when she went over the tapes of the meeting, she would find a thousand things to question, a thousand places where suspicion might be anchored. She trusted them as much as she trusted anyone, but in matters like this, trust was a luxury she couldn't afford. She'd watch them all, and the slightest hint that anything was not as it should be would bring all the force of her office down on someone's head.

"If a situation arises where you must transmit, you'll use this for encryption." She nodded to Devlin, who flashed an icon that would begin loading the proper programs into the guild-masters' brainware. She listened to the heavy silence as each of her guests envisioned the icons necessary to receive and store them. As she did so, she was intimately aware of the flaws in even that system, of that fragile instant in which the binary codes in one machine would slip through space to contact another. Could they be hijacked in that short a time? she wondered. What if there was an invading program in the room even now, collecting and recording their most private communications?

*So what's the alternative?* she asked herself harshly. *Shall we plug wires into our heads, like the ancients did? Isolate ourselves inside our skulls like the Terrans still do, hoping the invader won't zap our brains the one minute we do connect? You can't live in fear like that,* she thought. *Not every moment. If they get us to the point where we're feeling that paranoid, then we've lost a far greater battle than with this one virus.*

But she could feel the fear, a cold trickle of unease in her heart . . . and she knew that the others did, too.

## TENSAN

The *tensan* is restless, uneasy. It feels driven to do something, but it doesn't know what that something is. It feels dread, as if contemplating the loss of something it holds dear, but cannot tell just what it fears losing, or how that thing will be lost. It feels excitement, as if some bright new horizon is about to be revealed, but it lacks any insight into where it may travel once it gets there.

It senses, in the core of its being, that its life is about to change forever. It cannot know what the process is like, for only those who have submitted to the Changing and come out the other side can understand it.

It hungers to become something greater than it is.

It fears unbecoming all that it has been.

It knows, in its heart, that Change is unavoidable.

*KAJA: An Outworlder's Guide to the Gueran*
*Social Contract, Volume 2: Signs of the Soul*

# REIJIK NODE
# REIJIK STATION

IT WAS HARD to learn to take a back seat in your own head, to
let someone else take control of your flesh and allow his sensations to invade your soul. The first few times it happened Jamie
was so terrified she could do little more than cower in the one
corner of her brain that was left to her, crying and screaming
without sound, without comfort. Watching her body move as
one might watch a viddie.

A few of the Others were gentle. A few of them seemed to
understand what was needed. Even Derik, in his own coarse
way, seemed to sense that this was not the time for macho display, that the fragile mind sharing this body with him could
only handle so many challenges. So it was pretty much all right
with him, so far. That was a surprise. She had expected him to
be one of the worst. But if he was coarse-mannered and violent
and full of pent-up rage, that was all on her behalf, and at least
he wasn't self-destructive, like Zusu. No, he wasn't one of the
bad ones.

Verina helped a lot. She was a cold presence, but she did know
a lot, and sometimes when Jamie was most afraid, she would
hear that measured voice whispering facts to her, to ease her
fears. Like when Zusu took over for the first time, and Jamie
watched in horror as her own hand reached for the utility knife,
took it up in a trembling grip, and then began to scratch jagged
lines into the flesh of her own arm. *Self-hate, induced by Shido's
minions,* Verina whispered the words into her brain even as the
blood began to flow. *If not for her existence, it would have no outlet, and you would surely be overcome by it.* And as she watched in

horrified amazement, the cool voice assured her, *Don't worry, we never let her go too far.*

*Why did they do it?* she begged them all. Struggling to put the pieces together, to understand what Shido had wanted. Oh, she knew now what had been done to her, that was no longer a secret . . . but *why?*

They never answered that.

The most amazing part of all was that these Others who shared her body seemed to know each other pretty well. It was like some secret club that everyone belonged to except her . . . only now she had been taken in, and she was fighting to learn the rules before the very concept of what the club was about drove her crazy.

The worst of them all was Katlyn. Not because she was the most unstable; on the contrary, of all the many Others who crowded in Jamisia's head she was one of the sanest. And she never tried to take control if the moment wasn't right for it, which couldn't be said of all the others; in their hunger to experience life at its fullest there were more than a few who demanded prime time, pushing Jamisia to the back of her own brain at a time she most wanted to be in control. No, Katlyn always waited until the moment was right for her to take over. Jamie flushed as she recalled her last escapade, a meeting with the Captain-General's son in one of the hydroponic gardens. He'd managed to shut down the main portals so that no one would interupt them, and then, in the midst of all those exotic smells, heady high-ox air filling her lungs, Jamie had felt the raw heat of Katlyn's hunger filling her. . . . God, she thought, what shamed her more now, the memory of what her body had done, or the memory of how it had felt to do it? Even now it made her tremble.

*It's really about power,* Verina explained. *Sex is just the vehicle. It's about connection, breaking through the walls that confine us, defying the doctors who meant to stifle our freedom.*

But it was about sex, too, raw and clutching and wholly overwhelming to Jamisia's inexperienced soul. Yes, she knew now that her body was far from inexperienced, for Katlyn had shared stories of her adventures on the habitat . . . but Jamisia had no real memories of those trysts, and so they didn't affect her. Not like these did.

*We're a team now,* Katlyn whispered, in the same seductive tones she used to draw men into her web. *And this is so much better, no doctors to hide from, no more secrets to guard . . . so relax. Sit back. Enjoy.*

Hot memories. Shameful memories

*You'll have to function as a team,* her tutor told her in a dreamscape vision. It was one of many he had planted in her brain, to help her through this terrifying transition. She had them nearly every night now. Workshops in insanity. *It's your only hope.*

*I'm trying,* she told him. Tears in her eyes. *I really am trying.* Teamwork. . . .

"**J**amie?"

She looked up from packing and saw him standing in the doorway. As always, his presence brought a flush to her cheeks. For a moment she hesitated, waiting to see if Katlyn would take over—Justin was really her lover, not Jamisia's—but for once she didn't. Was that good or bad?

"Come in."

She looked up from the bag she had been packing, one of two that held her meager belongings. Despite the temptations of the metroliner she had purchased very few things, always aware that her resources were limited. Clothing, mostly practical. Jewelry, modest pieces that could be worn with anything. Cosmetics, enough to accent her features without adopting the bright and often hideous fashions that swept through the great ship at intervals. No music beyond that which she had brought with her from Shido. No books. There were libraries for those, from which she could borrow journals for Verina, suspense novels for Katlyn, combat manuals for Derik, space adventures for Raven . . . now that she was allowed to share consciousness with the Others it was all a mess in her brain, she could no longer remember who had read what.

For a moment it seemed that he might come into the room and kiss her. She braced herself not to draw away from him if he did. It wasn't that she didn't find him attractive herself, and the few times she'd been with him in her own right she'd rather liked him. But the memory of her involuntary intimacy with him made her skin crawl when he touched her.

Damn it, where was Katlyn?

"We need to talk," he said quietly.

She started to say something about long good-byes—and then looked up at him, and looked in his eyes, and the words died in her throat. This wasn't about her leaving the metroliner next E-week. It wasn't about two lives that were about to be separated, to Katlyn's frustration and Jamisia's great relief. They had been through all that, a dozen times over.

This was about something else . . . something more.

"Okay." She closed the cover of her bag and sat on the edge of the bed, not quite knowing what to expect. "Go ahead."

"Not here." He glanced around the small room—somewhat nervously, she thought—then gestured toward the corridor outside. "Come with me."

Mystified, she followed him. This kind of behavior wasn't typical of Justin at all. As she left the room, she flashed a quick thought to her Others—?????—but none responded. Apparently they were as much in the dark about this as she was.

*Be careful*, Derik warned her, as they walked down the corridor in silence. External silence, anyway.

One would think that after three years a passenger would know the metroliner by heart, but he took her to a place she had never seen before. Once he used an ID tag to open a sealed door; at another portal he hesitated, and she guessed that the ship's system was checking his brainware for clearance. Soon they were in a part of the metroliner where no passengers besides themselves could be seen, all stark corridors and simple door-frames with numbers beside them: cold, undecorated, unwelcoming. Something about the place made her skin crawl . . . could it be memory? Was this the place they had brought her when she first arrived, where medical tests had been performed on her, to guarantee that she was free of infection? With a start she realized that Verina had been present for much of that testing, her quick mind absorbing every fact within reach. Not an ordeal, for that one, but an education.

How different Jamisia's memories seemed, now that she

knew about the Others who were part of them. She wondered if she would ever get used to it.

"In here."

The door he opened led to a meeting room of some kind. She hesitated, then went inside. It was a small room, simply furnished, with a table and chairs set alongside one wall and a computer console along the other. No pictures. No labels. No fragments of someone's business left behind, that she could judge its purpose from.

He locked the door behind them and then walked about the room, peering into its corners. He had a sensor in his hand, which he referred to periodically, and at last he seemed satisfied with its readings. "It's clean," he muttered, and he put the box away. Only then did he turn to her, leaning back against the computer console as he did so.

"Clean?"

"Most of the metroliner has surveillance capacity. I shut it down in this room. They won't discover it till tomorrow at least, not with all the other stuff that's going on here."

"So you mean—" It hit her suddenly; she could barely whisper the words. "My room?"

"I said *capacity*," he stressed. "Under normal circumstances, passenger privacy is considered sacred we'd have a revolution on our hands if it weren't. But the Captain-General reserves the right to use surveillance if necessary to safeguard the ship . . . so all the rooms are wired, just in case. Don't worry," he said quickly, seeing the growing alarm in her eyes. "I know for a fact yours has never been turned on before today. No one's been watching you, Jamie."

"But you thought someone might be." Her heart had begun to pound in her chest. "Today."

He hesitated. "Let's say I didn't want to take any chances."

He came toward her, drawing a folded plastic sheet from out of his pocket. "This came yesterday. Mom doesn't know I have it."

She looked at him for a minute, then took the letter. And opened it. And read.

*To Viktoria Clarendon, Captain-General of the Earth Metroliner* Aurora.

*We have reason to believe there may be a fugitive hiding among your passengers. Her true name is Jamisia Shido, and she has been implicated in the terrorist sabotage which destroyed Shido Station three E-years ago. We are most anxious to find her, and have arranged for all access stations serving Earth to be on guard for her arrival. In addition, we would appreciate your assistance.*

*Ms. Shido was not present at the start of your journey, but would have come on board some short time later. She is a young woman, now nineteen years old; attached to this file are pictures of her when she left Shido Habitat, and a computer update of her probable appearance now. We do not know for sure what brainware she carries, thus we regret this cannot be used to verify her identity. Attached are the following additional files for your use: kinesthetic template, fingerprint and retina scans, DNA sequencing, betawave prints. We hope that some or all of this will prove useful to you in your search for her.*

*We regret that we do not have an agent on Earth's access station to take custody of Ms. Shido, which would be our preferred method of dealing with this matter. Instead we ask that you bring her back to Earth with you on your return journey, to be surrendered to the proper authorities when she arrives. If this is not possible, we ask that you ascertain which access station she is being shipped to and contact the appropriate authorities; a list of their names and eddresses has been appended to this letter.*

*Thank you for your assistance in this matter.*

She read the letter twice, and then finally the signatures and titles scanned in beneath it. *Earth Central Security. United Habitat Defense.* Two of the most powerful security operations in Earth's domain. They wanted her, these people, and they wanted her badly.

Suddenly the old fear was back. She wanted to run somewhere—anywhere—but where was there to go? So she forced herself to take in a deep, deep breath and hand the letter back to him. Waiting.

"Well?" he said quietly.

She swallowed thickly. It hurt.

"Jamie?"

She whispered it: "What do you want me to say?" God, they had her retina, her betawave . . . everything. What effort would it be for the ship's crew to scan the passengers as they left? Security probably did that anyway. She was trapped, trapped. . . .

"Tell me about this," he urged softly. "Help me understand."

How many dreams had she had, in which her tutor warned her about the enemy? How many times had he told her in dreamscapes that her brainware was worth a fortune to Shido's rivals, that they would come after her if they possibly could . . . and she had been foolish, and imagined herself safe here. She had forgotten the first rule of inspace, which he'd drilled into her from childhood: people can only travel so fast. Data moves at the speed of light.

It had beaten her here.

"Jamie?"

She drew in a deep breath, trying to assemble a plausible lie. What could she tell him? How much did she dare trust him? *Go for it*, Katlyn whispered, but Jamisia wasn't about to take her advice; Kat's brain was between her legs.

"I am from Shido." She said it slowly, picking her way through each word with care. "That much is true." Where could she lie safely, and where would he catch her? There might be more to this message, she realized suddenly, which he had not shared with her. She'd better stay very, very close to the truth. "There was a hostile takeover about the time the *Aurora* was leaving Earth. The habitat was destroyed. I . . ." She saw the look in his eyes and was suddenly wary. *He knows what happened to Shido*, she thought. *He researched that before he came to me.* She felt tears beginning to build in her eyes, and dreaded the moment they would begin to trickle down her cheeks, advertising her fear.

"I got away," she said at last. "One of my . . . family sent me here. To go join my outworld relatives." One more deep breath: shaky though it was, the rush of oxygen lent her strength. "My father was involved in research for Shido. He was teaching me about his work, he . . ." The first tear began a slow course down her cheek, and she decided to use it. "He's dead," she whispered. "He died in the explosion. All of my family died."

She broke down then, and wept openly; it was only partly for show, mostly it was genuine grief pouring out of her. It had been so long since she'd mourned the loss of everything she'd had, everyone she'd loved, she'd been holding it all in. . . .

*That's it,* one of the Others whispered. She didn't even know which one. *Let the tears flow, Jamie, he'll respond to that.*

And he did. After a moment's hesitation he came to her and gathered her tenderly into his arms. The embrace felt awkward—he was little more than a stranger to her, though a lover to Katlyn—but the warmth was good and the caring was genuine, and in the back of her mind a flicker of hope began to spark.

Verina began to feed concepts into her brain; she tried not to hesitate as she absorbed them, tried to make the words flow like her own. "His work was highly secretive. It's worth a lot to Shido's rivals. I don't know all the details, but I know—" *Careful!* Derik warned. "Enough to be afraid of them. Enough to know that they think I have information I don't . . . and they're not going to believe that." She met Justin's eyes then, and tried to pour all her desperate need for masculine support into that precious contact. "Shido's rivals will be looking for me. They want to bring me back to Earth; once we're there, corporate law gives them the right to what's in my brain. Only they'd have to . . . they'd have to . . ." She choked out the words. "It's . . . not a safe process," she said at last. "It might . . ." she hesitated, not wanting to push the truth too far. Then: *oh, what the hell . . .* "I might not survive it."

He fingered the paper in silence for a moment, as if weighing her words against the formal titles printed on it. *He isn't a corporate,* Verina judged. *Most likely a rockborn for whom this type of affair is the subject of viddies, little more. He probably doesn't know enough of corporate law to judge if what you're saying is reasonable or not.*

*But that could be an advantage,* Derik offered. *Brave mudder hero helps comely young victim to escape the clutches of an evil syndicate. . . .* Someone giggled. *Fuck it, if it works, go for it!*

At last he folded up the message. It took him a while, lean fingers pressing each crease before going on to the next. She held her breath while she watched, afraid to ask what he was thinking. What he intended.

At last he said, "When you get to these relatives of yours . . . you'll be okay?"

Her heart pounded wildly. She tried to sound calm. "Yes. Yes. Earth law doesn't hold in the outworlds . . . once I'm there, they can't come get me."

He said nothing more for a moment.

"Justin?"

"Mom hasn't seen this yet," he muttered. He slid it into the pocket of his jumpsuit; a faint smile touched the corner of his lips. "Guess she doesn't have to, does she?"

*Yes!* Zusu crowed, and Derik cheered, *You did it, girl!*

*Not yet,* Katlyn warned. *The deal's been offered, not sealed.*

Jamisia could barely make out her own thoughts, for all the voices inside her. "What if there are more?" she asked nervously. Half afraid to even broach the subject. "What if they write again?"

He took her by the arms, and pulled her gently toward him. "Don't worry, I'll watch for it. No one on this ship will sell you out, Jamie. I promise."

He kissed her then, and she could feel herself slipping away. No, not slipping away, exactly . . . slipping from this self into an Other. *Don't try to fight it, Jamie. This is our life now. Let go. . . .* So she let go, sinking back. Giving up. Granting control to one who understood the rules of this fragile moment, and could make the most of it.

"My hero," Katlyn breathed, smiling.

**T**he disembarkation went surprisingly smoothly, considering how many thousands of people were involved. That was no small accomplishment, when you took into account that the stewards overseeing the effort were, by definition, inexperienced; with two round trips providing enough pay for retirement, it was rare for anyone to dedicate their lives to metroliner service. All the ship's officers were doing their part as well, and anyone the officers could draft into duty . . . which meant that Justin was too busy to spend any time with her.

Just as well.

She had the Earth transmission hardcopy in her pocket, along with two others which had come later. Shido's enemies were determined to find her, all right. She tried not to think about what they would do to her if they did. For all of the dreamscapes her tutor had provided, none of them actually told Jamisia what they wanted with her, or even what the point of Shido's work had been. She had the impression he really didn't want her to know, as if he had thought the knowledge was more than she could handle.

*So I'll never know*, she thought as she closed her cabin door for the last time. *Because I sure as hell am not going back to Earth to find out.*

They said you could see the ainniq from the forward domes, but they also said it was so crowded up there that it was hard to see anything if you were merely human. She watched as Variants hurried past her, racing to the spot: Alegonki, with long, spindly legs that would raise them high above a crowd; Salvationers, whose prehensile feet made them perfectly suited for climbing the support struts of an observation dome; other Variants whose form gave them advantage and not a few true-humans as well, all rushing to the place where they could, if they were lucky, see that most marvelous of all natural phenomena. The rift in space which had given man the stars.

*We really should go look*, Raven began, but the Others shouted her down. In Derek's words, *Now is not the fucking time!* As for Jamisia . . . all she could think about was getting off the ship in one piece, and avoiding whatever dangers might be waiting for her. And apparently the majority of her Others agreed, for she heard no further protests as she turned away from the corridor that would lead her to the observation dome, and headed toward the bay.

She had both her bags slung over her shoulder; it was an awkward burden but a necessary one. She didn't want to get slowed up in baggage protocol, not with ten thousand people all claiming their household effects at one time. The fact that there was a hefty fine for every pound of baggage above a certain limit hadn't stopped these people from cramming the great ship with their belongings; most of them were rich, after all, and many of them were emigrants proper who would never be coming back to Earth again. You couldn't expect them to make a trip like this without all their property, could you? Stewards hurried past her with servocarts laden down with everything from furniture to architectural fragments. And that was just from the staterooms. God alone knew what there was in storage.

*Crazy,* she thought to the Others. as she made her way through the madness. Derik's word for it was considerably less refined. She could feel him come to the surface once or twice as the press of the crowd got too close, but he never quite took over. This wasn't a good time for him, he lacked patience. She could hear the Others chiding him as she made her way to the exit bay, and having an argument raging in the back of her head didn't help her own nerves at all.

*There could have been another transmission,* she thought as she slipped into a tube. Overloaded, the system started with a jerk. *They could be waiting for me.* What if Justin hadn't intercepted them all? What if her enemies had made contact with the station they were approaching, and the authorities there were ready to seize her?

*Unlikely,* Verina told her. *We'll be processed through emigration, which is in the hands of the Guild. I doubt the Guerans would cooperate with such a thing, and the price of lying to them is surely too high to risk.*

*Are Guildsmen so incorruptible?* Jamisia wondered.

It seemed to her Verina smiled. *No, my dear. But it's said that they hate Earth with a passion, so I doubt they would lower themselves to becoming a tool of corporate politics.*

*If they hate Earth so much, then why are they here? They're the ones who taught us about the ainniq. Without them we never could have left safespace.*

*Yes,* Verina mused. *Isn't that the question?*

And Derik added dryly, *Gueran ethics. Whatever the hell that means.*

At last she reached the exit bay to which she had been assigned. She shifted the heavy bags to a new and more comfortable position and gave her ID chip to the steward on duty there. He read it, nodded shortly, and gave it back to her. "Confirmation?" he asked. For a moment she didn't know what he was referring to, then she saw him holding out a small disk for her use. She placed it against her temple, flashed up her brainware's ID program, and had it reel off her personal specs into the small receiver. False specs, of course; in her months on the metroliner she had altered all of her ID programming, as per dreamscape instructions. Thank God for her tutor's foresight.

Apparently the subterfuge passed muster, for he nodded at last, took back the receiver, and gestured for her to move forward into the bay. He even managed to smile at her as she passed by, though clearly the day had tired him. "Hauck 9200, huh? That's a nice piece of circuitry to have." She smiled weakly back, but didn't answer. How could she? God alone knew what was really in her head. Considering that her brainware had to respond to as many as a dozen individuals at one time, each with his or her own agenda, it was amazing there was still any room for gray matter in there.

She passed through multiple checkpoints and had no problem at any of them. She even began to relax a bit, though several of the Others warned against it. God, if she could only shut them all up for just an hour, one precious hour of peace. . . .

And then she was ushered into a small room with two people in it. One was a woman, whose right arm and right leg seemed strangely twisted. One was a man.

Gueran.

It was amazing how powerful he seemed. In truth he was neither tall nor strongly built, nor possessed of any other attribute the mind might associate with power. His body was so swathed in loose black robes it was hard to get any physical sense of him at all. But even as she felt her breath catch in her throat, she knew where the feeling came from. He *was* powerful: not in presence, but in truth. His word could give her freedom, or bar her from the ainniq. His race could bring planets into the fellowship of human nations, or cut them off from it forever. And his face . . . she knew even as she looked at him that the fine black lines which seemed almost barbaric in origin—like the tattoos of Earth-primitives before the first age of space had begun—were in fact a language as rich as any spoken. A form of communication which (it was said) rivaled the telepathic in its ability to communicate fine gradations of mood and intention.

She felt suddenly lost, not knowing how to speak to him.

He was silent for a few seconds—she could almost see the fine transmissions linking him to the ship's computer, a spider's web of data—and then said, "Jamisia Capra."

She nodded. So far so good. They might suspect who she really was . . . but they didn't know.

"Medical records . . ." Again a pause. She hadn't boarded with the others, so she didn't have quite the exhaustive dossier the other passengers did; nevertheless, they had tested her pretty thoroughly before accepting her for passage. There were several dozen medical conditions, she knew, which would not be permitted into Guild-controlled space. The Guerans claimed it was because they were highly contagious, and could devastate populations that had lost their natural immunity. Detractors claimed that the Guild culled out genotypes it didn't like as well, sorting among the physical and mental types of old Earth for the ones it preferred, discarding the rest.

She held her breath, waiting for his verdict.

"Clean," he said at last. He held out a small instrument toward her; she recognized a DNA curette. "For confirmation only, Ms. Capra."

She held out her arm and let him touch it briefly with the instrument, garnering cells for examination. The curette hummed briefly, then buzzed. Whatever the sound meant, it seemed to satisfy him.

"Very well." The Guildsman stepped aside, signaling a far door to open. "Everything's in order, Ms. Capra. Please proceed."

She hesitated, then moved forward. Her path to the door brought her close to the room's other occupant; the woman gazed at her from a strangely twisted face as she walked cautiously past her, but she said nothing.

And then she was past the door and entering the docking bay proper. There were Guerans loading luggage into a mid-sized transport, with twenty to thirty passengers already inside. She accepted a hand up the entrance ramp and found a seat by one of the curved, clear windows. In the distance stars were gleaming, and there between them . . . was that it, that flicker of radiance? Was that the ainniq, signpost of her freedom?

*We made it!* one of the Others exulted. It didn't even matter who; for once, it seemed, they were all in agreement.

Jamisia leaned against the wall of the transport, exhausted by the tension of the last few days. But it was over now, at least for a while. Soon she would be in Guild space, protected by galactic law from the greed and the politics of corporate Earth. And then, for a time, she would be safe. The Guild had no interest in her. Shido's enemies couldn't reach her. Not until an outship brought her to the first access station would her enemies have a chance to get to her again . . . and by then she would think of some way to evade them. Somehow.

*Yes*, she agreed. *We made it.*

Fingering her icon necklace, she gazed out at the starscape, searching for the ainniq.

**"W**ell?" the Guildsman asked.

The Yin thought long and hard and then chose her words carefully. "She has secrets, that one."

"Many have secrets."

"She is pursued."

"We know that."

"She knows it, too."

The Guildsman shrugged; the motion was anything but casual. "And?"

The Yin paused, considering. "I don't think she herself understands why they're after her. If so . . ."

"Then we would gain nothing from questioning her at this point."

"Exactly."

The Guildsman drew out an item from the pocket of his robe. Hardcopy of an Earth transmission, folded in thirds. He unfolded it. Opened it. Read.

*We have reason to believe there may be a fugitive hiding among your passengers . . .*

"Let's see where she goes," he said at last. "Let's see who comes after her." He refolded the letter and tucked it away inside his robe once more. "Let's see if her knowledge increases."

"You'll warn the outship?"

He shut his eyes for barely an instant, flashing the icons that would link him to that ship. Thoughts became binary code became a signal beam . . . several seconds to span the space between where his signal began and where it would be answered. Several seconds more for the answer to get to him.

"It's done," he said. And he took up his place before the inner door once more. "They'll take care of it."

The door whisked open. A young man was waiting, baggage in hand.

*Next. . . .*

## ASSIVAK

The *assivak* does not speak, or cry out, or leap upon its enemies. Its customary appearance is as ore dead, for it is motionless, reserving strength. If one looks closely one might see the flicker of an eye or the twitch of a sensory hair, but even those things are rare.

It does not have to move, or scream, or rush about in any way. It is an architect, who builds what it must build and then waits for that structure to serve its purpose. It does not pursue food, for food comes right to it. It does not hunt, but receives. Its pattern is ordered, so finely designed that one who is not looking closely will never even see it . . . and by then it is too late.

No one can guess what thoughts are stirring within its brain. No excess motion betrays its purpose. It builds its traps just so, and waits. Nothing more. If the trap is right, if the prey is not alert to its existence, there is no doubt as to the outcome. No reason to waste energy.

It rarely goes hungry.

> KAJA: An Outworlder's Guide to the Gueran
> Social Contract, Volume 2: Signs of the Soul

# SERPENT'S REACH NODE
# SERPENT'S REACH STATION

IN THE WEB the spider waited: centered, silent. Crystalline strands stretched out from beneath her feet to node, station, outship and beyond. A thousand strands as fine as thought, to bind the human worlds together. They shivered now and then, as one event or another altered the tenuous balance of human power, and the creature at the heart of the web shifted her attention accordingly. Slender fingers stroking the web with loving care, coaxing maximum data from each frail vibration.

There were thick strands for each of the Guild stations, paths of shimmering data whose far ends lodged in the souls of the Guildmasters. Those were the most important strands, the armature of the entire structure. If Hsing so much as twitched in his golden palace, the spider knew it. If Ra took a lover who might prove her weakness, the news was carried along that slender thread, until it came within the spider's reach. If Kent or Varsav so much as drew a breath that might prove relevant, by darkshift the spider was tasting his exhalation. There were other strands that led to other Guildmasters as well, twenty of her strongest lines and over two hundred of lesser strength, but those were the four that mattered right now. Those were the four whom the Prima, in her wisdom, had declared the spider's rivals.

Hsing. Ra. Varsav. Kent.

They were not rivals for power, not in the traditional sense. Chandras Delhi had already reached the highest station that any human—save the Prima herself—might attain. Yet power might be lost. Only two hundred and twenty nodes existed in outspace, each with its resident Guildmaster. It wasn't a large number, when one considered the thousands of Guildfolk who fought for such an appointment, and those just beneath her were constantly seeking the chink in her armor that would allow them to unseat her. As for the other Guildmasters . . . they always bore watching. Her station at Serpent's Reach was a plum assignment, situated at the midpoint of several major trade routes, and she knew the others coveted it. She could taste how badly they wanted it, knew in her soul that a single mistake—even a fleeting moment of weakness—might find her rendering up her passcodes to a stranger, so that another might move in.

Hsing, Varsov, Kent, Ra. They all had stations of their own; not the equal of hers perhaps, but valuable in their own right. So there would be no competition from that end. Indeed, they probably expended as much energy guarding their own positions as she did with her own. Ra was not someone she feared; the woman was shallow, obsessed with her own pleasures, and was unlikely to be involved in the kind of political intrigue that Delhi and the others thrived on. Delhi kept a watchful eye on Ra's affairs, but expected no surprises. Kent had been a shell of a man since his accident, but a keen wit still lay coiled within that tormented soul, and people who underestimated him did so at their own risk. She did not intend to. Varsav . . . that man was a lit fuse, and there was no telling what might set him off, but he was a brilliant strategist, and his attention to detail made him doubly dangerous. People like that sometimes sensed the webwork in which she had bound them, and if they struggled hard enough and long enough they could damage the delicate strands of data which she used to control them. As for Hsing . . . the man was a capable adversary, and normally she watched him closely, but he had been away from his station for a year now. By the time he returned, there would be a dozen underlings vying for his seat, each with his own private plot to steal the mastership. It would take all his energy to consolidate his position and undo what damage those absent months had fostered. So she did not fear Hsing. Not yet.

Did they fear her?

She knew that Kent did. Kent was a creature of fear, and even the flood of chemicals in his bloodstream—she had a full accounting of it, the gem of her secret intelligence—could not negate the emotion entirely. She knew that his own dark senses had tested the borders of her domain, and she had not turned away all his efforts. Better to know where the enemy was, and feed him the data you wanted him to have, then to send him back into the nameless darkness to plan a better assault. Because the next one you might not catch. . . .

Her brainware flashed an alert: incoming shipment. She signaled it to go ahead and let the symbols of its efforts scroll upward in her field of vision. It was a data capsule, hijacked from Reijik Station. She keyed it to open, took a brief look at the coded contents, and then shunted it over to her decryption experts. She noted the cost of transmission—not cheap, but then, hijacked data never was—and flashed an icon to confirm that payment would be made. It wasn't necessary for her to visualize instructions to have her account debited the proper amount, or to see that it was forwarded to the proper agent. Nor was it necessary for her to oversee the process which disguised the payment as something else, so that an unexpected audit would not reveal illicit business. All of that was automatic, programmed deep into the recesses of her brainware and the living cells that surrounded it. Such methods were as much a part of her as breathing.

With a sigh of satisfaction she flashed a series of icons to her brainware, and the plasteel cage that supported her body began to move. She could have had her brain repaired long ago so that her body moved of its own accord, without the need for mechanical support, but there was risk in that; the same techniques which would reroute the neural pathways in search of more efficient cellular combinations might also do damage to the delicate systems she relied upon for thought. A woman from some other planet might have risked that, preferring to sacrifice a few fleeting thoughts rather than spend her life encased in this mechanized carapace, but no Gueran ever would. The legacy of Guera was in the minds and souls of her people, and like all her people, Chandras Delhi revered the human brain in its natural form. If the cost was to her body, so be it; she was a creature of mind, not flesh, and would willingly bear the sacrifice.

*Reijik Station*, she thought. That was one of the nodes that served the motherworld, Earth. There were some on her staff who felt she was mad to focus as much energy as she did on that forgotten planet, but that was because they didn't see the universe as she did. Earth was so finely wrapped in datalines that it appeared as a white cocoon to her inner senses: a network so closely tangled that only rarely did an outsider manage to pull loose a thread and examine it. Few bothered to try. To most Guerans, Earth was a waste of space and history, too tied up in its own internal politics to ever become meaningful in the larger sense. Those Guerans who did pay attention to their evolutionary motherworld generally did so with resentment. Earth was, after all, the homeworld of nine billion "true" humans, and the focal point of five billion more. Or so they called themselves. Humans whose ancestors had stayed at home while the colonists of Guera and Yin and Frisia went forth to claim the galaxy . . . and now they dared to feel superior to their Hausman cousins, and to flaunt that superiority at every turn.

In truth, Delhi mused, if Earth had been closer to an ainniq, there would probably have been war long ago. The Variant worlds were united in very little, but their hatred of Earth was a rallying point. Shortsighted fools. Just as the primordial melange of Earth's ancient oceans had once provided nature with the raw materials for life, so would its crowded datasphere now provide the spawning ground for new forms of technology, new gems of data, new dangers . . . she was alone in feeling that Earth had such promise, but that didn't bother her. Few watched the human homeworld as she did, which meant there were fewer rivals for her harvests. Her predations.

*Reijik Station*, she mused. Her fingers twitched in their plasteel cage as she wondered what manner of feast this harvest might provide.

**"D**amn it to hell," Stivan cursed.

His coworker looked up from the control panel where his own attentions were focused. "What's that, Stiv?"

"Nothing." His voice was a growl. "Nothing at all."

Line after line of code scrolled up on the monitor. You had to look at hijacked material like that—on a monitor—and you had to shut your brainware down, too, because you never knew when there was some kind of security virus embedded in that mess that would fry your circuitry as soon as it got into your head. Okay, so that was the job. He understood it, and accepted the whole thing. But this shit was encrypted out the wazoo. His decryption programs were sending him signals he had never seen before, and the only references he had on such things were in his own head.

"Shit." He struck the control panel in frustration and at last turned away from the monitor. One deep breath. Two. Take it in, hold it for a six-count, let it out. He'd made enough mistakes when his temper was short that he'd finally programmed his brainware not to accept the start-up icon unless he was calm—which was fine in theory, but a royal pain in the ass when he needed access to something quickly. Like now.

At last he guessed that he had reached the point where his internal monitors would be satisfied with the key readings—pulse rate, blood pressure, skin conductivity—and he envisioned the start-up icon. It was a red dragon on a black background, very dramatic. He had based it upon a tattoo he had once seen as a child, that had stuck in his mind ever since. It was complex and hard to envision properly—he'd programmed his head so that any line more than a nano out of place would cause the whole icon to fail—but that was for security. Stivan Dici was obsessed with security. Little wonder, since his primary job was to break down the security of other systems.

It took him three tries—apparently his blood pressure was still a bit too high, and he had to wait it out—but at last he was back in operation. The decryption data was in part of his permanent storage array, nestled against the inside of his ventricular wall. The information took up a large chunk of his permanent memory, but it was well worth the sacrifice. What was he going to do with his brainware otherwise, store viddies for replay?

With a spare headset he downloaded the information he needed, then wiped the headset clean immediately. With data like this, you didn't take chances. He'd put over thirty years into accumulating information on rare and alien encryption techniques, which was why he was one of the highest-paid hackers in existence. Of course, that could only take you so far. . . .

He tried not to think about that, as he set up his remote processor to deal with the new input. He tried really hard not to be impatient . . . but it was hard. Talent such as his was destined for bigger and better things, and although he knew his chance would come eventually, it irked him that no opportunity had come yet. Oh, sure, the Guildmistress lavished gifts upon him for his many services to her, and his coworkers all regarded him with something midway between admiration and awe. He could taste it while he worked with them, and he played up to it whenever he could.

"Well, what have we here?" he would mutter, as he entered the encryption office, "Another capsule from Danylon?" And his coworkers would look at him in stunned amazement, wondering how he needed no more than a glance to assess the chaos of foreign symbols which they had struggled with for hours. He loved that moment. He loved it even more because it was all showmanship, nothing more. Long ago he had wormed his secretive way into his Mistress' own private datalines, and could pluck a single fact from them so delicately that her security alarms never stirred. Of course, that was in part because he himself had designed her whole security system. . . .

Yes, he was living in a hacker's paradise, no doubt about it. Paid an immense wage to rape the galaxy of its most secret data, and festooned with Guild status for it. It should have been enough. It would have surely been, for any other code hack. But it wasn't.

He wanted the station.

She was only two ranks above him, in the hierarchy of Guild service. And he knew that you could skip a step or two if the Guild Prima wanted you badly enough. No man of his profession had ever gained a guildmastership, but that didn't mean it couldn't be done. For a man who had broken the war code of Termillian and hijacked pirates' freight on Paradise, let's face it, there were few challenges left.

Ironically, the one thing that could vault him into the higher reaches of Guild power was the same thing his Mistress had hired him to find. Data. He didn't know what he was looking for exactly, or how it would work, but he knew it was out there, his golden goose. Data that would threaten to topple the Guild—or strengthen it—so that the Prima must have it, or all would suffer. There would be rewards aplenty for the one who brought her that little tidbit, and Delhi was perfectly positioned to do so. And he was perfectly positioned to steal it from her when it came in.

"What do you want for this?" the Prima would ask in her dulcet tones, to which he would casually respond, "Well, my talents seem wasted where I am, perhaps I should move up to a higher level. . . ." And if she talked about raising him one level in rank, he would politely point out that one who had saved the Guild itself surely deserved better, perhaps—dare he suggest?—a station of his own. . . .

And it had to be Delhi's, of course. If he didn't take that woman down, and take her down hard, she would make him pay for such a betrayal. But if she lost her own status at the same time that he gained his, so the facilities of the Guild were no longer hers to command . . . it would be hard for him to manage, but it could be done. It had to be done. Her network was too vast, too perfectly managed, for him to play rival to it. It must be neutralized, if he was to come into his own.

*After all*, he thought to her, *we play the same game, you and I. And there can only be one who writes the rules.*

But first, he must have the data.

With a second glance to make sure the headset had really, *really* been wiped clean—he was compulsive about such things, which was part of the reason for his success—he started to scan the mysterious data packet one more time. So many instructions had been added to his decryption program now that its action was noticeably slower, and he tapped his stylus on the console restlessly as he waited it out. If he'd been on the big machines this wouldn't be happening, but you didn't work on hijacked data with any machine you valued. Just last week the safeguards on a Paradise packet had fried five remote units, one after the other. You didn't take a chance on that happening to something important.

A red light flashed on his screen, alerting him to a change in activity. Bingo. He leaned forward and studied the data that was now scrolling up for his perusal. And he grinned. Yeah, that was an Earth code all right, and a damned old one. No one but a collector would still have something like that on file . . . shit, either someone was playing a very complicated joke, or the data was damned serious stuff. He could feel his pulse begin to race as he started to neutralize the security safeguards built into the packet. They weren't focused on the whole package, he realized, but on one very small section, barely a few lines long.

As he got near it, one of his alarms went off, and he quickly backed away and took a second look. The packet looked unchanged. He reran the last part of the search program to check for contamination . . . and damn if something hadn't gotten into his own equipment. Shit.

He'd been through too much to get this far, didn't want to go grabbing a clean disk and starting over. Besides, whatever had zapped his first set of programs might just do it to the next copy. That meant he had to weed out whatever he had picked up. He called up a comparison program to go through the software byte by byte, comparing key sections of code to a copy of the original. The console buzzed softly each time it zapped a piece of intruding code. He was too preoccupied to hear it.

What the hell was this? Why was there a security program being triggered in the *middle* of the goddamned packet? It should have been there from the beginning, to protect the whole transmission. What sense did it make to protect this one small bit of code separately, as if it had come from some other source—

He stared at the screen. His heart stopped beating for a second. He didn't notice.

A different source.

Jesus Christ . . .

His decryption program had stopped. *Layered encryption*, it warned him. *Proceed?*

His hands trembled slightly as he typed in, *No. Isolate segment. Display.*

And he waited.

The machine whirred softly, an unusual sound. He was driving it hard, that was certain. After a while a series of lines appeared on the screen. They were, of course, unreadable. He set the encryption program on them, and got another five lines. Still unreadable.

His heart was pounding now. He felt as if he should look up

and see if anyone else noted his uncharacteristic excitement, but he couldn't take his eyes off the screen. Trembling, he gave it instructions for a new decryption scan, and when the computer indicated that yes, it could crack this code as well, he felt something in his gut tighten up in anticipation.

This was it, he thought. This had to be the one.

At last the computer signaled its success. The five lines of alien text disappeared from the screen. Five other lines took their place.

English.

PROJECT JANET CONFIRMED UAO
BELIEVE SUBJECT UNAWARE
LAST ID JAMISIA SHIDO
OUTPILOT ABILITIES UNEXPRESSED
FIND AT ANY COST

There was more, but that was supporting data. He didn't look at it yet. He didn't look at anything but those five lines.

*Outpilot abilities unexpressed.*

He managed to touch the control that would bring the screen down to darkness. This was no time to discover that someone was reading over his shoulder.

Jesus Christ.

At last he brought the contrast back up and typed, JAMISIA SHIDO. SEARCH.

It did so. Four minutes. Four very long, very tense minutes. THREE, it said at last.

The small number wasn't surprising. Corporate names were tightly controlled, it was rare that people would share both given name and corporate. PLANET/STATION OF ORIGIN? he typed. Hands still shaking.

The response this time was immediate.

EARTH
HELLSGATE
ELISIA

Earth. Reijik Station was one of the nodes that served Earth; if one wanted to intercept a woman fleeing from the motherworld's sphere of influence, Reijik Station was one of the very few places one would have to warn.

That had to be the one.

Stivan had the computer give him all the information it had on that Jamisia Shido. There wasn't much. Earth files were generally private things, not uploaded to the vast outernet system. But it seemed that with this woman there was even less than usual.

Little wonder, he thought, if she was involved in some secret project. Little wonder if that project involved outpilots. . . .

He pressed forward, feeding icon after icon to the controlling programs. Cut the data packet open, pluck out the twice-encoded section. Close the data packet up again, working with code as fine as a surgeon's scalpel to make it appear truly whole, as if nothing had ever been removed. *Be careful*, he told the stranger's hands before him, *be very careful, Delhi knows what she is doing. Leave nothing for her to find.*

When at last he was done, he set the encryption program to running again. Later he would go into his log and remove all traces of the operation, so that no one could ever discover what he had done. As far as anyone was concerned, he had devoted this hour to decoding a packet for the Guildmistress' use.

The small chip on which the message was recorded burned in his hand as he picked up a clean headset, trying to bring his brainware up at the same time. This time there was no doing it naturally; he used the headset to take control of his wellseeker, and injected enough sedative into his bloodstream that at last he was capable of feeding it the start-up icon again. Clearly the biological safeguard he had been so proud of was not a good thing to have around at moments like this.

He loaded the transmission's contents into his headset, and from there into his brainware's permanent storage. Five lines and a short packet of supporting data. Shadows of a project that was ultra-secret, that involved the outpilots and Earth, that might—just might—be the break he'd been waiting for. Reijik had hijacked it from Earth. Delhi had hijacked it from Reijik. And now he had hijacked it from Delhi. . . .

*And that*, he thought darkly, *is the most dangerous part of all.* But well worth it. God, yes. Well worth it.

**"M**istress?"

Delhi turned slowly; her mechanical carapace did not allow for quick movement.

It was Jovanne, her secretary. "I have that log you asked for."

"Yes, of course." She waved absently to an empty spot on the table, where she might set it down. "Leave it here, I'll take a look at it."

She did not watch as the data chip was laid down on the table, nor as the tall Anduluvian bowed and left. Her mind was on something else.

Her web.

She was perusing its lesser strands now, and it took all her concentration. Not vast concourses of data, these, but delicate lines built of single facts, that rippled like delicate cilia in her mind's eye. Each time a fact was added to her collection she saw it thus; if one was removed, she could sense the gap forming, as a true spider could sense some alteration in his own creation. At times she even lost sight of the fact that it was data she was looking at, and lost herself in the sheer beauty of it all: fractal patterns of interlocking facts, complex beyond all imagining. The outernet that most people saw was barely a reflection of this ultimate truth, a pale and clouded image in a distorted mirror. How many could see the world as she did? How many understood that the reinterpretation of a single datum could cause shivers to vibrate through the entire web, until the vast supporting strands themselves were threatened? She knew, and she could see the changes directly, without the need for intellectual interpretation. That was the gift which the Hausman Effect had given her, when it robbed her of her mobility.

She was more than content with the trade.

With care and delicacy she focused in her analytic programs on the anomaly she had sensed. There were over five thousand programs embedded in her headset which were running constantly, requesting and receiving data from her inhouse system, analyzing it, requesting data from the outernet, scouring it clean for safety, sorting the two sets together and searching for patterns . . . it was partly her own programming, partly that of a lover (now dead), and a security chief (now dead), and a favored hacker (still alive, but without any memory of his work). Only the end results of the data search were fed into her brainware, where her specialized senses devoured them and displayed them in this, her chosen metaphor. Through it, she had learned to spot data trails so fine, so hidden, that her own hackers had passed them by. With it, she had leveraged herself to the Mastership of this station. Using it, she would defend her seat to the death.

Not her death, of course.

The web resolved in her mind's eye, sparkling with activity not unlike the brain's own. After a time she could see the fine strand divide, and identify which part she needed. *It's on the station*, she mused, *how interesting*. Then, a few seconds later, new patterns resolved. *In my citadel. Even more interesting.* Her expression was dark as she studied the web further, looking for the anomaly's source. It was subtle indeed, this thing which her search programs had found, well beneath the level of data with which she usually concerned herself. Perhaps it would have no value at all. But she reminded herself of the first tenet of chaos theory—infinitesmally small input can alter infinitely large systems—and continued her search, wondering what it was that her brain and its attendant programs had found worthy of notice.

At last she was at the trail's end, and to her amazement found herself amidst the biologs of her employees. She glanced over the tables presented to her, but there was nothing unusual that she saw. She refined her vision further, using the search program for a guide, and found herself reading the biolog of one of her code hacks, a Stivan Dici. Like the others, he had no idea that she regularly tapped into his wellseeker's readings. Oh, he could figure it out if he wanted to; he had the skill to spot such a thing . . . if he looked for it. No one did. Who would think that one's employer kept an hourly watch on one's blood pressure, one's pulse rate, one's breathing?

And there it was, in just those terms. A spike the day before, and two at night. A long, tense plateau during REM sleep. And a series of spikes today, closer and higher and more significant than any which came before.

He had found something, she guessed. Or heard something. Or thought of something. A piece of data that excited or upset him, that tormented his dreams, and that today—right now— received his full attention. His pulse rate was well out of bounds for a man of his age and condition; she checked it against his medical files and whistled softly. *Well* out of bounds. He had always been something of a hothead, and spikes in his biolog were far from rare, but the intensity of these, and their sustained nature, hinted at some outside cause. And given his nature, she would have put money on it being some some choice piece of data that had come into his hands.

She called up the work he had been doing when the first spike hit, and found herself reading the Reijik packet. He had decrypted most of it, but it still made little sense, being mostly specifics of shipping and communication between Earth conglomerates and their Reijik counterparts. A rich harvest, to be sure, and one that her analysts would comb through for useful data . . . but there was nothing she saw that should excite the kind of agitation Dici's biolog had recorded. Delhi's hackers dealt with this kind of data all the time.

LOCATE STIVAN DICI, she instructed her headset. It took little more than a second for the request to be transmitted to the in-house computer, which responded, PRIVATE QUARTERS. She asked, ACTIVITY? Another second passed, then the words flashed before her eyes: DATA SEARCH/OUTERNET.

That wasn't like him. Usually her prime hack lived in his lab, where paper-thin monitors adorned the walls, and cabinets full of sterile equipment attended his most dangerous exploits. This wasn't like him at all, this . . . secrecy.

No, this *attempt* at secrecy.

Like so many who did not truly know her inner workings, Dici had underestimated her. She had the computer switch on the cams hidden in his quarters, and put their gleanings on screen. There she saw him sitting on his bed, with beads of sweat running down his face. Most uncharacteristic. His hand lay on a keyboard of some kind, marked in symbols she didn't recognize; most likely a personal code of icons he had developed himself. She brought a cam into close range and began to record the symbols themselves, and the dance of his fingers across them. There was knowledge here, and she wanted it, but the only way to eavesdrop on such an encoded soliloquy was to obtain its template directly from the man's brain. And while that was not impossible, its cost was considerable. One could not remove information from a dead brain, for the brainware systems expired upon death; one could not force it from a fully functioning brain, for a man like that would have safeguards in place that would erase sensitive data at the first hint of invasion. No, there was a way to get what she wanted . . . but only once. She had to make sure that she wanted it enough to sacrifice this servant, and then strike with stealth and surety.

She was receiving a feed from her house computer now, listing all the data requests that this man had made. She watched as he continued what was clearly some kind of private investigation, citing corporate names that were among the elite of Earth's power brokers. Something very big was clearly at stake here, and if her guess was right, the first hint of it had been discovered in the Reijik data packet. She called up the packet in her own head and compared it to a list of his search items. No match. So whatever it was that had inspired his investigation, had been removed from the packet before she saw it. And that—by the standards of her house—was a crime.

*You have betrayed me*, she mused coldly. If so, then there was nothing left worth saving, was there? Other than the data itself, which was lodged within his brain. It was commonly said that you couldn't get to such information without the subject's cooperation. That the brain invariably protected itself too well for such invasion.

How unfortunate that would be, if it were true.

**S**tivan visualized the search icon, and spelled out in his mind's eye: JANET.

> 1. PROPER NAME WITH VARIATIONS IN THIRTY-SEVEN LANGUAGES. FROM THE HEBREW JANE, MEANING "GOD IS GRACIOUS." 2. THE SEVENTH MOON OF HYDRA, NAMED FOR EXPLORER JANET WITHERS. 3. COMPANY FOUNDED BY TWENTY-FIRST CENTURY CLOTHING

DESIGNER, JANET DYMACEA, NOW A SUBSIDIARY OF MARANECK
CORPORATION. 4. TWENTY-FIRST CENTURY VIDDIE KNOWN FOR
EXPLICIT—

He scanned the twenty-odd definitions with a careful eye.
Any of them might have been right. None of them *felt* right. At
last he sighed, and signaled for the house computer to SEARCH:
UAO

ABBREVIATION FOR "UP-AND-OUT," A PHRASE USED ON EARTH TO
INDICATE OUTWORLD (AINNIQ ACCESSIBLE) CIVILIZATION. COMBINES
SLANG TERMS FOR OFF-PLANET (UP) AND PREFIX FOR THE AINNIQ
SYSTEM (OUT)

SEARCH/EARTHBIO, he directed it. JAMISIA SHIDO

MEMBER OF SHIDO CORPORATION, BORN 1.11.37 (EARTH
STANDARD CALENDAR) IN SOL CITY, USNA. PARENTS KILLED IN
COLLAPSE OF HAIDO CITY CENTER, 12.12.43. FORMAL ADOPTION BY
SHIDO INTERNATIONAL, 1.03.44. RESIDENT SHIDO HABITAT 1.30.44
to 3.21.54. LOST DURING HOSTILE TAKEOVER BY TRIDAC ENTERPRISES.
CURRENTLY PRESUMED DEAD.

*Not by everyone*, he thought darkly.
After a moment he visualized, TRIDAC ENTERPRISES. A
flurry of bright words scrolled into his field of vision.

EARTH CORPORATION, FOUNDED 2013 (OLD CALENDAR). MAIN
BUSINESS, BIOTECH RESEARCH. NET ASSETS—

No, this would get him nowhere; the file on a company that
vast would take hours to study, and the information he wanted,
if it was there at all, would probably be so buried beneath paragraphs of businesspeak he'd pass it right by.
Frustrated, he stared into space. After a minute his attention
saver kicked in and started to display enticing holos of nude
women, as a reminder that he was still online. He banished them
with an irritated snort and tried to think.
Janet. A name. The project had been named for someone.
Maybe not in the corporation that had started the project.
Maybe this was a code term used by those who were trying to
get control of it.

JANET TRIDAC, he visualized, interrupting its scrolling of financial statistics. HOW MANY EXIST?

It took the computer a good five seconds to go through all its databanks for that information. It could have taken as long as five minutes, if the data hadn't been stored on Delhi's station.

*15*, it told him.

PLANET/STATION OF ORIGIN?

CASPAR
EARTH (2)
EUMENIDES
HELLSGATE
LORD'S KEEP (2)
NEW HEBRIDES (2)
NEW TOKYO
NEW WASHINGTON (3)
OBANTU
SINCLAIR

Two from Earth. He called up their bios and studied them. Janet Austria Tridac was a research technician in Tridac's main lab, on Earth's surface. Janet Dian Tridac was a maintenance worker in the company's orbiting habitat. The one he wanted was unlikely to be the second one, he thought, why would they name such a vital project after her . . . but at this point he was not about to rule anything out. There was only a slim chance the project had been named after someone currently working for Tridac; Earth corporations didn't like to give that kind of recognition to a single worker, lest it inflate their own sense of importance. A worker who knew his own worth was a risk to security, the old axiom stated. Stivan called up all the data he could find on past Janet Tridacs—there were nearly thirty in the databanks, and probably more had existed on Earth whose files had never been outloaded to the nodes—and studied it all. There wasn't much. The corporate giants of Earth were notoriously secretive, and this one was no exception; the bios were short, superficial, and utterly unhelpful. He did the same historical search for Janet Shido, and again came up with nothing. Or perhaps the answer was there in front of his face, and he just wasn't seeing it. Damn.

He stared at the five lines again, tasting their mystery with a dry tongue as he licked his lips. This wasn't his forte. He was good at finding data, brilliant at decoding it, but when it came down to *using* the foreign bits and pieces that came his way, he had always been blissfully ignorant. It wasn't his job.

Now it was.

His security program flashed him a warning, alerting him to the fact that he had been online for an hour already. He had programmed it years ago to warn him of that, when he first realized that someday he might wind up doing research he didn't want Delhi to know about. An hour of research was high risk, in this situation; the house computer would have logged it, and anyone going over the records would surely wonder what a hack was doing in a data search for so long. He'd better erase his tracks, and fast. He visualized one of the icons that would give him access to the security programs Delhi relied upon—

—and a flash of pain seared through his brain. No, not pain exactly. Disorientation, so sudden and so powerful that for a moment it felt as if his brain had been put through a blender. The sensation was sickening, and though it didn't hurt in a physical sense, his inner senses reeled in agony. What the hell was going on? He tried to—

Tried to—

Tried to—

*Oh, God. . . .*

Didn't try.

Didn't do.

Anything.

Silence, within and without. Where thoughts normally scurried through his head, there was nothing. The sound of his pulse, now beating wildly, resounded in his ears. BLOOD PRESSURE/PULSE RED ZONE, his wellseeker informed him. CORRECT? He could give it no answer. After a moment the system defaulted to a health option, and he knew that instructions were being given to his heart, his brain, his adrenal gland. Seconds passed. The pounding slowed to a mere fevered thud. The pressure in his head seemed to ease a bit.

He couldn't think.

He couldn't think!

Emotions poured into him without analysis, without explanation. Primitive emotions, such as the lowliest life-forms must know, bereft of any rational trappings. Terror as raw as an animal knows when the scent of a hunter suddenly comes from behind it. Desperation such as would cause a trapped beast to gnaw off its own foot, in an effort to escape a trap. The emotions filled him to bursting, till tears came out of his eyes. But there was no thought accompanying them. No brain activity at all, that anyone would label *human*. He couldn't even wonder what had happened to him . . . for that in itself was a thought, and thought—all thought—was denied him.

After a brief time, an endless interlude of terror, he heard the door open behind him. He didn't turn around to see who it was— didn't even *want* to turn around, for *wanting* was a complex thought process—but fear stoked his blood pressure to new heights. CORRECTING, his wellseeker repeated. Whomever it was that had come in remained where he was for a moment, then began to move toward him. And it was with the terror of a trapped and dying animal that he recognized the almost inaudible hiss of Delhi's mechanical carapace.

After what seemed like an eternity she moved into his field of vision. Her expression was unreadable.

"Well, well. Stivan Dici. My most loyal servant." Her clear eyes fixed on him, icy in their depths; in the folds of her aged and mechanically supported flesh they seemed to almost take on a life of their own, and he cringed beneath their scrutiny. "Perhaps I should tell you a story, Stivan. Not that you'll be able to appreciate all its fine points, of course. Your mind is quite frozen in the here-and-now, and hardly in a state for speculation. But I think the points that matter most will be clear."

She began to move then, a bizarre sort of mechanical pacing, until the softly whirring carapace had brought her around behind him. He couldn't turn to watch her. He couldn't even *want* to turn. Some vital link had been severed in his brain, and he could only listen.

"You of course do not know," she began, "the ceremony that accompanies the rise to guildmastership. It's quite secret, and steeped in a symbolism centuries old. At the end of it, when the investiture has been completed, the new Master or Mistress stands before the Prima and is permitted to make one request. A sort of gift, to celebrate her new position. Also a test. Not all realize that, of course. The first free interaction between a new guildmaster and his superior says a lot about what their relationship will become. Few realize the potential of that moment."

Pictures began to form before his eyes, misty images which the house net was feeding into his optical center. Then, like an uploaded vidlink, the details slowly crystallized. He saw a room, all in shades of gray. A woman in black robes, with the mark of the Guild in gold upon her chest. A man behind her and to the side, some sort of waiting attendant not fully admitted to the circle of ritual. Delhi was visualizing her memories and using the house net to feed the images into his brain. It wasn't an unfamiliar technique by any means; what child of the outworlds hadn't done the same thing at some point, mimicking telepathy in order to transfer dirty or shocking pictures to a friend? But combined with his inability to edit the input—combined with his total helplessness—the sensation of having someone else's memories fill his brain was doubly terrifying.

"Some ask for but token things, thinking the point of that moment is to reaffirm their loyalty with the ultimate statement of selflessness. Those people are fools. Others may ask for the station they covet, backing in their first guild investments, a choice position for a loved one or ally. The list of requests is as long as the list of guildmasters. How does one make the most of such a moment? There is no preparation for this, you understand, the ceremony is kept such a secret that the answer serves as a test of sorts, to see what manner of Gueran has been raised to power . . . how quickly he thinks, how perfectly he weighs the various options, and what his political priorities are. . . ." She paused, letting Stivan's helpless brain absorb that final confirmation of terror: *Secret ceremonies. No one knows. She is telling me.* It didn't take rational thought to draw a conclusion from those bits and pieces; the connection was primal, as much a part of his neural circuitry as the desire to eat or drink . . . or flee.

"And so, you see, the question was put to me. And in that small eternity I wondered, what did I want most in the whole of the outworlds, and could the Prima give it to me? It wouldn't do to ask for the impossible . . . nor to understate the moment's

opportunity. Surely this moment was as much a test as a reward.''

He saw them waiting, the man and woman both. Strangely,
there seem to be fine lines connecting the two of them, that trembled in the still air between them like a spiderweb. The longer the
vision remained in his head, the more clearly he could see them.

''At last I said, *I want a program.*

''*What manner of program?* the Prima asked.

''My thoughts were racing; I took my time before speaking.
*Give me something that will remove a man's initiative*, I told her.
*Give me a program I can plant in a man's brain, which when acti-
vated will remove all capacity for self-motivation. Not only of the
body,* I added quickly, *but of the mind itself.*

''There was silence for a moment. Then she said, *There are
very few programmers capable of designing such a thing.''*

He saw as the woman turned back to glance at the man. Devlin Gaza? His nod was so slight as to be almost imperceptible.
The silken lines between them shimmered as he did so.

''At last she nodded. *Very well,* she told me, *if it can be done, it
will be done.*

''So you see,'' Delhi said quietly—the pictures vanished in a
flash of light, ''I can do that now. Burn out that part of the brain
which provides the spark of initiative. Make a man into something which can only react . . . and obey.''

She stepped around him, into his field of vision once more.
For a moment there was silence. Then: ''Raise your left arm,
Stivan.''

To his horror he saw his arm moving upward, as if pulled by
a puppeteer's string. When it had reached the level of his shoulder and it was clear he was not going to halt on his own, she
said curtly, ''Stop.''

He did.

''Put it down.''

He did.

''Excellent. Let us hope that internal commands work as
well.''

She walked around to where his keyboard lay, and studied
the hand-inscribed sigils on its keys. Customized icons, every
last one of them. Her silence, and her utter stillness, hinted at

some internal monologue . . . or dialogue, perhaps, with the computerized presence that surrounded them.

Suddenly one of the images formed in his mind's eye, placed there by an outside force. To his horror he could feel his brain stirring in response, a cascade of neural connections triggered by the familiar symbol. He couldn't stop it. He wasn't even part of it. He was a spectator in his own brain. watching his own secret icons appear and disappear before him as one would watch a viddie.

"Excellent," she said at last. "Gaza did well." She gazed at him directly—eyes so cold, expression devoid of all human sympathy—and said, "It's so hard to interrogate a human brain, since one single thought can shut down the brainware. One flash of an icon, prearranged, to alert the internal security systems that all input is to be rejected. I'm sure you have such safeguards, Stivan. So you understand, there was no other way to question you. I am so sorry. You were a good servant." She looked deep into his eyes, as if searching for something within him. The sensation was sickening, as if some huge predatory creature had flicked out its tongue to taste him. "Now let us begin, shall we? I'd like to review your most recent discoveries, and outload them for my records. I regret that your brain will be ruined in the process . . . but I'm afraid that the program does irreparable damage when it's used. Something one reserves for enemies, Stivan." Her expression hardened. "Or traitors."

The flow began then, secret data worming its way out of his brain in response to her electronic summons. It wouldn't have been so bad if he could have closed his eyes. The flow involved no visual processing; if he could have shut his eyes, he could have pretended it wasn't happening, could have cowered in some hidden little portion of his brain and pretended nothing was wrong, until it was over.

As it was, he had to stare at her until the end.

*T*he assivak crouches with its prey before it; the tiny creature is now immobilized, barely struggling. Silk wraps it tightly from head to toe, making any form of resistance impossible. Bright powdered *wings that once tamed the skies are now glued to its side, and its faceted eyes gaze helplessly out through a tangle of sticky strands.*

*It was doomed from the start, of course. Any creature who sets foot in the assivak's web belongs to her. She may not choose to feed immediately, but once she does, there is no question of the outcome.*

*Carefully, almost daintily, the assivak begins to suck out the life juices of its prey.*

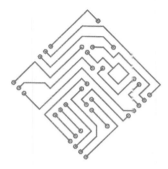

What is true genius, if not the perfect balance of inspiration and perseverence?

CHEULGU KIM
*Ancient Truths for a New Age*

# INSHIP: MERCURY

THE HARVESTER was a strange and wonderful creation. With silver wings that spread out for miles in every direction, shifting moment by moment as some new solar current tickled their paper-thin substance, it seemed more like a living creature than what it was, a man-made construct of plasteel struts and sheets. Out here the wings were mostly folded, of course; only within the bounds of a fertile solar system would they stretch out to their full length, like a bird of prey splaying out his feathers to catch the wind. Here the galactic breezes were quiet, mere echoes of the storms that had once sparked on some solar surface, billions of miles away. Here the vast creature was quiescent.

Beneath those wings, sheltered in a cocoon of paper-thin hydrogen collectors, would be more substantial cargo: elements harvested from the outer planets by tiny probes, who now lay tucked within the bosom of their mothership, sleeping the mechanical sleep of their flight. Precious metals and radioactives, gases compressed nearly to the breaking point, and anything else that the nodes needed for construction and energy were all stored away for the decade-long journey.

It was life, Hsing mused, or at least the source of life. As much as the sun of Guera made life on that planet possible, as much as Sol warmed earth so that life could prosper, these vast collectors made life possible in the nodes. Because you couldn't support living worlds with no new raw materials, no fresh energy input. The stations of the outworlds were nearly perfect closed systems, and even so, there was a limit to how often the same materials could be reused. An endpoint even to recycling, when metal and plastic had been reshaped so often that molecular integrity could no longer be guaranteed. The Earth Tithe made up for some of that, of course, with its requirement that every ship coming from the dirtworlds bring with it a mass of raw materials for the Guild to use as needed. But that just barely supported the building of new stations, new ships, and necessary repairs. Without the harvesters making their constant journeys to living systems for supplies, there would not be enough new energy in the outworlds to keep trillions of humans alive. Much less to keep them happy.

Hsing stayed at the viewpoint until the harvester receded into the distance, as did most of the passengers surrounding him. You could almost sort them into racial categories by the distance they kept from him: the Guerans close by, undisturbed by his Guild office; other Variants keeping a few steps away, wary and respectful; the few Terrans on the ship staying as far away from him as they could at all times. Was it his power that unnerved them, he wondered, or simply the fact that his Variation was hidden, causing them to imagine the worst? Or was it the "ferocious war paint" (as one Terran had labeled the kaja) which spoke to them on a more primitive level, warning them not to get too close? What did they imagine he was going to do if they did invade his personal space? Eat them?

It was doubly ironic, being that his own Variation had been corrected long ago. Some people made that choice. In his case it had been pretty simple, really, a choice between having a body that would respond to his commands and one that wouldn't. He'd had the procedure done as soon as he was old enough to make his wishes known, and had never regretted it since. Oh, there were Guerans who would accuse him of throwing away a rare opportunity, those who would remind him in no uncertain terms that some of humankind's greatest works of genius had come from minds that others would consider "handicapped." It was bullshit as far as he was concerned. Maybe relevant enough for folks like Masada and his wife, whose cognitive patterns had shifted into an alternate mode, but how did it benefit the human mind to be trapped in a body that couldn't respond to it? He thought Ra was crazy, for not having her visual circuits fixed. He knew that Delhi would trade in her current body in a nano for one that worked, if the operation required to do so didn't put her whole consciousness at risk. And even Masada had a wellseeker programmed to tune out the worst of his sensory distortions, at least when it would affect his work.

*We're all human, right?* But you didn't tell the Terrans that. God, no! One must preserve the mystique at all costs.

Today he had managed, for perhaps five minutes, not to think about what was happening back home. It took effort. For a Guildmaster to abandon his domain for a year meant leaving his holding in the hands of those who coveted it the most, and for all that the Prima herself had promised to protect his interests, she wouldn't even be aware of the kinds of subtle maneuverings that went on there, not until it was too late to stop them. No outsider could possibly know. You had to be in the middle of things yourself to catch all the cues, you had to be meeting with people who were plotting to bring you down so that you could see them with your own eyes, searching for that one quickened breath or awkward glance which would hint at a rebellion in the making. . . .

He felt helpless here, and frustrated, and at times even angry. There was no point in the last emotion and he knew it, but being human he suffered it nonetheless. The Prima had given him a choice. The Prima had told him he didn't have to go. The Prima had assured him that she could find someone else to carry the precious virus to Masada, so that he could be convinced to sign onto the project. It didn't have to be Hsing.

Only it did.

He knew that he had carried the whole fate of the Guild in his hands, and it was an awesome feeling. He knew that there were maybe ten people at most that the Prima would trust with such an assignment, and that he was the first she had asked. That was worth something, wasn't it? That was the kind of favor he could parlay into power at some later date, an implied obligation on her part that he would save until the day he needed it most. It had seemed, at the time, like that made all the risk worthwhile. But now, eight months later, he wasn't quite so sure. What if he came home to find that he had been ousted from power, and had to climb his way back up from the bottom again? Would he have to waste that precious favor just regaining what this mission had cost him?

*It'll all be worth it if we beat this virus,* he told himself.

He wished he could fully accept that. There was a part of him deep inside, a selfish part, that warned him that a dead virus would be damned little consolation if he did indeed lose everything he had. Was that something to be ashamed of, or was it simply part of being human?

"Guildmaster?"

The sudden voice from behind startled him. He turned to find one of the ship's stewards waiting at a polite distance, eyes averted. The man's *kaja* warned him not to read too much meaning into the lack of eye contact, merely to accept it as an accompaniment of his Variation. He quieted his *nantana* nerves and waited.

"The captain would like to see you," the man said, and then added, almost apologetically, "if you can spare the time."

It took little effort to interpret the man's tone and pick apart its hidden meanings. The captain's real words had been much more forceful, but the steward balked at delivering them precisely as ordered. The last words were strictly his own, meant to ameliorate the aggressive power of the implied command. Not an uncommon blend of messages, in such strained circumstances as these.

How very strange it was, moving into another man's territory, where the title of a Guildmaster meant so little. In any other setting a captain would have bent over backward to see that Hsing didn't take offense. In any other setting a Guildmaster's word was law. But when you locked up five hundred people on a single ship for six months, and gave one man the responsibility of keeping them from killing each other out of sheer boredom, the balance of power shifted accordingly. Hsing didn't like that fact, but he acknowledged it.

"Very well," he said. Was it his imagination, or did he see the steward's shoulders slump in relief? "Take me to him."

The captain was in one of the small briefing chambers at the front of the ship, flanking its bridge. Hsing knew it well. He had fought for more than a week at the beginning of the voyage to get Masada access to one of the well-equipped spaces, so that when his work required a more sophisticated display than the vid labs could handle, he could have it. Hsing had won that battle, but barely. No doubt resentment still lingered. No doubt that was half of what this meeting was about.

*They'd give him the whole damned ship if they knew what Masada's work was about. Unfortunately,* he thought with a sigh, *we can't tell them that, can we?*

The captain waited until the steward had shown him in and left them alone together. He was a sturdy man anchored solidly in the prime of his life, and the joint pleasure and responsibility of his office were written boldly in the lines of his face. Right now it was the lines of tension that showed the most, wrinkling his *simba* kaja. Not a good omen.

"Guildmaster Hsing." He nodded toward a chair at the far end of the table, but Hsing shook his head. He wouldn't sit while the captain was standing, it would put him at too much of a spatial disadvantage. He saw the captain's eyes narrow briefly as the *simba* assessed his defiance, but what did the man expect? Hsing was the man's superior in every forum but this one, and he wasn't about to let the captain forget it.

A real *simba* would have snarled its annoyance at him now, and stiffened in predatory posture. This man did neither of those things, but Hsing wasn't fooled by that. The reaction might be hidden inside him, but it was there all the same.

"I've been having reports from my stewards of problems on the ship."

Hsing waited politely.

"First it was the viddie library that was affected. Access slowed down by 10%, then 20%, now 40%. Then some of the vids became unobtainable . . . apparently the directory's been dumping its less popular offerings to save space for processing. Now my nutritionist says that *his* programs are slowing down, which means that meals aren't there when people want them. Not a good thing, on a ship like this. I need people calm. I need them happy. Keeping them that way is my job. Not interfering is yours."

For a moment he was tempted to simply say what he was

feeling: *What the hell do you think I have to do with all that?* But you didn't confront a *simba* like that. An *iru* might try it, or some other kaja that lacked social sophistication, but not a *nantana*.

Instead he did the social equivalent of baring his neck. "Of course, I would never interfere with this ship's functioning."

It worked; several of the harsher lines creasing the man's brow relaxed ever so slightly. "Perhaps you wouldn't. But your companion has."

"Dr. Masada?" He was genuinely surprised. "He brought his own equipment with him."

"You asked me a few weeks ago if he could use some of the ship's processing capacity for his research. I said yes, provided he didn't interfere with any of the ship's programs."

"I'm sure he didn't," Hsing said quietly. Then, when he saw the captain's expression harden, he added quickly, "Why would he? What would he have to gain?"

Grim-faced, the captain handed him a hardcopy readout, printed on thin white plastic. Fifteen pages: an inventory of net usage since the first day of their voyage. Hsing tried to make sure that his expression revealed nothing as he studied it.

The records clearly showed that Masada had been using the ship's innernet for data processing, and using it freely enough that the system had begun a partial shutdown of peripheral services. Food wouldn't be cut off entirely, of course. Nor would the viddie program, or any of two hundred other systems that the passengers relied upon for survival or entertainment. But the borrowing of a byte or two here, a few million there, had its price. Nineteen of the ship's primary systems were already affected. Twenty-seven more were soon to follow, assuming the current pattern of usage continued. At that rate of consumption, it was estimated that the average ship's program would be running at half-efficiency within days. He could see why the captain was concerned.

When he indicated by looking up that he was finished perusing the document, the captain said to him, "He's your charge. You asked for permission for him to use our system. Very well, you deal with him now. I don't know what the hell he's doing— you say it's top secret stuff, all right then, I won't ask—but I want him *out* of our system, and I want him out now. We've got more than four months left to this trip, and I'm not going to spend it on a crippled ship."

Aware that the very air was charged with social pheromones of dominance and conflict, he chose his words carefully. "Of course, Dr. Masada understands his responsibility to you and your ship. No doubt he was unaware of the effect his research was having on your system. I'm sure when I show this to him, he'll make the necessary adjustments."

"Make sure of it," the captain said gruffly, and he handed him the inventory.

With great effort Hsing managed to make his exit without any further confrontation. But inside he was seething. No one would treat him like that in his own node. *No one.* Had the captain forgotten that without the Guild there would be no outworlds to support his little ferry? Had he forgotten just what Hsing's title meant, the kind of power he wielded in his own right? What was a petty inship processor when compared with the kinds of priorities he juggled daily?

But you didn't fight with a man over things like that when the two of you were stuck on the same ship for months yet. It just wasn't worth it. Let him have his petty little kingdom; the stars would belong to Hsing, once he returned to the ainniq.

For now, all he had to do was deal with Masada.

Masada.

At times he wondered if what was going on inside the man's head resembled any process he would recognize, or whether common speech and cultural habits were disguising a conceptual gap so vast that they might well be from different species. But in that sense, all Guerans were aliens to one another, weren't they? The *iru* only seemed more alien than most to him because he was *nantana*, and all the signals of tone and movement which he relied upon for social intercourse were absent in such a man. Or distorted. Or exaggerated. You couldn't even try to read such a man beyond the surface, you just took his words at face value and tried not to look any deeper.

*Ah*, he thought dryly, *the joys of Gueran society.*

He wended his way through the public parts of the ship, back to the small cabins which were tucked into its rear. It was a pretty empty place this time of the shift; most passengers preferred the roomier public chambers up front, with their viddie screens and gaming tables and the thousand and one diversions provided for their amusement. Here in the back, in these smaller spaces, it was harder to forget that you were locked inside a finite vessel for the better part of six E-months, and if you didn't get along with your neighbors, or needed some new horizon to explore, or simply wanted to be by yourself for a time . . . tough luck.

He knocked on Masada's door. Three times in all, before the man responded. That was typical. The door finally opened to some unspoken command, and he saw exactly what he had expected to see.

The professor was sitting before the large vid screen he had brought with him, which was doubtless displaying some coded and incomprehensible interpretation of a computer program. The screen was angled so that Hsing couldn't see just what was on it, but that was all right; he had learned weeks ago that the types of visual patterning Masada used in his work were utterly meaningless to him. Which was just as well. He doubted the *iru* would take kindly to explaining the details of his work, even if Hsing were capable of understanding them.

"Come look at this," the professor said.

Hsing was startled. Masada wanted him to look at his work? That was a first. Usually the *iru* treated Hsing's bouts of curiosity as mildly annoying interruptions, and though he gave such explanations as the moment required, he was always anxious to regain the solitude which was his accustomed environment. To be invited to look at the Master's work . . . that was an honor indeed, Hsing thought dryly. Almost enough to make him forget that, look as he might, he probably wouldn't comprehend one line of it. Most of it looked like pure chaos to him.

But then he came to where the screen was fully visible, and saw what was on the surface. Not chaos. Not chaos at all. For a moment all other concerns were forgotten, even the one that had brought him to Masada's cabin in the first place.

"What is it?" he asked.

Masada pushed his chair back slowly; his eyes never left the screen. "That," he said quietly, "is our virus."

It flowed across the screen with fluid grace, a shape made familiar by every youngster's teaching program. The sheer familiarity of it took his breath away, and for a moment he couldn't even connect what he was looking at to what Masada said it was. A double helix? How was their virus connected to that? Was Masada trying to say that the damn thing had DNA, that it really was alive, in the sense of a biological infection? If so, then the world-famous holist had finally lost all touch with reality. Life was a metaphor for programming, not a description of its true state. Surely even Masada understood that.

"What is it?" he asked again. This time the question meant other things, deeper things. And it sheltered an ever larger question: *Have we made a mistake after all? Have we hired an extremist so lost in his holistic fantasies that he can no longer connect to reality?* The thought made Hsing feel sick inside. Had he put his guildmastership at risk for some fairy tale of a binary Pygmalion? God help this man if that were the case. God help the Prima if it were so, for asking him to come here. Saving the world was one thing. This . . . this was just crazy.

But Masada's tone was not the tone of a madman, and it was clear from his voice that he neither knew nor cared what was going on inside Hsing's head. "It's a programming chart of the virus. This is just a section of it, of course—but I assure you, the whole thing looks like this. Perfectly organized, from the first bit of data to the last." He looked at Hsing for a moment, and it seemed that he smiled slightly. "Life."

If Masada had been *nantana*, Hsing would have taken the word as mockery. But no *iru* could have gained such insight into his thought processes from one look alone to know what power that one word would have.

He moved closer and put his hand out to the screen, as if he would touch it. It was hard to look at such a thing in 2D like this, and not be able to rotate it at will in his mind's eye. It was turning slowly on the screen, giving him a gradual view of the whole, but that wasn't the same thing as being able to control it. "What's that thing?" he said, pointing to a slender yellow line running down the center of the helix. "That doesn't belong there."

"If it really were alive, no." Masada turned back to the

screen, and he must have fed the controlling program some command through his headset, for the double helix and its odd accessory suddenly increased in size and definition until he could make out the fine yellow struts connecting the central tube to the helix. "That's memory storage. Normally it would be integrated with all the other elements, not isolated like that. But the programmer put it there, separate from the rest, so that it wouldn't disturb the symmetry of the overall design. Which tells us just how very deliberate his choice of image was."

"You seem very sure of his motives."

He tapped a finger on the screen, touching segments of the helix one by one: blue, red, green, white. "Four colors, Master Hsing. Each one representing a different kind of processing sequence. Four colors in varying combination—just like the amino acids in a DNA string. Add one more color and the metaphor is no longer perfect." He shook his head in amazement. "He designed his whole program to mimic DNA. A pattern one would only discover by decompiling and then charting the entire thing. One can barely comprehend the effort that would take. The frustration that would be involved, as he discarded segments of code which would suit his purpose perfectly . . . except when viewed thus."

"Why?" he asked. "I mean, what's the point?"

"Good question. It certainly isn't a desire to show off, for the odds of anyone getting this far with it are astronomically small. I had to dismantle over a hundred traps to get the virus decompiled in the first place, and those were very effective traps, targeted at someone of my skill level or better. I've ruined over two dozen copies of the virus just getting this far. So whoever did this never expected any kind of recognition for his efforts, unless it was from a very select and secretive circle of colleagues."

"Hackers?"

Masada turned to him. Just that: no words, no clear expression, just a look that Hsing could not read, a sentence that was never voiced, and the clear impression—gleaned from nowhere—that the professor's estimate of Hsing's intelligence was not all that high right now.

"They fit the bill for secrecy," Hsing offered. "And ego."

"Not hackers."

"You're sure?"

Masada said nothing. After two months of sharing a ship with him, Hsing knew that he hated repetition of the obvious. What seemed obvious to *him*, anyway. The fact that sometimes redundancy might serve an emotional purpose—like reassuring someone that he did indeed have some basis for his judgments—was lost on him. Or perhaps he was aware of it, but simply didn't care.

"How?" Hsing demanded. "How can you know that?"

A faint expression that might almost have been a smile flickered across Masada's face. "This isn't a hacker's pattern, Master Hsing. It isn't how they think, how they act, how they program. Hackers are impatient creatures, hungry to test their skill against the world. They would never design a virus like this, that could disrupt all outworld commerce, and then hold it back for years while they worked to make it just a little prettier, on a level that no one would ever see. They would want to see it do its stuff."

"You think it took that long to finish?"

"E-months at least. Years, if the designer had other business to attend to." He turned back to the screen, and Hsing saw one section of virus give way to another, then to a third. "The programming charts of hacker viruses are complex, artistic in their own right, but they tend to be more chaotic in form, slapped together in bits and pieces as the muse of inspiration strikes. This is the product of a much more ordered mind. In fact I would say, this is the product of a mind that prides itself on order." He stared at the sequence of flashing images for a moment in silence, then added, "I'd be willing to bet our designer is the product of conventional education, well-schooled rather than self-taught. He's a perfectionist at heart, and that probably shows up in his day-to-day life as well as his programming. He doesn't require praise from others, but takes pleasure in the process of his work. And whatever he planned to do with this . . . I'd bet it was neither an impulsive move, nor a response to any outside event. He began work on it long ago and kept working on it until every byte was perfect. Then he set it loose. He's probably still watching it, which means that we may have a way to find him; I'm searching through his code now for any kind of homing sequence, or a pattern that might reasonably evolve into one. The fact that we're dealing with infinite variations makes it hard to find, of course; it may not even exist at this point. But I assure you, the man who created this masterpiece will want to see what it becomes.''

"He could just collect spores from the outernet," Hsing reminded him. "Eventually he'd get what he wanted, and there'd be no risk that way.''

"For another programmer that might be enough," Masada agreed. "Not for this man. His work is too ordered, too controlled; that kind of personality wouldn't put itself at the mercy of chance. He'd want to watch every variation as it evolved, and in the proper sequence, so that if corrections were necessary, he could make them in a timely manner. And he's made arrangements to do so. Of that I'm certain.''

Hsing stared at Masada for a moment—the professor was focused on the virus once more, and seemed unaware of his scrutiny—and at last said, softly, "You seem to have great insight into how this man thinks.''

Did Masada hear the unvoiced challenge in his words? *Iru* weren't known for their insight into other peoples' motives. In fact, they were notorious for their lack of such insight. It had been one of the things the Guild had argued about, when Masada's name was first brought up as that of a possible consultant. An *iru* might prove helpful in analyzing cold, dead code, but could he possibly give them insight into who and what had created it? In the end they had decided to hire him anyway, but they hardly expected him to turn in a personality profile on the virus' designer.

"It's all in the code," Masada said quietly. And it was to him. Cold code, clean and impersonal: of course, it contained the essence of the personality of the man who designed it. Of course, anyone who knew what he was doing could find those clues, and interpret them. It was all simple math to him, motivations dissected with the cool precision of a laser scalpel. *It's all in the code*. Yes, but who else would ever see it there?

It struck Hsing suddenly that Masada didn't even understand the nature of his own genius. To him the patterns of thought and motive that he sensed in the virus were self-explanatory, and those who could not see them were simply not looking hard enough. Yet he would readily admit to his own inability to analyze more human contact, even on the most basic level. That was part and parcel of being *iru*.

What a strange combination of skills and flaws. What an utterly alien profile. Praise the founders of Guera for having taught them all to nurture such specialized talent, rather than seeking to "cure" it. It was little wonder that most innovations in technology now came from the Gueran colonies, and that Earth, who set such a strict standard of psychological "normalcy," now produced little that was truly exciting. Thank God their own ancestors had left that doomed planet before they, too, had lost the genes of wild genius. Thank God they had seen the creative holocaust coming, and escaped it.

"True evolution is random," Masada told him. "This isn't. Someone had to decide when and how the virus would mutate, and if I can isolate the code that controls that, I should be able to gain more insight into how the designer thought. Which in turn should give me more control over his creation. As well as answers to some very important questions."

"Such as?"

For a moment Masada didn't answer. For a moment, it seemed, he was deciding whether or not he should answer. "It uses a segment of outpilot's code to gain entry," he said at last. "Right now it's using code it stole during its former invasions; that's how the thing works. I want to know what was there originally, the first time it tried to gain access to an outpilot's brain. That will tell us a lot, Master Hsing . . . including whether or not the designer had access to Guild files."

A cold shiver ran down his spine. "You think one of our own was involved in this?"

"I think nothing at this time," he said quietly. "But I must consider all possibilities . . . including the least pleasant ones. If I can regress the virus, I may be able to tell more."

"I thought you already did that."

"I *decompiled* it. Broke it down. Regression is a different process, an extrapolation of source code probability." He suddenly seemed to guess that he was moving into territory where mere untrained mortals could not follow, and started again. "I'm going to try to determine what earlier versions of this thing might have looked like. Depending upon what happens to the invasion sequence then, that may tell us something."

"Evolution in reverse?"

"Precisely."

"But if the thing really is that complex . . ." He fumbled for the proper words. "That's rather like trying to guess what a child's great-grandparent looks like, given only one glimpse of the child. Isn't it? Wouldn't there theoretically be thousands of possible ancestors for each version of the program?"

"Millions, at this point. And more as each new generation is spawned." His eyes fixed on the screen before him, he seemed wholly undisturbed by that prospect. "I'm hoping to find some underlying patterns which will enable us to prune the family tree. Reduce it to a workable number. That done, the most likely suspects for source code will be allowed to reproduce and evolve on their own, to see if the pattern of their growth is true to the original. Most of the false leads will reveal themselves within a few dozen generations. The remainder may enable us to draw some observations about the origin of our virus."

Hsing stared at him in amazement. "Do you have any idea how much raw data you're talking about processing?"

"Of course I do, Guildmaster Hsing." He shrugged. "I have four months here, after all. The Guild won't transmit current copies of the virus to us while we're in transit for fear of data interception, thus I have only what you brought me originally to work with." He looked up at Hsing. "Can you think of a more productive way for me to spend my time?"

"No. Of course not." He watched as the professor turned his attention to the creature on his screen once more. The image grew larger, sharpened, and coiled upward a few turns, responding to unspoken commands. Within a few moments it was clear that Masada's attention was elsewhere; Hsing wondered if the professor even remembered that he was in the room.

"Your processing requirements are crowding out the ship's own programs." He said it bluntly, plainly, though all his *nantana* instincts urged him to do otherwise. But you didn't beat around the bush with an *iru*. They didn't like it, and besides, it wouldn't get you anywhere.

A second passed, then Masada turned to him again. "Is anything disabled?"

"No. Not yet."

"Then there is no cause for concern." He turned back to his work.

Hsing took a step forward, edging into the man's personal space just enough to break his concentration. "Dr. Masada, the captain asked me to talk to you about this."

The dark eyes turned on him. Annoyance flickered in their depths. "Speak, then."

"You're monopolizing his processors. Ship's systems are slowing down."

"Guildmaster Hsing." The man's tone was slow now, infinitely patient, as though he were talking to a child. Or an idiot. If the man were *nantana*, Hsing would have taken great offense at his tone; as it was, he grit his teeth and didn't protest. "I've explained my work to you. You understand its importance. Now, I've promised the captain and his crew that my calculations won't interfere with the functioning of this ship. And they haven't, have they? I'm sorry if one program or another is running a nanosecond slower, but unfortunately this ship is ill equipped for my kind of research. I have to use whatever space I can find, wherever I can squeeze it out of something." His eyes flickered back to the screen, but Hsing's closeness made it impossible for him to tune the Guildmaster out. "The equipment we brought with us is sufficient for me to manipulate the virus itself, but I need much more than that. The things I'm processing on the ship's system are no security risk."

"That isn't the issue."

The dark eyes narrowed. He had rarely seen Masada angry; it was strangely refreshing to see a human emotion on that impassive face, one that he recognized.

"Master Hsing, you hired me onto this job because the Guild was threatened. A virus is loose in the outworlds which can take down your outpilots . . . and because of that, it threatens all of human civilization. Or at least, so you told me. It strikes me that a threat like that is a *little* more important than whether some rich tourist from Paradise can access the latest Ima Starshine viddie to go to sleep by. Now, if you feel I'm wrong in that assessment, you just tell me now and I'll withdraw all my data from the ship's innernet, and let the captain run his systems in peace. Otherwise, I would very much appreciate it if you would let me get back to my work."

*You bastard*, Hsing thought. *You knew exactly what systems you were crowding out, and exactly what the effects would be. Nothing you do is an accident, is it?* Anger was an impotent emotion in such a situation, but it rose up in him anyway, and it took all of his guild training and his *nantana* experience not to let it show. *Why the hell didn't you at least tell me, so I could be prepared?*

"Give the food programs the space they need," he told Masada. "At least let me give the captain that much."

"Everything you take away from me slows my work down that much."

The anger reached his voice at last. "Food programs. Wellness tracking. Anything else that deals with health or life support. I don't want those programs slowed down by so much as a nanosecond, Dr. Masada." He paused. "Or at least, not enough that any of the passengers will notice. You understand me?"

The dark eyes turned to him, unreadable once more. "And the rest?"

He started to say something equally angry, then drew in a long, hard breath. The man was right, damn him. What he was doing mattered ten thousand times more than the comfort of a handful of tourists, and both of them knew it. But where was that thin line drawn, between the liberties they could take and the peace they must have? The Guild had never been tyrants. If they became so now, then they would lose more in the long run than any data processing could gain them.

"You just make sure those programs get freed up," he said gruffly. "I'll deal with the captain on the rest."

God, he'd be glad to get back home, to the *nantana* who normally attended him. They'd be plotting against him, of course. He expected as much. They'd have spent the past year preparing for his return, and God alone knew what subtle and devious traps awaited him. Their machinations were complex, sophisticated, deadly. He dreaded discovering what they were. But it was a game that he understood, and if he didn't play it well, he wouldn't be where he was.

It would be a breath of fresh air after this assignment.

Cursing all *iru* under his breath, he went to find the captain.

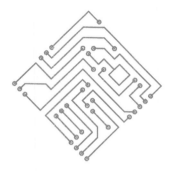

Each Node will provide a waystation, not more than ten hours' flight from the nearest exit point of the nearest ainniq.

This waystation must be of sufficient size and structure to house all travelers passing through the system, with amenities and services sufficient to sustain all known human types in reasonable comfort.

No human traveling the ainniq shall be denied access to the waystation.

Cost of services will be uniform for all humans. Laws and law enforcement will affect all humans equally.

Public behavior may be circumscribed within reason.

Private behavior may not be circumscribed unless it poses a threat to station security.

Any Node failing to provide the above services, or failing to comply with the conditions listed, will be suspended from outpilot service until the offense is corrected.

Failure to correct the offense, or a pattern of repeated offenses, may result in permanent Isolation.

*Master Contract of the Ainniq Guild, section 4*
*(also called the Law of Universal Access)*

# METROLINER: AURORA

**"M**S. CAPRA?"

Fuzzy thoughts. Hard to grasp. Mechanized voice speaking through piles of wadding.

"Ms. Capra. Can you hear me?"

She struggled up from the thick, warm depths to the place where her own voice resided.

"Ms. Capra. Please respond."

"I . . ." She drew in a deep breath and coughed; her lungs felt like they were filled with cotton. "I hear you."

"Are you all right, Ms. Capra? This program requires confirmation."

She glanced toward the place in her field of vision where the wellseeker display should be. It was blank. "I . . . don't know. My wellseeker . . ." It took so much effort to speak, those were all the words she could manage. She hoped the program understood.

Where was she?

"Your wellseeker was shut down at the beginning of suspension, Ms. Capra. That was necessary to keep it from interfering with the process. You can bring it back on line by using the proper icon. Please do so now."

It took her a minute, her mind was still fuzzy. The triple spiral design took shape slowly in her head; she traced its pattern three times in red, hoping her mind's eye was steady enough to make the icon work.

Apparently it was, for the program began to scroll through a host of biological measurements. Many of the readings were slower than usual, or colder than usual, or otherwise slightly off kilter, but none by so much that it mattered. ACTION? the program inquired when it was done. She hesitated, then flashed it a negative icon: NO.

She was beginning to remember.

"Ms. Capra, please confirm your biological status."

"It's . . . it's all right." The cotton was dissolving now, she could hear almost normally. In the distance there were footsteps, voices. "I'm okay."

"You perceive of no condition requiring external attention?"

She checked the wellseeker's display again; already the readings were much closer to normal. "No. I'm fine."

"Confirmation acknowledged. This suspension program is now terminated. Have a good journey, Ms. Capra."

Slowly, carefully, she opened her eyes. At first all she saw were blurry shapes, then those resolved somewhat. She blinked hard, trying to conjure clearer vision. She was lying in a contoured shell of some kind, affixed to the wall alongside dozens of others. . . .

The outship. Of course. She remembered now.

She pushed herself up to a seated position. A Guild technician glanced at her, then went back to his work. Several other passengers had just regained consciousness, as she had, and were staring about the ship in a kind of dazed confusion. Perhaps a dozen of the shells were still shut, no doubt with recovery programs droning inside, questioning the occupants. As she watched, the lid of one slid open, and its occupant—a young boy whom she had met on the transport—slowly rose to a seated position, blinking heavily.

Yes, she remembered now. The long trip to the Guild station. Final clearance. Her disappointment when it was explained to her that the outship was sealed tight, with no view of the outside universe, and that passengers would be put to sleep for the duration of the voyage. Some rich idiot from Earth had tried to talk the Guerans into letting him do otherwise, she remembered; he had offered millions in the currency of their choice to let him look at the ainniq while they were in transit, just for a minute. They had ignored his offer, then his protests, and then strapped him into a suspension shell just like everyone else. No one who was not of the Guild would be permitted to see the ainniq from the inside.

Jamisia had seen it from the outside, though. Just for a moment, as the transport approached the Guild station, it had been there—a flicker of maverick light, surreal, a shifting veil that took form, shimmered, and then suddenly was gone. She had kept her face pressed to the window, hoping for one more sight of it, but apparently the angle was wrong, or something. Half the people on the transport hadn't seen it at all, and they were quite upset to learn that she had. Apparently the position required for viewing was precise enough that being seated across the aisle, or farther toward the prow of the transport, kept one out of proper alignment.

"You're lucky," a steward had told her later. "Few ever get to see that much."

With a groan she levered herself out of the shell and onto her feet; there was gravity in the ship, just enough to let her steady herself. The Guild claimed that all their precautions were required to protect the passengers, but she wasn't sure she believed them. She knew that there were creatures inside the ainniq that would attack any human invader—everybody knew that—but she really didn't see how a lack of windows was going to save people from that. Or why the passengers had been forced to sleep through the journey. Was it just to protect them from fear, or to keep them from interfering with official business in midvoyage? It had been decades now since the Guild had lost a ship, so it wasn't like they were really in any kind of danger. She suspected the Guerans just didn't want to have to deal with so many "dirt-born," and so they drugged them and shelled them and stowed them in the main chamber like so much baggage.

At any rate, it was over now. She stretched her stiff limbs, noting some bruising along her right arm. The wellseeker would deal with that automatically, she knew; within hours the damaged cells would be repaired, and the discoloration would be gone. She wondered what had caused it. Other passengers seemed to be similarly damaged, so it must have been something that had happened during the journey. Well, she thought, that was what happened when people weren't awake to take care of themselves. She wondered if anyone ever sued over it, then remembered the releases she'd had to sign before they would let her on board. . . . No, the Guild apparently thought of everything. No lawsuits.

By the time she felt fully alert again, the last of the shells had opened, and the aisle was filled with jumpsuited passengers working out the kinks and cramps of the voyage. One woman seemed to have some difficulty breathing and needed assistance; apparently it was a common side effect of the suspension process, for the stewards seemed to know exactly what to do, and had clearly practiced their response many, many times. A quick adjustment to her headset, some kind of program feeding in from the ship's medical bank—she watched as the woman drew in one long, tortured breath, testing the capacity of her lungs. Then a second one, more easily. A guarded smile spread across her face, and the stewards moved on to other problems.

"Ms. Capra?"

She turned about to find one of them behind her, waiting for her response. "Yes?"

"Would you come with me, please?"

It took her a moment for the words to sink in. She looked around, saw that none of the other passengers were being approached with such a request. Something in her chest tightened.

*This isn't right*, Derik warned.

Her wellseeker warned her that her blood pressure was rising; she almost asked it for a tranquilizer, then decided against it. It might soon be more important to be alert than it was to be calm.

*No*, she agreed with him, *it isn't right, but what can I do?*

"What . . . what is this about?"

"Just a few questions, Ms. Capra. It won't take long."

"Let me get my bags," she said. Partly to make sure her possessions stayed with her, mostly to stall. She needed a minute to pull herself together. Was she overreacting? The fears of half a dozen Others were pouring into her brain; it was hard to think clearly, much less act.

God, there was nowhere to run. . . .

"That's not necessary," the steward told her, and he took her gently by the arm, urging her forward. "The crew will take care of your things."

"I want my fucking bags!" The venom poured into her soul with such force that she felt like she'd choke on it if she didn't spit it out at him. "You got that, you bastard? Take your hands off me NOW."

Stunned, the steward stepped back. The other passengers had stopped their stretching and were watching her, all of them. *Fucking idiots.*

*Derik. . . .*

*Just a helping hand,* he thought gruffly. *Go get your bags.*

Shaken, she went to the forward compartment where carry-on luggage was stored. What the hell was that? Usually the Others either took control or they didn't, the change was always a shock, but at least it was clear-cut. God help her if they started inserting thoughts in her brain while she was still herself.

*Don't sweat it.* Derik was grinning, she could hear it in his voice. *We're all on the same team, remember?*

*Oh, God,* she thought, *I just want this to end, I just want to be normal again. . . .* She shouldered the heavy bags, took a deep breath, and then turned to face the steward. "All right," she said. "Let's go."

Had she *ever* been "normal?"

Forward they walked, past the passenger compartments—there were twelve in all—into the command section of the ship. When they passed the place where workers were fixing an exit tunnel in place, she was tempted to simply break away from the steward and run down that tunnel with all possible speed, but that would only take her as far as the first customs barrier, she knew, and then they would have her again. No, it was better to pretend she didn't know anything was wrong. That way at least she'd have time to figure out what to do.

He led her into a part of the ship clearly not meant for passengers; black-robed Guerans brushed by them, intent upon the business of docking. She shivered a bit when they came in contact with her; it was an involuntary reaction, and she was embarrassed by it. If she could stand the sight of Variants with truly repellent deformities, why did these people scare her? They looked human enough, and as for their minds . . . it was said that all the Gueran Variations had existed on ancient Earth, so her ancestors had dealt with them. You couldn't say that about the other Variants. So why did their painted faces and black-robed bodies make her skin crawl?

To her surprise the steward led her off the ship, guiding her away from the customs checkpoint and down a narrow corridor which she guessed served the command crew of the vessel. To her right as she exited she could see a line of passengers gathering outside the checkpoint portals. *Visas*, a sign said at one gateway, and at another, *Immigration*. The steward took her to neither, but instead led the way to a small group of offices; opening a door, he ushered her inside.

"In here, Ms. Capra."

Trembling, she entered. There were two men in the room, both of them Gueran. The figures painted on their faces were so fierce and strange she could read no human emotion in their expressions.

*Who are they?* one of the Others whispered in her brain.

*What do they want?*

*How much do they know?*

"Jamisia Capra." One of the men gestured toward the room's only table; after a moment she realized what he wanted, and placed her bags on top of it.

"You're from Lansing Habitat, yes?" He paused in the manner of one consulting an internal list. Or else . . . she looked at his headset, then at the small transmission nodes set into the corners of the ceiling, and it suddenly struck her that she was in outernet territory. Here and now. If she'd thought to have her headset on, she could link up to it right now, just like these two men undoubtedly were doing. For a moment sheer wonder banished all fear. God, if she could only get through this meeting, who knew what wonders were out there?

Lansing Habitat. It was part of the false history her tutor had created for her. Were they questioning that, did they sense it was wrong? She tried to look calmer than she felt as she nodded. Maybe it was time for tranquilizers, after all.

"I have a few questions for you, Ms. Capra. Nothing to be concerned about. In the meantime," he nodded toward his companion, "my assistant will do customs clearance on your bags, to save you additional inconvenience. I understand these are all you have?"

She nodded somewhat numbly, watching as the man checked through her jewelry, her clothing, her very few keepsakes. What did they expect to find? God—she almost laughed—did they think she was a smuggler? Was that what this was all about?

*You are, though,* Verina reminded her. *You smuggled from Earth a brainware prototype they'd give their right arms to find—*

*—Only they ain't gonna find it in your bags,* Derik added.

She tried to watch what the one man was doing with her things, but the other one had questions which required her attention. How long had she lived on the habitat? When was the last time she'd left it? Had she visited Earth proper in the last ten years, and if so, where and when and for how long? Some of those questions she could hardly answer, she had to apologize and hoped they were patient while she tried to locate some internal log that would have dates on it. At last she simply called up her diary and adapted the relevant sections. The closer she stayed to the truth, the safer she would be. She tried not to become distracted as other paragraphs scrolled before her eyes, mysteries that had once obsessed her . . . lost time, unexplained possessions, a stranger's face staring back from her mirror. Once she had thought that if she could only understand those things, her whole life would come together. Little did she know.

There were surprisingly few questions, overall. Was that truly strange, or was it only her fear that had caused her to expect worse? "All right, then," her inquisitor said at last. He looked at the man with her bags, who nodded. "That's all, Ms. Capra. So sorry for the inconvenience."

"That's all?" The words were out of her mouth before she could stop them. Her surprise was undisguised.

"That's all," the man assured her. An expression that might have been a smile twisted the patterns on his face, and as the other man gave her bags back to her he offered, "It's not often we have folks complaining that we didn't harass them enough. Here you are, Ms. Capra." Despite her protests that she didn't need assistance, he insisted on helping her hoist the thick straps to her shoulder. One of them pinched her painfully until she twisted it so it fell right, but she winced and bore it with a half-hearted smile; he was *trying* to help.

And then they let her go. Just like that. Like she was anyone else, nothing to hide, no secrets. . . . They opened the door and ushered her out and even said good-bye to her, like this was some kind of social visit. Pretty strange. She started to move toward the portal marked *Immigration*, but the nearer Gueran caught her by the arm and stopped her.

"No need," he said. "Your file's been cleared for immigration. Enjoy the outworlds."

She stared at the line, then at him. And at the line again.

"Everything is taken care of," the other man assured her.

There would be dozens of officers in that other area. Hundreds of passengers, if not thousands, would be processed in the next few hours. If someone were watching for her arrival, they would expect her to pass through that portal. And the crowds would be such that if someone tried to get to her there, to do God knows what, very likely no one would notice. Or care. They could even figure out exactly when she was coming through the checkpoint if they hacked into Immigration's files, because no one entered the station without being processed first. How easy it would be to set up a trap. Anyone who was hunting for her was probably right in there, trying to sort her out from among the crowd.

She started to run . . . then stopped, and forced herself to drop to a brisk walk. She didn't dare draw attention to herself, not when her pursuers might be so close. As she passed through the portal the Gueran crew normally used, she waited for one of the Others to protest that she was being too paranoid. But no one did. It was a very, very bad sign.

*Those men knew something,* Katlyn whispered.

*Damn right they did!* Derik agreed. *So why the fuck did they let us go?*

Why indeed? She tried to come up with a reason—and was suddenly overcome by the whole situation, the sheer complexity of what her life had become. Only by pushing the whole question out of her mind could she even keep walking, much less functioning mentally. As it was, she felt nauseous; not a physical malady, but pure spiritual vertigo. *Got to make it out of this area while I can,* she told herself sternly. *Got to find a safe place before I lose it.*

Her shoulder still stung where the strap had pinched it; she shifted the bags as she walked, then ordered her wellkeeper to kill the pain. Under one security arch and then another she walked warily, machinery humming as it checked her for the dozen or so contraband substances on this day's watchlist. No drugs, she thought, no weapons, no explosives . . . only a few ounces of brainware that she would rip out of her head if she could, and a dozen more personalities than any one body should contain. Only that.

The arches did not protest her passage.

The promenade of the docking ring was a vast, curving corridor teeming with travelers of all Variants and destinations. The crowd jostled by her with hurried indifference, each individual headed toward a different gate, a different station. *They call them worlds here,* she reminded herself. *Just like they were real planets.* The far wall was lined with viddie screens, each one blaring a different advertisement. *YOUR FIRST TOUR OF THE OUTWORLDS BEGINS WITH US!* one announced, and below the scrolling description an eddress blazed in fiery orange. *A THOUSAND AND ONE NIGHTS OF WONDER* another beckoned, and that one offered an icon proper as well as the more prosaic text eddress. Triddie letters blazed overhead, scrolling through empty air as passengers hurried underneath. It was all too much for her, her brain ached from trying to make sense of it all. God, was anyone supposed to actually *read* all those things? She had to shut her eyes for a moment just to think. Was this what all the outworlds were like? A new wave of vertigo overwhelmed her, and she had to reach out a hand against the nearest screen to steady herself. *ROOMS TO SUIT THE MOST EXOTIC TASTES,* it proclaimed. Words scrolling over her hand. . . .

Where was she supposed to go now? What was she supposed to do? Oh, she'd come up with some ideas on the metroliner—more ideas than any one person deserved, for most of the Others had spent the last three years bickering over their communal fate—but this was *real,* this was *now.* This was standing in the middle of an unknown station some zillion miles from Earth, and not having family or friends or a home or job or *anything.* Oh, God—where did you even start? She felt tears coming to her eyes and tried to fight them back; she didn't want to start crying here. A set of four identical young men passed by, glanced her way, and then hurried on. She couldn't even remember the name of the planet that Variation came from, though she'd learned it in grade school. Then there was another creature who looked like an insect and a pair of Variants with what looked like snakes sprouting from their shoulders. She forced herself to ignore them and stagger onward. Her only hope lay in putting sufficient distance between herself and the checkpoint so when her enemies realized she had gotten away, they could no longer find her. And for that she needed to keep moving.

She passed more than twenty gates, each with its own crowd of humans and Variants embarking, or disembarking, or . . . whatever. Some walked, some crawled, others used automotive devices of a dozen different types; some of the latter seemed to be necessities rather than luxuries, the beings encased within them hardly capable of independent locomotion. Once or twice she stopped to stare at one, and had to force herself not to, to move on. God, they were so *alien*. . . . Was it that there were simply more of them here, which made the sight of them so unnerving? The metroliner's population had been mostly true-human; as frightening as the Variants were, they had always been outnumbered by creatures more familiar. Not so here. She passed by a gate which must be assigned to some planet; nearly all of the people there were of the same somatype. Long limbs covered with some kind of natural armor, more insectoid than human. She forced herself not to look, to keep walking. How far was it to the nearest place where she could exit the ring, and try to lose herself in the station proper? As long as she was trapped in this simple corridor, it would take little effort for her enemies to find her.

If her enemies were here. If the letter Justin had waylaid had in fact been delivered to someone. . . .

*Count on it,* Derik said harshly. *That shit back at customs was no accident. Something's going on that we don't know about, which means we need to get out of here FAST.*

Jamisia agreed. But where? She couldn't get through one of the gates without a passcode; only legitimate passengers would be allowed into the docks themselves. What else was there? She searched the ring with anxious eyes, and to her surprise—and relief—saw that up ahead its configuration changed. The corridor widened out, into a plaza lined with sales cubicles. Food, tools, and all the necessities of life were laid out in neat displays for travelers to peruse. The sight of food made Jamisia's stomach growl, but she had more important things to take care of right now. The vendors could answer her questions, the vendors could tell her where to go—

And then she saw the sign.

OUTERNET SUPPLIES, it said. Bright gold letters floating over a crowded booth. HEADSETS FOR ALL BRAINWARE CONFIGURA-TIONS. INTERFACES. GUIDECHIPS. She elbowed her way to the counter, ignoring the bright displays, and looked for the vendor. It was a triddie figure, but that was all right; now that she knew what she wanted, a holoclerk would be good enough.

"I need an outernet link," she said, rummaging through her bag to retrieve her headset. "For . . ." She couldn't read the fine print on it, finally just held it out to him. The figure was silent as somewhere, somehow, cams recorded, stored, and analyzed the corporate markings. "Shido 9135," he said at last. "An ex-cellent model for the inworlds. For the outernet, however, I would suggest not only a Nagoni model 476B Interface, but an additional software package—"

"Just the interface for now," she interrupted. She began to pull out her debit chip—and then stopped, suddenly afraid, as she realized what that could lead to. What if someone was watching for her codes to turn up on a vendor log? She would have to spend money sooner or later; it was the surest way for anyone to find her. Oh, God—what was she going to do! She rummaged in her bag for some alternative, found a handful of cash chits at the bottom. God willing there were enough. She poured them onto the counter and counted them quickly; on both sides people were staring now, watching the strange and primitive transaction take place. One hundred. Two. That was enough. She gathered up the chits in her hand again and offered them to the vendor, heart pounding. With any luck his program could handle cash chits. If not . . . then she didn't know what she would do.

He stared at it for a minute. She held her breath. "Terran corporate," he said at last. "I must inform you that there will be a 12% charge for processing, above and beyond current exchange rates.''

"That's fine." The stranglehold on her heart loosened up a bit. "Just give me the total."

It was almost more than she had. In the end there were only three chits left in her palm, of such denominations as would hardly buy her lunch. If the food vendors even took chits, which she doubted. She was going to have to find someone who could alter her debit chip, and soon. Or at least get far enough away from this place that she didn't envision her pursuers lurking behind every corner.

She found a corner of the vending area which was less crowded than most and took refuge there, feeding the software into her headset. Her hands were shaking, and she couldn't stop them. God, this wasn't how she had dreamed of entering the outernet for the first time, this half-baked race for data. At last it was uploaded properly, and she put the headset in place; tiny icons flashed their approval as contact after contact lined up with the ones embedded in her skull. Then came the blessed words ALL CLEAR, and she visualized the icon that would start the software running.

*** WELCOME TO THE NAGONI 476B INTERFACE ***

IN ORDER TO SERVE YOU MORE EFFECTIVELY, NAGONI CORPORATION WOULD LIKE SOME INFORMATION REGARDING YOUR PAST NETWORK EXPERIENCE. THIS WILL BE USED TO

"Fuck that!" Derik had taken control, but it only lasted a moment. Then he was gone and Raven slid neatly into place, taking control not only of the brain they shared but of the brainware as well. With blinding speed she fed a dozen icons and text codes into the visual processor; half of them were things Jamisia had never seen.

. . . TO USE IF YOU WISH TO DO THAT LATER. COMPLETE LISTING OF NAGONI'S PRODUCTS CAN BE OBTAINED BY . . .

Now Raven swore. It was less colorful than Derik's usual expletives, but under the circumstances, even more unnerving. Raven understood programming better than any of them; if she couldn't get the interface to do its job quickly, none of them could.

God damn it, all they needed was a simple map of the station; if she was back home, Jamisia could have accessed it by now. Why the hell wasn't planetary Earth on the same headset standard as the rest of the universe?

*** WELCOME TO THE OUTERNET GATEWAY ***

"Yeah, yeah." Raven flashed through half a dozen displays impatiently, messages designed to soothe the rockborn into feeling comfortable with the vastness and the vagueness of the electronic entity they were about to become part of. She had no time for any of that crap. At last she got to one display that mattered, ENTER YOUR BRAINWARE SPECS FOR REGISTRATION, and she gave it the false specs her tutor had provided: Hauck 9200, model 42A. It wasn't the name of what was really in her head, but it was still hellishly impressive; not one in thousands would have a current-model Hauck, and as for the 42 series—

*Shit.*

*Shit.*

*Shit.*

Jamisia tried to shut the program down. But it had already made contact with the outernet registration programs, and was uploading the data she had given it. *SHIT!* Only one in ten thousand might have brainware like she did, and if her enemy had gotten any information on her at all, he might know what to look for. He could have hacked into those programs and set up a sniffer, how hard would that have been? He already knew when and where her ship was coming in. It was a good bet she'd sign on to the outernet as soon as she got an interface program, and this was the closest supply point—

Jamisia ran. Somewhere in the back of her head, using her own little corner of their brainware, Raven was still searching for data. Jamisia just concentrated on running, on getting as far away from that vendor area as she possibly could, in as little time as she could manage it. Deep inside she knew that it was a mistake, that running made her stand out from the crowd and put her in even greater danger, but she couldn't stop herself. The sudden feeling of being trapped, of finding herself surrounded by faceless enemies at every turn, had triggered memories that were even more terrifying. Like being buried beneath a mountain of rubble. Like feeling the air squeezed out of her lungs with every tortured breath. Like knowing that she was trapped, trapped forever, there wasn't now and never would be any way out—

Someone grabbed her, strong hands on both arms jerking her to a stop. For a moment she couldn't even respond, as her mental circuits struggled to switch gears from terrors of the past to those of the present. Derik took over their flesh then and almost managed to pull himself loose, but despite his dreams of male bravado, it was only a small and slender body he was wearing, and not a very strong one at that. The hands held her tight.

"Easy, girl, easy! I'm trying to help. Calm down."

Gasping, she subsided. The man holding onto her looked mostly human, though his skin was streaked with blue; she couldn't tell through her frightened tears if that was a Variation proper, or just some alien cosmetic custom. "Calm down. It's all right. Tell me what's wrong."

"I . . . I . . ." She was back in control of her body now, and gasping for breath. What should she say? She could hardly dare trust this stranger, whose only contact with her thus far had been to witness her panicked flight. God alone knew who he was, or what he would do if he even guessed at the truth. But she needed someone to help her. She couldn't get away from her pursuers by herself. "I need to get off the docking ring," she gasped. "Away from here." God, if he would only help her do that it would be enough, it didn't even matter right now where she went. "Fast. . . ."

He hesitated only for an instant, then straightened up and moved through the nearest gate. His strong hand on her arm would have made it hard for her to break free, but right now she was happy to stay with him. "I don't have a—" she began, but he whispered "Shhhhh" to quiet her. He paused for a moment when they reached the gate, and she realized that he was feeding it a passcode through his headset. ACKNOWLEDGED, the display confirmed. SECOND CODE? With a start Jamisia realized it was asking for her passcode. "I can't—" she began . . . and then she realized that he was in communication with the gate's security program once more. CAPTAIN'S OVERRIDE ACKNOWLEDGED, it said at last. And the gate irised open.

He led her through with a firm grip, and she heard the door hiss shut behind them. The dock they had entered was a small one, and it led to a sleek private vessel being prepared for flight. His ship? She glanced up at him, saw him nod ever so slightly. His ship.

She looked behind her, back the way they had come. The gate was closed now, and no one without a suitable passcode would be able to make it open. For the first time in too many hours she managed to relax a bit. *Safe for now,* she told herself. Granted, it was a small safety—in the presence of strangers, in a dock about to be emptied—but in contrast to where she'd been a few minutes ago it seemed like heaven.

The pilot's hand was still on her arm; not until her breathing had slowed and her heartbeat was close to normal did he release her. "Now," he said, and his tone was gentle, reassuring, "want to tell me what all this is about?"

She hesitated. It was tempting to imagine she could trust such a man, spill her secrets, gain aid . . . but only a fool would actually do so. She hurriedly tested a few lies in her mind, but none sounded valid enough that they would assuage this man's suspicions. At last she decided the best thing to do was put off the issue . . . hopefully until after he got her out this place.

She put on her best helpless-young-girl face and murmured, "I can't. I'm sorry. But I can't." Hell, sometimes it worked.

If he meant to question her further, he didn't get the chance. Another man was coming up to them, this one a slender figure in a no-G jumpsuit.

"No more time for girlfriends, Allo." His face, sculpted in sharp angles, was softened somewhat by a teasing grin. "Ship's almost ready to go." As he nodded toward the ship, she saw his Variation: a half-dozen tendrils cascading down from the back of his head in the place of hair, which twitched and curled as he spoke. She remembered that Variation from her schooling, and knew that the slang name for his home planet was Medusa; what the real name was, though, she couldn't recall.

"Found this one running along the concourse, scared of

something. Says she needs to get off the docking ring, fast, but won't tell me why.''

She watched while the Medusan absorbed that. "Is that so?'' he said at last, and to her, "Where are you trying to go?''

Jamisia bit her lip, wondering what to say. At last she ventured, "Doesn't matter.''

He raised an eyebrow. "Got money?''

She nodded, then dared, "Enough for passage.''

"Ah!'' The Medusan laughed; his skull tentacles jiggled in time to the sound. "So she wants to be a passenger, does she? And what does our illustrious captain say to that?''

The blue-faced man studied her; she had the queasy feeling that his eyes were somehow looking right into her brain. At last he said, "We've got the room. Won't be the first time we've taken someone in at the last moment, or the last.'' He paused, studying Jamisia. "Not sure I want to get involved in this, though. Not without knowing what's going on.''

The gate chimed softly; someone was trying to come in. She listened, breathless, but only silence followed; whoever had sought entrance had lacked the proper codes.

She felt the Other slide into place, and for once was grateful to take a back seat. Her body controlled by another soul, she heard herself say, "I'll pay double what the trip would be worth.''

The captain said nothing.

She waited.

"That's not enough,'' he said at last. "Not if there's trouble in your wake.''

"That won't be a problem for you.''

"Oh?'' He raised an eyebrow. "I don't know that now, do I?''

She met his eyes with a steady gaze. "Then name your price.''

The captain stared at her. Inside, Jamisia cringed. Then he laughed, long and heartily.

"I like this one, Sumi. Program a bunk for her, will you? I think we have a passenger.''

He hesitated. "You sure this isn't a mistake, boss?''

He smiled but said nothing. There was an odd pause then, a heartbeat in which all sound seemed strangely suspended. Then Sumi nodded slightly, giving his approval. With a strong hand on Jamisia's shoulder, the blue-faced captain propelled her forward, toward the small ship. "You do understand that I'll expect more information than that, don't you—"

"Raven," she said quickly. It was the first time any one of the Others had given a real name to an outsider; the sound of it was unnerving to Jamisia.

"—Raven. I'm letting you off the hook now, we're all in a rush, but later I'll expect some real answers."

"Later," she said evenly, "you'll get real answers."

He looked strangely at her for a moment, as so many people did these days—sensing something in her had changed, but not knowing how to define it—and then turned his full attention to the ship. "You heard her, she wants off the docking ring NOW." He grinned. "So let's move it."

*You sure this is the right thing to do?* Jamisia ventured.

*Nothing is sure anymore,* Raven answered calmly. *This'll get us off the station. Nothing is more dangerous than staying here.* And she added gently, *Relax.*

Foreign voices greeted her as they approached the ship. Variant accents from half a dozen planets. Those who saw her seemed startled by her presence. Was that because she was a Terran, so rare in their world, or just because she was a stranger? No doubt the captain by her side was feeding them information on what had happened, via the outernet. She had been told that under the right circumstances, a quick exchange of visual information could seem almost like telepathy. It was unnerving to walk up into the ship like that, knowing that messages discussing her were even now zipping through the air about her head. When she got the interface program up and running, maybe she would be able to listen in.

"All right," the captain said, "I want out of here within the hour. Tam, run the gateway programs. Calia, make sure those new charts are loaded. And Sumi—" He glanced down at Jamisia and smiled. "Show our passenger where the guest accommodations are, will you?"

She hesitated only a moment, then nodded and began to follow him. With only one glance back toward the gate, now silent.

*Safe,* she thought. *At least for now.*

Then she moved into the depths of the sleek little ship, and left her enemies behind.

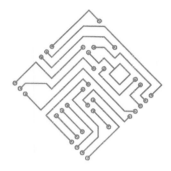

Let every government see to it that each child is implanted with the tools it needs to communicate, calculate, and process data. Let each government make sure that rich and poor alike, dirt-born and outworlder, Terran and Variant, all have equal access to the outernet and its resources. Let them do that, and we will see something the galaxy has never seen before: a time of true equality, unequaled prosperity, and the kind of conceptual innovation that can only take place when every human being is functioning at peak capacity, 100% of the time.

*New Horizons: Social implications of Cerebral Technology.* (Historical Archives, Hellsgate Station)

# PARADISE NODE
# PARADISE STATION

**T**HE MEDS were there within an hour, but it wasn't soon enough. Phoenix had waited too long to call.

He'd known it, too. That was the part that burned worst of all. He'd known there was something seriously wrong with Torch, and he hadn't done anything about it. The guy had started twitching in that spastic kind of way, and that should have been warning enough. But when you walked the firewalls in your spare time, that kind of thing happened, you know? Something crummy would get into your circuits and then from there it would shunt into your brain, and before you knew it your grayware had gone into virus-alert and shut down everything it didn't need, to focus all its efforts on cleaning you out. Sometimes that meant a few body parts went offline for a while, which was pretty spooky, but who in his crowd hadn't experienced it at least once?

So that's what he'd thought it was. Torch was working right next to him when the shit hit, and all of a sudden his arm had started twitching, and it was pretty spooky, but not out of line with the kind of thing that happened sometimes. You didn't really need things like arms and legs when you were 'netting, so if the grayware needed a little extra space to run things, it might preempt the circuits that ran extraneous systems. Not for enough time to do serious damage—the wellseeker made sure of that—but even a nano was enough time to scramble a few neurons here and there. Hell, they'd all been through it. Phoenix remembered one time he'd gotten really deep into the security system of Hellsgate and run into trouble. He'd been playing a war of nerves and speed with the megacomp there and every nano counted, so his 'ware had switched over a whole part of his cerebral net to data processing, which screwed the lower half of his body for well over an hour. Man, how he'd had to pee when that was over! If it wasn't for the contraband 'ware that ran a flesh-check and told him everything was okay, he might have panicked and called the meds . . . but like they said, shit happened. The minute you stuck that first contraband circuit inside your skull and let it hook up to your brain, you'd damn well better know there was trouble coming.

That's what he'd thought it was. The twitching. He'd glanced over once or twice to make sure nothing worse had happened, but Torch looked alert enough. As alert as anyone could when their eyes were shut and they were kind of snoring, but Phoenix knew that was how the guy worked, so it didn't fool him. Torch was so into what he was doing he would kind of let his body go on vacation while his mind soared free through the datalines. At least that was how it seemed to him. Sometimes when you were hacking you had to remind yourself that your mind wasn't really going anywhere, it was just the whole outernet dumping shit into your brain so fast that the only way you could deal with it was with all these bizarre fantasy trappings, dreamlike settings that the brain created to give you some illusion of control. Phoenix hated them. He had a master program whose only job was to clean them out of his head as soon as they appeared, so that he could hack clean and sane. Torch got off on it, though. He'd had these theories about how those supposedly random images were actually visual access codes to deeper levels of consciousness, and he regularly recorded his own in the hopes of decrypting them later. Never did, though. The code key, whatever it was, had eluded him.

And now it was too late.

The med standing next to Torch's body stood up at last. There was all sorts of electronic crap scattered around Torch, things they'd tried to use to get him started up again. No dice. You could tell by the look on the guy's face that he was dead and gone, his brain having opted out for some data-fantasy far sweeter than real life ever was.

Then the med turned to Phoenix and said, "This guy a moddie?"

For a moment Phoenix could only just stare. What did he expect, this idiot med? That anyone would answer yes to such a question? Late-life modifications were as illegal as it got, and if they knew the half of what was in Torch's brain, they'd start asking all the wrong questions, in all the wrong places.

Then the med put up his hands in a gesture of innocence, and said, "Just trying to help, man."

"Don't know," Phoenix said warily. "Why? You think something fried him?"

"I think his wellseeker's a scrambled mess. We tried to download a mort log, and all we're getting is nonsense." There was another med present, a girl, and she began to pack up all the electronic 'ware they'd used on Torch. Coiling cords neatly, so neatly, as if one coil out of place might cause some vital control not to work. In the middle of Phoenix's hyper-cluttered abode, it seemed almost a ludicrous effort. "Can you shed any light on that?"

He spread his hands in a matching gesture of innocence. "Hey, he was just a friend. Whatever he was into . . . he didn't share it with me." Then he took in a deep breath, tried to choose the tone of voice that would sound the least confrontational, and dared, "Can I get a copy of the mort log?"

The med's eyes narrowed. The girl looked up. "You kin?"

He hesitated only a nano. "Yeah. Only living." When the med didn't say anything he added, "Cousin."

"What's your name?"

"Randol. Randol G. Harrington. Like his name. Father's side." He figured by now they had run Torch's ID, so that wasn't giving away anything they didn't already know. When they stared at him in what was clearly a disbelieving manner, he added, "Honest."

"Well, Mr. Harrington. I'll tell you what." The med tapped a button on his jacket collar and the door slid open; two white-garbed assistants appeared with a stretcher rolling between them. The med glanced down at the body, assured them, "It's clean," and then looked back at Phoenix. "We're going to take him back to the station lab and outload everything we can, to see if we can isolate the cause of this fellow's demise." The two men gathered up the body and placed it on the stretcher, strapping it into place. "When that's done with, if indeed you are legitimate kin of his, I'll see you get a copy of all the logs. Mort included."

It was the best he was going to get, so he put a fake smile on his face and nodded. "Thanks. I really appreciate that."

Such service didn't come free, of course. He flashed up an icon that gave him access to his most legitimate-looking debit account and bundled up a nice bit of cash as baksheesh. The med didn't bat an eye when his grayware informed him of its delivery—he was so *very* smooth—but Phoenix knew from his own program that the offer had been accepted. He stuck a piggyback on the next message the med sent out, figuring that it was headed to his bank. Just in case the asshole didn't come through as he promised, Phoenix would have his financial passcodes to play with. It never hurt to be prepared.

*Torch is gone.* It hit him suddenly like a blow to the gut. Watching them bundle up his friend's body onto the auto-stretcher, watching it wheel itself out, he felt a stabbing grief, and a sense of total dislocation. Was this the guy who had broken into Dormia Station's penitentiary databank by his side, changing the code heading of each inmate's file so that the system was totally mucked? Was this the guy who had broken into the secret archives of the Sons of Perdition, committing a blasphemy for which (the Sons claimed) they would burn in hell forever? Was this the guy who'd hacked into Phoenix's own files on Hellsgate, the fourth or fifth time he'd been arrested, so that by the time they got him printed and booked, there was no complaint left on the books to keep him? God, they'd had fun. He couldn't even imagine what it would be like without Torch. First Chaos had been downed by a virus, then Deth Warrior went down, now this guy . . . the last of his little pack was on his way out the door, and Phoenix couldn't even bring himself to look at Torch's face. There were tears in his eyes—real emotional stuff, not the faux shit his bioprograms churned out when diplomacy demanded it—and it was pretty hard to focus.

He had to get hold of those logs. He had to see what had taken out his friend. If it was the same virus that had screwed up Chaos, and then Deth . . . well, there'd be hell to pay. And if it really *was* a government plot to take out the moddies, as Deth had claimed . . . well, then that hell would shake the known universe to its roots! He had lost too many friends too fast, and no longer cared what the hell the establishment thought of his methods.

The door whisked closed behind the meds and their burden, leaving him alone in the dark and cluttered apartment. With a sigh he forced his attention back online, to the task of the moment. By the time Mr. Baksheesh got back to his station there would have to be records proving that Bent Harrington really did have a cousin named Randol, and that meant breaking into the Census files and MedCom and whatever other systems Torch's family tree was logged on, and adding himself to one of its branches. It wouldn't hurt if he could whip up a will really fast and get it into the databanks, too, just in case someone was stupid enough to try to claim the guy's possessions. That would take an hour, maybe, a bit more if there was trouble.

He wondered, as he started to work, if they would let him claim Torch's modware.

*Yeah. Right. Dream on, Phoenix.*

**"A**ll *right now, Mr. Devon. We're ready to proceed."*

*It's a fake name, of course. Who'd give a real one? He tries to nod, but the straps holding his head down to the table don't allow for it.*

*"One last time, for the record . . ." The med's hand goes somewhere out of sight, and there's the soft click of something being turned on. "You understand the risk involved? It's not just a question of whether or not there will be damage. There will be damage. It's only a question of which cells get damaged, and how badly. I can't access your current brainware without going through gray matter, and that means risk. You understand that?"*

*His head is fuzzy from the drugs. "Just do it, okay?"*

*But no laser scalpel moves towards his skull; the med's voice drones on like this is some recording stuck on automatic. What does he think, that having a tape of this little speech will somehow save him if the station goons seek him out? Like they care if a moddie was warned or not.*

*But the drugs have made Phoenix mellow, and they dull the edge of his impatience. Fine, he thinks. Whatever. Let the guy have his say.*

*"You're going to have internal pressure for a while. That can't be helped. It's going to take a while for your body to figure out that it doesn't have room for as much ventricular fluid as it used to . . . if it ever does. An infant's brain adapts as it grows, an adult's . . . sometimes doesn't."*

*Oh, yeah. He knows the truth of that one, better than this med does. He's already seen a friend taken to the morgue because of bio-ware run amok. You stick the stuff in your head and then you wait with fingers crossed to see if it stops growing when it should, and if your brain figures out it's there and adjusts for it, and what kind of damage the meds did putting it there in the first place. Not to mention whether it will prove compatible with the rest of the junk in your head, and hook up to it like it's supposed to. Hardware proper is even worse, that has to be imbedded in its finished form, which means gray matter from somewhere has to make space for it. And the brain isn't all so nicely labeled that a med knows for sure what he's cutting.*

*But what's the alternative? Go through life with an outdated piece of shit in your skull? Hell, maybe the rich folk liked what they got in the birthing center enough to be happy with it all their lives, but they were a whole different story. State-of-the-art wiring from the get-go, happy little babies hooked up to special monitors to make sure every biocircuit which grew was just where it should be. Little wonder they thought the stuff in their heads was perfect. It probably was. But what about the rest of the population? Node law guaranteed that every child was implanted with brainware upon birth, at state expense if necessary, but that didn't say anything about the quality of what they were given, or how careful the meds were about placing it. Shit, he knew one guy whose processor seed had been placed in a crease in the ventricular lining, it grew about a micrometer and then hit the wall and figured it had no more room to expand. Intellectually the guy was okay, but his inner circuits couldn't process much more than a cheap viddie. What was someone like that supposed to do, just smile and live with it?*

*No way. That's not what the brain was for. God might have meant gray matter for thinking, but thinking man knew that its ultimate purpose was as a biotech interface. Could God send human thoughts buzzing across the universe at nearly the speed of light? Could He inload a copy of an ancient document so fragile that the original pages were never exposed to light, and cut and paste in new text, and outload the finished product to hardcopy . . . all in the blink of an eye? Well, maybe He could, but He sure as hell hadn't given those abilities to His children. So mankind had worked them out for himself.*

*Slice the gray stuff up, Phoenix thinks. Put those circuits in place and give them room to grow and let's see what the human brain can do with 'em. And you may as well put hinges on that piece of my skull you're cutting out, 'cause you can bet that when Sitech or Omniware comes up with something new to add, I'll want that installed, too. You've only got one life to live, right? So why waste it on outdated ware?*

FINAL REPORT ON THE DEATH OF BENT HARRINGTON, the paper said.

It was real paper, the plastic stuff. You could hold it in your hand, stick it in a pocket, pass it along to someone without need for 'netting. Clearly the station authorities were trying for class, or . . . something. Phoenix preferred the confines of his own brain for reading, but what the hell. Someone, somewhere, had decided that a piece of paper was more compassionate, and had sent out the notice that way. Maybe Torch's family would take comfort from it.

PROBABLE CAUSE OF DEATH: WELLSEEKER MALFUNCTION.

PROBABLE CAUSE OF WELLSEEKER MALFUNCTION: SOFTWARE INFECTION.

ILLEGAL MODIFICATIONS TO THE VICTIM'S BRAINWARE MAKES FURTHER ANALYSIS UNADVISABLE. FAMILY SHOULD NOTIFY STATION FORENSIC LAB WITHIN 24 HOURS IF THEY PLAN TO ARRANGE FOR PRIVATE AUTOPSY.

BE FOREWARNED THAT ANYONE HIRED FOR SOFTWARE AUTOPSY MUST BE WARNED OF THE PRESENCE OF ILLEGAL MODIFICATIONS IN THIS SUBJECT, AS PER STATION CODE

3410-97-9E. FAILURE TO DO SO WILL RESULT IN FINES AND/
OR IMPRISONMENT.

Software infection. Wellseeker malfunction.

*Shit.*

He had a sick feeling in the pit of his stomach, a cold and clammy and downright ominous sensation. Because they'd been screwing around with a major software virus right before Torch went down. It was something Chaos had found on the outernet, massive and complicated and as intelligent as a virus could get. Awesome stuff. She'd looked at it too closely herself, and gotten fried. Poor Chaos. She was good at what she did, but she was never very careful; she relied on intuition to decide when to take precautions and when not . . . and this time, apparently, it had failed her.

They'd posted her death notice on the moddie networks, and a thousand faceless friends from throughout the outerworlds had sent in obits or roasts or whatever to commemorate her brief life. She'd become well loved among them, as befit someone who once made all the Hellsgate Pol computers churn out yellow smiley faces whenever they were asked for mug shots. Man, that was a classic. The best part was that she'd once slept with this guy who worked for the Pol there, some ex-hacker they'd later bribed into doing data security, and she probably could have gotten him to just give her safe access to the system, if she'd wanted it . . . only she didn't. She wanted to do it the hard way. Which was why they all loved her like they did.

So the death notice had gone out and the responses came in, and along with all the notes of grieving and sympathy came an odd little packet from Lisalia. Seems the crowd there had picked up a few samples of a nasty little virus, and it looked very much like what she had been playing with. It took Phoenix's crowd a week to yank its teeth so they could even copy it without getting burned, but at last they had a copy they could take a close look at, safely. Sure enough, it matched up with the one she'd in-loaded, at least in the parts that mattered. This was Chaos' killer.

He was willing to bet that's what Torch had been working on, too. Maybe all its teeth weren't out, after all. Maybe it was nasty enough to grow new ones. He could feel a cold knot of hate growing in the pit of his stomach, a kind of hate he'd never felt before. If this was what had taken Torch down . . . then there would be vengeance. One moddie death might be an accident— *maybe*—but two meant that someone or something was targeting their kind. And that would not be tolerated.

Was it possible the government was conspiring to take the moddies out? Torch had thought so. It was no secret that the augmented hackers were a thorn in everyone's side, from the loftiest Guild authority down to the lowliest shipping clerk. Everybody'd been hit at one time or another, be it with a playful infection that translated all their private documents into Pig Latin, or a subtle, insidious mole that ground government functioning to a halt when it finally broke out. When you had a central processing system to which everyone and their mother were plugged in, such pranks were inevitable. The majority of problems were caused by youngsters who really didn't know what they were doing, of course, out to prove their fledgling manhood by screwing with other people's data; they generally got caught, and their wrists were heavily slapped by the Powers That Be. Most quit the game at that point. Those that didn't tried again, and tried harder, and in the end they got good enough not to get caught any more. Which was a good thing, 'cause that kind of behavior could get you put away for life. Which is why Phoenix was damned glad that Torch had fixed his own files, the one time the pols had picked him up. If they'd ever figured out just how much havoc he was personally responsible for, the goons would have canned him, for sure.

So maybe this virus was somebody's way of getting back at them. Maybe somebody got hit by an electronic prank and didn't appreciate it for the art form it was, and decided to exact his own revenge. Torch had always believed that the virus which took out Chaos was a government plot, a way of dealing with hackers through their own choice medium. What if he'd been right?

*Then there will be hell to pay*, Phoenix swore silently.

There was a code of behavior common to all hackers: unwritten, unspoken, but absolute. You didn't hurt people. Their businesses were fair game, their possessions, and even their governments—but not people. You might shut down the whole Paradise shipping ring just to watch the state of electronic panic which ensued, but you didn't screw with a med center. You might target a politician known for anti-mod campaigning, and add a few thousand live-sex calls to his vid bill (alerting the press, of course,) but you didn't do that to a politico on whose reputation some disaster relief bill was riding. You might even rig a bank executive's account so that when he woke up one day he discovered that every cent he possessed had been donated to the Friends of Earth, or some other such fringe group. But you never, *ever*, took money that was needed to feed a hungry child, or purchase medication, or otherwise save a human life. That just wasn't done. And likewise the government's attempts to crack down on the hackers—an effort that went on constantly, with notably little success—always fell short of the ultimate penalty. It was an unspoken agreement, to which both sides had adhered since the beginning of electronic time. *Thou shalt not kill.*

Until now.

He stared at the thing on his monitor, hating it, loving it, needing to dissect it in that primal way that animals need food and water. He hated working on a monitor, but he sure as hell wasn't going to load the damn thing into his head. Had Torch done that, had Chaos? It was always tempting. You could manipulate code much better internally than you could through a stone-age mechanism like this. Had Phoenix's packmates gotten frustrated one day, decided they could handle the consequences, and let the monster in? Modware was notoriously sensitive to such assaults, it lacked the kind of safeguards that came with legal implants. That's what you got when you added to a system piece by piece, rather than planning it out from the start. Had they figured they could handle it, neutered the virus and then inloaded it only to find out that it hadn't been neutered at all?

He was going to find out. He was going to take this sucker apart bit by bit if he had to, squeeze it until its secrets ran out like blood, and find out where the hell it had come from. And God help the feds, if they were behind this thing. Or the politicos. Or . . . whoever.

The full destructive potential of Phoenix and his kind hadn't been unleashed for generations, not since the terrorist hacking of the third new century. God help the deadheads if they had forgotten their history lessons, and thought that people like him would sit back and submit to their petty extermination efforts. Did they really believe the moddies would die off one by one in silence, never asking who their enemy was, never striking back?

Fat fucking chance. If the hackers went down, they'd take the outworlds with them. Anyone who thought it couldn't be done needed to go back and run their history chips again.

*God help you all, if Torch was right.*

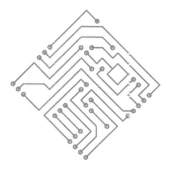

Trust is a luxury to those in power, and those who indulge for no better reason than a hunger to taste its sweetness will know the full power of its poison.

# GUERA NODE
# TIANANMEN STATION

THE PRIMA knocked when she reached Devlin's office. She didn't have to (and with some subordinates never did, it kept them on their toes that way) but Devlin's rank deserved the courtesy.

"Come in."

The door slid open in response to his words. When she entered, it slid shut behind her, leaving her in near-darkness. Most of the room was taken up by a holographic display, some bizarre kind of star map that provided the only light in the room. She recognized the icons representing Earth and Guera at opposite ends of the holo, with a fine webwork of glimmering lines connecting them to the three or four dozen stations between them. It was a large display, the kind you could walk through to get a better perspective, and Devlin was in the center of it. His vision was focused on a pattern of fine white lines so thickly gathered about one point that they looked like a mass of tangled silk. He looked up and saw her then, and the pleasure on his face that it was her and not some annoying subordinate was unmistakable. "Lights to half," he said aloud, and the room went from dark to semi-lit. He was smiling as he walked toward her, the holo patterning his body as he moved, but she could see from his tightly knit brow and the tension of his shoulders that he had been stressed, was stressed now, and would remain stressed for some time to come.

"Working, I see."

"Always."

The display looked chaotic to her, but of course it wasn't. Nothing he did was ever chaotic. "What is it?"

"Patterns of communication. Compliments of your loving and loyal subjects, whose only purpose is to serve you." His tone was dry. He reached into the display and pointed to one of the most active icons. "Delhi." Then another, linked to it by a number of bright lines. "Kent." And another, some distance away. "Varsav." And on Paradise, "Ra."

"You're monitoring them."

He smiled darkly. "Of course. Didn't you tell us that even our own people were suspect? I'm watching them now, as I'm sure they're watching me."

"Perhaps if they had the technology they would," she said, smiling slightly. "As it is, I think you have a slight advantage in that arena."

He didn't smile outright, but the comment clearly pleased him. "That's as it should be, don't you think? God help this office, the day your Guildmasters know *all* my tricks." He looked back at the display once more. "Still, Delhi has some hackers I'd like not to duel with, and Varsav's security is downright Moebian in logic. Or so I've heard," he added quickly.

She took a few steps closer to the display and studied it herself. From here she could see that the seemingly empty space between station icons was webbed with even more delicate lines, each of them pulsing with its own secret rhythm. She knew that the thickness of each would have meaning to Devlin, as would its luminosity, its rhythm, and its duration. Another programmer might have rendered the same data in a list of numbers, or some other more prosaic form. Devlin preferred a more abstract format, that hinted at complexities no mere list of figures could capture. That was his strength, and the facet of his intelligence which had allowed him to rise above all his would-be rivals. She couldn't always understand what he was doing . . . but could she have relied upon any programmer whose work *was* fully comprehensible to her? He was a programmer; she wasn't. She expected mysteries.

Her predecessor had been different, of course. He had ruled the Guild with an iron fist, a *simba* among *simbas*. Such lack of subtlety can become a weakness, if exploited properly. Identifying such weaknesses was her own field of specialty.

Which is why she was where she was, and her predecessor was . . . gone.

"So what does this tell us?" she asked him.

"That Delhi's more active than usual. I think she's got some special project going, and knowing her, that bears watching."

She caught the cautionary edge in his voice and mused, "You think she's dangerous."

He looked up sharply at her. "They're all dangerous, Alya. These are the ones most likely to get your job if anything happens to you, and don't think that a day passes without them thinking about it. If something like this virus were to bring you down. . . ."

Her expression darkened ever so slightly. "Don't think that a day goes by without my being aware of that, Dev." She nodded toward the display. "Go on."

"Kent's also increased his com activity. He started the day after you met with them all, before he even got back to his station. Now, he's always been the quickest to respond to any threatening situation, but in this case his speed was truly noteworthy. Perhaps it's the subject matter here which inspires him; he still thinks of himself as an outpilot, you know. No doubt he sees himself as their natural protector in this crisis . . . so his activity is probably Lucifer-linked. Something to watch, not necessarily something to worry about."

"Perhaps," she said quietly. She considered whether she should tell him what she'd heard, and if so, how to word it. At last she said, "It's been suggested to me that Kent might be . . . connected to all this."

"Based on what evidence?"

"There is none . . . yet. But it's been pointed out to me he does have a possible motive." Her eyes were fixed on him now, and she set her brainware to record what she was seeing. It wasn't as good as a full-view cam, but it was the best she was going to get. (*Damn* this virus, which forced her to treat her own loved ones like suspects!) "It has been suggested . . . perhaps his resentment over his injury. . . ."

There was a long silence. She could read nothing in his face.

"You think he might strike at the other outpilots? Out of jealousy? Resentment? What?"

She spread her hands wide in speculation. "It's simply been suggested at this point." She watched him for a moment, his brows drawn together in contemplation. Quietly she said, "What do you think?"

He took a deep breath before answering. "I think . . . it's possible of course. Anything is possible." He processed his own thoughts in silence for a moment more, then shook his head. "It's good we sent for an independent to help with this. Yes, Kent could be guilty. So could I. So could any of us. We'd be better off tracking this thing to its source than trying to second-guess its maker's motive, don't you think?"

"I think right now we have to do both," she said grimly. "Which brings us to the next question, one I didn't want to ask in front of others. How sure are you of your staff?"

"Suspicious of them all, of course." A faint glimmer of dark humor touched the corners of his mouth. "Just as you have to be suspicious of yours."

Yes, she thought, all of her staff. Her guildmasters most of all, because they had a motive to bring her down. Her lover, because he had the means. And every programmer and pilot and secretary who served them, because Earth would pay billions to have the Guild's secrets, and someone might have wanted riches badly enough to sell out his own people. Who could she trust in this? No one. But you had to have someone to work with, you couldn't do this kind of thing alone.

God, there were times she hated this job. Not what it was, but what it had done to her. You should be able to run the Guild and still remain human. You should be able to shuck off your responsibility at the door when you came home to your lover, and enjoy the sweet refuge of companionship without being strangled by the paranoia of your office. Maybe someday she'd learn how to do that. In the meantime . . . well, it was a sweet dream. He understood. Several other men hadn't, and they were no longer part of her life.

She walked into the display herself, and put a slender hand up to where Delhi's icon hung in the air. As if she could touch it. "Are they serving themselves, do you think, or the Guild?"

"Probably both," he said dryly. "Isn't that the way it's done?"

She looked at him sharply. But there was no hint of accusation in his tone or manner. There never was. *I know how you got here,* his expression seemed to say. *I know what bodies were left behind you when you started your own rise to power.* But there was no criticism in the thought, not anything but acceptance. Perhaps even admiration. He'd have left an equal number of bodies behind him, if he'd needed to. Fortunately, his skills had made that unnecessary.

*We are such cold creatures, all of us. Power robs us of our humanity. It's an ancient formula, hard-wired into our brain cells, and any attempt to circumvent it is an exercise in futility.* Devlin had not had to fight so hard for his position as some others did, but she valued him all the more for that. There was still a spark of humanity in him, which the climb to power generally crushed. The day that she described her plans to him and saw horror in his eyes, that was the day she would know she had gone too far. He was, one might say, the litmus test of her own humanity. And he was priceless to her, for that reason if no other.

"Hsing will be home soon," he told her, gracefully changing the subject. "I've plotted out his probable com pattern and will compare it with the real thing when he gets here. I expect no surprises there; he'll be too busy reinforcing his power base to worry about much else. We know the general pattern of his alliances; I don't expect to see much else out of him for several E-weeks at least."

"And Masada?"

He started to speak, then stopped himself.

"Devlin?"

"You sure about this man?" he asked quietly.

"Sure that I can trust him, or sure he can do his job?"

"Both."

"Well, then . . ." She hesitated. How much should she confide in him? Yes, she felt in her heart that Devlin was loyal . . . but she also knew that loyalties could be complex, and the only kind of Guild officer without secrets was a dead one. How much did she trust Devlin because he deserved that trust, and how much because she just needed to trust someone? It was a question that haunted her constantly.

But in this case, there really was little question. Clearly there had to be an independent investigator in this matter, she had insisted upon it. Of all the choices available he had agreed that Masada was best. If he had his doubts now, as the man approached outspace, that was only natural. Such doubts needed an outlet sometimes, and he could hardly share them with his staff.

His *suspect* staff.

She said it quietly, simply, knowing he would understand everything the one word entailed. "No."

"You sounded very sure of yourself in that meeting."

"I have to sound sure of myself in meetings. It's my job." When he said nothing in response, she sighed and added, "I'm sure he won't betray us. I'm all but sure he's careful enough not to give away our secrets by accident. In his home environment there were no doubts, of course; he's one of our most trusted consultants. But the *iru* doesn't adapt well to new environments. And he isn't alert to all the subtle social signals that might warn you or me of trouble in the making. So . . . can he be bought? No. Corrupted? I doubt it. Tricked?" She drew in a deep breath. "Possibly. That's a risk we chose to take. Let's hope it proves worthwhile."

He said nothing, but came to where she stood, moving close enough that she could feel the warmth of his body against her skin. When she didn't move away—a necessary sign—he reached out a gentle hand and squeezed her shoulder. She shut her eyes for a moment, savoring the contact, then reached up her own hand to cover his.

"God help whoever designed this virus," she whispered. There was hate in her voice now, a raw and venomous hate unfiltered by any polite social conventions. She treasured the fact that she could be so open with him. "Because that bastard is going to need the help of a deity when I get through with him."

She moved closer to him then, and he put his arm around her. And for a short while, in the seat of Guild power, there was nothing but silence.

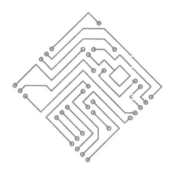

Those who support the concept of a direct interface network don't take into account the price they would have to pay for it, in privacy and safety and a thousand other areas of concern. Do you really want a machine to know where you are every minute of the day? Do you really trust the people who design these things, and program them, enough to let their work directly into your head? Don't you realize that every time you let this creature come in contact with your brain, you are leaving your mark upon it as clearly as fingerprints upon glass, which any clever programmer can decipher?

MAXWELL ONEGIN, *Think Again!* (Historical Archives, Hellsgate Station)

# INSHIP: EXETER

IT WASN'T until they were well clear of the station—and clear of the traffic surrounding it as well—that Allo finally leaned back in his chair, drew in a deep breath, and said, "So. The girl. What do you think?"

Sumi glanced up briefly to see the expression on his face—it was bland and uninformative—and then looked back at what he was doing. "Not much to think yet, is there?" The Medusan's tentacles twitched slightly as they tested the air for particulate clues as to the captain's state of mind. "You think she could be important?"

"I think she could be worth money. A lot more than she herself would pay us." He flashed a command to the commissary program: visual icon for a cup of heller tea. "Tam picked up some buzz on the high security lines right before she ran into us. That's an interesting coincidence, don't you think?"

"Could mean something," Sumi said quietly. He adjusted one of the engines slightly, his slender fingers moving sinuously over the controls, like tentacles themselves. Sumi preferred manual switches to visual icons. Most Medusans did. "Could mean nothing." He glanced up at Allo again. "You want to wager on it?"

The commissary port slid open, revealing a cup of steaming liquid. Despite the lo-G lid which covered most of the contents, guarding against spills, the scent of mixed spices and alcohol quickly filled the small chamber. Allo took it from the port and sipped from it, slowly. Before him, on the main viewscreen, the crowded skies of Reijik Station were giving way to the peaceful black of empty space. Only it wasn't empty, not really. At any given time there were more than a billion transmissions buzzing through that darkness, chronicling everything from a grand-child's first words to the kind of secrets that could unseat gov-ernments. Jewels in the darkness. If you pointed your receptors in the right direction, you might even pick up the skip from other nodes, messages bounced off the surface of the ainniq as a stone might be bounced off smooth water. Those were the most valuable transmissions of all. Without them the nodes would be isolated, like true planets, and no outernet would be possible. There couldn't be a universal network of data if it took years for stations to share their input with each other.

The warm drink filled Allo, and the alcohol began its work of soothing his nerves. Down in the hold the crew had enough contraband drugs stashed to buy half a station, and he was anx-ious to get it unloaded safely. Usually he limited his "acquisi-tions" to less tangible goods, but this deal had been just too good to turn down. And if they got away from Reijik Node without trouble over it, he thought darkly, that would be too good to be true. They'd gone over it five times for tracers and not found any, but that didn't mean there wasn't one. He'd done two years hard time once, for learning that the hard way.

"No betting on this one," he said at last. He glanced back to where Tam was working—one of the Tams, anyway, the other was off duty somewhere—and asked, "Any luck on those secur-ity transmissions?"

The Belial twin shook his bald head quickly. He was short and wiry, and moved with that jerky quickness which was typical of small animals. "Not yet, boss. It wasn't logged in the usual manner. I'd say top secret, though, by the feel of it."

Top secret. If that was so—and if the buzz on the security lines was connected to their guest—the girl might be worth quite a bit indeed. "It'll be encrypted, then."

"I'd expect so."

Security codes took time to break. How long could they af-ford to stay at this node, tempting fate with their cargo? It might be best to leave as soon as they had the transmissions in hand, and worry about interpreting them later. "All right. Let me know as soon as you've got them."

"Of course."

He finished the tea, then chuted the cup and eased himself out of the contoured pilot's chair. "Anything you can't handle?" he asked Sumi.

The Medusan shook his head placidly. "So far so good."

"Tam—"

"I'll call you as soon as I get anything," the Belial promised. His bald head gleamed in the monitor's light as complex codes appeared on his screen, and just as quickly disappeared.

"Good." He watched them both for a moment, took a last glance at the viewscreen—all was still peaceful—and nodded. "I'm going to go see how our guest is doing."

**S**he was pretty . . . or would have been, if recent tension hadn't bled her face of color and made her skin look dull and dry. Her hair was a rich copper color currently stylish in Paradise circles, long and wavy and soft enough when it moved that if it wasn't the real thing it was a damn good fake. Her body looked unaugmented, slender but not without a curve or two in just the right place. Big eyes, delicate nose, mouth neither too thin nor too full for her face. He liked that. On the whole she was attractive, even though she was clearly Terran through and through. Normally he wouldn't spare the earthborn a second glance; they carried so much psychological baggage it wasn't worth the effort of dealing with them.

She was also scared out of her mind. That much was very clear, though she was doing her best to hide that fact. He could see it in the backs of her eyes when she first noticed him standing in the doorway, before she had gotten her guard back up. It was the look of a frightened animal, expecting hunters to close in from any quarter. Big hunters, he guessed. Clearly her panicked flight down the corridors of the docking ring had been everything he'd assumed it to be, and more.

*Yeah, this one's worth a hell of a price,* he told himself. *Question is, who's going to pay it?*

He nodded a greeting and moved into the small room. He knew how to walk with the fluid grace of innocence, and how to make his voice devoid of any threat. It was a guise he used a lot during customs inspections.

"Raven, is it?"

She seemed strangely startled by the question, and hesitated before nodding. "Yes," she whispered. The timing of the response was oddly wrong, as if she didn't even know her name. Or couldn't remember what name she had given him. *The latter's more likely*, he thought. A pseudonym was a damned good sign that something unkosher was going on. This got better and better.

"My name's Allonzo Porsha," he said, offering her his hand. "I'm pilot and captain here—as you've probably guessed." No answer. The large eyes were fixed on him, measuring him. They were a startling blue, the one thing about her that couldn't be real. Earthie eyes didn't come in that color, did they? "Allo to friend and crew."

Finally she moved; her small, warm hand clasped his in a ritual handshake, then quickly withdrew. "Raven Capra," she said quietly. Watching him. Waiting for . . . something.

"Where are you headed, Raven?"

She shrugged, and then glanced nervously about the room; he got the feeling she was trying to avoid looking directly at him. So that he wouldn't read too much in her expression? "Anywhere," she said at last. "Doesn't matter."

"No friends to go to?" She said nothing. "Family?"

She shook her head. She wasn't going to give him a single clue.

*All right, you little vixen, I can do a data search as easily as anyone. Better, with Tam-Tam at the screen.*

"But you've got enough money to pay for this little jaunt."

She nodded, then clearly realized that more was required of her. "My parents were wealthy." It was odd watching her speak to him; it was as if she were testing the words as she said them, watching his face to see how well each one would work. "They're dead now. Corporate accident. I . . . came out here to live with relatives, but they're gone. Died while I was on the metroliner."

A simple lie, so awkwardly voiced that he didn't even question its veracity. He let it go unanswered for a minute, waiting to see if she would say more, but no further facts were offered. "You were pretty anxious to get off that station."

He watched as she bit her lower lip but she said nothing.

"Raven . . . I told if I gave you passage I'd expect some answers. Why don't we get that out of the way now?"

She stood up suddenly and took a few steps away from him. Her movements were sharp now, no longer fearful and nervous, but somehow aggressive. The transformation was jarring. "You'll have the answers you need for this trip," she said sharply. "But I have business which doesn't concern you. Don't press me on that."

For a moment he said nothing. The chemistry in the room had just changed, and with startling suddenness. The girl who looked back at him now with defiance bright in her eyes was a whole different creature than the one he had just been questioning. What had just happened? Usually he was good at reading people—a man in his line of work had damned well better be—but this girl defied his best instincts.

He decided to forgo that line of questioning for now. They could always return to it later. It wasn't like she was going to leave the ship before he got another chance to talk to her.

"You said you could pay for passage."

In answer she pulled out a debit chip from an inner pocket of her belt. Holos flashed across its surface, expensive little icons that promised lots of corporate money in a heavily guarded account. "I can pay."

He reached out his hand for the chip.

"When we arrive."

He shook his head. "Now."

"It's my chip."

"And my ship. Thus my schedule." When she still didn't hand it over, he softened his voice, and said quietly, "Look, I did you a favor taking you on, right? Now how about a show of good faith on your part?"

He saw her hesitate . . . and he saw her try to hide the hesitation. *Okay,* he thought, *the chip can get her in trouble. Why?*

He waited.

"Not in this node," she said at last.

Of course. If there was someone looking for her, they'd be waiting for her to access her accounts. You can't travel far without money, and you can't get money without connecting to a database somewhere. The minute that chip made contact with the outernet, her pursuers would be tracing the signal.

Whoever they were. Whatever they wanted. However much they would pay to get hold of her. . . .

He briefly toyed with the idea of leveraging the moment to try to gain more substantial information, but a glance at her expression told him it wouldn't work. Whatever vulnerability he had sensed in her before, it sure as hell wasn't there right now. He was better off waiting for another time when she was less guarded.

"All right," he said amiably. "Fair enough. But let's log the transaction now, and transmit it later." He spread his hands in a gesture of utter reasonableness and innocence. "We won't send it out until we've reached another node, I promise you."

She hesitated. He could see the hard-edged fear inside her giving way to exhaustion . . . and the need to trust. That was the chink in her armor, he thought. Her defenses were good, but they were far from perfect. She wanted to trust somebody . . . anybody.

He could work with that.

"Okay," she said at last.

His expression betrayed nothing untoward as he showed her the nearest data port. Not until she had turned away from him to use it did he flash the icon that would connect him with the ship's innernet, and through that to Tam's headset.

SHE'S ABOUT TO CONNECT, he sent to the twins. GET A COPY OF EVERYTHING.

He didn't know which of the twins would respond to him, or even how they would decide which one should. The inner workings of the Belial mind were a mystery to him . . . and to any sane man. He'd known the Tam twins for five years now and he still couldn't tell them apart, in looks or in actions or in any manner of thought process. With a pair it wasn't too bad, but he knew the Belial typically birthed their young in matched sets of three, four, even five and six. All answering to the same name, all sharing a single identity. One of Mother Nature's stranger creations . . . or Father Hausman, more accurately.

The girl slid the slender chip into the input slot. Evidently she didn't choose the option of headset control, for the computer asked her, VOICEPRINT VERIFICATION?

She hesitated. "Capra."

CONFIRMED. TRANSACTION?

She looked up at Allo. "Ten thousand," he said. That was high enough to make her think she was paying him good money for his services, low enough that the fancy little debit chip should be able to handle it. She flinched a bit, but nodded. "Ten thousand Corporate Standard Units," she told the computer. She was talking aloud for his benefit, it was the icons in her head that would enable the actual transaction. "Transfer to—"

He gave her the proper routing code and she repeated it in her own voice; a well-designed chip would accept nothing less. He was willing to bet that this one was state-of-the-art, to judge from the looks of it. She'd been a rich kid once, whatever she was now, and he was willing to bet that whomever was looking for her didn't deal in play money either.

When the transaction had been properly confirmed by both parties he added his own instructions to the data string, letting her hear with her own ears that all was to be held in storage, not acted upon, until his ship left Reijik Node. "You see?" he reassured her, as the ship's computer confirmed his instructions. "As I promised."

She nodded, but she didn't relax. She wasn't ever going to relax around him again, he realized. By questioning her as he did he had made himself into the symbol of authority on this ship; if she was going to fear anything about this journey, he'd be the symbol of it now.

TAM? he visualized. WHAT'VE YOU GOT?

Response was immediate; the Belial had clearly been waiting for him. CHIP'S IN THE NAME OF JAMISIA CAPRA. PROGRAMMED ON EARTH, LANSING STATION, A LITTLE OVER FOUR YEARS AGO. NOT USED MUCH, FROM THE LOOK OF IT. I CAN'T ACCESS THE ACCOUNT ITSELF WITHOUT USING THE OUTERNET, AND I GATHER FROM YOUR INSTRUCTIONS THAT THAT WOULD BE BAD.

She was looking at him suspiciously, sensing his mental absence as he read the words scrolling before his eyes. He smiled and deliberately, clearly, focused his eyes on her. "I'll leave you for a while now, Raven. There's a com port to the left of the bed—'' He gestured toward it, and while she turned to see where it was, visualized quickly: YES, THAT WOULD BE BAD. By the time she turned back, he had flashed an icon that ended his link with Tam, and she saw only an expression of carefully orchestrated concern. ''Why don't you get some rest now?'' He suggested. ''You look like you could use it.''

She looked back at the bed, clearly tempted. It wasn't much—a pallet with minimal cushioning and pillow all in one, typical spacer issue—but after you'd been on the run for a while it must have seemed like heaven. And he was willing to bet she'd been on the run for quite some time now.

''Where are we going?'' she asked. Then, flustered, ''I mean . . . where is the ship . . . ?''

''We've got some local business in this node,'' he told her. ''After that we'll be heading out to Paradise Station. We can let you off there, if you'd like, or make other arrangements after that.''

''Paradise?'' She scowled slightly, as if trying to remember something about the name. ''Don't know it,'' she said at last.

''Tourist node, mostly. Massive waystation. You'll find just about every race there, and can make contact with . . . well, with whoever you want. It's a good place to lose yourself,'' he offered.

*And to sell rare commodities.*

''That's good,'' she whispered. She suddenly looked very, very tired, and older than her years. Which he was willing to bet did not top twenty. ''Thank you. Thank you very much.''

He felt a twinge of guilt, right then. But only a twinge. Men in his line of business couldn't afford much of a conscience.

''Sleep well,'' he told her.

*You can trust him, Jamisia.*

*Hell you can! Don't listen to her—*

*You have to . . .*

''Shut up, shut up!'' The words were barely whispered, but Verina's stern warning followed nonetheless: *Say nothing out loud, you don't know who may be listening.*

God, if this went on much longer, she was going to go crazy for real.

*Listen.* It was Verina again, always calm, always rational. *We've gotten away from the station, that was the most important thing. Whomever was looking for us doesn't know where to search next. The fact that the ship is changing nodes is a stroke of real luck. That'll muddle the trail even further. We've got a little time to think now . . . and to come up with some kind of long-term plan.*

*I want to see the ship,* Raven sulked.

*Later,* Verina told her. *For now, can you alter that debit chip so it can't be traced as easily?* Raven was the closest thing they had to a programmer.

*It's a fucking debit chip!* Derik snapped. *It's got a fucking account at the other end that it's got to connect to, and if it doesn't, there's no money. What the hell do you think she can do, conjure credit by magic?*

*I'd like to see that,* whispered one of the child-voices.

*Shut up, shut up, SHUT UP!!!!!* Jamisia put her hands up to her ears as if somehow that could shut out the noise. *Look, Verina's right. We need a plan. Now.*

Startled by Jamisia's uncharacteristic aggression, the others subsided.

*I don't think he believed our story,* Jamisia told them. *So he's going to keep asking questions, or else maybe get someone else to do it. Right? So we need some kind of story that he'll really accept, for a cover.*

*He'll know it's a lie,* Zusu warned. *We're not good enough to fool him.*

Jamisia could feel Derik bristle angrily. *Speak for yourself, twit!*

Katlyn, normally silent in such debates, moaned in exasperation. *Hello! Remember teamwork? Working TOGETHER? Isn't that what we're supposed to be doing here?*

That quieted them all for a moment. Thank God. Silence.

*Look,* Katlyn said, *We need an ally on this ship. Someone who'll work for us, maybe warn us of trouble coming our way. Cause we sure as hell can't trust them all, and I don't like the fact that we're helpless out here.*

*A "friend?"* Zusu said suspiciously.

Derik was less inhibited. *Jesus fucking . . .*

*We know what kind of friend YOU mean, Katlyn.*

Jamisia thought of what it would be like, to sit back and let Katlyn take control, to watch her work her games on one of the crew members. To her surprise, the thought was less sickening than usual. Was she getting used to it? That was a very, very frightening thought.

Katlyn demanded, *Look, does anyone have a better idea?*

For a moment there was silence. Then: *No*, Raven grumbled. A few Others reluctantly followed suit.

*Jamie?* Katlyn asked.

Jamisia was startled. Never in all their time together had any of the Others asked permission to take control, or attempted to gain her cooperation in . . . well, in anything. Was Katlyn really concerned with how much her actions might upset Jamisia? If so, that was a new development. She hardly knew how to respond to it.

*Whatever we have to do*, she thought at last. She could feel her heart pound as her brain formed the words, and she sensed that she and the Others were now moving into a new realm of relationship. Katlyn had made the gesture of asking for her input; now she had to prove that she could work with the Others, as opposed to merely enduring them. *I . . . I trust you.*

New words. New feelings. She could feel them sinking into the depths of her mind, where a dozen strangers absorbed them. Only not quite strangers any more. Not quite family. Something else.

*Okay*, Katlyn said. *If there's an opportunity, then, I'll take it. In the meantime I suggest the rest of you try to learn what you can from this ship.* And with a half-amused smile that the others could sense, she added, *Variants, huh? That'll be a new twist.*

Jamisia tried not to shudder.

It was Sumi who was given the job of befriending their passenger. Any one of the crew could have done it, of course, but Allo had already come off as too aggressive, and Tam-Tam would probably confuse the poor Earthie, and as for Calia, she had a pretty strong distaste for the Earthborn, which might make things difficult. So Sumi it was.

Truth be told, he wasn't unprejudiced himself, and he knew he would have to work hard to keep an edge of hostility from his voice whenever he addressed her. This was, after all, a member of the race that had abandoned his own people when their need was greatest. Oh yes, he understood that the Hausman Effect had been terrifying, that the sudden divergence of human evolution into a thousand different directions was more than Earth could handle . . . but did that mean all lines of supply had to be cut so suddenly? Granted, no living creature should ever have been subjected to the Hausman Drive again, for fear of creating monsters . . . but did that mean that robots couldn't have made the trip? His people had just put up their first crude homes when the curtain of Isolation fell, they still needed seeds and embryos and medical supplies from home to insure their success as a colony. Supplies which would never come. That first winter was hard, so hard. Earth had made it hard. Callous Earth, who wrote off its injured children, rather than supporting them in the few ways she still could. Oh, yes, Sumi hated Earth as much as any Variant did, as much as Calia, if not more . . . but this girl hadn't been around back then. She wasn't part of all that, except by an accident of birth. And so he tried to divorce his feelings about Earth from his feelings about her, and he was a fair enough man in his heart that for the most part he succeeded.

There was another advantage to having him approach her. The unique Variance which his people suffered had evolved in time into a sensory advantage, which might give him insight into her true nature. He remembered the last time he'd been in her presence, tasting the sour tang of fear rising up from her skin, molecules of hormonal exhalation that drifted through the air to be caught on the moist surface of his tendrils. Few humans knew just how acute the Medusan particulate sense was, or how much it could reveal of an individual's state of mind. Allo knew. Which is why Allo gave him assignments like this, where emotional insight was a key factor. Usually Sumi was the one who dealt with customs officials, and other situations where diplomacy was crucial; today it had netted him this job.

If only she weren't an Earthie.

Her door was closed, so he raised a hand and knocked on it. "Who—" she began, and then she seemed to realize that it hardly mattered who it was. "Open," she commanded, and the door obliged.

Her smell was different than before; he noticed that immediately. There was still the lingering taste of fear in her exudate, but now other things were mixed in as well. He felt his tendrils begin to glide forward instinctively to catch a better sample, then saw the look on her face as they did so. So. The Earthie wasn't used to Variants. He stiffened, and forced the fleshy appendages back to the rear of him, where his own scent overwhelmed anything he might pick up from her. All right. He'd be subtle, then, and spare the Earthie from having to confront his "deformity." Which was a good deal more consideration, he thought darkly, than her ancestors had ever shown for his.

"I came to see if you were comfortable," he offered.

She had unfolded the monitor screen and was in the process of reading something on it, he saw. He'd have to warn Tam to make sure that all their private files were inaccessible. They so rarely had guests on the ship that it wasn't something they normally worried about.

It was strange to see her sitting there, without a headset on, reading thus; like a vision from another age. But that was often true of Earthies, he'd heard; they used their brainware for specific tasks, having not yet made that mental adjustment which turned it into a natural appendage. Without even thinking, he flashed up an icon in his own field of vision which gave him access to what she was reading. General information from the ship's library, mostly on Paradise Station. All right, that was safe enough. He flashed a quick note off to Tam about limiting her access to their database, then turned his full attention to her again. Outworld etiquette said it was rude to indulge in lengthy internal dialogue when there was a real person sitting right in front of you. Not that folks didn't do it all the time anyway, but with strangers he liked to be proper.

"I guess," she said. Then she smiled; it was an expression of genuine gratitude, if not true relaxation. "Thank you so much for taking me aboard. I don't know what I would have done if you hadn't."

There was his opening, clean and simple. And he didn't take it. She'd be far more off her guard if he didn't question her immediately. That was the mistake Allo had made, and he didn't intend to repeat it.

"You said you'd like to see the ship. I can give you the tour now, if you'd like."

She stared at him for a minute, her eyes weirdly vacant. He might have assumed she was accessing the ship's net, if she'd had her headset on. But she didn't. Very strange. Was Earth producing brainware that could access a network directly? It had been tried once before, with disastrous result. You needed some kind of portal mechanism to weed out garbage, lest some teenager's pet virus made it into your brain and started rearranging your neurons. Yet she had no headset on, and was clearly accessing . . . something.

Was that why she was being hunted, for something that was in her head? *Shit*, he thought, envisioning the tangled mess of bioware and brain matter that was inside his own skull. You couldn't get at one without pretty much destroying the other. *If so, I'd run, too.*

But when she finally said, "I'd like that," she picked up her headset from the room's small folding table. Which meant that she needed it. So that wasn't her secret.

He took her on a tour of the few parts of the small trading vessel that a stranger was allowed to see . . . all in all, not much. It was a functional ship with little room to spare, and half of its chambers were now filled with boxes of contraband. But if she noticed anything missing in the tour, she didn't mention it. She seemed almost more interested in him than she was in the ship . . . and the result was a strange mix of signals, which he couldn't quite interpret. She was pretty clearly obsessed with his Medusan mutation, and he caught her staring at the proud crest of sensory tentacles whenever she didn't think he was watching her. He knew that their natural movement disturbed most Earthies, sinuous twining and unexpected flicks not unlike the movements of a cat's tail. He'd braided them into a mohawk pattern today—mostly to keep them away from his face—so they rose from his skull like the crest of some exotic E-bird, waving slowly as if in some unseen breeze. So all right, she had every reason to stare (by Earthie standards, anyway) and even to be marginally repelled. Given her background, he pretty much expected the latter. But she also stood very close to him, closer than normal, and that seemed very strange. Was it an Earthie habit? He'd met very few people who came from the planet itself, maybe this was normal for them. It was said the motherworld was hellishly crowded, maybe people there weren't used to having the room to spread out. She wasn't so close that he had to move away, or ask her do to so, but she played at the border of his personal space as if she knew exactly where it was . . . oddly disconcerting, that. It made him intensely aware of her, even when she was walking behind him. Good thing she wasn't more familiar with Medusans, or she'd be able to read his agitation in the twitching of his tendrils.

Then, when they reached the bridge, the whole formula changed. Suddenly he was all but forgotten, and the suddenness with which she moved away from him was so unexpected that it felt almost physical. Quick and curious, she moved with eager steps from one control panel to another, pausing only to take the measure of a screen readout, muttering things to herself as she moved. There was nothing wrong with such behavior per se, but the suddenness of the change was . . . spooky.

Calia was the only one there at the time, and she shot Sumi a quick flash: IS THIS WISE? He didn't answer. He was too intent on watching the Earthie, on trying to figure her out.

She was making comments about the equipment now, as she walked about the small chamber. "You have an Austin navicomp . . . that's rare in a ship this size . . . coupled with Microtech's 912-EX amp . . . that's not really compatible, is it? Must be a customized interface . . . bet that has a hell of a kick when you get moving. . . ." She continued to rattle off technical terms, many of which he only half understood. Even Calia looked up from where she was working, and flashed him a quick thought. ENGINEER? He flashed back, DON'T KNOW, then checked the ship's innernet to see if the girl was requesting any information from their database. She'd put on her headset on the way here, so it was possible. But no, that link was silent. Whatever detailed knowledge she was drawing on, it was all in her head.

She was a strange one, all right.

At last he had to almost physically drag her off the bridge, so intent was she upon studying everything within it. She seemed almost angry with him for forcing her to go . . . and then, as soon as they exited the control chamber, that mood was gone. As if anger, too, was a mask she simply put aside, her whole mood banished in an instant.

"Where did you study tech?" he asked. He didn't necessarily expect a straight answer—no one who worked the ship had credentials they'd discuss with a stranger—but he figured she'd at least reveal something of her background in how she chose to answer him.

But what he got wasn't helpful at all. She turned to look at him with those strange blue eyes—they *had* to be artificial—and seemed almost puzzled herself.

"I read a lot," she said at last. And it was clear from her tone that this the closest thing to an answer he was going to get.

Their tour completed, he led her back to her own room. It was little more than a closet with a bed, in size, but he supposed that when you were running from someone you didn't much care how big your bedroom was. Calia flashed him a message that she had copied the security transmissions from Reijik Station into the ship's own database, and was struggling even now to decode them. Soon enough they'd know what the situation was with this girl . . . and how it might benefit them to exploit it. Sumi had worked with Allo for over twenty E-years now, and knew how the Castilian's mind worked. Everything that came on this ship paid for itself . . . and that included passengers.

A pity, with this one. He rather liked her, for all her strangeness. She intrigued him.

At the door of her room he muttered a polite leavetaking, and began to move back toward the bridge, where he had work of his own to do—but she put a hand on his arm, gently, tentatively, to stop him.

"Yes?"

She seemed about to speak, then shut her mouth without making a sound.

"Raven?"

Strange, how she looked at him when he said that name. Almost as if she didn't recognize it.

She drew up a hand to his shoulder, curved gently, like the hand of a dancer. After a few seconds, one of his questing tentrils brushed against her. The taste of her skin was a not unpleasing mixture of tension and female essence; he wasn't all that sure of his ability to interpret the exudate of Earthies, but there seemed to be a hint of sexual interest, too, barely discernible on her skin. Was that really possible? He should have been repelled—a Terran was hardly a desirable sexual partner in his circle—but something about her manner made the thought more arousing than repellent. He could feel his tendrils stiffening in response and flashed a quick, somewhat embarrassed instruction to his wellseeker, which drained enough blood from the offending appendages that their appearance returned quickly to normal.

*Gotta be careful there*, he thought. *Don't want to scare the poor little Earthie too much.*

A cryptic, minimal smile curved the corners of the girl's mouth, hinting that perhaps she had guessed at his train of thought and no, it was not repellent to her. Then she drew back her hand from his arm, but slowly; slender fingers stroking the fabric of his jumpsuit with just enough pressure to be felt. Such a simple motion, not suggestive in any obvious way, but his heart started to pound nonetheless. So he told his wellseeker to deal with that as well, and felt the sharp bite of mechanical activity in his arm as the autopharmacy embedded in his flesh released a drop of the proper medication into his bloodstream. Thank God for modern medicine. He'd have to make sure he had enough sedative compounds for future use; he had a feeling he'd need them.

"Thank you," she said quietly. Almost a whisper. "For the tour."

There was nothing more to say. He mumbled something that might have amounted to "you're welcome," then nodded a stiff leavetaking and backed out of the room.

**W**orms. That's what they reminded her of: moist, repellent worms, like the ones they had studied in Earthbio 101. She remembered her tutor encouraging her to reach out and touch one, to experience its nature through all of her senses, not just the computer-enhanced visuals she usually relied upon. It was cold and clammy and soft in a squishy, nauseating way. Later he had shown her pictures of worms mating, wrapped in some gelatinous gook, and she had pictured touching *that*, and the sickness had welled up inside her. Only the prompt action of her wellseeker had kept her from throwing up right in the class-room. Could it help her now? She wasn't so sure.

*How can you even think about him that way?* she asked Katlyn. Scrubbing her hand as she did so, trying to scour away the memory of contact with Sumi's moist, repellent appendages. The thought of having any kind of sexual contact with the Variant, damp and snakelike tendrils against her naked skin . . . she leaned over the side of the bed suddenly and did throw up, her whole body heaving as if trying to force out the image. And no bottie was going to clean it up for her, either. She was going to have to deal with the mess herself.

*You've got a lot of growing up to do, kid,* Katlyn told her.

God, if only the Others would go away. Just for an hour. Just one blessed hour of being a normal human being, *one* human being in all her parts—not trapped in a body that did things which repelled her, or endangered her, or . . . or anything.

"I want to be normal," she whispered. "Oh, please, I just want to know what that's like again. . . ."

*This is normal now,* Verina thought gently. *There's no going back.*

To which Derik added, *So fucking get used to it.*

Hands shaking, senses reeling, she dialed up a towel from the commissary outlet and slowly, shakily, began to clean up the evidence of her sickness.

**"G**ot it," Tam announced.

Allo and Sumi both looked up from the work they were doing as soon as the Belial spoke. They'd been waiting for such an an-nouncement.

"And?" Allo asked.

"Take a look."

An inloading query flashed in Sumi's field of vision. He answered with a go-ahead, and the ship's innernet began to feed text into his brainware. He shut his eyes so as to see it more clearly.

There was a picture, first of all. It was clearly the same girl they had on board, though taken when she was younger, and she looked every bit as prosperous as Allo had guessed her to be. Sumi quickly assessed her lo-G formalwear and matching jewelry to be in the neighborhood of a thousand corporates in value, and that was if there wasn't a designer label inside to boost the price. He was willing to bet there was.

He scrolled past the encrypted text of the message itself—Tam always included a copy of the original in his reports, he was a little bit anal in that respect—until he got to the translation. It was short and sweet, and all that Allo had hoped it would be.

SUBJECT: JAMISIA SHIDO (MAY BE TRAVELING UNDER ALIAS)
FUGITIVE FROM EARTH CORPORATE COUNCIL
SUSPECTED STATION TERRORIST, WANTED FOR QUESTIONING IN
    CONNECTION WITH THE DESTRUCTION OF SHIDO HABITAT
SEARCH AND DETAIN
CONFISCATE ALL COMPUTERWARE
DO NOT PERMIT SUBJECT TO HAVE OUTERNET ACCESS UNDER ANY
    CIRCUMSTANCES
NOTIFY OFFICE IMMEDIATELY UPON CAPTURE. FURTHER
    INSTRUCTIONS WILL BE GIVEN AT THAT TIME.
ADDITIONAL DATA BELOW.

"So," Allo mused, "our little passenger's a terrorist. Any thoughts on that, Sumi?"

For a moment the Medusan did not respond. "Hard to believe," he said at last. "But not impossible."

"She fits the bill," Tam pointed out. "If terrorists were recruiting, they'd look for someone with an air of innocence, who wouldn't draw suspicion. Someone just like her. Don't you think?"

"I think," Allo said slowly, "that someone wants her very badly. I think there's one hell of a crime involved, if an Earth Habitat was destroyed. I think there's someone out there willing to transmit any lie it takes, to get hold of her." He looked up at Sumi. "How about you?"

Sumi didn't answer right away; he was trying not to think about his own memories of the girl, for they were ill suited to the current conversation. The touch of her fingers, the taste of her skin . . . he forced those images out of his mind and struggled to recover his objectivity. "I doubt she's a station terrorist," he said at last. "That being the one unforgivable crime in outspace . . . who would give her refuge, once the truth was known? She doesn't seem the kind to risk that. She isn't . . ." he struggled to find the right word.

"Focused enough?" Allo suggested.

"Gutsy enough?" Tam offered.

"Polished enough," Sumi said. He was thinking of her vulnerability, then how it gave way to a strange intensity on the bridge, and that in turn to a more seductive aspect. "A terrorist would have her act down better than this girl does. A real one wouldn't have run through the docking ring like that, no matter what the cause. She'd have had a better story prepared to cover her ass than what she gave us, and she'd know how to access funds . . . or how to do without them."

"True." Allo nodded thoughtfully. "If so, then the contact data given here is a fake. And whoever sent this out is pretty damn confident . . . because someone who saw her might lose track of this eddress and contact the real ECC. So they'd have to have their bases covered there, too, just in case that happened."

"That's one hell of a high-level contact," Tam mused.

"Which means . . ." Allo drew in a deep breath. "Whoever wants her is probably powerful, and probably rich, and willing to do just about anything to get her."

He let that sit for a minute, then asked, "Any comments?"

There were none.

"Any questions?"

None.

"All right. Sumi, you keep an eye on her. Win her trust if you can, see if you can get her to disclose something useful. We still have to track down just who it is that's looking for her, and do it very carefully. You keep her out of the way while we finish off our current business, then we can focus on her."

"Allo, I—"

Silence.

"What?"

"Nothing," Sumi said quietly. His tendrils were held rigid in a submissive posture, communicating nothing. "It doesn't matter."

"Tam, try to trace this transmission back to its source. In the meantime I'm going to get that shit in the hold unloaded, and if we have to cut price to do that fast, so be it. We've got more valuable cargo now."

"You think she's worth that much?" Sumi asked.

For a moment there was silence. The pilot's eyes shut halfway as he scanned through the message again, letters bright against the darkness of his inner lids.

"No question about it," he finally assessed. "The only question is, to whom?"

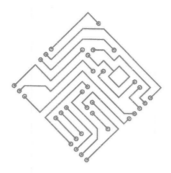

God save us from an Earth in which all men are the same. God save us from a colony where that is the goal, or a culture which assumes that for its norm. Give me a thousand people speaking different tongues, worshiping different gods, and dreaming different dreams, and I will make of them a greater nation than you can make with ten thousand of your gengineered duplicates. For mine will have the spark of greatness in them, while yours will live for conformity, worship mediocrity, and take their carefully modulated delight in predigested dreams.

*Reigning in Chaos: the founding of Guera Colony* (Historical Archives, Hellsgate Station)

# GUERA NODE
## TIANANMEN STATION

THE FEAR didn't really hit Masada until the waystation was in sight.

He was good at ignoring things; it was a skill all *iru* had. A lifetime of dealing with senses that tended to go haywire had taught him how to shut down the part of his awareness that was causing irritation. Never mind that now he had his brainware do the job of correcting things, so that he was hardly even aware of the process taking place. He'd done it often enough as an adolescent that his mind still remembered the trick.

So until the waystation was in sight he was capable of ignoring it. When Guildmaster Hsing came to tell him it was time to pack his equipment for transfer he managed not to think about why. When the steady hi-G of the trip became the slightly nauseating complex gravity of compensated deceleration, he released a few grains of a remedy into his bloodstream and went on with his work as if nothing were happening. Even when the ship gave out its instructions on what to do and where to do it in preparation for disembarkation, he managed to shunt that information to a part of his brain that wasn't connected to the hotwires of fear and incapacity.

But now . . . now it was impossible. As he gazed out at Tiananmen Station—seat of Guild authority, and therefore the ruling center of all the human worlds—it was impossible to ignore the implications of where he was. It wasn't so much because of the station itself, but the change in his traveling associates as they approached it. Even his limited *iru* sensitivity was capable of sensing the change in them . . . and intellectually, of course, he understood its cause. They were within reach of the outernet now, and most of the passengers had clearly connected up to it. Children who had previously run wild now sat tucked quietly in corners, busy with their favorite multiworld games. Adults whispered comments to nothingness, as their favorite outernet drama coursed through their brains. Those who stared out the window did so with an intensity that told Masada their view of the station was augmented by scrolling facts about Tiananmen, or the latest economic report, or maybe simply words of welcome from a loved one who was waiting for them.

Guera had its own network, of course—as did all the civilized planets—and every transport that left the outworlds was capable of feeding data and entertainment to its passengers through their headsets. But though there was little difference in actual fact between Guera's planetary network and the system that linked the outworlds, there was a universe of difference in how people used them. The outernet did more than provide data and communication, after all. It linked worlds, skipping messages along the ainniq with a speed that made the concept of "distance" almost meaningless. It linked cultures, feeding the databases from a thousand colonies into a grand gestalt consciousness which any human mind could access. It saturated daily life in ways the average human was not even aware of, so that a single casual thought broadcast on Hellsgate Station, meant for no more than a local audience, might affect the manner in which stock funds fluctuated on Sanctuary, five nodes away.

It was chaos, plain and simple. A system so vast, with so much living input, that humankind could no longer predict exactly how it would function, or even understand exactly what it was. It had its own tides of connection and efficiency—much as the planets had weather—and humans could no more predict those tides than the planetbound could tell in one year if a tornado would form in the next. It was a truly living system, Masada had theorized, and like the biological systems whose terms were used to describe it, it could no longer be controlled by humans, only nurtured, goaded, cajoled. And people knew that, deep inside. They sensed that when they connected to the outernet they were becoming something more than human. They knew that the vid games and the stock scrolls and the group chats were but the surface markings of a creature with a heart and a soul all its own. A creature that might just as well be alive, for all that its systems mimicked life.

He had spent his life studying it. He understood it better than any other man alive.

It scared the hell out of him.

They were strangers to him now, the humans on the observation deck, made alien not by the stream of messages feeding into their brains, but the casual way in which they absorbed those messages. Conversations went on with seeming normalcy, but too many eyes were focused inward. Words left unspoken were supplemented by phrases sent brain-to-brain, turning speech into a string of seeming non sequiturs. One adolescent walked through the observation chamber growling and snarling half-animal challenges to all who came near; clearly he was in the grip of some fantasy program, which translated all his surroundings into the venue of his choosing. It was an eerie world, enough that it affected even the *iru* in him, to whom the universe was always somewhat strange. And it confirmed his fears about coming to the outworlds, and intensified them, until he finally had to order his wellseeker to flood his system with sedatives in order to calm himself down. It wouldn't do to arrive at Guild headquarters in such a state. They had *nantana* galore in the Guild, and at least a dozen other kaja who could read meaning into the slightest hesitation of speech, or the slightest hint of bodily tension. If they didn't respect him when he first arrived then his work here was doomed from the start.

With a start he realized just what he had been thinking. Did he fear the *nantana* now? That was a new concept, and a highly disturbing one. The *nantana* were his own people, after all, and they respected the rules of social interaction which governed all Guerans. This trip must really be getting to him, if he now thought of them as something to be feared.

He drew in a deep breath and shut his eyes, imagining that he could feel the subtle flow of sedatives into his blood. Already his pounding heart had quieted somewhat, and his wellseeker had given up on bright red warnings and settled for a cautious gold. *Yes*, he told it, when it asked if it should adjust his adrenaline levels. *Yes*, to normalizing hippocampus function. *Yes. Yes.*

*Yes.* What had it been like to live in a natural world, in the days before brainware and wellseekers and conscious control of one's own body? He shuddered even to think about it. Terrifying horizons lay before humankind, but an even more terrifying primitive helplessness lay behind him. In some ways this was the only sane moment in human history, mind and machine as perfectly balanced as they would ever be. God help his species when the balance shifted once more.

*Living systems always change,* he had written. *And that change is never predictable.*

Not a comforting thought.

*You must learn not to think too much,* his wife had told him. *You must learn just to* be. *Taste life and enjoy it. Don't analyze. Live.*

Impossible.

She was no less driven than he was, though she'd never have admitted it. The difference was that her thoughts were voiced in music rather than language, notes rather than binary code. When she sat in her meditative silence with "no thoughts" disturbing her peace, there were symphonies stirring inside her soul. Notes fit together in her brain like facts did in his. She could not have lived in a world without music, any more than he could have lived in a world without logic.

Had he loved her? Gueran science wasn't sure if an *iru* could love. The chemicals were there for it. Sometimes they even combined properly. Wellseekers couldn't tell the difference.

But subjective experience? No one was certain. No *iru* understood the language of love well enough to confirm or deny it.

He missed her terribly.

**T**he Prima met with him in person, of course. Privately. Given that she was *simba,* such an invitation was replete with social implications. *This man is mine,* it told her staff, as surely as if she had urinated on Masada to mark him with her smell. It made little difference to Masada. Status was the least of his concerns.

If they had just picked him up at the dock and delivered him to his new workstation, instead of providing an honor guard to accompany him to her audience chamber, that would have been fine. As it was, he tolerated her *simba* need for precedence and ritual, as she was no doubt tolerating his own *iru* idiosyncrasies. Gueran society was a complex webwork of such tolerances, as natural to them all as breathing.

Devlin Gaza, now . . . that was a different matter.

Masada knew of the man's work, and had immense respect for his skill. He knew the standard that Gaza's staff was held to, and was amazed at how often they met it. Masada wasn't the kind of man to be impressed by rank, or wealth, or social grace, or any of the other superficial qualities that *nantana* obsessed about, but Gaza was rich in the one coinage he did value: the ability to *think*. The last program of Gaza's which he had worked on had been a creation of true brilliance, and he had regretted that afterward he'd had no opportunity to see the man's next project. But that had been Masada's last commission for the Guild, at least until Lucifer raised its ugly head.

Gaza programmed only rarely now. The staff of several hundred who answered to him took up most of his time, as did the thousand-and-some-odd electronic assaults which were launched against the Guild each day. Most of those were amateur efforts, would-be hackers buzzed on their own importance, trying to break into the most guarded system in the outerworlds just for kicks. Some were more serious threats, requiring targeted antibodies to be launched in return, or, occasionally, a rewrite of the security programs themselves. A few were so destructive that portions of the net had to be shut down for several seconds while a clean-and-strike program swept through suspect nodes, seeking their source.

And then there was Lucifer.

Masada knew that the best efforts of Gaza and his staff had already been assigned to the problem for an E-year now. He also knew they had made little progress. The coms sent to Masada's ship had been short and nonspecific, due to security concerns, but even so they had expressed growing frustration with Lucifer, both from Gaza and his staff. *Your fresh perspective is welcome,* the last com had said. *I hope to be able to help*, he had responded with equal caution.

The door at the far end of the chamber whisked open and Devlin Gaza entered. Masada recognized him from his holo: lean, light-skinned, with aquiline features that played up the bony angles of his face, and a short crop of naturally blond hair above surprisingly dark eyes. His black jumpsuit was informal in its cut, but the insignia above his pocket spoke of the highest rank there was, the Prima's Inner Circle. The combination of images—straightforward, unpretentious—pleased Masada. A man who believed in omens might say that things promised to go well.

Gaza nodded slightly, a tight smile on his face. "Dr. Masada. We're glad to have you here at last." He didn't offer his hand or in any other way seek physical contact, no doubt in deference to Masada's kaja. Nor did he come as close as another man might. There were decorative squares on the chamber's floor and he planted his feet precisely in the center of two of them, a feat managed without him ever seeming to look down. In another man Masada might not have noticed such things, but he had read enough about Gaza to know the nature of his Variance, and to see it reflected in such choices. It was, of course, what made Gaza such a master in his field. All Gueran Variances were like that, dark and light combined. Yin and yang. Pleasure and pain.

"It's a great honor to meet you," Gaza said.

Assuming the comment to be sincere—he lacked the social acumen to tell if it were otherwise—he responded, "The honor is mine." And just in case his tone of voice failed to communicate his own sincerity, he added, "I've admired your work for years."

Something in the man's posture seemed to ease up a bit. Had he expected . . . what? Competition? Confrontation? "And I yours, Dr. Masada. I've waited a long time to meet the man who designed the Hellsgate-909 antibody. When they approved your coming here . . . well, let's just say that when this job is finished, I'd welcome a chance to sit down and talk shop with you."

There were few people in the outworlds whose praise could affect Masada; Gaza was one of them. "That would be an honor indeed." His face had grown slightly warm at the praise, but he had his wellseeker put a stop to that. Biological display of any kind was distasteful to him. "I have some figures I'd like to check with you, and simulations to run—'' He stopped suddenly, aware that in his haste to get started he might have missed some fine point of protocol, and added, ''Assuming we move right on to business, of course.''

Gaza smiled a tight smile, replete with tensions of its own. ''Business is fine, Dr. Masada. We eat, drink, and sleep Lucifer here. Let me give you a tour of the place, and an update of what we've come up with while you were in transit. Not very pleasant, I'm afraid.''

He told Masada of the most recent mutations, while they walked through triple-secured portals into the heart of Guild processing. He told him of the pilots who'd been injured by the virus, and the half dozen more who'd been saved just in time. ''The damned thing evolves faster than our antibody programs can adapt to it, and each new generation seems to be increasingly deadly. I believe it's only a matter of time before Lucifer attacks someone or something out of the Guild . . . and God help us all when that happens.''

''Chaos in the streets,'' Masada mused.

Gaza shook his head grimly. ''Worse than that. Chaos in the outworlds means chaos in enclosed corridors, with no escape. Implosion, rather than explosion. On a planet you can have time to deal with such a thing, places to allow its energies to diffuse, and if worst comes to worst, places to escape to. Here we have none of that. Social dynamics shift accordingly. Panic . . . is death.''

A final security program confirmed Gaza's identity, then took a brainware profile of Masada for future reference. ''I think we're on borrowed time now,'' the Guild programmer said as a final silver portal split open to admit them. ''Rumors have gotten out about the virus, and already my people are picking up signs that civilians are searching for it. The thing is well designed enough that I doubt anyone will find it by accident, not without having some inkling of the codes it was designed to infect. We didn't find it ourselves till it broke out in a pilot's brain. But still. You never know. And all it would take was one . . .''

''And you may have a leak,'' Masada said quietly.

Gaza put a warning finger to his lips, gesturing for silence.

Beyond the silver portal was a room that glistened spotlessly, consoles and workstations lining the walls. Several men in black uniforms looked up as the two of them entered; all were wearing identical skullcaps of silver and black, with bands of circuitry running across them like the markings of some strange metallic animal. At a short gesture from Gaza they turned and left, pausing only long enough to flash the images that would save their work, shut down their programs, and withdraw them from the system. Not until they were gone, and all the doors in the room sealed shut, did Gaza speak again.

"This is your lab, Dr. Masada. Sealed and secure and discrete from all other systems on the station. We've got a Hauck Model 6700Z Overseer for you—the Z line is experimental at this point, yours is one of only five existing units—and enough bandwidth to run five million copies of the virus simultaneously. You can't access the outernet directly from here—for obvious reasons— but we've got a three stage relay that can dump information for you, or collect it, without anyone from the outside being able to follow your signal home."

No direct access to the outernet. He felt a knot in his chest loosen up the tiniest bit . . . and hated himself for it. What kind of a programmer was he, if he feared the very programs which held the outerworlds together?

He walked into the room and studied each panel and machine there, one by one, nodding a slow and studied approval of each. "All sterile, I assume?"

"Brand new, in most cases, and then sterilized five times over just for good measure. All the programs we loaded for you are verified clean as well, matched against the master copies which are kept offline in my office. Samples of the virus are stored separately," he placed his hand on one of the consoles, "so you'll have to transfer what you need the old-fashioned way." A slight smile creased the corners of his lips. "That seemed far safer than any direct transmission."

"I agree," he said. He remembered the warning on the first copy he'd seen: *Grade A Contagious Material.* Grade A meant a program that might infect anything it interacted with, and not necessarily in an ordered or predictable manner. Nothing which touched Lucifer could be allowed back onto the outernet without first being matched, byte by byte, with a copy of its original. Or simply destroyed. Sometimes with highly contagious material the latter was the easiest course. "How about copies of the virus itself?"

"There are over thirty thousand examples stored in here, representing two thousand seventeen different spores. The collection is updated daily, with new spores culled from all Guild stations in the outworlds. The damn thing's prolific as hell," he said dryly, "which doesn't make our job any easier."

Masada's brow furrowed as he considered the number. It wasn't quite what he had predicted. Had his calculations been wrong, or had Guild simply failed to gather as many spores as they should? The latter would surprise him, as it would imply that Devlin Gaza was inefficient. And he knew the man's work well enough to know that such an adjective could never be applied to him.

"We've found what seem to be generational markers," Gaza told him. "That's simplified the sorting process greatly."

"Good," he approved. "I'm looking forward to seeing what you've gathered."

The truth was that he wanted to start working. The truth was that he already *was* working, his mind having half-abandoned Gaza's informal briefing to explore the convoluted maze of data which that briefing had unveiled. It took all his self-control to keep from shutting Gaza out entirely, and even so the next few words were lost on him as he flashed a quick command to the nearest terminal and saw data begin to scroll upwards in response. *12.12.57. 9 spores collected from the following stations: Hellsgate, Etherea, New Hope (2), Anachron Nova—*

". . . that we have a leak?" Gaza was saying.

Masada forced himself to look back at him, shutting the data stream out of his brain. "I'm sorry?"

"How sure are you that we have a leak?"

He said quietly, "I would bank my career on it."

Though he was far from adept at reading human expressions, Gaza's response was anything but subtle. The dark eyes narrowed, the brows drew together, and the thin mouth tightened in an unmistakable grimace. Since he didn't speak for a few seconds, Masada took the time to scan his image into his brainware's social database; within seconds his primitive observations were elaborated upon. Gaza was tense, the program informed him, and hostile, and probably angry as well. The negative emotions were most likely not directed at Masada, the program informed him, but internally motivated.

Well, that made sense. If someone on Gaza's staff proved to be a traitor, might the Guildsman not imagine that it reflected upon him? And perhaps it would. Perhaps this man, one of the most powerful in the outworlds, could be brought down by a leak in his own department. That would certainly explain his reaction.

*There is more at stake for these people than a virus*, Masada realized. *Careers will be made and destroyed over this, positions gained and lost, outworld politics altered forever.* For the first time since signing onto the project he sensed the true magnitude of the situation, and was humbled by it. No wonder they wanted an outsider. No wonder they needed someone from outside the Guild to handle this matter, to guarantee that politics and prejudices and the simple instincts of job preservation didn't interfere with the search for the truth. He alone, in all the outworlds, had nothing to gain or lose from this thing. Which was fortunate, as he lacked the type of cognition required to sort out complex human motives.

They knew all that, of course. They had chosen him carefully, with all his strengths and weaknesses in mind. For the first time now he understood just what had gone into their decision, and how correct that decision had been.

"Tell me about it," Gaza said evenly.

As they walked down into the chamber itself, Masada found his attention wandering once more to the vast array of equipment before him, and wondering at its capacity. That was bad. He knew all too well how easy it was for him to lose track of a conversation when he was thus distracted, and how easily people took offense at it. With a quick icon he called up his master sensory program and ordered it to step down his visual acuity several points. The program was one he'd designed himself and used many times, that made everything look dark and gray and slightly unclear. It was easier to stay focused on Gaza that way, and ignore the sensory stimulation which surrounded him.

"I regressed the virus," he explained. He saw Gaza raise an

eyebrow in surprise, and he could not entirely repress a smile of pride in response. What a rare pleasure it was to discuss his work with someone who appreciated its true complexity! "Once the false leads were weeded out, that resulted in several approximations of the virus in its original form. I did an analysis of the programming elements those samples had in common, which distinguished them from all the false regressions. The resulting summary gives us a true profile of *Lucifer Prime*, the virus as it was originally designed."

Gaza's expression was dark, unreadable. "How reliable is this profile?"

"Some parts are necessarily more precise than others. I have a complete breakdown of the entire project available for you to look at, including my error estimates for each section. It's in the briefing material I delivered to the Prima."

Gaza nodded. "All right. I'll go over it. Now tell me about the leak."

Masada drew in a deep breath, knowing that what he was about to say was nothing Devlin Gaza wanted to hear. "In the course of testing thousands of proto-viruses, I found that those which evolved true to form all had one thing in common. At the core of their search program was a fragment of Guild code. Very well hidden, almost indecipherable . . . but Guild code all the same, without question."

Gaza looked at him for a long moment without saying anything. Finally, softly, he said to Masada, "The thing was made to seek out our programming and copy it. Surely that's where these fragments came from. Former assaults—"

"No."

"Can you be sure of that?"

"Yes. All regressions point to it. I'm sorry to say this, I know what it implies . . . but I believe the conclusion is inescapable. This thing may have come from outside the Guild, but it invaded Guild files with the help of someone who had access to your most secure programs."

Gaza turned away from him. Just that, for a moment: no words, no gestures, no hint of what was going on inside his brain. Not that Masada could have interpreted such signs anyway, but his social programs might have stood a chance. This way there was no insight possible.

"If this is true . . ." The Director's voice was low, but infinitely tense. "We're talking about someone betraying the Guild."

Masada said nothing.

"But why? Why give out that one portion of code, and nothing else? Why not just give our enemy what he wanted in the first place? Surely that would have been easier."

"Perhaps," Masada said quietly, "this way, he didn't think he'd get caught."

Gaza turned back to him.

"Perhaps he thought that this way the data transfer could never be traced to him. Perhaps he felt he was safe this way, sheltered by the sheer complexity of his creation. The virus could collect its data and deliver it and he would never be blamed . . . because no one would ever do the kind of regression that was necessary to prove that not *all* the Guild code Lucifer contained was stolen."

"Regression of such a complex virus is theoretically impossible," Gaza reminded him.

Masada smiled tightly. "Nothing is impossible to someone who's willing to wade through enough data, Director. Who knows? Perhaps if the trip to Tiananmen had been shorter I would never have gotten far enough to isolate this bit of code. Perhaps if you had sent me more fresh data to work with, I would have gotten involved in analyzing that and let the regression project slide. As it was . . . this is what I found. I leave it to you to analyze its implications. I'm no expert in human motivation, I can only tell you what's visible in the code itself. The rest I must leave up to you."

"And we will look into it," Gaza promised him. Even Masada could hear the darkness in his tone. "My God, it could well be one of my own staff. . . ." He shook his head sharply. "It's one thing to discuss such possibilities in a general sense . . . quite another to contemplate proof of it . . . I must look at your data. . . ."

"I think you'll find it quite convincing."

"What about the code itself? Who would have access to it?"

"It's a segment of outpilot programming. Your own staff

would have access, of course, and the Prima herself. Some guild-masters might. Outpilots certainly would. Others might on an individual basis, if their security clearance was high enough, but there's no other group who would have such access as a matter of course."

"Then we not only have a traitor among us," Gaza said quietly, "but probably one of rank."

Masada said nothing. It was not his way to confirm the obvious.

"Who would do this to his own people? This thing is killing outpilots—"

"That was a later development, Director. Or so you tell me. Lucifer's designer might not have anticipated that it would evolve into such a deadly invader."

Gaza's eyes met his. The man's gaze was hot, very hot, fired by a turmoil of emotions Masada couldn't begin to interpret.

"No," he said. The anger in his voice was unmistakable. "He knew. Any man intelligent enough to design this thing knew damned well what it might turn into. He just didn't care. Somebody paid him enough money that he just didn't care."

Suddenly, without warning, he struck out at one of the walls in fury. The blow was hard; the faceplate of a nearby console was jarred loose a fragment of an inch, and the blow echoed audibly in the sleek-surfaced chamber.

"When I find the one responsible for this," Gaza swore, "I will tear him apart with my own hands. He will suffer more than any man has ever suffered, for betraying the Guild, and for betraying *me*. And as for whatever agency corrupted him . . . I will see to it that they never see the inside of an ainniq again. Let them rot on their fucking homeworld, whatever the hell that is, without the Guild to rescue them. Let their ruined and deserted stations be a warning to anyone else who thinks he can take on the children of Hausman and get away with it."

"I don't think this is a Hausman issue—" Masada began.

The look on Gaza's face cut him short. For a moment it seemed like the outburst of fury might be turned against him, then the Director's face relaxed ever so slightly, his rigid shoulders eased, and the angry flush in his cheeks began to fade.

"I'm sorry," Gaza said. "But you understand—security in

this area is my domain. This incident . . . it's like spending your whole life building and fortifying a citadel for war, only to find out that some bastard on the inside has thrown open the gates and invited the enemy in." He drew in a deep breath. "We have to find out who did this. That's all. We have to find out who is responsible and see to it that his fate serves as a warning to all. The Guild is not to be trifled with."

"All I can do is analyze the code," Masada said evenly. "Others will have to deal with questions of motivation."

"Of course, Dr. Masada. Of course." While speaking, Gaza noticed the jarred faceplate. It was barely a millimeter out of alignment, but even that much clearly disturbed him. With steady hands and the deadly serious expression of a neurosurgeon he reached out and eased it back into its proper position. Perfectly even, perfectly parallel to every other horizontal surface in the room. Not until it was solidly fixed in place did he release it, and even then he checked to see that the friction of his withdrawing hands didn't jar it loose again. Apparently not. "Again, I apologize. Much as you were undoubtedly frustrated by being cut off from current news while in transit, we here at Tiananmen have been waiting over a year to have the benefit of your counsel. Tell me what you need for your work and you'll have it. Equipment, funds, personnel, whatever you need."

"Thank you, Director."

"As for the rest of us . . ." He shut his eyes for a moment. "All we have to do is figure out who in the Guild hierarchy would turn on his own people, and why. No small task, my friend." He looked about the room, at the wealth of machinery and programming committed to the effort. "We *will* find him," he swore.

It wasn't the kind of statement you questioned.

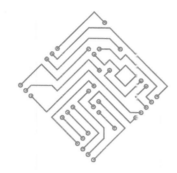

## BAKIRA

Black as night, black as death, the *bakira* slinks in shadows unseen, following the scent of prey. There is no terrain so dangerous that it will turn aside; there is no enemy so fierce that it will give ground.

It hunts where it wishes, and none bar its way. If its prey flees into territory marked by another living creature, it does not acknowledge those markings. It journeys where it pleases, hunts as it pleases, and steals prey from others without fear or apology.

It is the shadow-killer, red of heart and claw, black of soul.

It is hunger.

*KAJA: An Outworlder's Guide to the Gueran*
*Social Contract, Volume 2: Signs of the Soul*

# HARMONY NODE
# TRIDAC STATION

**T**HE BOARDROOM was dark.

A single holo glowed in its center, a blue-and-brown globe of Earth with all its clouds removed. Stations and habitats and a thousand tiny pods orbited about it like a cloud of tiny asteroids, each with its own pinpoint of reflected light. The display was small and not very bright, and it did little to illuminate the room. Nevertheless, Miklas Tridac had the distinct impression of a figure sitting somewhere behind it, a shadow among the shadows.

He cleared his throat, more to see if there would be any response than because he had to. There wasn't.

At last he dared, "You wanted to see me?"

The display clicked off. The projector nodes withdrew into the conference table, leaving its surface flat once more. A dim light came up—very dim—that allowed him to make out the form of a woman at the end of the table. Her features were in shadow.

"Tell me about the girl," she said.

He took a step forward, to where the end of the long table stopped him from going any farther. There was a chair there, turned out to receive him. He chose not to sit in it.

"We've lost her."

If there was anger in her, it wasn't visible. But of course not, he thought. You don't rise to the vice presidency of a Terran corporation by giving out emotional data for free.

"Give me details," she said quietly.

"She was on the metroliner as Jamisia Capra. We've got her records going through Immigration under that name. We lost her after that."

"I sent out enough people to cover Immigration."

"The Guild took her out of line. They processed her privately, and got her into the ring before we knew what had happened."

He could sense the anger rising in her. At him, at the Guild, or at the girl? "We should have had the whole ring covered, then." He started to answer, but she waved him to silence with a short and angry gesture. "Twenty-twenty hindsight. Immigration was a guaranteed bottleneck, we counted on it." He heard her draw in a deep breath as she considered the ramifications of what he had said. "So," she said at last. Her voice was like ice. "The Guild knows."

"How much, do you think?"

"They know she's important. That's all that matters. They know they need to have control of her."

"They let her go free."

He could sense her eyes on him: cold, uncompromising. Unforgiving. "So it would seem" she agreed. "Perhaps to see where she would go. Perhaps they're not sure just what exactly she is, and hope that she'll reveal herself."

"Do *we* know what she is?" he asked.

There was a long, long silence after that. The invisible eyes were fixed on him, and he could feel their scrutiny like a cold caress along his skin. You didn't ask for information from the Corporation, not if you valued your job. Then again, he was one of the few she trusted.

"We know," she said slowly, "that she is an experiment. We know that if the experiment proves successful, it will put the Guild out of business. And we risked a lot to get hold of her, for that reason." There was a long pause after that. Was it true that the Corporation's masters could access the wellseekers of their underlings? He felt himself being dissected mentally, and wondered just how much data she had on him. "That's enough for you to know, I think. Any more would be . . . dangerous for you."

"I thank you for your trust."

"It isn't a question of trust. We have to find the girl. You're in charge of that effort. You need to understand what the stakes are here, and just how far we're willing to go to accomplish our goal."

She stood, then, and for a brief moment the light in the room played over her features as she moved. Eyes and lips carved out of ice, an imperious nose, blonde hair slicked back tightly against her scalp. The corporate logo was bright on her lapel, three interlocking triangles in gold with a star at their center. The Star of Earth.

"You will find her," she said. "Period. I don't care what you have to spend, I don't care whom you have to hire. Do it."

"But—"

"*She is somewhere.* She will use the outernet, she will access her money, she will walk and talk and breathe the recycled air— and every minute she does so, she will leave her mark on some data system. Find her. If you can think of no better way, then go through every security tape in the outworlds with a face recognition program. Hire some moddies to put sniffers on the outernet, I'm told they can find anything once they put their minds to it. Pay them whatever it requires. Just don't give them information. *Nothing.* You understand me?"

"I understand."

"Expect the Guild to be making a similar effort. Watch them closely, for they may have access to data that we don't. I'm tapping into every data line I can, and if I hear of anything relevant, I'll forward it to you." She paused. "In the meantime, remember this. *We need this girl.* We need her alive and we need her undamaged, so that we can study what Shido did and benefit from it. She does us no good dead . . . and she probably knows that. But as for the Guild—I doubt they've heard anything more than rumors of what Shido was doing. Right now they would like to get hold of her and see how accurate those rumors are . . . but if that becomes too much of a luxury, if the choice comes down to letting her go free or removing her from the picture . . . she is no threat to them if she's dead. And if she leads them on a long enough chase, if it looks as if she might really manage to escape them for good, then it's only a matter of time before they decide to end this little game, while the odds are still in their favor. A dead experiment benefits no one, and they are the default victors in this scenario."

"I understand."

"Make sure you do." She leaned forward over the table; gloved hands splayed out to rest on its polished surface, displaying the corporate logo on their cuffs. "Make sure you grasp that this may prove our most important campaign since the end of Isolation. If there's a chance—even the remotest chance—that this girl can help break the Guild monopoly, then we have to control her. Period. Failure isn't an option."

"I understand."

She leaned back again, drawing herself up to her full height. At nearly six feet, she was an impressive figure. "Do what you must. I expect a better report next time."

"Of course." He bowed slightly and began to back up, but a raised hand from her signaled him that the interview was not yet over.

"There are legal parameters to such a search," she said quietly. "If you act outside those . . ." The sentence went unfinished, but the words were clear enough even so.

*Don't get caught.*

He cleared his throat; this time it was for real. "The Corporation, of course, would not support me in such a case."

"Of course not," she said quietly. "I'm glad you understand." They were speaking for the record now, and both of them knew it. He wondered how many separate recorders were taking every word down for posterity. To be disassociated from their previous words, of course. "We all must obey the strictures that the Guild has set, you see. For as long as their monopoly holds, they are the ultimate authority in outspace. Do nothing that would . . . displease them."

He felt a faint thrill then, the first one he had allowed himself in all his time on this project. If the Guild monopoly were broken at last, so that they no longer had the power to impose their will on all the citizens of outspace—good God, what a revolution that would be! And with his corporation at the head of it. . . .

"Thank you for your time, Miklas." Her head inclined slightly, a cold but regal gesture. "Keep me informed of your progress."

"Of course."

He bowed and took his leave. He'd need new plans, and maybe new equipment. The search would clearly not end just because the girl was lost; it would not end until she was in the Corporation's hands, or dead. And if he could be the one to deliver her to the company . . . then next time it might be him at the other end of that table. Miklas Tridac, giving orders to *his* subordinates.

As he left, he could see the Earth holo flicker back to life before her.

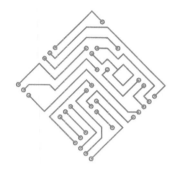

That which is alien repels us.

It also draws us, fascinates us, obsesses us.

How many wars have been fought down through history, for the sake of those two conflicting instincts?

DUAEN CORREN,
*On Human Nature*

# INSHIP: EXETER

THEY FINALLY unloaded the drugs, at a small private station at the far side of the node. Some billionaire tech baron owned the place, but Sumi suspected that the man who gave them their entrance codes to the estate and later paid them in unregistered cash chits wasn't working for him at that moment. It was a pretty bizarre setup, with fantastic, glittering air-lock gates that looked like they belonged on an amusment station, and surreal architecture to match. But when you were rich, Sumi thought, you could have whatever environment you wanted. Wasn't that why so many of Earth's financial elite had moved out here, when outspace was first colonized?

The price they got for their cargo wasn't half of what they could have gotten elsewhere, and Allo clearly was having second thoughts about the sale. Sumi watched him stand silently with furrowed brow, no doubt weighing the buyer's bottom line against the manifold risks of keeping the drugs on board. In the end he nodded stiffly, and the station's bots began to move the crates out. Sumi thought of warning their contact to wipe the bot logs clean when he was done, so that there'd be no record of the unloading—for all of their contact's tough attitude, he didn't seem like a professional smuggler, and might not realize the importance of that—but Allo caught his eye and shook his head sharply, slightly. The man had dickered price with them well past the point of polite negotiation. If he was so stupid that he didn't realize that a simple bot log could be used to convict him at some future date, let him pay the price for his ignorance.

They had Tam do one last scan for surveillance activity—as promised, all cams had been turned off for the duration of the delivery—and then they took off again, to deal with their next order of business.

The girl.

She was the real reason for the sale, of course. Allo could have gotten a much better price on Paradise for what they were carrying, but Sumi knew his captain, knew he liked his business clean, knew that he wouldn't want to deal with a puzzle like this girl while his holds were stuffed with enough contraband to earn them all life sentences from the feds. And so he had accepted lower profits on one deal in order to focus all his attention on the other . . . which said much for what he thought of her potential value in the open market.

The girl . . .

Sumi couldn't stop thinking about her. He'd done so even during the unloading, when his attention should have been focused on their work, and on watching for trouble. That wasn't like him. He liked women well enough—he enjoyed them immensely when the shipping schedule allowed for indulgence, and when station custom was obliging—but it was rare that one of them got under his skin the way this one had. Was it those strange blue eyes, or something in the taste of her skin? Or was it the unfathomable mystery of her, those strange mood changes, her secret past? Or was it (this was really alarming) that she was an Earthie? That she was the first Earthie who had ever responded to him with something other than revulsion, and he was curious to see just how far her tolerance would go?

He shivered and tried to focus on the screen before him, watching numbers scroll across it as the small ship made for open space once more. Allo liked the fact that his first mate was steady, reliable, unshakable. Allo wouldn't like the fact that right now Sumi was thinking about the soft touch of Earthie fingers, the musky smell that lingered about her flesh. No, he wouldn't like that at all. Sumi felt his wellseeker stir as he input the data for the next leg of their flight, scouring his biological systems for any sign of sexual arousal, chemically compensating for his fantasies. One thing was certain, he sure as hell didn't want Allo to guess what was on his mind. The captain would imagine . . . well, all sorts of things.

Worse than the truth?

He had dreams that nightshift. Strange dreams, that mixed together sex and guilt and racial hatred into an odd brew indeed. Was it the lure of the forbidden that drew him to her, the fantasy of having Earth itself between his strong hands, of forcing the heat of his body into the hated mother race itself? He'd always laughed at people who talked about things like that. He knew some men who who hired Earthie whores on a regular basis, just to vent their racial hatred. He'd always looked down on them, feeling himself above such things. Was that what he wanted now? Was the hunger inside him as well, two thousand years of racial resentment just waiting for the proper forum to express itself?

If so, that was yet another reason not to indulge himself. The poor girl was hardly responsible for all the evils of Earth. He knew that intellectually, even if his glands argued otherwise. It was better not to mess with a mix of feelings like that. Better just to focus on work, put his wellseeker on automatic, and hope nobody noticed his agitation. It was only one dive to Paradise Node, and then she would be gone.

But he couldn't stop thinking about her.

The bed had straps attached, tough plastic bands that pulled out from one side, wrapped over the top, and clipped onto a narrow bar on the far side. Jamisia looked at them dubiously, nervously, then at Calia again.

"It's for the dive," the Calistan said impatiently. She was clearly tired of explaining things to Jamisia, and spat out the words with the kind of disdain one usually reserves for morons. Tall, broad-shouldered, lean and muscular, she was physically well-suited for arrogance, and the sleek striped fur which the Hausman Effect had given to her people only added to her feral aura. "The headset will run all the programs to put you to sleep. In the meantime you want to be held in place, don't you?" When Jamisia said nothing, she snapped, "Or would you rather be pitched to the floor if things get rough, maybe break one of those precious Earthie bones?" She snorted in disgust and turned away from Jamisia. "Do as you like, girl. Tam'll be in later to program the headset. You can ride it out standing on your head for all I care.''

The door slid shut behind her with a finality that seemed almost personal. Jamisia stared at it for a moment, then looked back at the straps on the bed. Yes, there was apparently a damned good reason for them being there, but their presence still seemed ominous. Or was that just her paranoia speaking?

*Damn,* Raven observed, *she really hates Terrans, doesn't she?*

*They all do,* Verina answered. *She's just the most open about it.*

*Not like we had anything to do with Isolation.* Derick snorted. *Okay, so our ancestors were assholes. They're dead and gone now, and we're here. Why blame us for their mistakes?*

*That "mistake" killed millions, and sent some colonies back to the Stone Age.* Verina's tone, as always, was utterly reasonable, even when she was discussing such volatile issues as race hatred. *There are cultures still paying the cost for that mistake. Don't ever forget it.*

*It's not like we did anything wrong,* Zusu said miserably.

*That doesn't matter. Identity's a genetic thing out here, and we've got the genes of the race that betrayed them. We're an infection to them, unclean, an insult to the worlds they struggled to save.*

*There were reasons—* Raven began.

*Yes,* Verina interrupted. *Earth reasons. Try explaining them to a colony that starved for two centuries, because Earth cut them off. Try telling such people that the reason they haven't been able to raise their population above the point of minimal survival is still because billions of people once rioted, planet, and their leaders decided to cut off the Hausman colonies so they could pretend they didn't exist, to quell the tide of panic. Tell them that, and see if they understand.*

She paused for an instant, then continued in a quieter tone: *How can they know what it's like to have ten billion people crowded on a single planet, with the only hope for escape suddenly cut off? How can they understand the mindset of such a world, or the extremes to which it might have to resort, for the sanity of its masses? Rats in a cage will kill each other, you know, if there are too many of them confined together. Terrans aren't so very different. Our ancestors understood that, and they knew that when the cage door was suddenly slammed shut again, after two decades of hope, there'd be hell to pay. I'm not condoning what they did, mind you . . . but neither can we condemn them, without understanding their world.*

*The Variants like to believe they're superior to us, that under the same circumstances they wouldn't turn on one another, wouldn't cut off their own children. Perhaps . . . but I suspect that's only because they haven't yet been locked in a small enough cage. To them every Terran is a diseased individual, heir to a genetic heritage of violence and irrationality—a heritage they imagine themselves freed from by virtue of their cultural trials. Little wonder they hate us! It's a marvel they let Terrans come to the outworlds at all. And I'm pretty sure they wouldn't, if the Guerans didn't force the issue. Most Variants would much rather leave us to rot in our own home system.*

*I would have been very happy rotting away on Earth,* Zusu mourned.

*Easy for you to say,* Derik snapped. *We weren't on Earth, remember? Plenty of space on the habitats, since they don't let anyone reproduce without a permit.*

Their words and images filled Jamisia's head, battering her imagination from a dozen different sources at once. That was the problem when the Others argued, or even just discussed things; she felt like a battleground. "All right," she muttered. "This is all very interesting, but it's getting us nowhere. We can hit the history books later, okay? For now, can we get back to making plans?"

To her surprise they all went along with her. *That* was a first. All of the rational ones, that is. She could still hear the most frightening one of all, the crying one, whose muffled sobs had become a counterpoint to all internal conversation. When the Others had first made their presence known, she'd almost never heard him, but by now the soft cadence of his terror had become a backdrop to almost every conversation. She didn't want to know what had frightened him. She *really* didn't want to know why his presence was slowly becoming more obtrusive. She tried to block out of her mind the day her tutor's dreamscape had shown him to her, naked and trembling and oblivious to the world around him. What would happen to her if *he* ever took over?

She drew in a deep breath, trying to shake off that image. "Look, we've got to decide—"

Her words were interupted by a soft knock on the door. She caught her breath, wondering if whoever it was had heard her whispering to herself. If so, would they think she was crazy, or something worse? At last she mustered her voice and asked who was there.

"Sumi," came the answer.

She could feel Katlyn taking control of her body with silken ease, like a hand sliding into a cool satin glove. "Come in," she said, and Jamisia could hear her exulting silently, that such a chance had come before the skip. Many of the Others had thought the Medusan would not come back, although Katlyn had insisted otherwise.

The door slid open and he stood there. She could see at once in his eyes that he was not wholly comfortable in her presence. Jamisia felt sorry for him, but Katlyn assured her that it was a good sign, that men always felt that way when a woman manipulated them. As if they could sense the nature of the game, without quite understanding how to exit from it.

*They're easier to control when they're like that.*

"Come in," she said softly. It was the kind of tone one used with a frightened animal, luring it close with a promise of safety.

He stood in the doorway for a minute, then took one step into the room. A token concession; it was clear he would rather keep his distance. "Allo told me to check up on you, to see that everything was all right here, before the ainniq." When she didn't respond he shifted his weight uneasily from one leg to the other, then offered, "Is it?"

Katlyn looked at him as if she wasn't quite sure, then glanced back at the straps on the bed. One glance was all it took: hesitant, frightened, female. Instinctively he took a step toward her, which brought him far enough through the threshold that the door whisked shut behind him. Inwardly Katlyn smiled.

"They're for the dive," he said. "Nothing to worry about, standard procedure on a private vessel."

This one was easy to play, Katlyn thought. Almost too easy. If the stakes weren't so high, it would be downright boring.

"So where are we going?" she asked, honing her voice to a perfect blend of bright curiosity and hesitant dependency. "You said ainniq, so I assume. . . ." She let the rest trail off into silence.

"Paradise Node." His eyes flickered about the small room, she noticed, focusing on her bag, her headset, her brightly lit computer screen . . . anything but her. "The waystation is a major commercial hub; you can contact your people from there."

Katlyn took the words at face value, but something in his tone made Verina suddenly wary. Raven stirred inside her. *Something's wrong, Kat, you'd better let me talk to him.*

*No way.*

*Kat—*

"Paradise," Katlyn mused aloud. She took a step closer to Sumi, one small step in an instant when he wasn't looking directly at her. Oh, he could back away when he noticed, but this way it would be obvious. Men were the most vulnerable when they felt self-conscious. "I've heard about that station, even on Earth. Is it as . . ." She fumbled delicately for a word ". . . interesting as the tour pages make it out to be?"

"Interesting?" He seemed to have noticed that she was closer, but he didn't back up. "That's a curious way to describe it. I suppose for a Terran it would be."

"How would you describe it?"

She didn't even listen to his answer, but flashed up a choice cut from a porn viddie; the images danced before her eyes as she watched him speaking. Some of the Others, repelled, tucked themselves deep inside Jamisia's mind and refused to watch. Derik muttered a curse and then withdrew in a huff, as he always did when the girls expressed their sexuality. That was all fine with Katlyn, she'd rather do this without them anyway.

He was telling her something about Paradise. She wasn't even listening, though she nodded her head attentively now and then, and kept her eyes carefully focused on him. Instead she was remembering what she had read about Medusans, and the way their strange particulate sense worked. And she was watching the viddie, its erotic images transposed like a fine veil between her eyes and his. It was one she often ran when someone else had control of the body, enjoying its artistic lewdness in the privacy of her own soul, using the circuits and pathways of brainware that had been assigned specifically to her. Now, however, she was not just watching the viddie itself, but remembering all those other times, and linking up to all the fantasies it had ever inspired. It was a heady tonic. She could feel her body stirring in response, skin suddenly made sensitive by the flush of heat along its surface. He was telling her something about the relative lawlessness on Paradise Station proper, how that was the public perception, but in actual fact the resident Guildmistress had eyes and ears everywhere, and it was said that nothing escaped her notice . . . and all the while Katlyn nodded at him, and smiled on cue . . . while the rythym of the bodies moving in her field of vision inspired a similar fevered rhythm in her own heart. ACCELERATED PULSE, her wellseeker warned. ADJUST? She flashed an icon that told it to mind its own business, and smiled.

And now . . . yes, she'd guessed right. Her visual wiles might not have gotten much notice from the Medusan, but other signals were coming through loud and clear. Particularly the scent of desire which must even now be rising from her skin, too faint for a Terran to notice, but rich and tantalizing to the Medusan senses.

He seemed to stammer then, as though losing his train of thought. Or perhaps his control? Deep inside her she was aware of Jamisia marveling at the flush of elation this little game provided, and despite the girl's own revulsion at where this was heading, she could sense her crouching close to the border which separated Katlyn's mind from hers, watching with a feverish intensity.

"It's an indulgent place, I hear." She was close to him now, so close that the nearer tentacles could feel the touch of her breath on their moist surfaces; she could see them quiver, their surfaces contracting for a second, tasting the chemicals of her life through that precious breeze. Sumi drew in a deep breath and for a moment his eyes seemed to focus elsewhere; she held her own, guessing that this would be the moment in which the whole game was decided. Would he let his body follow the course that instinct preferred, or override it with commands to the med programs, cutting short the flow of hormones which had surely begun? Her heart was pounding, as much from the elation of the hunt as from any more prosaic arousal. Men like this were a sport too precious to deny.

He exhaled slowly, somewhat hoarsely, and a number of tentacles slid forward over his shoulders, daring a more intimate proximity. They seemed ruddier than before, flushed with fresh blood, and they twined about each other endlessly, restlessly, hungry for sensation. A strange and disturbingly alien heat flooded her body, familiar and yet not so. She was distantly aware of Jamisia's horror, as the girl realized that the man's very alienness aroused Katlyn now. How could she help the poor girl understand that? It was the thought of tasting the Unknown on her lips, of embracing the Forbidden. What was it like, Katlyn wondered, to feel those gifts of Hausman touching one's naked skin? Were there other deformities, more secret, which fingers and tongue and eyes might uncover in the course of intimacy? Oh, this was going have rewards all its own, she thought.

"So it's said," he whispered hoarsely. She couldn't even remember the question that had prompted it. Slowly she put up a hand to his face, and touched his cheek, oh so gently. It was a small gesture, but it broke down the last of the barriers between them. As she had intended. His hands moved to her shoulders—large hands, strong hands—and then down to her upper arms, where he grasped her forcefully. She sensed an instant's hesitation in him, as he satisfied himself that her behavior was indeed the invitation it seemed to be. Or perhaps instead, he needed to satisfy himself that he meant to answer it. Then he leaned down toward her until his lips met hers, and she put her arms up about his broad shoulders in response. Half a dozen warm, moist tendrils began to slither up and about her arms, sliding into the sleeves of her jumpsuit and spiraling down towards her body. It was at once repulsive and unbearably erotic, a cocktail of sensation almost too much to bear. Even the taste of his lips was alien to her, a mix of chemicals born not of Earth, but of some tortured realm far from any human shore. She could sense the last barrier of self-control in him coming down as he moved in closer to her, the scent of his own desire now sweet in her nostrils; and his hands moved up to her shoulders to caress her, pulling the neck of her jumpsuit open—

Then pain. Just an instant of it, a stinging sensation, quickly gone. She hardly flinched. But he noticed, and drew back, and looked at her. His right hand stroked her shoulder again, where the reaction seemed to center, a lot more forcefully. And this time a short gasp escaped her lips, as something that felt like a needle stabbed into the tender flesh beneath his thumb.

He stared into her eyes for a moment as if seeking explanation there, and then, when none was forthcoming, reached up to the neck of her jumpsuit and pulled it open, baring her shoulder for his inspection. Several snaps down the front of the garment broke open as well, baring the flushed, warm curve of a breast. He didn't notice that. His attention was wholly on the tiny red circle he had found on her skin. "What is this?" he asked.

"Nothing. I pinched it. About two days ago. Nothing to worry about." She reached for his hand, to urge him away from the spot, but as she did so a flicker of doubt suddenly took root inside her.

*The wellseeker should have healed such a thing by now. Shouldn't it?*

His tendrils were cold now, and they withdrew from her arms. The alien lover was gone, and in his place stood a man who was all too familiar with unnamed threats. And his concern over this one was all too clear. "Where were you hurt? How did it happen?"

"Why does that matter?" she demanded. He didn't answer, so at last she said, "I was going through Immigration at Reijik Station, someone handed me my bag and helped me put it on and the strap pinched—just for a moment—"

*It shouldn't have lasted this long.*

He prodded the spot with his thumb, pressing downward. The pain was sharp, and her cry of surprise let him know it.

"Shit," he muttered. "God *damn*."

"What?" she begged him. She was scared now, and the Others who had been cowering within now came to the surface, adding fears of their own. "What is it?"

"Something that should have healed," he muttered. "Only it hasn't. You have a wellseeker online? Automatic?"

"Of course," she managed. She was more and more unnerved by where this was leading, and just about ready to give over her control of the body to Jamisia again. Or whoever. This wasn't the kind of scene she handled well.

His eyes unfocused for a moment, and she was sure he was

sending a message somewhere, relaying the details of his discovery. "What?" she begged.

He didn't answer, but asked, "Who was with you then?" The level of tension in him was palpable. "Who helped you?"

"I don't know their names. There were two of them, both Guild—"

He cursed more dramatically then, in a language she didn't understand. Quaking inwardly, she didn't know how to respond. "Guild! That's all we need now."

The door slid open; it was Calia, with a medkit in hand. "What is it?"

"Some kind of implant, I think. Take a look." He pushed Katlyn toward the woman, the jumpsuit still pulled low off her shoulder. Calia spared one low glance for her half-bared chest—a look of utter disdain flickered across her face, that encompassed both Katlyn and Sumi—and then focused on the red spot.

"She says she's had it two days. A spot she pinched."

Calia prodded the center of the spot with a sharp fingernail. It hurt. "Damage from an external source would have been healed by now."

"That's what I thought."

Their conversation, cold and impersonal, took place as if she were not in the room. Or as if she were some slab of meat being dissected on a cutting table, that couldn't possibly hear what they said, or care what they meant. "What is it?" she demanded, as much to declare herself a part of the scene again as to get any kind of answer.

They both looked at her; Calia's eyes were cold, cruel, but Sumi's held something of sympathy; she clung to that. "Something inside you, I'd guess. Something your Guild friends put there. Calia will dig it out."

The woman turned away, snapped open the white plastic box she had brought, and laid it on the room's small table. "Sit her down," she ordered. The door slid open again as Sumi maneuvered her to the small bed, gently forcing her to sit down on it. It was Allo, and he didn't look happy.

"What the hell is going on here?" he demanded.

"We may have one more passenger than we knew about," Calia said, as she withdrew a short silver tube from the case.

"An implant," Sumi explained, and then added, "maybe."

"I didn't know—" Jamisia began.

"Whose?" Allo demanded.

"Don't know yet." Calia adjusted some rings at the base of the tube, then nodded her satisfaction at the result. "We'll find out soon enough."

Katlyn was gone. And even Jamisia herself wasn't in full control. An Other stirred, taking up the reins of volition, and Jamisia let her. Fine and good if someone else wanted to handle this, she sure as hell didn't.

"I didn't know," Zusu whimpered.

"Hold her still," Calia ordered. Something flickered in her eyes that was more than mere efficiency; hate, perhaps? Pleasure that the Earthie was in such a position, restrained by alien hands while she, a Variant, prepared to cut into her flesh? The woman said nothing more as she moved into position, putting the narrower end of the tube against Zusu's skin, centering it on the red spot . . . but Zusu could sense her hatred all the same.

Then something bit into her flesh, and she cried out. Sumi's fingers gripped her arms with a strength that was painful, as the silver tongue of the probe cut down into her flesh, following some alien signal. She felt it descend an inch, maybe two, probing around inside her as if searching for something—and then there was an almost inaudible *click* and Calia muttered, "Got it!" She twisted the tube then, and pain burst inside the muscle of Zusu's arm. DAMAGE TO LEFT OUTER DELTOID, her wellseeker warned, ANALYZING NOW—She shut it off, not wanting to see the details of the damage scrolling up before her eyes, and whimpered softly as Calia withdrew the tube. This was what she deserved for not being careful enough. This was what she deserved for leaving Earth at all—

And then the tube was gone and so was something else, a small bloody bit that dangled from its tip. It was hardly as thin as a hair, and not even an inch long. As Zusu watched, it seemed to her that the thing squirmed slightly, as if alive, and a small circle of barbed tips flexed open like the struts of a parasol, then closed again. She felt suddenly sick, at the sight of what had just recently been inside her flesh.

"It's a trace," Calia announced.

Sumi cursed.

Allo's voice was all business, cold and clean and utterly devoid of emotion. "Guild?"

"Can't tell yet. Have to clean it off first." Calia held it up to the light, where the sharp highlights of direct illumination made it somewhat more visible. "Biotech, I'd guess. It'd have to be, to bypass the wellseeker programs." She glanced at Zusu, then fixed her eyes on Allo once more. "She really may not have known it was in her."

"What is it?" Zusu dared. Her voice was trembling. *Don't cry in front of these people. Don't. It would be bad, bad, bad. . . .*

"A *trace*," Allo said harshly.

"Someone's been following you," Sumi explained. "Or someone wanted to be able to follow you in the future. Probably Guild, from your description. They must have slipped this into you under cover of your little accident; within a day or two you'd never have known it was there. It must have picked up a germ or two on the way in or there wouldn't even have been that much sign of its existence."

"Nasty little sucker," Calia observed. "So what do we do with it now?"

Allo studied Zusu. She could sense the unspoken question inside him, could feel just how close it came to being voiced. *Why are they after you?* But there was no point in asking her that, and perhaps he sensed that. At last he turned away from her, and seemed to dismiss her not only from the conversation, but from his entire consciousness. "We'll stop at some hub station long enough to get rid of it. Slip it on some tourist headed out to nowhere. Damn!" He struck a fist into his open hand. "They may have traced us to that last stop—"

"You want me to warn them—"

"No. No. They probably won't take any notice of it, not if the girl wasn't left there. Safer not to draw their attention to things. If they ask, we'll say it was a social call. I'll have Tam draw up a dossier on the owner of that station, just in case we have to fake some details for the Pol. Damn!"

He turned to Zusu, his blue-streaked face scowling. "You may have cost us an awful lot here, *Jamisia*. I think you'd better give some real thought to letting us know what's going on."

Sumi started to protest; Allo waved him to silence. "At least as much as you know. We can hardly protect you if we don't know who we're protecting you from, now, can we?"

*Is that what you mean to do?* Derik demanded. *Protect us?* His tone was dry, but he wasn't in control of the body now, so his sarcasm went unheard. Zusu was in control, and her own response was to whimper softly and draw her knees up to her chest, wrapping her arms around her legs in a posture that was purely protective. As if someone was about to hit her in the gut, and she couldn't stand the pain if he did. That was how she felt.

"She doesn't know anything," Sumi said softly.

Allo's lips tightened in a hard line, but he nodded finally, accepting that interpretation. "All right. We'll talk it out later, see if she does know anything that can shed some light on this situation. For now . . . Calia, get that cleaned and IDed and ready for transport. And keep it at body temperature, just in case they're scanning for possible removal."

She nodded and started to put her hand around it, but the tiny barbs flexed, and she clearly had second thoughts about touching it. "Let me get it down to med, then."

He nodded. "Go."

He looked at Sumi, and at the girl. There were tears running down Zusu's cheeks, channels of glistening fear that spoke volumes for her state of mind. If it occurred to Allo that such a total breakdown was uncharacteristic for the girl they had taken on board, he didn't say that out loud.

"You're turning into a lot of trouble for us, Jamisia." He was trying to make his voice gentle, it seemed, but the tension underriding it was too marked for that subterfuge to work; Zusu's self-embrace grew even tighter as he sat down by her side. "You will help us try to figure all this out, won't you? We can't help protect you if you don't."

The lie was so blatant that even Zusu understood what was behind it . . . and the danger so evident that even her young mind, normally oblivious to the fine gradations of social dishonesty, caught on. "I'll tell you all I can," she whispered. "But really, I already told Sumi everything." To her surprise, Allo seemed to accepted that. Perhaps it was the tears in her voice; some men, Katlyn explained, mistook that for honesty. Perhaps it was simply that he needed to be elsewhere, and saw no further use in pandering to her fears.

*Well done,* Verina told her. *We'll get through this yet . . . together.*

With a muttered word of leavetaking Allo quit the room, leaving her alone with Sumi. The Medusan had placed a gentle hand on her shoulder in comfort, but when they were alone together, he withdrew it.

"I'm sorry," Zusu whispered. Sorry for causing him trouble, sorry for his obvious sexual embarrassment, sorry for everything. It was a generalized guilt, rather than a specific apology, and she hoped he understood it that way.

He didn't meet her eyes. "Look, we've got a few more hours in Reijik Node because of this mess. Try to use it to relax, all right? Calia will find out exactly what that thing was, and who made it. Then maybe you can help us put two and two together, and we'll figure out what to do about it."

He didn't go on to the part of the speech that should have come after, about how he was going to help her. Maybe that was too much of a lie for even him to stomach.

Jamisia felt sick inside. So did Verina. So did most of the Others who were watching now, their consciousness crowded about Zusu's own like tourists at a small viewport.

"I'm sorry," she whispered again. No answer.

He got up silently from the bed and walked to the door. For a moment it seemed he might leave without even looking at her, but he did glance back, and there was as much sympathy as frustration in his expression. "It'll be okay," he said shortly, and then he stepped close enough to the door for it to open. In another second he was gone, and the door slid shut once more; she—*they*—were alone.

Jamisia could have taken the body back then, but Zusu wanted it for one thing more. One thing she needed more than anything else, to deal with the emotions that had built up inside her. Frustration and despair and a thousand other things she didn't know how to handle. The Others had their ways of dealing with such things. She had hers.

The Others understood. The Others sympathized. They were family, after all.

They let her cry.

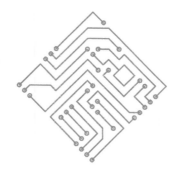

Terran man being the creature that he is, it should not surprise us that the first thing he wishes to do when venturing into out-space is build walls and doors and station boundaries to shut his fellows out. Is not Terran history but a series of attempted Isolations, and most wars fought on that battered soil for the sake of racial or cultural boundaries?

MARO TALRAND,
*The New Isolationists*

# ADAMANTINE NODE
# ADAMANTINE STATION

Guildmaster Anton Varsav was calm.

It scared his people.

He knew that.

It pleased him.

They knew him well enough to worry when the frenzied motion of his restless body eased, for it signaled that his brain had found something to focus on so closely that it couldn't be bothered with extraneous motion. They knew that when his language flowed smoothly and easily it was because there were no inappropriate phrases being edited out by his brainware, the usual case. And they knew that he only found such focus in danger, and conflict, and vengeance. So when they saw these signs, it scared them.

As it should.

He had spent the last E-week buried in Isolationist research. Saturating his mind with images and arguments from the two most hateful station colonies in civilized outspace. Tract after tract of the New Terran Front passed before his eyes, proclaiming the natural superiority of humankind's hated ancestors. As always, he wanted to take them by the shoulders and shake them violently, demanding, "Why did you come out here if you hate Variant space so much? Why not stay at home and nurture your precious barbaric genes in peace?" As for the New Aryan Nation, merely looking at a picture of them was enough to make one's bile rise in disgust. It wasn't enough for them to declare Earth stock superior, but they must cordon off a small section of Terra's gene pool and declare it sovereign over all that Earth had ever produced. To see a picture of them standing together, with their meticulously engineered features, perfectly matched in color, height and form, beautiful on the surface but cankerous with hatred underneath, was to understand just how corrupt ancient Earth must have been to have given birth to such a movement.

How they must hate him, all of them. How they must hate his race in general, but him most of all. This alien who ruled their node, who forced Guild law down their throats, and who flaunted his Variation before them as if it was not some kind of deformity, merely a normal state of being. How he hated them, and how he wished that Guild law would allow him to squeeze the life out of their colonies, so that the universe could be cleansed of such garbage forever.

But the law was the law, and he was sworn to uphold it.

Until they transgressed.

He hoped they had done so. He prayed nightly that they had done so. He dreamed of discovering that they were behind Lucifer—of being free to wreak vengeance upon them for that unspeakable crime. He would grind their stations to dust, and then package that dust and sell it to tourists, so that it reached every corner of the universe with its message: *Your kind is not wanted here.*

It was going to happen.

He had done all the things that were asked of him, and more. He had placed so many spy programs in his node's network that one could hardly buy a pod ticket without tripping over one of them. He had all the mail from both those problem stations diverted, analyzed, and tagged for a trace, and even the regular correspondence from more worthy humans was being watched as well. It was a monumental effort. Another person would have despaired of coordinating it all. Another would have been overwhelmed by the sheer mass of data, unable to give it order and focus and purpose. But for him it was merely an exercise of intellect, more challenging than most but not at all daunting, and the diverse parts of the investigation fit together in his head like the pieces of a puzzle.

That was Hausman's gift to him, a precious talent he expressed all too rarely. Setting his brain to this project was like stretching muscles too long unused, and he gloried in the sensation. Others noticed nothing, save that his walk was easier, his hands roved less in search of sensation, and he wrestled less with his language inhibitor programs to get speech out. Those who had served him for a long enough time knew what that meant, of course. And they knew to fear. He could see it in their eyes as they passed him in the corridors of the waystation, their glances quickly averted . . . but not quickly enough.

They were afraid of him.

Good.

Day after day he went over the data, giving his people key words and phrases to search for, never giving them quite enough information to know exactly what he was looking for, or why. Unlike Ra and so many others, he never trusted his hackers. He never forgot that the same talent which made them so valuable also made them unpredictable as well, and that more than one Guildmaster had been brought down by a disgruntled employee with access to confidential files. Like so many before him, he had learned that hiring conventional programmers was not enough, that one needed a mind hungry to devour secrets, in order to find secrets out. Unlike so many before him, however, he was not going to make the mistake of ever thinking they were loyal to him, or giving them a chance to work their mischief.

But they could sort through this mess in search of key patterns, and weed out the ten million letters that were of no interest whatsoever. Meanwhile his more prosaic programmers could come up with sorting programs for what was left over, searching for that all but invisible hint of insurrection in the making.

The hint would be there. He knew it.

If they did not find it for him, he could always create it.

What power she had placed in his hands, the Prima! Did she even know? Did she think in those terms? One hint of Lucifer, and he could sent an army into Destiny Station. And not his own army either; an army of the Guild itself, hot with the hunger for vengeance, ready to make an example of the isolationists for all to see.

One station to be destroyed, for the crime of setting Lucifer loose in the galaxy. The other to quiver in fear down through the millennia, as the dust of their neighbor and cohort circled endlessly through the system, as a warning. Now *that* was a lesson he could never have managed on his own.

They *were* guilty. He was sure of it. And even if they weren't . . . it didn't really matter, did it? The only thing the Guild would see was the data search, and what came of it. And he was in charge of that. How closely would they question his report? How little work would it take to add a small fact here or there, and seal the fate of the Isolationists forever?

He passed by a picture of the Prima and saluted it, a tight smile twitching across his face. *Thank you*, he thought to her. *For all of this.*

Power was such a sweet elixir.

The ambassador from the New Terran Front was predictably hostile. They were always hostile. They considered it an affront to be asked to share the same air as a Variant, and their speech and manner and expression all showed it.

"Our station space has been invaded."

Varsav had started the meeting sitting, but quickly rose and began to pace. They did that to him, these Isolationists, overriding even the calm that his med programs could produce, driving him to a frenetic display of wasted energy. God, how he hated them.

"Invaded, you say."

"Yes."

He snorted with what he hoped was suitable disdain. "By what? Tourists? A harvester? Some poor little transport jarred off its course, that came within a million miles of your outer ring?" He'd heard all those complaints before and dealt with them as his duty demanded, but that didn't mean he had to like it. Or pretend that he liked it.

There was fury in the man's eyes, but for now he was keeping it under control. "A pod."

"A pod?" He stopped pacing and faced the man. Did he sound as incredulous as he felt? "And you came to my office to complain to me personally because this pod, this tiny thing, passed within . . . what? A million miles of your station? Two million?"

The answer came between gritted teeth. "Six thousand."

Six thousand miles. Really. That was actually a legal offense, he mused, and not just some instance of Isolationist paranoia. Unusual.

"A pod, you say."

The man held out a sheet of plastic. Varsav took it from him, resisting the impulse to make physical contact as he did so. God alone knew what the man would do if he did, probably go home and have all the skin removed from his hand, for fear of some dreaded Variant infection. Maybe they'd even kill him when he went home, just to keep the station pure. Damn it, the moment was tempting . . . but he refrained from making contact. Duty above pleasure. Maybe next time, he promised himself.

Varsav looked over the figures recorded on the sheet, and frowned as he did so. This was not good. Not good at all. Something really had come into the Front's station space, and that meant he had to do something about it. The law was the law. "How long ago was this?"

The ambassador hesitated. "Nearly two Earth days now."

Varsav snorted derisively. "And you expect me to do what now? Track the thing?" Oh, he could see them wasting two days, all right, while the intruder made his merry way home. A grand council meeting or two to discuss how to deal with such a threat, followed by a host of committee meetings to decide if it was worth sending one of their own into Variant-controlled space, followed by a long discussion of who . . . if there ever was a war between Earth and her Variant offspring, and if this station was any example of Terran competence, Hausman's children had nothing to fear.

Which was not true, and he knew it. The Terrans had invented terrorism as a strategy of war, and if hostility between Earth and its descendants ever flared into open conflict, he did not doubt they would use it to their advantage. Whereas Variants were raised to consider terrorism an unacceptable strategy under any circumstances . . . the result of lifetimes spent on space stations, where a million lives might be lost in the wake of one well-placed explosion. That would be an ugly war indeed, he thought.

"We *expect* you to defend the sanctity of our station space. As our station treaty says you will."

For a moment he said nothing. His fingers, already exploring the surface of a statue near his desk, gripped it tightly. "Very well," he said at last. "You're quite correct. Your space was invaded. Did this . . . this pod do anything to damage the station?"

"No."

"Did it hinder your communications in any way?"

"No."

"Did it do anything else you are aware of, which might have harmed your station or any of its people?"

The fury on the man's face was unmistakable. "It could easily have spied on us. Intercepted transmitted data. Half a dozen things that we would never find out about. That's your job to determine, isn't it?"

Varsav scraped his nails along the statue. Scratch marks joined a hundred others already there. "Did you attempt to trace it? Backtrack its trajectory."

"We did what we could," the man said stiffly. "The figures are there." His very tone said they hadn't accomplished much. That wasn't a big surprise. They might have the equipment to track things through Guild space, but he doubted they used it often enough to be very adept with it.

"Very well. As you say. I will investigate." He paused. "Is that all?"

The man drew in a deep breath, and was obviously struggling not to let loose what he was really thinking. Which might even prove refreshing, Varsav thought, if he did let go. He could shut down his own speech inhibitor programs and let loose on the man with the kind of language he would *really* like to use. That could be . . . interesting.

But the man backed down. With a look in his eye like a wary dog, he muttered, "Yes. That's all." And added, "There's an ed-dress there for your report on the matter."

"Of course." He glanced down to note where it was, and nodded his official attention to the matter. The man glared at him but could find no concrete cause for further confrontation, so at last, like a snarling dog being forced to give ground, he backed, scowling, out of the door.

Varsav wanted to chute the damn report and the Terran isolationists along with it, but he knew that he couldn't. The Front would have been within their legal rights to shoot down any intruder who came in that close to their station space, and if they hadn't done that, Varsav was sure it wasn't due to any sense of mercy for whomever was inside the pod, merely the fact that they didn't have guns pointed in the right direction at the right time. Well, he was sure that was being corrected right now. In the meantime the Guildmaster had better just be grateful that he was dealing with a two-day-old complaint about an off-course pod, rather than the press closing in because some innocent tourist strayed off course on his holiday and was shot down by extremists. That had happened once off Destiny Station, and it was a scene he hoped never to repeat.

If only you could demand that people were *civilized* before you let them settle in outspace. . . .

With a grunt he called in his aide and gave him the sheet of data specifications. Let him see what he could find out now, two days after the fact. He suspected the thing was far gone, probably on a station somewhere, or maybe out of the node entirely. Two days was a long time in outspace. Oh, well, they'd try. And he'd file a report for the Front and they would bitch and moan . . . in short, business as usual. These Isolationist stations from Earth might be nasty and hellishly dangerous, but they were certainly predictable.

As for the pod, it was probably some teenager out for a joy ride. *Buzzing* a station, they called it. Each generation had its own particular stupidity, and the current one seemed to encourage reckless behavior when it came to transit law. He'd check the records from the educational circuit and see what the young ones were being arrested for these days. Maybe add a class or two on *Why I Should Not Annoy Isolationists*. Or even better, he thought darkly, *How Not to be so Stupid In My Youth That I Will Never Reach Adulthood*.

Maybe he could force all the would-be hackers to take that class, too. Some of them could use it.

It was his downshift when the message came. That was all right. He didn't mind his sleep being interrupted, if it was for a reason.

He tapped the com and muttered, "What?"

"You wanted to know as soon as we got something off the Front's station," a voice said hoarsely. It was his Director of Programming, and his long hours of labor sounded clearly in his voice. "I think we just did."

He was awake at that, and putting on the headset. Magnetic contacts snapped into place and the start-up icons filled his field of vision. He brought his interface online and said, "Let me see what you've got."

It came directly into his head, and spread itself out across his field of vision. He shut his eyes to make it clearer.

TROUBLE COMING. THE ENEMY SEEKS CHILDREN. SEND ALL HOME ASAP. LUX AETERNA.

Sleep was gone from his brain in an instant. His hands on the coverlet flexed and unflexed, as he read the message again. And again. Damn, but it looked promising.

"Where did you get this?" he demanded.

"Being sent out from the Front's main processor."

"Do you know where it's going?"

A pause. "We have the codes. We're working on them. I thought you would want to see this right away."

"You're right. I did. Thank you." Jesus Christ, they'd caught the bastards at something, at last! Was it Lucifer? The signature certainly implied that.

If so . . . he drew in a deep breath, feeling the flush of impending triumph flood his system. He'd watched two pilots killed by this thing. One of them had died in his arms, struggling against the plasteel bonds that kept him from tearing out his own throat. Varsav had sworn vengeance upon the maker of Lucifer, above and beyond anything the Guild might seek. Those were *his* people who were killed, outpilots supposedly in *his* care, for whom he was responsible. The man who had attacked them attacked him as well.

And now perhaps they had a way to take the bastard down.

He read the message again. There was no mistaking the conspiratorial tone. And it had come up in response to one of his search clusters for Lucifer . . . he glanced at the date and time to see just when the original message had been sent. With the monumental backlog of correspondence his people had to sort through on this project, it could have been hours ago. Days, even.

He looked at the date given for transmission. It was some time ago, all right. Nearly two days. Long enough for the data trail to be stone cold . . . as if they could follow it anyway. The Front wasn't likely to let him search their station computers, not without a warrant from the Prima, and even then they'd fight about it.

Two days . . .

A thought nagged at him. He tried to ignore it, focusing once more on what a pleasure it would be to prove that the Isolationists were connected with Lucifer. What if they were the ones who had launched it in the first place? What if he could find evidence of that? Or perhaps . . . create evidence of that?

Two days.

He tried not to remember the man who had stood in his office only hours ago, complaining of a pod in the Front's station space. He tried to ignore that, because it wasn't at all connected to this.

Was it?

With a muttered groan he flashed up a general control icon and called for his personal files. The Front's complaint was there, waiting for him. He read it again, and looked for the part that told when the spatial transgression had taken place.

And then he called up the letter his people had intercepted.

And cursed, rather loudly.

"Sir?"

He struck the com hard enough not only to turn it off, but to jar its control switch out of alignment as well. He also flashed up the icon that would shut off his language inhibitors, and indulged in a stream of invective so fierce and so hostile that letting it loose was like cleaning out all the garbage in his soul.

After that, he could think.

The pod had come into station space about the same time that letter was transmitted. Not exactly the same time. The link wasn't clear. If he ignored it now, and simply reported the stolen letter to the Prima, no one would know to question it. It was clear enough that the Front was engaged in some calumny, wasn't it? Wasn't that enough? Hell, he'd been all but ready to make up false evidence to get those bastards in trouble. Was it such a little thing to fail to mention that this obviously offensive document might be somehow connected to the act of an outside agency?

He wanted this letter to be from the Front. He knew in his heart that it *had* to be.

But what if it wasn't?

He rose up from bed with a groan and started pacing. Sometimes it helped him think, to let his body move freely. He passed by the mirror and saw his reflection in it. It was strange to see himself thus, without a uniform. He was Guild through and through, always had been, and now he felt doubly naked for not wearing the Guild sign somewhere on his bare skin.

If he lied about this . . . *no, don't call it lying,* he urged himself, *call it a creative oversight* . . . then there would be no further investigation.

And the real source of Lucifer would never be found.

He remembered the pilot who died in his arms, remembered swearing at the time that if it was the last thing he did, he would see the virus' designer brought to justice. He hated Lucifer's maker even more than he hated the Front, for the latter was just an offensive blot on his station space, while the former . . . the former had killed his people. People for whom he was personally responsible. That virus had snuck into Adamantine Node and attacked his outpilots right before his eyes. That was a deeply personal affront, and one that would not be forgotten.

If he let the investigation end now, by causing the Guild to think that it had found the culprit . . . then that affront would never be answered. Which enemy was worse? Which one was more of a threat to the Guild? Why had God dumped all this power in his lap, just to prevent him from using it?

He stopped before the mirror and stared into it, eyes darting from point to point within the reflection. He knew what his duty was. He also knew what his heart demanded.

*Don't call it conscience. Not if conscience isn't enough. Call it . . . vengeance.*

With a growl of resignation he called up a blank memo screen in his mind's eye, and began to jot down instructions for his people.

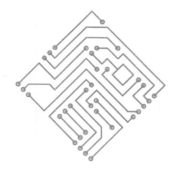

## TANJI

The *tanji* is not afraid. Fear is for creatures who are alone. The *tanji* is never alone.

When it is weak, others will support it. When it is strong, it will support others. The ebb and flow of interdependence is as natural to it as the pulse of blood in its veins.

Community is safety.

Loneliness is fear.

Isolation is death.

*KAJA: An Outworlder's Guide to the Gueran Social Contract, Volume 2: Signs of the Soul*

# INSHIP: EXETER

**E**VERYTHING HAD CHANGED.

Allo and Sumi and all the others still spoke to her politely, and even made what seemed like sincere attempts to be friendly, in between all the questions they asked her—most of which she couldn't answer, some of which she *wouldn't* answer—but it just didn't ring true any more. Was that because something in them had really changed, or was she just less able to accept their efforts at face value? And if the latter, why?

She knew when it had begun, of course. The minute Calia dug the probe out of her arm—the minute the words "Guild trace" were voiced in her cabin—some intangible, unnamable transformation seemed to have taken place in all of them. Her relationship with them had changed at that moment, but she couldn't say how. The words were the same, the looks, all the subtle moves and gestures, but the emotions underlying those things had altered. And she lacked the social acumen to define just what was different, or even to understand how she knew it. One thing was very clear, however.

She had to act. Soon.

It was Derik who told her that first, his tone as always imperious and hostile. Then Verina agreed, adding validity to the thought. In the end even the child-Others agreed, making for a truly rare consensus of spirit. Only Zusu held back . . . but Zusu was so afraid of the consequences of her actions that she preferred to huddle in a dark corner of their shared brain, lost in dread of what others would do to her. So she was hardly a fit counselor in matters like this.

It was no longer enough to be reactive, the voices warned

Jamisia. She had to move on her own now, analyze the situation, and determine how she was going to get control of it. She had already let the enemy drive her from her home, restrict her movement on the metroliner, and now she was letting it control her here as well. That had to stop. That faceless, nameless corporate enemy whose shadow hung over her life like a pall would control her whole life if she let it, until such time as it demanded that very life in sacrifice. That mustn't be allowed to happen.

She had to take control.

She had to do . . . *something*.

But what?

It wasn't an easy mental adjustment for her to make. In all of her life she had always been dependent upon others, and had been content to stay that way. First, for six years in a comfortable childhood with her parents, and then, when they died, with Shido Corporation. She'd been content to lead the life of a teenager in that indulgent environment, partying with the other young corporates and assuming that her company would always take care of her. Assuming that nothing ever would go wrong.

Only it had. It had gone very wrong.

And now she had to deal with that.

She ordered the monitor to give her a silvered screen, which served as a functional, if somewhat hazy, mirror. In it, she studied herself. There was no longer any secret about why she had always seen faces in mirrors that were not her own; they crowded about her now, ghostlike in her mind's eye. The phenomenon was still shocking, but it no longer horrified her. *No,* she thought, reaching out to touch the screen with a slender finger. *I'm not alone.* Surely with all those minds inside her, she could come up with some plan of action. Or at the very least, some plan of *reaction* that would let her take control of her life again. It was time for that, wasn't it?

*Well past time,* Derik agreed.

Allo had said it would be a few days before they could make the skip. He wanted to make sure that the Guild's trace was far, far away before he put himself—and Jamisia—into their hands. He'd told her how Tam had slipped the barbed trace into a tourist without her noticing, some heavyset woman from some hi-G world, out for a holiday. They'd stopped at one of the hotel stations for a while, and Tam had caught sight of her there. The Belial had talked to her briefly to ascertain her intentions—and her relative lack of intelligence—even while his twin hacked into her travel itinerary and confirmed her as a suitable stooge for their purposes. She was on her way to five different stations in Reijik Node, a leisurely tour of the health spas and tourist resorts for which the node was known. That was good. It meant that the trace and its current host wouldn't wind up in Guild hands for at least an E-month, so it would be that long before anyone realized that the precious mechanism was now lodged in the wrong flesh. In the meantime the woman would flit her way from station to station in much the same way a fugitive would, making for a convincing profile in whatever computers were keeping watch.

All of which meant that Jamisia was safe, for now.

From the Guild, at least.

She heard no hint of direct threat from the small ship's crew, but she knew it was in the air. There were whispers she didn't quite hear in the corridors, which hinted at trouble to come. Things were left unspoken when she entered a room, so pointedly she could not miss their absence. The crew of the ship spoke as many words to her as before, but those words carried less meaning. It was as though they were all marking time now. Waiting for . . . what?

Maybe there was an answer she needed to find. Or maybe . . . maybe it was all her imagination. That was a very real possibility. What if these people meant her no harm, and it was merely the unease of some paranoid Other that was causing her to think otherwise? Their concerns did have a tendency to bleed into her consciousness, and not all of them were justified. The one who cried constantly was acutely paranoid, and every now and then when his mind touched hers, she cringed beneath the weight of its terror. Could he be responsible for her fears? Was she doing these people a disservice? How could she even know what she herself thought, in a world where the awareness of half a dozen pressed constantly against her brain?

*Don't be an idiot,* Derik growled. *They're planning something. Figure out what.*

In the end it was the sheer consensus of the Others that convinced her. In all the time she had known them, they had rarely agreed on anything. They did now. *Something is wrong,* an inner voice warned, and in her mind's eye she could sense a dozen individuals nodding in sage agreement. No one argued, not even the children. That was damn convincing.

*Time to take control of my life,* she thought grimly. And then added, before anyone else had a chance to correct her: *My lives.*

She hoped it would be easier than it sounded.

**T**am came to her five hours before they were due to reach the outstation. He was a brusque little man who didn't look at her often, and his fingers bristled with special tools that were worn like false fingernails on his slender, pale fingers.

"Came to do your headset," he told her. His eyes scanned the room, fixed on her briefly, then flitted away again. "For the ainniq. Get you ready."

She hesitated, then handed it to him, as she asked, "What are you doing, exactly?"

"Programming." The quick little fingers snapped open the housing of the headset, and tapped something glittering and crystalline within with a metal rod attached to his index finger. Whatever the headset did in response, it seemed to satisfy him. He snapped it shut again, put the contraption on his own head, and closed his eyes; she could see his eyeballs twitch back and forth as he scanned some internal vista. He seemed wholly unaware of her, lost within some internal computerscape. She waited silently. At last he took the crescent-shaped device from his head and handed it back to her. "All right, you're ready to go."

She tried to keep the unease out of her voice as she asked him, "What did you do to it?"

A brief hint of irritation passed across his face, and for a moment she saw his eyes unfocus, no doubt marking some internal conversation. Explaining to his twin that the difficult Earthie girl was keeping him longer than she should have, perhaps? "Programming downtime."

Raven nudged her mentally, and she asked, "Which means what?"

He scowled. He had every right to. Any schoolchild should know what downtime meant, and be able to figure out why he was programming it into her headset. But Raven wanted to hear how he worded his answer, and Jamisia wasn't in the mood to argue with her.

"We're going into the ainniq," he told her. His tone was crisp, curt, not unlike the sharply defined voice of a public address computer. "We've got class C vessel status, which means we can stay on our own ship—they'll tow it—but the Guild requires that all human passengers be either sedated or chilled during passage."

"Would they know if someone wasn't?" she asked.

He seemed startled by the question. "It's rumored they have a program that will scan for beta waves on board. Maybe not. But would you want to take that chance? Considering that any-one who offends the Guild would be banned from the ainniq for-ever? That's a pretty harsh punishment." He shook his head; clearly he found the mere thought of such defiance incredible. "It's not like you can see anything anyway. We'll be completely enclosed during flight."

She tried to make her voice sound as naïve as possible. "And what did you program for me, exactly?"

"Theta-sleep. It's the best choice by far, everyone but the Captain will do it. Sedation's a pain to program, and it doesn't clear out of your system all that fast." His sharp eyes fixed on her with all the intensity of a predator. "Haven't you ever been through an ainniq before?"

"Once. From Earth to Reijik. I slept through it."

"Best way to go. Trust me. Most of the ships, everyone just goes under, easier that way. You need a special license to do oth-erwise."

"And Allo's got that license?"

He hesitated for only a fraction of an instant, then nodded. She was willing to bet the affirmation was at least half a lie. Had Allo stolen a license? Forged one? Two and two suddenly added up to four in her head, and she knew what it was that the ship's crew did for a living. She'd have guessed it sooner if they hadn't so carefully kept her away from their business, back when they were unloading their cargo. Now, lots of little small hints suddenly snowballed into a very clear, very comprehensible picture.

"Of course," she murmured. Of course smugglers would have such a license. Of course they wouldn't trust themselves to be put to sleep during Guild transport. She was willing to bet Allo wouldn't really be sedated either, though she didn't know how he'd slip that one by the Guild authorities. They seemed to be thorough in checking everything. "He has everything covered, doesn't he?"

She regretted the edge to her voice the minute she said the words, but he didn't seem to notice it. "He tries to," he agreed. "Anyway, it's five hours to immersion by our current clock, so figure the last warning will come through about thirty minutes before that. You'll need to have all your gear stowed for no-G by then, just for safety's sake. Then lie down, strap in, tell your wellseeker to inload . . . and before you know it we'll be on Paradise."

He turned to leave, but she still had questions. "Why do they do it?" she asked him. "Why do they make us sleep? Are they so afraid we might . . . what, exactly?"

He turned back and stared at her; clearly amazed at the level of her ignorance. She could almost hear the words spoken aloud: *Didn't they teach you anything on Earth?* "There are predators in the ainniq," he said at last. "You know that much, right? Things that will rip your soul right out of your body and eat it for lunch." She nodded. "Well, rumor has it they're drawn to certain types of brain activity, in the same way that Terran sharks are drawn to blood. The Guild won't confirm that, of course. They're not about to tell us anything about what *really* happens out there." For a moment hatred flashed in his eyes, undisguised by societal pleasantries. Like most Variants, he had no love for the Guild. "I've been told that the reason they put most of us in theta-sleep for passage is so that the dragons won't hear us coming. Same thing with a sedation program. It doesn't stop the brainwaves, but it skews them a bit. A kind of disguise."

"The outpilot will be awake," she offered. "He has to be, to steer the ship. Right?"

"Yes," he told her. "And maybe that's why not all ships make it through." The hostility in his eyes subsided, but it clearly took effort. "This is all just rumor, you understand. The Guild isn't about to let us share their precious secrets. All we know is that they can get a ship through the ainniq uninjured and no one else can. What else really matters? They say sleep, so we sleep." He shut his eyes for a second, apparently to consult his timekeeper. "Immersion at 0728 Standard Time," he told her. "Just be sure you're running the program by then, okay?"

He looked at her then—really looked at her, not past or through her like he usually did—and it seemed to hit him just how unnerving his little speech had been. His eyes unfocused for a minute as he indulged in some internal dialog, then he said, "Look, the program will rouse you within an hour after passage. There's nothing to worry about. Really."

*Nothing to worry about.*

The words were cold comfort. Even as the door slid shut behind him, a half dozen voices inside her head were whispering warnings of where the danger in this plan might lie, describing the various things that Allo and the Guild might do to her while she was chilled and helpless. Her hand trembling slightly, she picked up the headset. Was there something else in there now, besides the program he had told her about? How would she ever know? Raven knew more programming than any of them, and even she was no expert. How could she analyze what Tam had done, much less alter it? Her fingers closed about the thin plastic band, and a cold fear began to take root in her heart. She was in over her head here. All the voices crowding inside her head couldn't give her access to impossible skills. She knew from things she'd overheard that Tam was the kind of programmer accustomed to breaking the rules. Could a normal person even figure out what he'd done to her equipment, much less undo it? The fear became a chill despair that clutched her heart like a fist, and her hand spasmed tightly about the headset as if crushing it would solve all her problems. Within her soul she could feel one of the Others rising up, consciousness reaching toward the surface like a desperate swimmer struggling for air . . . Zusu? *No,* she begged, *no, no, not now, I need to think this through, just let me do it, please.*

And then there was something else. A presence like fire that exploded through the many layers of her consciousness, butting aside the Others that got in its way. Zusu took one look at it and fled in terror; Jamisia wished she could do the same. In all her time with the Others, she had never seen one in such a rage. So alien was the newcomer's fury, so mind-numbingly intense, that not until he took direct control of her senses did she even realize who it was.

"Fuck all this shit!" Derik snarled. The rage was like a whirl-wind inside him, a storm of frustration and anger that was directed at all of them. "Is this what you call action? This bullshit? I'll show you action!"

In horror Jamisia watched as her own hand took the headset and threw it down onto the floor, hard. The plastic frame hit the floor with a sickening sound and then bounced some feet up, its resilient surface and the lo-G of the ship combining with the force of Derik's pitch to give it almost ludicrous flight. Then it settled back down to the floor, and he slammed his foot down on it, hard, crushing the delicate components—

*No!!!* She surfaced and took control of the body again, to stop him. Or tried to. But his mental grip on it was more than secure, and he had no intention of relinquishing control. "Stay out of this!" he snarled. "I'm doing what has to be done!" He ground his foot, intending to crush the headset, but she'd pulled him off balance enough that he missed it by inches. With a muttered curse he threw her off and struck out at the instrument again. But this time Jamisia wasn't alone in her efforts to stop him. Verina was helping her, and Raven, and after a moment even Katlyn and Zusu joined in. They'd never tried to control the body together before, least of all against the might of one of their own kind. And damn, he was strong! With all that fury unleashed, he was stronger than the rest of them put together. But that was his nature, after all. He was the one who had raged in fury when the doctors fed hurtful memories into Jamisia's brain; his was the role of avenger, protector. And he had never been released to vent his indignation, not at a time when it would do any good . . . until now.

*Derik!* It was Verina, the voice of reason. *Don't be an idiot! If you break the headset they'll know we've caught on, don't you see?*

He hesitated. In the sudden silence, Zusu whimpered, *I don't want to go into the ainniq without the headset—*

*Shut up!* half a dozen voices told her.

*Derik?*

He could scarcely see through all the wellseeker messages in his field of vision. He flashed the goddamn thing to shut down and didn't answer anyone till the last red warning was gone. "Yeah?"

*First, don't talk out loud. You know we're probably being watched. Keep it internal.*

He drew in a deep breath. The force of his rage still boiled inside him; Jamisia kept a careful distance between him and her, afraid that she'd get sucked into it. Zusu cowered, terrified.

*Derik . . .*

*Yeah.* God, he hated to admit when one of the others was right. Damn girls! With a growl he put his foot down on the ground, a good three inches from where the headset now lay. He could sense them all inside him, tense, ready to fight with him again if he tried to do something stupid. Damn them all!

*Okay.* It was Verina, as always the voice of reason. *Now listen to me. We won't wear the headset if you're that set against it. Okay? But if you break it to pieces, they may know—we don't know what they have linked to it—and certainly they'll see it, if they stop in later. All right? So just let it be.* When a minute went by and he didn't answer she prodded gently, *Derik?*

*Yeah,* he growled. *I got it.*

Zusu began to cry. So did one of the children, and then another. The combination of their tears and Derik's rage and her own fear was sickening, and Jamisia knew that if the body had been in her control at that moment she'd be sure to vomit.

*Look,* Derik said sternly. It was clear he was struggling not to speak aloud; silence didn't come naturally to him. *I won't do anything more to the headset, okay? But we're not putting it on for transit, or for anything else. Fuck those bastards! God knows what they did to it. So screw this concept of taking a nap, we're doing the dive with eyes open and that's all there is to it! Got that, girls?*

There was silence. Dissension was considered, then left unvoiced. There were doubts, of course, in all of them. He ignored them.

At last one of the children murmured, *What about the drag-ons, Derik?*

*Dragons be damned*, he retorted. *If they get us, at least we go down clean.*

*They eat souls*— one of the others began.

With a cry of frustration he threw the headset against the nearest wall. It rattled as it bounced off onto the bed, as if something inside it had broken loose. *Fuck the dragons, fuck this ship, fuck everyone and everything that's on it! You said you wanted to do something, right? No more sitting back and waiting for other people to take control of our lives. Right? RIGHT?*

A second passed. A few voices, hesitant, whispered confirmation.

*All right, then. So I'm taking control. If one of you feels more qualified to do that, you can fight me for it. I'm sick and tired of listening to all of you bitch, you understand? So I'm in charge now, and you all can just deal. Is that clear?*

This time several seconds passed before there was confirmation. When it came, it was hesitant, tentative. It was clear the others weren't all that happy about what he had done . . . and equally clear that they didn't want to take over themselves. Even Jamisia found a strange comfort in his fury, as if he were voicing emotions she herself had been keeping bottled up for too long. Yes, it was all right if he took over for a while. It was a relief, in a way. He scared the hell out of her and she didn't trust his judgment, but Verina would surely ride herd on him, and in the meantime. . . .

In the meantime she could rest. Relax. Shut down. Wasn't that what the others did sometimes, when there was something they didn't want to be involved in? It would be nice not to have to worry for a while, or deal with anyone else's worries. How did they do it? Verina had explained once. Something about letting go, so that the sensory feed ceased and there was only mental input . . . a kind of sleep, she'd said. Sometimes you needed that, when a dozen voices were in your head all the time.

*Here,* a gentle voice whispered. *I'll show you.*

Take her by the hand. Follow her into darkness.

Peace.

**T**here was a knock on the door just as Derik was buttoning up his jumpsuit. Startled, he fumbled for a moment, then gritted his teeth and forced the small plastic disk through its hole. It wouldn't do to have anyone see him when he wasn't fully dressed; that would spoil everything. "Come in," he muttered.

It was Sumi.

*Derik, you want one of us to—*

*Fuck off,* he told them. All of them. He managed a smile for Sumi, while thinking to the Others, *and thanks for the show of confidence.*

"We're approaching the outstation now," Sumi told him. "I came to see if everything was okay."

He saw the Medusan looking over his body and he sat down on the edge of the bed; there was less to see, that way. "I'm fine. Thanks."

"Anything you need?"

"No." When that didn't seem to be enough, he turned his smile up a few degrees of warmth and assured him, "Really."

*Derik, you're missing signals here.* It was Katlyn. *Maybe I should help.*

He kept the smile on his face, and sent her a firm denial. He was damned if he'd be sharing his bodytime with a girl. Any girl. Besides, what was Kat going to do? Get this guy so worked up that he tried to make physical contact? What then? *There's too much at stake here to play games,* he snapped at her. *Let me handle this.*

"All right, then." For a moment Sumi just looked at her— trying to define the change in her manner, perhaps, trying to come to terms with it?—and then he nodded toward the headset that sat beside her. "Immersion in thirty. You'd better put that on."

From somewhere he dredged up his best charming smile, and picked up the headset. "Thanks." Then he cast his eyes demurely down, trying to look embarrassed. "Sumi, I'm a little bit tense is all. After the dive I'll be okay. . . ." He left him to fill in the rest.

"That's all right." He seemed to relax a bit. Whatever he had come for, now his job was done. Derik could imagine the captain's orders to him: *Get her in the fucking headset, whatever it takes. Make sure she wears it.*

No, he wouldn't have said that. Only an idiot would go into the ainniq unchilled and unsedated, endangering them all. And the Earthie girl wasn't that stupid. Right?

One of the children snickered.

Sumi waited until she had put the headset on her head (so maybe that was it, after all) and then nodded his leavetaking and left him alone.

*Not alone*, Derik thought with satisfaction. *Never alone.*

Raven was still sorting through the files he'd inloaded from the ship's library. She had her own section of brainware to do it in, so it wasn't bothering anybody. Verina and Katlyn were holed up with some viddie of life on Paradise; he could see its ghostly images flicker in his field of vision, a necessary annoyance. Even the kind of brainware they carried didn't have totally separate visual tracks for everyone. Still, after years of playing hide-and-seek with each other in Jamisia's brain, they had pretty much learned to tune each other out. He did so now, ignoring the half-dozen efforts going on inside his head which, hopefully, would lead them all to safety when they finally got off this ship.

With a sigh he visualized the icons that would make sure his brain accepted *no* input for the next few hours, not from the headset and not from anywhere else. Raven had showed him how to disconnect its processor—it still worked despite his abuse of the instrument, though not well—but even so, this was not a time to take chances. His gut feeling was that some kind of trap had been set when Tam played with the thing, and he was damned if he'd give it half a chance to work.

*The dragons will find us*, a child whispered. *They'll eat us.*

He ignored that.

When the time came, he lay down on the bed and pulled the straps across his body, fitting them into place. Ankles first, then knees, then a pair across his torso. They withdrew slightly after he snapped them shut, tightening across his body. Like he was going to fall out of bed without their help, or something. The things he'd stuffed into his pockets dug into his body from all angles, and he had to squirm around a bit to get the pair of shoes in his thigh pocket aligned so they didn't dig into his leg.

Sumi hadn't noticed all those bulges, had he? Derik hoped to hell not. That would ruin everything. God damn those straps. . . .

Jamisia shot him a picture of the thing they'd put her in the first time she'd gone through an ainniq. a kind of padded cocoon. Also of the bruises on her body afterward, and the ones she'd seen on other people.

He shrugged.

It was just him, then, him and this female body with its fearfully pounding heart. The wellseeker begged him to let it adjust something, anything, and at last he let it put the reins on his pulse, and neutralize some of the adrenaline pouring into his system. He'd need that back later, but right now all it was doing was making him restless. *But the minute these straps come off, you quit all that.* He made sure it understood that instruction, then tried to relax. But it was impossible. So much was riding on this little gambit, and the risk involved in trying it was so very great. What if the creatures who lived in the ainniq really could smell human thoughts, or hear them, or whatever? He knew that in the past manned ships had sometimes come back into safespace with the crew all dead. It didn't happen a lot anymore, but the odds were still there that it might. What if his little game skewed the odds enough to turn this into a doomed flight?

*Shit.* He called up a few drops of sedative to still his nerves. It bothered him, how much this was getting to him. The girls got scared like this often enough, that's how they were, but him? Fine example he was setting.

Then he felt the ship shudder, and a sound that was not quite a sound reverberated along his nerve endings. Something had grabbed hold of the vessel, he guessed, and was now dragging it along into the belly of a Guild transport. If that were the case, then everyone else on board would be asleep by now, or pretty heavily out of it. He wondered just how alert Allo was, and if he'd bother to check on the headset readings of his passenger. Probably not. He had enough things to worry about on his own . . . like two hours of having his life in the hands of a Guild he hated, who'd probably arrest him on the spot if they knew even half of what his business was about.

*The Guild wants us,* someone whispered. *Why?*

*Time enough to find that out later,* he told her. *On Paradise.*

The ship shuddered again, and this time he could hear something straining against its surface, a low squeal that made his skin crawl. He slid his arms beneath the straps and waited. There were clangs in the distance, which he felt more than heard, and he almost thought there were human voices. Were the Guildfolk that close to the ship, or was he catching the echoes of some kind of public address system? It must have been from something in contact with the hull, he realized, for the compartment Allo's ship was in would have no air in it. No point in air. If they got into trouble while in transit, then no mere evacuation could save them. You either lived or died in the ainniq, period; there was no middle ground.

Better to sleep through that kind of death, he thought grimly.

There was a long time of silence, then, and with a sinking feeling in the pit of his stomach he realized that they were all set to go. MORE SEDATIVE? the wellseeker queried. He told it to go fuck itself. Enough was enough. He needed to have his head free and clear when they got to Paradise, enough so that he could beat out Allo if he had to. And if that meant riding out this thing with his heart beating bruises against the inside of his rib cage, so be it.

The ship jerked.

He caught his breath.

It started to move forward. The sensation was weird, not the kind of thing you usually felt in space travel. If the vessel had been moving on its own, it would have had its own G-web up to compensate for such things, which didn't mean that you wouldn't feel the acceleration, but it would have been . . . well, different, somehow. This was kind of like what you felt on Earth, where all the gravity was natural. Or so Jamisia told him. She was the only one who remembered that sensation.

He felt a cold knot form in the pit of his stomach as the ship moved forward toward the ainniq. Would he know when they entered it? Would he sense the dragons, as it was said they could sense him? Panic started to well up inside him at the thought of lying there, strapped down, while the universe's most deadly predators homed in on him, but he refused to let his wellseeker do anything about it; finally, when it insisted once too often, he shut it down. It wasn't a question of safety, any more, or even common sense, but of sheer masculine pride. He could hardly bitch at the girls for their cowardice and then act like a baby himself, now, could he? He gritted his teeth as the ship jerked again, and he felt a faint queasiness stir in his gut at the *wrongness* of that motion. Safespace shouldn't feel like this. . . .

Passage took an eternity.

Yes, he was sure he could sense things outside the ship: hungry, circling. Maybe it was just his imagination, but that didn't make it any easier to deal with. Worst of all, he could feel every lurch of the small vessel as its outpilot pulled it into one evasive configuration after another. Once he even felt something touch his soul—or so he thought—something colder than the deepest reaches of space, something so horrific that his skin crawled where it brushed against him. He thought for that one moment that he was surely gone, that he had taken one chance too many and was about to pay the price for it. But then the moment was gone, as quickly as it had come. Was that really some life-form of the ainniq, or just his overheated imagination? Sweat was running down from his face in rivulets, pooling on the synthetic mattress beneath him. What if you went into the ainniq awake, and the sheer terror of it drove you insane? Was that why everyone had to be sedated? Was that why no one was allowed to go through this journey with all his senses online? The ship jerked suddenly, so hard that the strap holding his left arm down cut cruelly into flesh. *This was a mistake,* someone wailed. Zusu? "Shut up!" he growled, as another wave of sickness welled up in his gut. Damn it to hell, they needed to be awake, they *had* to be awake, so they should just stop their bitching and deal with it. Another sickening lurch brought hot bile into his throat, and he swallowed back on it, hard. The ship would fly straight for as long as it could, so any time it didn't meant that something was out there. Right? And a series of rapid adjustments of direction and speed, like he was feeling now, could only mean one thing. . . .

He shut his eyes and tried not to think of what was following them. Did they hunt in packs? Did they enjoy the chase? Were they intelligent, or just fast and hungry?

*Some ships don't make it.*

One of the children started crying.

Maybe this had been a mistake.

He shut his eyes and started counting backward from ten thousand . . . which should, if he did it slowly enough, get him to Paradise. More of the children were crying now. He wished he could make them go away. He wished he could do his usual routine and yell at them to shut the fuck up, and they'd do it. But there was too much fear in his own mental voice now for that to work. He had no authority, and he knew it.

Nine thousand . . .

Eight thousand . . .

Seven . . .

A heart-wrenching lurch was followed by what could only be the ship pulling into a sharp turn. Something must be close, very close. His heart was pounding so hard he was surprised it didn't break a rib or something. Sweating profusely, he forced his mind back onto the numbers, envisioning them as he muttered their names. *Six thousand, five hundred and ninety-two . . .* How did the outpilots deal with this? What kind of nerves did those fuckers have, that they could dodge monsters for two whole hours without losing their shit? And this was only a short trip by Guild standards, he knew; some of the trips the Guild ran were more than five hours. How could a human brain handle that?

*They're not human anymore,* someone answered. Verina? *The Hausman Drive warped their brains so they could live in this place. That's why we have to have them for space travel, because no "true human" can manage it.*

He swallowed back on something hot and nasty in his throat and started his counting again. Eternity passed, measured in seconds, stinking of fear. When he finally heard the grating sound of a docking mechanism rubbing against the hull, he practically wet his pants. Which, given the dynamics of being in a female body, would have been really embarrassing.

He waited until the ship stopped moving and all was silent, then began to unclasp the straps that bound him down. The jumpsuit was plastered to his skin along with everything under it, but he hardly noticed. Shit, he just hoped he'd read the signals right and they were really in safespace once more; if not he was about to do something really, really stupid.

He went to the door, listened for a moment, and then opened it. He could sense two or three of the girls looking back, regretting all the stuff they were leaving behind. Souvenirs from teenage high points, memories almost too precious to part with . . . hell, he thought, they knew why it had to stay here. They'd discussed it till they were blue in the face, and all but the children had agreed. If the crew came here and found nothing, they'd know this whole thing was planned. If they came here and found Jamisia's bags instead, and if those bags looked like they were full, then they'd be looking for a young girl running in panic, without change of clothing or other supplies. Big difference.

*It's gotta be this way,* he muttered to someone who was sulking. *Trust me, okay?*

The ship was empty. Still too early for the crew to be about? He moved through it carefully, silently, trying to remember that he was bulkier than usual and couldn't squeeze through small passages like he should be able to. This was the most dangerous part, these first few minutes, but it was a danger he was ready to face; the pounding of his heart energized him now instead of draining him, and adrenaline shot into his brain like a drug. The girls couldn't pull off this kind of shit, he told himself, only he could. It was a heady tonic, being needed that badly. He savored it for a moment, until someone gave him a mental kick and told him to get his mind back on the job at hand. *Fuck you,* he told her, but his voice lacked its usual venom. Because she was right, damn her. This was no time to be enjoying himself.

There was noise from the bridge. He eased toward it, and heard the soft murmur of a voice he thought was Allo's. Okay, that made sense, the man was still awake. He had to bring the ship into port, after all; the Guild transport wouldn't take him that far. Derik listened closely, but there was only silence now; evidently the pilot had started dictating his orders through his headset. All right, all he had to do now was wait—

He heard a sound from the far end of the corridor. Startled, he pressed himself into a service alcove near the bridge and held his breath. Footsteps approached, somewhat unsteady, and he prayed that whoever was making them didn't turn to look to the right as he came down the hall. If so . . .

*Then all is lost,* Zusu mourned.

*Fuck that!* He told her. *Then we fight!*

But the footsteps came within a few feet of him and then turned toward the left, heading in the direction of the bridge. He caught sight of flesh tentacles behind the man, all hanging limp now in the aftermath of his enforced snooze. No one else seemed to be moving on the ship yet, which made sense. Only those who had to be awake would rush the process, it tended to make one weak and disoriented; the rest would take their time.

So far, the plan was still good.

"Tam?" it was Allo's voice. "Calia?"

"Due up in ten."

"The girl?"

"Tam said she'll be out a good two hours more. More than enough time."

"You're optimistic."

"Not at all. I just know how you work."

Someone chuckled.

Derik moved cautiously down the corridor, toward the main door of the ship. There was an air lock which had been wide open when he first came aboard, but it was shut tight now to keep out the vacuum of space. He'd have to wait until that was unsealed, otherwise they'd catch him in it while it cycled him out. That was no good.

His pulse was a drumbeat, a soundtrack, like music. He felt weirdly like he was in some viddie, instead of in real life. An action viddie. He sure hoped the bloody scenes weren't coming up yet, that would be no fun at all.

He waited.

There was a viewscreen beside the door. He watched as they approached the station proper—God, it was *immense*—and held his breath as Allo and Sumi maneuvered them past the main docking ring, toward one of the subsidiaries. That was okay, he was prepared for that, too. There were six of them in all, circling about the main body of the station like the electron rings of an ancient nuclear symbol. He waited until they headed toward one in particular and then made sure Raven saw the symbol that was on it. God willing she was doing her job in there, because soon enough they'd be depending on her. This wasn't the kind of job one person could pull off.

The small ship approached an open dock, brimming with blinking lights. He could hear voices conversing on the bridge, probably Allo trading details of their route with an operator on Paradise, but he couldn't make out what they were saying. It didn't matter. Soon enough they'd be on solid flooring again, and he could make his break for it.

The mouth of the dock was narrow, hardly larger than the ship. Obviously it wasn't taking them to the kind of open dock they'd been in before, but a less wasteful space. Air cost money, after all. Some kind of track rose up from beneath them and grabbed hold of the small vessel, and clamps came at it from the sides. He could hear the engines shut down as they took over the work of driving the ship forward. He dared to draw in a deep breath, exhaling slowly. So far so good. They were sliding down into a flickering darkness, like some kind of bizarre amusement ride. If he'd been in less danger, he might have enjoyed watching it, but as it was, he only had eyes for the sign above the air lock. *Caution*, it warned. *Lock sealed. Pressurize before opening inner door.*

And then they stopped. There was a dull thudding noise against the wall of the ship, a faint vibration, and then nothing. He held his breath. Would they open the lock now, or let it stay closed until they needed it? If the latter, then he'd have to take a chance and break the seals himself. He waited as long as he could stand to wait, reached out to the control panel . . . and then forced himself to wait some more. Now was not the time to do something stupid.

There was someone else awake on the ship now, approaching the bridge; he could hear the sound of footsteps. Damn. He'd thought he'd have more time than this. What if he wound up having to fight them after all?

A hiss by his side made him jump. The bright red sign overhead flashed to yellow, then green. The lock on the inner door popped open. He hesitated only an instant. The voices on the bridge were louder now, and he thought he heard one of them coming his way. He couldn't get the outer door opened that fast, not by himself. With a pounding heart he ducked into a nearby service access, high-heeled shoes digging into his thigh as he pressed himself into the small space.

It was Calia. Just his luck, the one who hated Terrans the most. She came and checked the lock, opened it, then moved beyond it to the outer door. After a moment he heard the whir of a motor, and alien light spread into the corridor. He heard no voices from beyond the door, which meant they were probably in some kind of transitional space; the ring itself would be noisy.

He found himself holding his breath as she turned back to the bridge, and started to move as soon as she was out of sight. All right, if he did this right, they wouldn't even realize he was gone for an hour or more—

He did it right.

She didn't.

She had forgotten something in the lock, or something she had to do, or . . . well, something that involved turning back the moment he moved out into the open. He heard her gasp and curse beneath her breath even as he reached the threshold of the ship. *Shit.* Was she armed? Would she shoot him? He took off across the portal with a force that carried him halfway down the loading ramp in one step; thank God, the ring was lo-G.

The chamber beyond was maybe twenty feet long, with an iris portal at the far end. He was willing to bet it would open automatically when approached from this side. In fact, he was willing to bet his life on it. He tried not to think about the frenzied messages that were flashing through the ship's innernet as he ran, or the fact that the two men were bigger and probably stronger and faster than the body he was stuck in. Damn it to hell, he was doing the best he could! Calia was coming after him, he could hear it. He threw himself toward the door—

And it opened! It opened for him and he bolted through. Calia was still far enough behind that it began to close behind him— she'd probably stayed behind for a second to report Derik's flight to the others—and that was great, it was the break that he'd needed. Slamming into some tourist who clearly didn't expect to be blindsided, he used the impact to halt his forward progress and turned to the side. And he ran. He ran as if his life depended on it. He ran as if he was some stupid girl who thought that running would save her, a stupid Earthie who didn't realize that by doing so she made herself ten times more conspicuous—

Okay, the door was opening again, he could hear it. Let it. He turned down a side corridor and dropped out of sight before any of his would-be captors could catch sight of him. Sure, one of the touristas would point him out . . . when they pulled themselves together enough to stop sputtering in anger and be helpful. That could take seconds.

*Where is it?* he asked Raven.

She flashed him a section of station map. She'd inloaded it all while they were on the ship; this time they wouldn't be fleeing blind. He took a quick turn at the next fourway, praying that they hadn't yet gotten close enough to see where he was going. All he needed was a few hundred feet, and he was home clear.

Maybe.

Passersby were staring at him as he ran by. Fine, that couldn't be helped. *Where is it?* he demanded of Raven. *Where's the nearest one?* She whispered directions into his ear, and he ran—

and turned a corner and slowed to a normal pace, albeit hurried, so that no one in that corridor saw anything amiss—

and passed by the first washroom door, cursing the *occupied* sign overhead. The second was free, and he struck it with his hand, as if there was really a human operator who might hear the urgency in his knock and open up faster. The door slid open slowly. He squeezed inside and slammed his hand on the lock, wishing he could will it to move faster. They had to not see him come in here, or all was lost. . . .

As soon as the door was shut, he began to strip. The heavy jumpsuit came off, and with it his few spare belongings. The metallic skirt he wore beneath it swung free with a shimmering sound, likewise the short-cropped blouse he wore on top. He kicked his shoes off with the jumpsuit and fumbled in the pocket to get Jamisia's dress shoes out. Right about now they would have figured they'd lost him and be asking questions . . . would they stand guard outside the washrooms? Hide someone by the nearest corner to watch without being seen? There were more than a dozen washrooms in a row, they'd have no way of knowing which ones were right or wrong until someone came out. He had to get out of his before all the others were emptied.

He rolled up the jumpsuit around his lo-G shoes and stuffed the whole package into a collapsable purse he'd brought along.

All that was left was the hair. He tried not to look in the mirror as he brought up the safety knife and snapped it open, one of the girls would probably just get upset and start bawling if he did. He started cutting by feel, hacking away at the thick copper tresses. *Hair grows. Deal with it.* The dispose-all was open and he threw the discarded locks into it handful by handful, hearing it grind up the pride of Jamie's womanhood. No one said a word. They all knew how much this mattered, apparently. Good. Finally he had to look in the mirror to finish the job.

It was short, downright stubby, and far from even. That was fine. He paid for some water—it took his last cash chit—and ran wet hands through what was left of his hair. Thus soaked, it turned a darker brown, far less conspicuous, and made weird little spiked shapes all over his head. Good. He hesitated, trying to sense just how much time he'd used up. How many cubicles had been emptied so far, how few were left for them to watch? If he came out of the last one, it wouldn't matter what he looked like, they'd know there was something wrong. He reached into the bag for a small container of silver powder—

And Katlyn took over, *thank you very much, this is no place for a man anymore.* Two swipes with a finger streaked metallic silver across her brow, nothing more or less than her outfit deserved. She slid her feet into the lo-G shoes—strappy little things with high, high heels, the kind of thing no sane girl would wear in *real* gravity—took one deep breath, and opened the door.

No one was waiting.

No one she could *see.*

She sauntered forth with all the arrogance of a woman who had nothing to hide, and fell into step with the throngs of tourists who filled the corridor. Her bag hung at her side, with all her meager belongings stuffed into it. Her skirt was a thing of glittering mesh, hi-G in design, and she'd rolled it up at the waist so that its hem was crotch-high. The grav in the ring was just low enough that it rode up with each step, hinting at treasures not well enough hidden. Likewise with the cropped top, riding up high enough with each bouncing step that the round underside of a breast was just visible. She smiled as she walked, falling into a gait that would accentuate the movement of both. No one would be looking at her face, that was for sure. God, she loved hi-G clothing.

She didn't look for Allo and his crew. She didn't look for anyone. She looked for signs of where she was going, and tried to keep in mind always that she *was* someone, she *belonged* somewhere. If they looked her straight in the eye, they'd probably realize who she was, but she was willing to bet they wouldn't look that closely. She was willing to bet they thought she was still running from them, or hiding somewhere, or doing something else in which she looked just like herself, wearing that stupid jumpsuit. A search of her room on the ship by now would have revealed the fact that she'd left her bags behind along with all her clothing, and they had no way to know that she'd chosen a few items from them before stowing them away for passage. Just enough to get by. That was crucial, that they would think she bolted in terror without thinking this thing through. They would look for a frightened animal, and thus would be searching in vain—because she wasn't that, not anymore.

That was the plan, anyway.

Tourists passed her on all sides—or maybe Paradise natives— and her glittering party outfit was hardly noticeable in that context. She'd counted on that. Raven had inloaded all sorts of visual data on Paradise, and she and Katlyn had studied it before coming up with this costume. Dressed like this she would be downright inconspicuous in the station's overdressed crowds . . . or so she hoped.

So far, so good.

A pair of women passed by her wearing nothing but bodysuits, one painted with swirls of rainbow colors and the other covered with vast, staring eyes. Someone else wore a headdress of synthetic feathers (now *those* must have cost a small fortune), that cascaded down around her shoulders and breasts and offered minimal compliance with decency laws. Something with six breasts held hands with a nine-foot-tall creature who had something alive wrapped around his loins—she didn't look too closely at that—and a crowd of tiny Variant women, no taller than her waist, ran down the corridor with a bouncing step that set their crystalline headsets jingling. All in all it was a crowd of humanity and unhumanity that made Reijik Station look downright empty by contrast, and all of it was colorful and bright and visually audacious. Including her.

Then she turned a corner and saw Allo.

She almost stopped walking—almost turned back the way she'd come—but no, they'd be looking for such a pattern of movement. And there was no telling who was behind her now, watching for it. With pounding heart she moved into the crowd heading toward him, wondering just how good her disguise was. It wouldn't pass close inspection, she knew that, she'd just hoped it would buy her time while she lost herself in the crowd. She paused at a display of food items, tried to look hungry, and then turned away from him as if to inspect its wares. She had bet everything on the fact that they wouldn't assume her to have managed such a complete change of look so quickly; if they did, and were looking closely at the faces that passed them, this outfit wouldn't help her at all.

Shifting her weight from leg to leg, she leaned over slightly at the waist to peruse something on a lower shelf. Her skirt didn't have a lot of clearance for that kind of maneuver, and she knew it. She sensed a couple of tourists stopping behind her, heard their smiling whispers. Men. They were so funny, so predictable. They could pass by a dozen nudes and not pay attention to one, but hit them with a piece of clothing that *might* slip out of place and their eyes became riveted. It must be some evolutionary thing, survival of the fittest and all that; maybe from the days when a woman in a fur sarong *might* have been hiding an extra banana or two beneath her wrap, whereas a nude offered no food at all. She giggled to herself and leaned down a little lower, enjoying the game. Too bad she couldn't really buy food, but the water had taken up the last of her cash, and she could hardly use her debit chip now. Or her headset. Or anything, in fact, but her brain.

After some time had passed, she turned away with a sigh— *not hungry after all*—and glanced surreptitiously at where Allo had stood. He was gone. The knot that had been forming in her chest started to unwind, and she had to remind herself, *Be careful. He may still be around here somewhere.* But it was a good omen, at least. Sometimes you needed omens.

She walked. Far, far, following instructions whispered to her by Raven, confirmed by consensus of all the Others. Walked with a swinging gait that spoke of sex and leisure and wealth and said nothing of fear and flight. Men smiled at her as she passed. Some women, also, and a few creatures whose sex she wasn't too sure of. She smiled back at all of them. *A creature of pleasure am I, inhabitant of this lovely station, addicted to its many delights.* Three corridors became five, became ten, and at last she began to relax. They couldn't have followed her this far. They couldn't get help from the authorities either, no matter what story they came up with to explain themselves, because their own business was so suspect they just couldn't risk the contact.

At last she took a side corridor to where the flyways were anchored. It was going to be a hell of a flight in this outfit, but that couldn't be helped; she could hardly change clothes here. She kicked her shoes off so at least she could get some traction if she needed it, then ducked into the circular portal and gave herself a good shove to start. It was a public flyway, wide enough for a dozen support lines in each direction, and travelers grinned or smirked or shook their heads at her as she went by. Well, that's what happened when you wore G-dependent clothing in a free zone; she hoped they enjoyed the show. She rather enjoyed the shock on their faces herself, and was willing to bet that if questioned later, they, too, would not remember what her face looked like. Oh, had she worn scarlet underwear? That must have been a mistake, how could she choose anything so bright . . . ?

The flyway brought her to an inner ring, from which point a free tube took her down to the station itself. Raven had all the maps of Paradise organized for this journey, and she brought them up one by one into Katlyn's field of vision as she walked. God, but she was tired; the journey, the tension, and the pressure of the heeled shoes were bleeding all the strength from her body. She was hungry, too, and wished she could afford food. The tube let her off in a mall that was ringed with delicacies, but no cash meant no food. At least until her financial problems were dealt with.

For a moment she just stood in the middle of the mall, hardly able to absorb all that had happened to her. People rushed by on every side of her: adults, children, humans. Variants. All going somewhere, all doing something. She should have been over-whelmed by the chaos of it all, but she wasn't. She was over-whelmed by something else.

She had *made* it.

Her enemies were behind her. They didn't know where she was. If she'd played her cards right, then even the Guild didn't know where she was . . . thanks in part to Allo and his crew. God alone knew why the Guerans wanted her so badly, but for the time being she didn't have to find out. She had lost herself in a crowd of millions, and if she was careful enough they'd never pick up her trail again.

All right, so she didn't have food or friends, money, shelter, or any of the other hundred-and-some-odd things you needed to get along. But those could be acquired, in time. Safety couldn't. Safety was a prerequisite to all other achievements.

And she had managed that.

Tired, hungry, she asked Raven for the map for the next phase of her journey and started walking. It was only four miles on foot to the place she needed, and that was a distance she could manage. When she got out of the shopping district, she'd change her shoes to make walking easier, and after that she should be all right. The hi-G of the station proper was hard on five-inch heels.

Safe. She was safe. The word had a strange taste in her mouth, as she whispered it aloud to make it seem more real. She was safe, and in control, and for the first time since leaving the metroliner she actually thought she might manage to get through all this somehow. It was a new feeling, and a strangely refreshing one. Hopefully, if she nurtured it right, it would en-dure.

With a sigh of resignation—and a faint growl of hunger in her stomach—she began to walk toward the less prosperous districts.

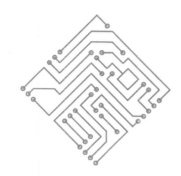

The propensity of young men to engage in mischief is increased many times with each new advance in technology. Those devices which seem to us a remarkable convenience are to them no more than new and delightful toys, whose disruption is merely one more way for them to test their young and rebellious spirits against the tenets of established Authority.

HAROLD E. RUTHERFORD, ESQ.
*The Perils of Progress: a Warning Against the New Telephonic Machines and Other Modern Contrivances.* (Historical Archives, Hellsgate Station)

# PARADISE NODE
# PARADISE STATION

**S**LEEP. PHOENIX vaguely remembered it. That was something you did when you didn't have a virus dancing inside your head, right? Something you did when there was no pressing business.

If such a time had ever existed. If it ever would again.

He was obsessed, but that was okay. There was a gene for obsession, and all the hackers had it. He could measure his own by the crumpled packages of instant food that littered the floor around his workbench. Wrappers from Energee! bars, shredded envelopes of Lo-Munch, boxes of some godforsaken soft drink that he was currently addicted to, the straws sticking out like Veridian eye stalks. He couldn't remember eating any of it, but that was normal for him. Food was fuel, nothing more, and at times like this he paid no more attention to it than you would pay to the compressed fuel you put into your pod.

The virus was all.

He could see why Chaos had been obsessed with it. He could even see why she had let it into her head, and Torch also. It was just that good. Sometimes he would reach out with his hand to the monitor as if he could touch the thing, wanting to run his virtual fingers across its surface, hungering to fold it and turn it and manipulate it as only the mind's eye could do, to see what made it tick. But that was suicide, plain and simple. He'd already sent out a warning to the other stations about what this thing could do, and how they should never, *ever*, let their people inload it. How could he make the very same mistake he was warning them against?

But he wanted to. He wanted to so badly.

With a sigh he reached out for the nearest drink box, cursing softly when he found it to be empty. At times like this he resented the five steps between his workbench and the chiller. He picked up another one from the shelf over his desk and forced himself to move, cramped muscles emphatic in their protest as he crossed the small room and opened the chiller door. Five seconds was all it would take to make the stuff palatable, so he set the chiller for that, put the drink box inside, and let it do its stuff. Five seconds. You could skip a message to Hellsgate in that much time. You could push the button that set off a cascade of destructive programs and watch their effect. You could feel the bite of a foreign virus in your head and know yourself doomed, you could feel the panic rising as your brain shut down, bit by bit, and have time to imagine what the end result would be. . . .

Five seconds was a long time, in his world. He hated to waste it.

He shook the box when it came out of the chiller, to even the temperature, and then pierced it and took a deep drink. The contents were a sugar-and-stim mix, disguised with a little food coloring and a dollop of some weird synthetic flavor. The taste wasn't a thrill, but the coldness of it chilled his tongue as it went down, and it felt good. He drank it all, then crushed the box in his hand and threw it toward the recycler. It missed. No surprise there. His attention was already on the monitor once more, and the monster that lurked behind it. Perhaps if this time he tried one of Chaos' testing sequences . . .

The pattern that was on his monitor suddenly disappeared and a square of white light took its place.

*Fuck.*

He stared at it for a few seconds, waiting for it to resolve itself. When you processed as much illegal shit as he did, sometimes glitches just happened. He even hit the side of the monitor once, in a strategy as old as mankind himself, to see if that would clear the problem.

No dice.

With a muttered curse he flashed his brainware an instruction to come online again, and started feeding it the control codes that would reclaim his system. Someone was screwing with his stuff, that was clear, and it had damn well better not be one of his own people. Or rather, he thought grimly, it had better *be* one of his own people, because if this was some stranger fucking with his system, he'd better kiss his own 'ware good-bye right now—

Numbers appeared in the center of the screen. 10 first, then 9, then 8 . . . the pattern was clear. He watched the countdown with a mixture of annoyance and real frustration. Goddam whoever was pulling this shit, if he actually screwed up any of Phoenix's work. The only thing worse than a war between hackers and the government was a sniping vendetta between hackers themselves.

Then: 0. The dot exploded into a circle of black smoke, which in turn became a rising column, which in turn became capped with a thick mushroom head that spread across his screen—

—which answered the question about who it was, anyway.

He flashed up the icons needed to send a message to him. FUCK YOU, MAN.

The mushroom cloud faded from his screen and block letters appeared instead. IS THIS A MONITOR I SEE? WHATCHA, PROGRAMMING FOR DINOSAURS NEXT?

He flashed back: JUST SENDING OUT VIRUSES TO GUYS WHO PISS ME OFF.

OOOOH, I AM SOOOO SCAAAAARED.

Despite himself, he smiled. It was hard, really hard to hate Nuke. The guy was an irritant extraordinaire, but so was half of Phoenix's crowd. It came with the territory. Still, he really did want to get back to that virus, and he wasn't all that comfortable with having someone else access his system while it was in there.

IS THERE A POINT TO THIS?

POINT? UH. YEAH. POINT . . . A frowning face appeared on the screen. I THINK SO. . . .

CUT THE SHIT, MAN.

OOH. BAD MOOD. NO NEW PROJECT FOR YOU, P. I'LL GO FIND SOMEONE ELSE. . . .

LIKE HELL YOU WILL. WHAT'S UP?

There was a long pause. He knew Nuke well enough to know what that signified, that the subject being discussed might really be serious. He leaned closer to the screen.

SOMETHING IN FROM DOCKING RING GREEN. RIGHT UP YOUR ALLEY.

He frowned. That was one of the inner rings, dedicated to smaller ships. It handled mostly local traffic, pods from the many habitats in Paradise, smaller shipments from nearby stations . . . and smaller ships that wanted to slip into Paradise unnoticed. Customs kept a close watch on Green, but not close enough; it was a known fact that half the contraband that passed through the waystation came in through the juncture. So if something was happening out there that was interesting enough for a hacker to contact Phoenix . . . interesting enough for him to hack all the overrides that protected Phoenix's current work, so that he could take over the monitor screen for com use . . . that might be worth sparing a minute to hear about. Maybe even more than a minute, depending on what it was.

SO WHAT IS IT?

Numbers scrolled across his field of vision, flashes of code, commands in English. Halfway through, he realized he hadn't put his recorder back online, and cursed the loss of all that had come before as he did so.

SLOWER, OKAY? WHAT THE HELL IS THAT CRAP ANYWAY?

DON'T RECOGNIZE IT? SHAME ON YOU. The frowning face stuck out its tongue. IT'S EARTH CODE FOR DAMN IMPORTANT SHIT, IS WHAT IT IS. IT TURNED UP ON A FINANCE CHIP.

Finance? He ran the last section of code before his eyes again, then stiffened as he saw where this was heading. WHERE DID YOU GET IT?

GIRL FROM REIJIK NODE. NEWBIE, I THINK. PAYING FIVE THOUSAND FOR ME TO DOCTOR THE CHIP FOR A CLEAN WITHDRAWAL. ODDS 50–50 RIGHT NOW FOR ME, I FIGURE. I KNOW YOU SPECIALIZE IN THIS KIND OF THING.

He considered carefully before responding. I COULD DO IT.

WOW. REALLY? HEY, MAYBE THAT'S WHY I COMMED YOU?

He ignored the sarcasm. WHERE ARE YOU NOW?

95 BAY WEST, 36C. The address was false, of course; one never knew when the law was listening in. The real address was in the code he'd been sent, next to a marker Phoenix would find later. YOU COMING?

MAYBE.

MAKE IT FAST. THIS ONE'S HOT.

THE CHIP OR THE GIRL?

YES.

Then the face was gone from his screen, and the words also, and in its place the slow and stately dance of the foreign virus had begun once more. He watched it for a minute and then muttered "Damn!" He knew he'd been hooked, and good. How like Nuke to give him barely enough data to draw him into something, too little for him to assess the possible risks—or rewards—without showing up himself. Damn it all, the guy lived halfway across the waystation. Why couldn't they just 'net this stuff back and forth, like sane people?

With a sigh he saved all his work, picked up his backpack, and ordered his grayware to decode the directions he'd been sent. *This had better be good.*

It was three tubes, two flyways, and a damn long walk to where Nuke was holed up. Or a docking tram, if you had the money. That was the problem with 'netting for a living. You could be working with people halfway across the node for all you knew, which was fine until you had to have lunch with them or something . . . then it was a bitch and a half. He started toward the tram and then his wellseeker kicked in, reminding him that he got *so* little exercise these days, and didn't he think that once, *just once*, he could do the right thing for himself and walk a little? He could hardly object to its nagging, since he'd programmed it himself, and with a wry smile he set off on a hike along the periphery of Paradise. At least the guy was on the same station as Phoenix; give thanks for small blessings.

The address that had been sent to him was on the waystation proper, near the middle of one of the vast public malls that encased Paradise like a colorful candy shell. Whatever had come in on Docking Ring Green to find Nuke, it had traveled a long way since then. Phoenix took a crowded public tube to the proper level and then made his way through the familiar chaos of ten thousand locals and a hundred thousand tourists, all shopping at once. Anyone living on Paradise was used to such a press of crowds, and to the buzz of a station net overloaded with local traffic. He'd been down in the processor chamber once—strictly illegally, of course—and knew from that experience just how much equipment had been dedicated to tourist services alone. Which was what kept Paradise afloat, of course, when several hundred rivals had sunk under their own weight. Paradise knew that data flow was the lifeblood of any station, and made sure that the riff-raff chatter of its million daily visitors didn't jam the channels that were needed for legitimate business. Phoenix flashed an icon that would segue him to a private channel, and could almost feel the signal speed up as he did so. One nanosecond instead of two. Any hacker could sense it.

SO WHERE THE FUCK ARE YOU? he sent.

There was a momentary delay—Nuke must have been working on something in his own head, usually he kept the com link open otherwise—and then the answer came. WHERE THE FUCK ARE *YOU?*

He looked around, at the stores surrounding him, the holo ads flickering brightly above, the distant flash of a directional sign. MATA HARI CONCOURSE, BY SOME BIG ARCADE.

THERE ARE FIVE ARCADES ON MATA HARI.

He muttered a picturesque curse under his breath and looked for a more helpful sign, trying to make out details among the hundred or so flashing advertisements that competed for attention in the airspace over the arcade. As he did, he heard someone inside the arcade suddenly squeal in delight, and a blast of holo rockets took off from the roof, blinding all who watched for several annoying seconds. BIG WINNER—BIG WINNER—BIG WINNER flashed overhead, drowning out everything else. Already the mall police were moving in to guard whomever it was that had hit whatever jackpot . . . she'd have to pay them off later for their service, but that was only to be expected. You wouldn't last five minutes in a mall like this, with that kind of cash in your account.

Finally he just visualized the façade of the arcade, and hoped that Nuke would recognize it. Apparently he did.

THAT'S CAESAR'S DEN. GOOD, YOU'RE CLOSE. HEAD WEST FROM WHERE YOU ARE . . . HERE.

A map sketched itself out line by line in Phoenix's head, which meant that Nuke was creating it for him, not just flashing him something from storage. He responded with an affirmative icon, lidded his eyes halfway to shut out the worst of the visual distractions, and began to follow the route indicated.

It was no big surprise that he was soon squeezing between the gaudy tourist shops and gambling dens, to the narrow service corridors which lurked behind them. Autobots rumbled by him, their armored exteriors marked with a small shield which guaranteed that not even a thief with a death wish would try to break into them. All the denizens of the vast station—low-life, high-life, and everything in between—knew better than to screw with the businesses that kept Mama Ra happy. You saw her sigil on a bundle of merchandise, and it was strictly hands off from then on. Which meant, of course, that the small shields with their engraved Guild-sign were themselves worth a bundle . . . but a girl had to make her profit somehow, right? Paradise Station was big enough and free enough that there was something on it to make everyone happy, and its grateful tenants policed their own.

The 'bots drove by him, delivering rare foodstuffs to the back doors of restaurants, precious gems to legal and illegal jewelers . . . whatever. He stepped aside to keep them from having to slow down as they maneuvered around him. It was a passing token of respect to the woman who ruled them all. Why not? Paradise was a haven for moddies, and he'd been in enough places that weren't to appreciate what that meant.

A narrow and low-ceilinged avenue gave access to an open space that must have once been meant for storage; certainly it had not been designed for the ragtag assortment of cubicles that had since been stuffed into it. He didn't even want to know what some of them were here for. The place looked much the same as his own street, truth be told, but he was willing to bet that here, this close to the center of tourist activity, there were far darker goings-on than ever took place in his sector.

The map indicated a door to his left and then blinked out as he put his hand to the lock. Apparently it had been programmed to accept him, for it opened even before the person inside could put a hand to it.

"Hey, Phoenix." A hand clasp of ritual warmth welcomed him into a dark and somewhat cluttered abode. An office, he guessed, rather than a home, and probably not Nuke's own. There was too much shit around that wasn't hacker stuff, and he knew from his time on the net that this guy lived, breathed, ate, and probably even dreamed on the outernet. He'd met Nuke several times before, and always in a place like this, filled with someone else's stuff. Maybe the guy didn't even have a real home, Phoenix mused. It was possible. There was a waiting list a mile long for apartments on Paradise Station, and it wasn't like you couldn't manage to live without one if you had to. Especially if you had enough friends . . . or did enough favors for people that friends weren't necessary.

"What's this all about?"

Nuke nodded toward a back door, a cryptic smile on his face. He was pale, pale as the bundles of fiberoptic that coursed through the central processor chamber; you could almost see the veins pulsing blue beneath his eyes and along the side of his neck. No solar chambers for this boy. "She's in the back room. I'll introduce you in a minute. What did you think of that stuff I sent you?"

"Damned nasty security shit. That was on her chip?"

"Those were the gateway programs. You haven't even seen what was beyond that yet." He glanced toward the back of the room, where the door to the next room waited. "I don't think she knows. Which means . . . shit. Someone programmed all that for her and then didn't tell her?"

"Maybe it's stolen." He said it in a matter-of-fact tone, not much caring whether it was true or not. Theft might complicate this job a bit, but he'd never let a factor like that affect whether or not he took on the project. Leave that to the politicos, who had to pretend they had morals.

"Don't think so. No proof there, just a gut feeling." Nuke reached down for a drink box on the table beside him and sipped it dry of its last few drops. It looked like it had been around for quite some time. "Doesn't look like the type."

He smiled dryly. "Oh, and you're a great judge of women?"

"You'll see. Trust me."

"So how did she find you?"

"Pawn sector in Green. Not a bad move, actually. Hinted around that she needed some help with unusual programming, someone adaptable, capable of dealing with equipment that had been, well, sorta modified . . . like you might find in one of those shops." He grinned. "I don't think she knew how loaded that word is around here . . . but anyway, Petroy put her in touch with me."

"Shit, she could be a Pol."

"Petroy didn't think so. I trust him. Besides, she was subtle, that's an after-the-fact summation. Never told anyone what she wanted, just let them understand that she needed . . . one of us. They figured it out."

"So they sent her here? Sheesh. Real discreet, those guys."

"You don't deal with them a lot. I do. Sometimes interesting business comes in that way . . . hey, some of us really do earn a living, you know? How do you think I find clients?"

*Clients.* Jesus, that was a laugh. His amusement must have shown on his face, for Nuke's own colored a bit. "Hey, some of us have a real business, you know?"

He put up his hands in a no-contest gesture. If that was what Nuke wanted to call his online games, so be it. They all had their own pretty names for what they did. He himself was on the Yellow List as a *Technology Consultant.*

"So does she know I'm helping you?"

"Ah . . . sorta . . ."

"And sorta not. Okay. So why does she think I'm here? Just passing by and stopped in to say hello . . . and oh, do you happen to have any high-security debit chips lying around that I could glance at while I'm here?"

"More or less, yeah."

"Jesus." He shook his head in amazement. "You really are something. All right, show it to me."

"Don't you want to see the girl first?"

For a moment he just stared at him. Then he realized that Nuke was right. Of course he would want to see the girl first. That was the human thing to do, wasn't it? "Sure."

She was in a back room, nursing a drink box of her own. She stood up when they entered, with a kind of awkward politeness that spoke volumes for her lack of experience in this kind of situation. Whatever she'd come to the moddies for, it was pretty clear she'd never done this kind of thing before. Or dealt with this kind of people, he was willing to bet.

"Hey, Kandra, this is a friend of mine. Phe . . . Michal." He stifled a grin at his own near-carelessness as he substituted Phoenix's real name for his outernet monikker. The name wasn't something kept a close secret in their crowd, but it wasn't something he'd want to advertise to every stranger either. THE NAME ON THE CHIP IS JAMISIA CAPRA, he flashed to Phoenix. Phoenix shrugged. If she wanted to use an alias, what the hell. He had several himself—including the one he was now using—and at least half a dozen he'd had to retire because they had a criminal record attached to them. That was the price of being too careless in your youth.

Damn, Nuke had been right about the girl. She was lean and leggy and dressed in some hi-G getup that didn't hide very much. The fabric was a metal mesh with lots of little holes in it, and he found himself forcing his eyes away from her bustline, where primitive male instinct urged him to search for a hint of rouged flesh at the tips of her breasts. It was a strange response to have—he could stare at nudes any day he wanted, down at the bathhouses—but sometimes the primitive parts of your brain sent out messages that had nothing to do with logic. Which was why he generally preferred cold circuitry.

He forced his eyes up to her face and saw that she really was very pretty. Rotten haircut, though. *Really* rotten haircut. What world had considered that a decent style, he wondered. He'd bet she had really pretty eyes when all that silver shit was wiped off; it was hard to focus on them as it was. Strange, how there was no heavy makeup on the rest of her face. It seemed . . . wrong, somehow.

"Michal's good at this kind of thing," Nuke was saying.

She was a little nervous, he could see that. Probably never did anything like this before. Maybe she was worried that these two unknown guys would take advantage of their isolation, and . . . *yeah, right*. The thought was almost laughable. Still, it was the kind of thought she inspired. Nuke was right, he thought; she was hot.

"Mind if he takes a look?"

She hesitated, then shook her head.

With a brief look of triumph Nuke handed Phoenix the chip. "She'd like to get to her money without the transaction being traced," he said. His voice made it clear that he had his doubts about whether the money was hers in the first place . . . but that went without saying. He nodded toward a little nook in the back corner of the room, which Phoenix could use to work in. Unlike the rest of the apartment, that one spot was clean: a desk without drawers, with the bare essentials of illegal programming arranged upon its surface. Phoenix ignored all that shit and uploaded the chip directly into his head, figuring he had enough safety programs there to handle whatever this thing might have on it. ICON ONLY, he told his internal systems; now they would accept his instructions, but load nothing from the foreign chip into his brainware. It was what Chaos probably tried to do with that killer virus thing, and Warrior also. Usually it worked, and he generally took its efficiency for granted, but in the wake of their deaths he felt a small stirring of nervousness in his own stomach as the chip's security program began to scroll across his field of vision. Damn it all, you couldn't let something like this get to you. If you did, you'd wind up in front of a monitor twenty-four hours a day, and that was no way to work. He might as well make his appointment at the terminal recycling center now and save himself the suffering.

He walked over to the alcove and sat himself down on the worn mock-leather seat, shut his eyes, and let the program take over. In the distance he could hear Nuke talking to the girl, her answers voiced in soft murmurs, volume low enough so that she wouldn't disturb Phoenix's concentration. Nuke knew better. Nuke knew that when Phoenix was working on something, the whole damn station could come down around his ears and he wouldn't know it.

The security on the chip was heavy, all right. Anyone trying to use it illegally—even someone with moderate hacking skills—was certain to trip over one part or another. He nearly got caught himself, in an intricate loop-the-loop of passwords and protocol. Periodically he needed information, but rather than stop what he was doing he flashed the question to Nuke, who got an answer from the girl and flashed it back to him. Once she had to flash him something herself, a personal icon embedded in the program. The voice recognition part was especially interesting, with a section of cadence-recognition that was easily ten times the length and complexity of anything he'd ever seen before. He couldn't figure out the point of it, but it was well done. The whole thing was well done. Whoever did this girl's programming knew his stuff, and it was a good half hour before he felt confident enough in his control of the chip to move on to the next part of the job.

Nuke had left his notes online, and Phoenix retrieved them. The first problem was that the money was on Earth, which meant that some outstation bank was going to have to make the transfer and then get reimbursed. All of which would take a good three months, allowing for round-trip transmission to that backwater planet. So under normal circumstances, that kind of transfer was going to carry ten times the security of an outworld transaction, which could be confirmed and reconfirmed in seconds. Okay, that he could deal with. The chip was programmed to route through the First Bank of United Terra, which apparently had an office on the Guild's outstation. Now *that* must have cost a pretty penny. He rode the skip into there and poked around a bit, making sure that its security wasn't any more or less than a normal financial office would have. It was, actually— quite a bit more—but not state-of-the-art stuff, more like dinosaur programs that overlapped in function, messy and wasteful bits of programming that had apparently accumulated for centuries without being cleaned up. Well, that was Earth for you. Normally, when he worked the skip, he had to be triply careful, because that meant a delay of a few real-time seconds, which was enough time for a security program to nail you, but this stuff wasn't even alert enough to take advantage of that.

When he thought he had the lay of the land—and had assigned his password programs to start testing combinations for a few things he was going to need access to—he decided to take a look at the account itself. Security wouldn't let him get into it without a good deal more work, but he could probably pick up enough peripheral data to tell him how hard the job would be. He didn't use the girl's chip to get in, but lifted the data he needed and chose a route of his own. It was always safer that way. He found an accounting program running on automatic, that would let him scan the numbers in her account without letting him change them. Good enough for now. He gave it her account code.

—And every single alarm system he had, from the wires in his head to the nerves twined around them to the primitive instinct of *turn and flee*, went off simultaneously. He trusted his own instincts well enough to know that meant something nasty was coming down the line, and he broke off contact as quickly as he could, dumping all the code he'd pieced together on the way in. Even that wasn't fast enough, and he knew it. The skip delay meant he was seconds behind whatever was going on, and only the fact that it was coming from another node gave him any time at all to save himself.

He had routed through Reijik Node on the way in, just for safety. Now he cut that trail short. Even as he did so, he could sense a powerful security sniffer searching for some sign of him, and he nearly tripped over it as he raced to erase the clues it might use to find him. He'd been careful—he was *always* careful—but he also had known that he wasn't yet doing anything that should excite this kind of attention, so he had been . . . well, maybe a little overconfident. Just a bit. He could feel his body sitting rigid in its chair now, and somewhere in the distance Nuke was asking him, "P? What's wrong?" He didn't answer. It took every neuron he had to think as fast as the damned thing that was tracking him, and to stay one step ahead of it.

At last he got it trapped in a logic loop on Reijik. It would figure that out in a minute or two and get itself freed, but at least that gave him time to maneuver. He made up a trail leading back to one of the public gateway programs, and from there sent out a thousand false leads that would bounce around on automatic until something caught up with them. Let the sniffer burn itself out on that job for a while. He took his time making damned sure then that every trace which could lead back to him was erased, and that the path documenting the erasure was erased, and so on and so forth until the constriction in his chest eased and he could breathe freely again. Damn, that was close.

"I'm okay," he croaked. Not knowing if it was an hour or

merely minutes since Nuke had asked him the question. His throat was as dry as chalk. "Get me a drink, will you?"

His brainware had copied a copy of part of the code of the thing which had intercepted him. With care he inspected it now. It was security, all right, and not the normal bank stuff. It wasn't even connected with the bank, he was willing to bet, but placed there from the outside. And it was one of the most vicious pieces of sniffer programming he'd ever seen.

*You have nasty enemies, girl.*

At last he let all that stuff fade from his vision, and he opened his eyes again. They were dry, and crusted with stuff he'd squeezed out during that last wild ride. A lot of real time had passed, then, probably while he was doing cleanup. Nuke was standing there with a drink and he reached up and took the box from him gratefully. Something warm and red and nasty was inside, but it wet his tongue and felt good going down.

"You've got one hell of a mess surrounding that account," he said at last. "The bank security isn't all that bad. I've broken into worse. But someone is watching for any activity that touches your account, and whoever it is has set some stuff up that's damned nasty. *Damn* nasty."

The girl shut her eyes for a minute, absorbing his message, and then leaned back in her chair. For a moment she looked weary and utterly disheartened. Did she think just because the job was tough, they wouldn't help her?

Then that mood passed. It was very strange, almost like a shiver passed through her and left in its wake another set of emotions. And new posture as well: stiffer, more upright, and much less vulnerable. She opened her eyes, and for a moment he had the fleeting impression that it was someone else he was looking at. Someone totally new.

In a tone that was cool and utterly controlled, she said, "So the money's not accessible."

"I didn't say that."

Her eyes were fixed on him: waiting, hoping. They were the oddest color, a clear blue that didn't seem like the right color for eyes. Probably not natural, he decided. Then for a moment her gaze became distant, unfocused . . . the sure sign of some internal conversation. But she had no headset on, so of course that wasn't possible. Was it?

*Nothing is impossible*, an inner voice whispered.

Was she hooked up to the net directly, without the need for a headset and interface? He wasn't sure he liked that thought. There was a reason no one plugged an outernet feed right into their head—actually about a thousand reasons, but viruses that could fry your brain started and ended the list. The thought of taking that kind of chance—and what it would imply about the stuff inside her head—was enough to spook even his kind.

It would sure as hell explain why someone was after her, though.

"I can get you money," he told her. And then, with a smile, "I can probably get you your *own* money." Okay, so he liked to brag. What hacker didn't have an ego? "The question is, what's going to happen after that? If you've got someone on your tail who's good enough to track you like this, it's only a question of time before he catches up with you again." He met those blue eyes, and held them. "I could maybe help you. . . ." He let the suggestion trail off into whatever she might wish to add to it.

"And what would you want for that?"

"More data."

"Like what?"

It was now or never, he thought. How much would she tell him?

"Who's after you?"

A faint smile, sad and frustrated, twitched at the corners of her mouth. "Don't know. Sorry."

"Do you know why they want you?"

She shook her head. There was no way to know if she was telling the truth or not. The latter would be no surprise; he was pretty much a stranger to her now. Hell, as far as she knew, he could be part of whatever high-tech gang was on her tail. He was surprised she'd trusted him this far.

*She has no choice*, that inner voice whispered. *No money, can't touch her own resources, and God knows what other traps are out there, waiting for her . . . she needs you, or someone like you, and she knows it.*

What if it was something in her head they wanted? Jesus.

That didn't even bear thinking about. He caught that flash of inner concentration again and wondered at its source. So subtle, so fast; he doubted any deadhead would notice it. Was there really something strange going on inside her, or was she just accessing some internal program? Hell, for all he knew, her well-seeker was urging her to go get lunch, and she was telling it to fuck itself.

MODDIE? he sent to Nuke.

DON'T THINK SO, came his answer.

OTHER BRIGHT IDEAS?

Nuke shrugged ever so slightly. He was clearly in the dark himself on this one.

It was dangerous stuff, for a moddie to be screwing with security like that. Doubly dangerous when he didn't know what he was doing, or why. The last time Phoenix had seen a program that nasty, it was after him. It had nearly gotten him, too. He still had nightmares about that one.

But if she had some kind of high-tech mystery inside her head, there was only one way to find out about it. Which meant there was never really any question about what he'd do.

MIND IF I TAKE THIS ONE OVER? he asked Nuke

A yellow face with a sad expression filled his field of vision. HELL, I FIGURED YOU WOULD. YOU'RE PREDICTABLE AS SHIT, MAN. The face disappeared, replaced by a fisted hand with its thumb pointing upwards. GO FOR IT.

He turned his attention to the girl again. "Going to be hard for me to work like that."

She shrugged, and seemed genuinely regretful about the whole thing. "Sorry. I really don't know anything about this." Then that vulnerability came into her eyes again—it seemed to come and go without warning, like someone was flicking a switch on and off in her brain—and she asked, very softly, "Can you help me?"

REALLY THAT NASTY? Nuke asked him.

SHIT, YEAH. Phoenix sent. NASTIER.

IF YOU TAKE THIS OVER, I EXPECT TO KNOW EVERYTHING.

OF COURSE.

"She promised me five thousand," Nuke said aloud.

The girl looked at Phoenix. It was a question.

"If we get the money," he said, smiling slightly, "you're in for five." Those words were for the girl's benefit, so that she wouldn't guess how much more was going on here than a simple financial transaction. Nuke was as capable as he was of lifting that much cash if he needed it; it was lesson one in the moddie's handbook. Then again, Nuke could be pretty lazy sometimes. Maybe he'd like to have that much money just fall into his lap, so he could spend his time doing other things. Nuke took pride in his ability to dodge the Pol—they all did—but he didn't go out of his way to egg them on. He didn't actively enjoy the risk, that knife-edged dividing line between trouble and triumph.

Phoenix did. Phoenix loved it. Dodging the Pol was great sport, and if something even nastier than the Pol had come to Paradise, and if it was focused on this girl . . . that was too much of a challenge to resist.

Nuke knew that about him. Probably that's why he'd called him in the first place. Certainly that's why he was willing to turn the girl over to him now, and settle for secondhand reports on what was going on. Maybe it wasn't as much fun as doing the job himself, but when three Paradise hackers had already gone to the reprocessor in the past few E-months, safety looked pretty good, too.

Not to Phoenix. There was a reason he'd chosen the name he did, in memory of an Earth-bird that plunged down into the fire of its own destruction, only to rise up anew from the ashes. This girl's story tasted of that fire. He wanted to see just what was burning.

"Where are you staying?" he asked her.

As soon as he said the words, he realized what the answer was, of course. And also why she looked so physically drained. *That was one fucking stupid question, Phoenix.* Still, he waited to see how she'd handle the moment.

To his surprise, she smiled faintly. "Well, I haven't got a place yet . . . but if you'd like to recommend a hotel that doesn't require any money, I guess I can take a room."

That was when he decided that he liked her. No: more accurately, that was when he realized that she was a real person, rather than just a programming problem to be solved. It was a pretty large leap for his moddie mentality, and not one he made very often. Generally he didn't acknowledge anyone as human whose brain wasn't wired directly to their headset.

"I've got a spare room," he told her. "Chaos used to—" He took a deep breath, trying to swallow back on the sudden knot of pain that had just formed in his throat. "A friend. Used to stay with me a lot. Kind of cluttered," he warned her.

"That's all right." Again that faint smile.

"Nuke?"

"Fine with me."

TAKIN' ALL THE PRETTY ONES?

He blushed. He actually blushed. It was by far one of the weirdest things he'd ever done, and he was someone who thrived on weirdness. Where the hell had that reaction come from? When the hell had it ever mattered to him whether a client was pretty or not?

*That will not happen again*, he told his wellseeker, in a personal patois of symbols and abbreviated English. *Ever. You see to it.*

"Thank you," she said to them. Her voice so gentle, so sweet. So perfectly appreciative. What was her secret? What was the name of the fire that burned within her, toward which his electronic wings were even now carrying him? Her voice and bearing offered no hint of it, but that hadn't stopped him before. "Thank you so much."

*I won't get burned*, Phoenix promised himself. *I'll be careful this time.*

He didn't flash that thought to Nuke. The guy would only laugh, and remind him of what had happened on Hellsgate. And Lampada IV. And . . . well, a lot of other trouble spots on his resume, places he'd rather forget. There wasn't exactly a college course in hacking, a guy had to learn from his failures.

Hey. Shit happens, you know?

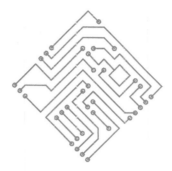

Each new technology will bring with it new forms of crime, demanding innovative security. That is the dynamic which drives our modern progress: not dreams, not ideals, but the simple desire on the part of criminals to take what is not theirs by law, and the determination of others to keep them from doing so.

DR. AMY LAN,
*Brave New Battles*

# REIJIK NODE
## INSHIP: *WAYWARD*

*M*AYDAY . . . *MAYDAY* . . .

The much dreaded icon of safespace emergency flashed red and bright in all their heads. The captain of the *Wayward* adjusted the contrast on his message so he could call up details without being blinded.

*Medical emergency . . . med programs down . . . assistance needed . . . emergency . . .*

"Transport vessel," his pilot told him. "Class six private. I've got the ID if you want it."

"Not now." The scarlet demand throbbed in his field of vision. Damn it, why did this have to happen now? They had too much work to do to stop for something like this. He had a full packet of high security data to skip, and he didn't like to stop for anything.

But you didn't leave someone stranded in space like that. Not ever. If the stationmaster didn't break your head for it, the Guild was likely to dump you in the ainniq without a space suit, and that overbore any considerations of time or security.

"Hail them," he ordered.

The mayday icon flashed twice more, then subsided. Its afterimage glowed with ghostly fire as the message was sent. Several seconds passed, then the pilot told him, "They say a data glitch in med programs fried the brainware of an officer, and enough basic programs that they can't stabilize the damage. They're asking for access to our med programs, long enough to put him into stasis."

The captain bit his lower lip, considering. Giving aid to a stranger was one thing. Letting that stranger onto their ship—

and allowing him to hook up to the ship's innernet—was a risk he didn't like. He had enough high-security data tucked away in that system that he'd just as soon keep strangers away from it.

Shit. It wasn't like they had a choice.

"All right," he said. Not liking it a bit. "Arrange for rendez-vous. Tell them we'll take the patient on board and one other, that's all. Limited med access. Frank, you get on this and close off all our other programs; I want a seal so tight that Hell's own hackers couldn't break through." Frank started to protest, but he waved him to silence. "Yeah, I know, but *pretend* it's possible, okay? Jesus."

He really didn't need this now.

The pilot turned them around, away from their target course, toward the distant distress signal. He flashed up figures on the distance and grunted. Damn, they'd lose time for this. He hadn't earned his data security clearance by taking deadlines lightly, and the thought that they'd show up late at the skip station was less than pleasant. But what could you do? Civilization had its rules. You couldn't leave people stranded out here, could you?

Well, maybe you could, but the Guild would get you for it.

He looked over the ship's ID and found it unexceptional. Private transport licensed for outspace business, probably some dayrunner doing courier work for the big boys. Plenty of them around. Sometimes those guys operated on a shoestring budget, which meant they couldn't afford the kind of backup programs he himself carried. Fair enough. Frank would get the med programs isolated and they'd let these guys connect to it, and then when they were gone he'd sweep the whole ship's processor five times over to make sure nothing had been left behind. The captain of the *Wayward* might be compassionate—or at least dutiful—but he wasn't stupid.

Coordinates flashed in his field of vision, not long enough for him to read them, just a quick confirmation from his pilot. He nodded, then glanced at the ceiling where electronic nodes shunted the signal from his brain to the ship's innernet, and back. *Have to shut those down, too,* he reflected. Couldn't let an outsider have access to their system. Damn, this was going to be a pain.

The ship wasn't all that far away, which was one good thing, anyway. Standard air lock and docking mechanism; it took a little over ten minutes to get the two ships sealed together, once contact was made. Not long for him, but he wondered how the injured man was taking it.

Then the portal hissed open and a null-grav stretcher wheeled itself into the ship. On it was a small humanoid, hairless, who twitched and pulled against the restraining straps in the grips of some kind of seizure. *They should have sedated him,* the captain thought. Or maybe they did, and this was the best they could do. Two more figures came through the door together, one diminutive in stature and one pretty Earth standard in form, though brilliant blue lines were streaked across his face. He opened his mouth to protest, but the blue guy spoke first, offering his hand for a ritual clasp as he said, "Allonzo Porsha, captain. I'm so grateful for your assistance." Then the hand was quickly withdrawn and the stretcher whirred impatiently. "Where should we take him?"

From somewhere the captain found his voice. "I said only two people. Including the injured."

Maybe it was what he said, or maybe it was just timing. But at that moment the other visitor, a short Variant as bald as the one on the stretcher, moaned in what seemed like agony and threw himself over the body on the stretcher. And damned if they didn't match. That, and their height and hairlessness, gave him his first clue.

"They're Belial," Porsha said.

"Yeah." He didn't like it, but he knew outspace custom well enough. The two matching Variants were supposed to be one guy, though how they managed that was beyond him. He started to tell them he didn't give a damn—then stopped, feeling somewhat foolish. Arguing fine points of Belial twindom was like buying a suit of clothing on the mall station and arguing about whether the price chip said it had one, two, or three pieces. He wasn't going to win.

"Okay. Okay. Come with me."

He waited long enough to see that the portal was sealed shut once more and locked—no sense in taking chances—and waved for Frank to lead the way to the med console in the back of the ship. He himself would watch the strangers from behind. Was he being paranoid? Pirates were few and far between, but he knew a guy once who'd been nailed by some, and this was how they'd gotten him. Once they were on board, there wasn't much you could do.

A warning icon flashed in his field of vision, and the tiny indicator in the corner of his eye blinked, indicating loss of innernet connection. Okay, so his crew was on top of things. That was good. Whatever these two wanted—these *three*—they weren't going to be able to rifle through his ship's files on the way there.

But it looked like the little guy was genuinely hurt. Either that or he was one hell of a good actor. Frank helped Porsha plug him into the console with a realwire connection that should override any damaged parts of his headset, then watched like a wary hawk while the blue-faced man made various adjustments. Frank nodded; he was watching it all, and no doubt recording it as well; if there was anything amiss about the process, any attempt on the part of these three to break through from the med complex to the ship's other systems, they'd know it before any damage could be done.

Suddenly, with a cry, the Belial on the stretcher began to convulse. His twin ran forward to help him, but Porsha thrust him aside. Somewhat belligerently, the captain thought. It was as if he'd been losing patience with the healthy twin for some time, but if that was the case, why had he let him come on board, where he'd only get in the way? Then he remembered the details of that particular Variation and nodded to himself in grim understanding. You couldn't separate Belial twins, not forcibly. You shouldn't even try. If they chose to split up that was one thing, some did and some didn't, but if they wanted to be together and you tried to separate them, it was like . . . well, like asking a man to send one hand and a leg of his out of the room, and keep functioning. Or so it had been explained to him in grade school. Truth is, humankind had so many Variations he could barely keep track of them.

Finally the injured twin settled down into the stretcher, seemingly asleep. His double was whimpering in the far corner, where Porsha was clearly happy to ignore him. He and Frank were both silent as they manipulated the innernet to heal the injured man—Porsha doing the work, Frank watching his every cybermove like a hawk. At last Porsha nodded, and took off his headset. The captain had seen no change take place in the patient that he could put his finger on, but now that he really looked at him, his color did seem marginally better.

All right. So this whole thing was legit. *And* it hadn't taken all that long. Maybe he'd be lucky, and they'd get through the rest of the day without interruptions.

"Listen," the blue-faced man said, "I can't thank you enough—"

"Just simple courtesy," the captain said gruffly. *Required courtesy.* "I'm glad we were able to help him."

"No really, I owe you—"

"Forget it," he said. And then, when it didn't seem like that was going to be enough for the man, he said it more emphatically. "*Forget it.*"

That ended the attempt to establish further conversation, anyway. Good thing. The captain might acknowledge his responsibility to help a traveler in need, but he had no responsibility to stand around shooting the breeze with a total stranger when there was work calling to him. He'd be polite, but that was it . . . and even the politeness had a limit.

They saw the strangers to the air lock, opened it, and let them pass through. His people were ready for trouble, he saw, weapons hidden behind them as they flanked the three strangers. But there was no trouble. It looked like the visit was purely legitimate, just some guy who'd needed the aid of a passing ship to clean out his head. But just to be sure . . .

"Check it," he told Frank. "Check it all. I want the gateways to the med system probed inside and out. If there was an attempt to break in, even one test against the password system, then you tell me and we'll start going over it bit by bit, until we know for sure it's all clean."

He wasn't going to tolerate some yahoo's virus on his ship, that was for sure. Or overlook any attempt to copy the data he was carrying. Probably their visit was nothing, just what it seemed . . . but in his business you couldn't be too careful.

It was an old pirate's superstition, not to count your loot until you were well out of earshot. Of course, the whole concept of earshot was irrelevant in space, so God alone knew how the custom had gotten started, but it was still considered traditional to put good distance between you and your victim before you exulted over his stupidity.

Which in this case had been massive.

"Tam?"

"No problem," the Belial told him. "Right where I was standing during the med stuff, under the console. No one was even looking at me, so I got a good placement. They won't find it by accident, that's for sure."

"Excellent." They'd stay a safe distance from the *Wayward*, but not so close that low-strength transmissions couldn't bridge the gap between them. In a few hours Calia would send out the codes that would bring their hidden transmitter to life, and Tam could bounce a signal off that right into the *Wayward*'s innernet. Which he could then hack into at his leisure, long after anyone aboard had stopped watching for such interference.

It was the kind of trick you couldn't use too often, but when it worked right, it could net a treasurehouse of data before anyone caught on. If they were lucky, no one ever would. Sometimes you were that lucky.

"Allo, I've got a signal coming in." It was Sumi. "Customs, it looks like."

It was a cold word in the otherwise jubilant atmosphere. Allo felt his mood deflate quickly. "What do they want?"

Sumi closed his eyes to better envision the message. His tentacles twitched slowly as he read.

"Permission for search," he said at last.

The words hung there in the air for a moment, heavy with connotations of trouble. It wasn't unheard of for a Customs team to go out and aggressively search independent vessels in the vicinity. Most smugglers knew enough to dump their loads at private docks before showing up at the waystation, so it was pretty much the only way they were going to nail anyone. But still. It wasn't that common. And now? Bad timing.

Allo bit his lower lip, considering. At last he said, "Your take?"

It was a long second before Sumi answered. "If we say no, it's trouble. You know that."

Yes, he did. It shouldn't be that way, but it was. In the space-lanes you were considered guilty until proven innocent, no matter what the laws said to the contrary. On a station he might argue. Out here in safespace, there was no one to argue with.

*Never forget they carry guns,* he thought.

*Never let them find out that you do, too.*

"Calia?"

"We've got nothing to worry about on board," she said coolly. "You did a scrub after that last drug shipment. We haven't carried anything else that would leave signs."

"We've got logs of legitimate business," Sumi added. "As always."

God, he hated this. You wanted to turn them away, to tell them to go off and mind their own business . . . and they might even do that, if they didn't have a proper warrant. You'd be within your rights to refuse them. But you could bet your ass that they'd be waiting at the next station you visited, and the next one, and the next one after that. If Allo and his crew were really legitimate, then it would just be a nuisance. But they weren't. And God knows, like Calia said, the ship wasn't ever going to be cleaner than it was right now.

"Tam, I want all our programs—"

"Erased from the main banks," the Belial said. "Already done."

His crew was good. They knew how to think, and they knew how to move fast, and most of all they knew how to lie. Sumi best of all. He'd let the Medusan play guide to the customs crew. That would give this little invasion the attention it deserved, not too little and not too much. It was important to get those gestures right.

"Check their ID," he said at last.

Sumi shut his eyes and started trading codes with the distant ship. After a moment he nodded. "Checks out," he pronounced. "Looks like they're the real thing."

He didn't know whether that was good or bad. An enemy might have been easier to deal with. "All right," he said. He could hear the frustration in his own voice. "Tell them to come on in."

Sumi looked up at him; he nodded. They knew each other well enough for no words or flashed messages to be necessary. After all, they'd been through such searches before. Allo hated it every time, but it was hardly unfamiliar ground.

It took the customs ship half an hour to reach them, and almost that long again to dock. Inwardly Allo was seething, but he knew the game for what it was. Node law forbade any truly invasive search without just cause and a warrant. But the minute he made any move against these people that could be read as defiance, a warrant was no longer needed. If they could frustrate him to the point of losing his temper, he'd be playing right into their hands.

He hated this game. But he usually won it.

The officials who entered his ship were crisply dressed, fresh from easy duty on some pleasure station, he'd bet. Their uniforms were emblazoned with signs of local rank that Allo didn't recognize, but the sheer number indicated considerable authority. He wasn't sure yet if that was good or bad.

"Allonzo Porsha?"

"Yes."

"This is your ship?"

He stifled a nasty retort and said simply, "Yes." Like they didn't have the ownership records already loaded into their heads.

They introduced themselves. He introduced his people. They stared at nothing while checking off the names against some list inside their heads. Then their leader asked to see the ship, and Sumi moved forward to lead them—

And there were weapons in their hands, appearing so suddenly that Allo barely had time to react. Even as he pulled out his own, a spray of some chemical enveloped him, an acid fog that burned his eyes and his throat and set off a spasm of coughing so violent that he couldn't even see straight. Damn! Blinded, doubled over as his body fought to heave up the poison it had breathed in, he didn't dare fire for fear of hitting his own people. *Jesus Christ!* He sure hoped Sumi and the others were on top of this situation, 'cause he'd been blinded but good. He tried to get the innernet to feed him something visual from a cam so that at least in his mind's eye he could see what was going on, but the poison spray had kicked off spasms so terrible he couldn't visualize the icons clearly. With a grunt of pain, he dropped to the floor and felt something sharp and nasty bite into his arm as he hit it, hard. His wellseeker flashed him a warning that was all blurred, probably about some new poison the shot had injected into him. *Damn. Damn. Gotta fight this. . . .* The sharpness became a burning that began to spread through his torso, and his whole body started shaking. All around him he could hear the sounds of battle, the hot buzz of electrical contact, the soft whir of darts . . . but even the sounds were blurred, as if his brain would no longer accept clean input. Was that poison in his veins? Something worse? He heard cries and crashing and the garbled curses of his crew. Jesus Christ, where had these bastards come from?

There was a final crashing sound, and then a hand grabbed him by the sleeve, forcing him upward a few feet. The motion proved too much, and he started vomiting; the bile was like acid on his tongue, as if whatever they'd shot into him had corrupted his own body fluids. They knocked his weapon out of his hand and then dragged him across the bridge to the place where their own ship waited. He banged into something on the way; a body? Moist tentacles were ground underfoot as his captors forced him into the air lock, and a trail of sticky blood marked his progress like the slime trail of a slug. Was anyone from his crew left alive? He tried to call to them but gagged on the words, his throat clogged with bile and worse. Desperately he tried to cough some of it up so that he could breathe.

And then someone hit him on the back of the head, hard.

And then there was darkness.

Sounds. Distorted colors, slowly coalescing into shapes. Bright lights, too bright. He tried to turn away. Couldn't. Motor control offline. Or was he paralyzed?

He blinked hard, trying to focus. Something stirred in front of him, other shapes following. People?

"He's awake."

The voice was gruff, and it was followed by a stinging in his arm and the hiss of a medspray. Something gripped his heart and squeezed it, hard. His wellseeker, which should have protested the move, was silent. He tried to call it up. No good. The fist around his heart loosened up a bit, but each beat that followed banged against his rib cage with unnatural force. He could feel a spark of life coming back into his brain, as the drug they'd given him forced his body into a more active state. He suspected that he'd have been better off staying asleep.

"Time to wake up now." It was a male voice, harsh and cold. Something chilly wafted across his nostrils and a sharp, stinging odor brought him suddenly into the here-and-now.

Big room. Mostly empty. Two men standing. Him sitting. Bound. Or maybe just shut down below the neck, like a program that wasn't needed.

The light was turned into his face, blinding him. Something buzzed inside his skull; brainware response to alien instructions? He tried to shake his head hard enough to throw off the headset, but of course it was locked into place.

—And pain, blinding pain, seared through every nerve in his body. Not as if he'd been hurt, nothing so centralized as an injury. It was as if all his blood had suddenly started to boil, and the flesh around it melted, and the skin over that dissolved in acid. It was hot and it was sharp and it was crushing and it was tearing, and every other word that had ever been associated with pain, or ever might be. All at once.

He didn't scream, but that was only because it was so fast he didn't have time to. It just lasted for a second—less than a second—and then it was gone.

He was left gasping for breath, his whole body shaking. The room spun about him dizzily, his brain too stunned to make sense of what it was seeing.

"Very good, Mr. Dietrich," the harsh voice approved. The lights moved closer. He could make out details now, in the room and of the men, but his brain could still make no sense of them.

Aware that he was fighting for his life, he struggled to find his voice. "Look, whatever you want—"

Pain again. Agonizing nanoseconds of it. He couldn't breathe when it ended, and there were bands of hot metal wrapped around his heart.

"You want the wellseeker on?" The voice from the back of the room was male.

"No. Not yet."

Oh, Jesus. Let this be a nightmare. A real sleeping-type nightmare, the kind you could wake up from.

"Now, Mr. Porsha. We have a few questions to ask you. And as you may have guessed by now, cooperation would be far more . . . comfortable for you."

He tried to feel strong, but the mere memory of that pain was enough to set his whole body to shaking violently. Any façade of courage he might have tried to erect could not stand up to that memory.

"I see you understand."

There was a pause then, enough time for images to flicker through his brain, hot and painful. Sumi's body on the floor. Someone's blood underfoot. Poisonous smoke drifting in the air.

A face appeared before him. Pale-skinned, aquiline, with piercing gray eyes. He was Terran, Allo noted, in that part of his brain that was still capable of rational thought.

"Let's talk about Reijik Node."

Reijik? What mattered about Reijik? That was—

Shit.

The drugs.

Shit.

"What?" he whispered. Stalling.

Jesus. He was going to die.

He tried to struggle against his bonds. His body didn't respond to him. Whatever program they'd launched into his brainware, it had shut down everything below the neck.

"Casalz' place. Do you remember that?"

The words confirmed his worst fears. Frederico Casalz was the man whose station they had used to transfer the drugs. Damn it to hell, that careless fucking idiot of a servant had gotten himself caught and spilled the whole story—

A bolt of pain, quicker than a heartbeat, cut short his reverie.

"Casalz."

"Yes." He gasped it, hating himself for his weakness, his fear.

How could you fight a pain that was injected directly into your neural circuits? "Yes. I remember."

"You transferred some goods there. What?"

For a minute he didn't answer, clinging to an illusion of free will. Then he saw the man's hand flicker up in a subtle gesture, and pain filled his universe again.

Longer, this time. Almost a second. Longer than eternity, when you were trapped inside it.

"What goods?" the voice demanded.

Had he stumbled into some drug lord's territory? Handled goods that belonged to someone else? Or just really, genuinely upset customs officials that much? He doubted it was the latter. Customs didn't generally use torture to find out what they needed to know.

He saw the man's hand stir again and knew there was no way out. They could have the answer now or they could squeeze it out of him with neurally induced pain; either way, he was keeping no secrets. "Sana," he said hoarsely. "It was sana." A nasty, nasty drug. If they really were customs people, they weren't going to be happy about this.

"Your crew knew?"

Were they still alive? Sumi and Calia and the Tams . . . were they being interrogated like this, their mental guts squeezed out for all to see? At least he could try to save them.

"No. No. They knew we had cargo . . . not what it was." He struggled to make himself sound more confident than he felt. "I don't tell them everything. Safer that way."

He saw the man's hand move upward, and braced himself for the pain. But the motion went uncompleted. The steel bands around his chest loosened an infinitesmal amount in relief.

"You'd better not be lying to me, Porsha."

"I'm not. I swear it."

"Who was on your ship, that run?

He hesitated. A moment too long. When the flood of pain had washed over him and was gone, he could barely breathe.

"Minor fibrillation," the voice in the back of the room warned. "Correct it?"

The gray eyes met his, and Allo knew what was in them. Death. That was the merciful option, the one that would happen if he cooperated. If not . . . what would a full minute of neural-induced agony feel like? Ten minutes? An hour?

No wonder the technique was outlawed on all civilized stations.

Small consolation for him.

"Porsha?"

What did it matter? His crew, his friends, were all on that ship. Dead at the worst, or captive at the best. Or maybe it was the other way around. What did their names matter?

"Sumi Ireta," he said slowly. "Calia Donelly. Tam-Tam."

"Is that all?"

He stared at the man.

"*Is that all?*"

"My crew," he began. "I—"

Pain. Pools of it, oceans of it, blazing, searing galaxies of it.

"Let's try that again," the man said calmly. "Who else was on the ship at that time?"

It was as if the pain had cleared his mind suddenly. He understood.

*The girl . . .*

"Let my crew go," he whispered. "They don't know anything."

His interrogator glanced back behind him. With the lights in his eyes, Allo couldn't see what he was looking at.

Finally he turned back. "All right. You tell us what we want to know, and we won't . . . question the others."

Were they lying? Could he tell if they were? Were his friends already dead, or locked up in rooms like this one, with strange programs rummaging through the cells of their brain, awakening primal fears of pain and dissolution?

"Life for them and death for you," the man said quietly. "Or far, far worse for you all." He glanced back to the unseen figure behind him, who was undoubtedly in control of whatever was triggering the pain. Porsha flinched. But no pain was forthcoming, not this time. The man turned back to him; his gaze was like ice. "Your choice."

"There was a girl," he whispered.

He could feel the change in the room with those words. This,

this was what they wanted. Lives were worth nothing to these men, compared to this information.

"Tell us about her."

He tried for a moment to think of how best to answer them, to gain something from this tenuous moment. A quick burst of pain reminded him that he wasn't in control of this interview, and never would be.

"*Tell us about her.*"

"Her name was Jamisia Capra. She called herself Raven. She was running from something—I don't know what!" he said hurriedly. The man was scowling: clearly he was reading evasion into Porsha's tone. Jesus Christ, Porsha thought, he couldn't take the pain again. Each breath was a struggle now, against a weight on his chest that grew and grew and grew. He couldn't handle it again.

The voice in the back of the room warned quietly: "Blood pressure redzoned."

The gray-eyed man stared at him.

"She came running down the docking ring and we took her in. That's all I know, I swear it! We got her name off her finance chip and were going to trace her at the next station."

"Why?"

"Why?" It was hard to think. He felt strangely light-headed, and his thoughts wouldn't arrange themselves properly. "Someone was looking for her. Someone . . . she was worth . . . money. . . ."

The gray eyes glanced to the back of the room.

"He doesn't know," the other voice assessed.

Hard to breathe. Chest wouldn't expand. Whatever they'd wrapped around him was too tight.

"Where is she?" his inquisitor demanded.

Where . . . ? He tried to think . . . had to think, or the pain would come back. . . .

"Don't know." Shallow, shallow breaths barely gave him enough air to speak. "Lost her . . . on Paradise."

He was dimly aware he had told the man something he wanted to hear. Good. Good. Maybe he would make the pain go away. It was like fire in his chest now, and every new breath hurt worse than the last. There was a roaring in his ears as well,

and a strange sense of being distanced from everyone and everything in the room . . . even his own body.

The unseen man said something—he couldn't make out
what—and stepped forward. His face was unfamiliar, but Allo
recognized the insignia on his jacket. All too familiar. Every pilot
knew it.

Guildsign.

Then the roaring darkness swept him away at last, to places
where not even the pain could reach him.

## OUTERNET FORECAST

Processing will be slow today in the Five Nodes, in response to a pressure system triggered by yesterday's stock market crash on Hellsgate. Consumers should expect delays in product services, debit routing, and investment analysis. Data redundancy is advised.

A backup warning is in effect, particularly in areas of travel and tourist services. Northstar Hotels, one of Salvation's most prestigious chains, has reported the loss of reservations data from its Aires office. If you have routed reservations through Northstar Aires in the past twelve hours, please check with the main office to see that your data arrived safely.

# GUERA NODE
# TIANANMEN STATION

**T**HERE WEREN'T enough spores.

Dr. Masada looked at the data five times, ten times, a hundred. Still the numbers weren't right. Still they didn't match what he knew must be out there.

With a sigh he pushed his chair back and shut his eyes, rubbing the ache out of his head with a weary hand. His wellseeker sensed the change in focus and took the opportunity to remind him that his caloric requirement for the day was far from met, and in fact yesterday's had gone at a deficit. He was about to shut it down again—for the fourth time today—but then he stopped and thought, why not? He needed a break from this damned screen, and the even more frustrating data displayed on it.

Mankind wasn't designed to stare at a screen all day, and handling data like this in such a frustrating format hour after hour was almost enough to make him load Lucifer right into his head, just so he could deal with the damned thing directly.

Almost.

Not quite.

With a sigh he visualized the icons that would shut down his programs and save all his data. He had a set of five high-security icons that he was using, dense and complicated visual designs that not only had to be formed in his mind's eye, but rotated properly as well. The likelihood of anyone managing to guess at such patterns was astronomically small, and not one he worried about.

Although someone could do it, theoretically. The security system didn't exist which *someone* couldn't break into. Who knew that better than Kio Masada, who had written the book on data security?

There were half a dozen Guild folk in the nearest commissary, two *nantana*, three *natsiq*, and a *yuki*. Programmers, all of them, who wore the sign of Gaza's department proudly on their left breast. He might have gone over to the *yuki* if he'd been alone, just to hear another human voice—sometimes even an *iru* needed such things—but the closeness of the group and the energy of its laughter dissuaded him. How he missed the ordered ranks of his students, the comfortable security of the educational ritual: human company without the stress of individual contact. Not for the first time since coming here he felt a wave of vertigo, as if he had suddenly been transported to a mountaintop barely inches wide, miles over the land which others inhabited. His wellseeker flashed a query, and he gave it permission to go ahead and adjust his brain chemicals to compensate for the sensation, but he knew from experience that mechanical adjustment alone couldn't make the feeling go away. It was part and parcel of who he was, and the price he paid for his special talent.

He flashed a request for a sandwich of some local synthetic meat, marinated "Paradise style" . . . whatever that meant. That and a cup of tea would satisfy his immediate appetite. His wellseeker processed the order while he ate, and informed him that he had 1237 calories yet to go to make his day's quota. So he ordered another drink, something fattening and frothy that sent the target number down to 829. Good enough for now.

And he thought about Lucifer.

He had spent the last E-week tracking the virus himself. Gaza's preparatory work had been excellent, of course, providing samples of every generation of the damned virus—every generation they knew about, anyway—but after a day of working with his figures, Masada had realized that he needed more data than Gaza had thought to provide. Perhaps on an intuitive level he'd sensed the numbers were all wrong, and gone to search for the right ones.

He'd designed sieve programs and sent them out to all the nodes, a repetitive and exhausting job, especially since he couldn't deal with the outernet directly. He'd sent out sniffers of his own, keyed to Lucifer's memory storage sequences. And then he'd waited, studying the most recent and deadly mutations while his programs scoured the outernet for spores of the elusive virus.

And there weren't enough of them. There just weren't.

He knew how many times Lucifer had replicated to date, give or take a generation. He knew what the parameters of that replication were. He knew—*knew!*—the numerical range that should define its current population. And that number was off from the real thing, by a good factor of ten.

Those extra spores were somewhere, he was certain of it. But where? And—more important—why weren't they still cruising the outernet, doing their destructive duty?

When his tea was done and his wellseeker was satisfied that no more caloric input was immediately forthcoming, he walked slowly back to the triple-locked workstation, running the numbers through his mind. Most programmers would have said he was crazy for focusing on a numerical discrepancy like this. Gaza wouldn't. Gaza's mind was like his own, ordered and precise, and like Masada he had utter certainty in his work. When Masada told Gaza that his projected numbers didn't match reality, the man hadn't asked—as Hsing might have—whether Masada had perhaps erred in his own calculations. He had simply said "What do you need?" and, when told that, provided it.

It was good to work for a man who didn't doubt him every step of the way. Even in the Guild, that was a rare pleasure. Gaza seemed to have utter confidence that he would beat this thing. He wished he shared it.

*Be confident, Masada. The answer is out there. You just have to figure out how to find it.*

Frustrated by the failure of all his other search methods, he had finally sent out special versions of the virus to all the major nodes, with homing patterns woven into their substance. It was a dangerous move—anything that released more copies of Lucifer into the outernet was dangerous, no matter how much care you took to see that your versions could neither harm people nor reproduce—but it had to be done. All other methods had failed thus far, and every hour in which he failed to bring Lucifer under control, it was spawning new and deadlier spores. Any day now it might evolve into a form that would attack civilians, and then . . . well, in Gaza's words, all hell would break loose.

Actually, hell would break loose the day the press got wind of this. Masada was amazed that hadn't happened yet. But then, why should it? Lucifer's creator would have gone to great lengths to assure that his program would remain a secret. No one in the Guild could possibly benefit from the matter being made public. So it hadn't made the newsies . . . yet.

One small thing to be thankful for.

He wondered if Lucifer's creator knew that the Guild was searching for him. No doubt he would assume it; any sane programmer would. And he would have taken precautions, setting programs in motion to mislead the Guild, to confuse them . . . well, thus far they had all worked. If Masada was going to track this damned thing to its source, he was going to have to think of some angle Lucifer's creator hadn't thought of, some element of data he hadn't thought to disguise.

Like the numbers?

*Maybe.*

He brought up the screen again, hating its limitations, and watched the cold code scroll across it in response to his mental commands. Every time he thought he had a handle on what made Lucifer tick, another mutation would surprise him. He understood now why Gaza was so tense about the thing, and that tension was infectious.

*All right. Check the numbers.*

He sent out a request to the Guild's data node to collect anything which had arrived with his special icon embedded in it, and deliver it to him. It was frustrating having to deal with such a system, but necessary. Direct contact with the outernet would mean that if Lucifer's designer realized he was being hunted, he could ride Masada's signal right back up the line to Masada's own head. You couldn't take a chance like that, not with a programmer of such obvious skill and malevolence. This way, if Masada's tracking programs were detected, the most anyone could learn from them was that they were being collected by a processor somewhere on Tiananmen Station. That was a far different thing than having some hacker in his head, real-time.

The data began to come in. Sieve figures from Hellsgate,

Reijik, Salvation. All wrong. Still. Then some private mail from various Guild officers whom he had queried, mostly amounting to some diplomatic version of "I don't know." It amazed him that people so dependent on the outernet could be so ignorant of its workings. Guildmaster Delhi had invited him out to her station if he felt that would help him in his research, as had Varsav. Kent had not yet responded to his query on outpilot conditioning. There was a sealed packet, neatly bundled, which he opened with an icon—

And there it was.

He stopped breathing for a minute. His own code. His homing program, come back to roost. He drew in a deep breath, then flashed it the command to transfer to his screen, where he could see its message unfold.

He had prepared several thousand truncated versions of the virus, too weak to do any damage, and had added to their substance a sequence which would report back to him if it was interfered with. Any collection program which was gathering up random spores would have triggered such action, sending back a signal to Tiananmen that in this place, and at this time, a spore of Lucifer had been yanked from the outernet.

And it had worked.

He wondered if he should report it to Gaza yet, or wait until he knew more. It could be mere coincidence, after all. Perhaps some antibody program had simply been scouring the outernet for viruses, and had caught his. Or his "Lucifer-X" had accidentally wandered into some system where security programs inspected all foreign material, and had gotten trapped.

Perhaps.

Or perhaps the enemy was out there, even now.

He felt a rush of elation in his soul, a flood of chemicals in his brain such as other humans might know in a moment of love, or perhaps religious insight. It was a rare experience in *iru* psychology, that left him dazed for a good minute or two. Then, with meticulous care, he reeled in the precious code, and began to dissect the message that it carried.

Something had grabbed hold of his spy-spore, all right. Its response had been immediate, triggering the signal to Masada before any real analysis of the threat could be completed. That was all right. What mattered was that now he had a way of tracing exactly where a spore had disappeared, and could search for the program that had intercepted it.

He called up a locator program and fed it the information that his spore had gathered. A good second passed while it consulted its files, which seemed like eternity.

Then the words appeared before him.

SOURCE NODE: SALVATION
SOURCE STATION: AIRES
SOURCE SYSTEM: NORTHSTAR HOTELS, INC.
SUBSYSTEM: RESERVATIONS

He stared at the words in silence for a minute. A hotel chain? Perhaps a *nantana* could have made sense of such information, armed with the proper instinct for such things. He couldn't. Fortunately, it wasn't his job to. Once he confirmed that spores were disappearing into the bowels of Northstar's computers, and he could hand over the data to Gaza in a nice ordered packet, the Guild could sort through questions of motive and means until the next step of this search was defined for him. That was their job, for which the gift of Hausman had prepared their brains.

A *hotel* chain?

*All right, that doesn't mean Northstar is guilty, it just means the capture program is sitting on their machine. An employee could have gained access to their system. Management could have traded access to some other company. A hacker could have broken in. This is the first step to the enemy, just the first step, and the trail is going to be long and winding, and it could well lead through every node in the system.*

He wanted to track it himself.

For a long moment he sat before the silent machine, studying that thought in his head. What had prompted it? Pride? Curiosity? Or even . . . boredom? Too many days spent staring at a screen, instead of interacting with the wealth of data that was out there?

Going after the trail of this thing meant hooking up to the outernet, plain and simple. It couldn't be done any other way. It meant letting the touch of that vast beast into his head, that living thing so unlike other living things that no man truly understood it. Tides of data no man could control. Hungers and diseases and tensions and conflict—

He shut down the screen and turned away from it, eyes shut. His hands were shaking. Data still filled his field of vision until he shut that down, too. Then there was only darkness.

*You have to do it someday.*

It was only data. He had given it other names, he had called it *alive* in the hopes of understanding it, and he had used the language of life to help others learn how to program for it. That didn't mean it was really alive. What did he think that it was going to do if he connected to it, eat him?

Silently, without further thought on the matter, he rose up from his seat and stretched. A ritual stretch, allowing him to concentrate on each muscle rather than the thoughts that might otherwise be in his head. Sometimes he could shut down like that, sometimes when he was very tired . . . or afraid.

*There's nothing to be afraid of. You know that.*

It was only data. Right?

**S**he came to him in his dream, just as he remembered her. Dressed in blue, as always. Perfectly coifed sleek black hair. Meticulously groomed, as always.

He watched her as she played the keyboard for a while, aware that she was dead, strangely undisturbed by it. She was playing a Bach fugue, and for a while he lost himself in the overlapping cascades of melody. Data. It was all data. All the world was data, codes and patterns rearranged into a thousand different forms. Even living flesh broke down to the same simple codes, if you looked deep enough.

He heard the rustling of her dress before he saw her move. He looked up and saw her dark eyes fixed on him, strangely soft.

"And love?" she asked him. "What is love?"

He smiled faintly. "Data of the heart."

"And hunger?"

Such wonderful eyes. He would never forget them. "Data of the soul."

"And fear?"

He had no answer.

She kissed him on the tip of his nose then and, even as she did so, began to dissolve. Pink lips fragmenting into fractal patterns of light and dark, skin breaking down into an array of chemical symbols, dark eyes giving way to a glittering display of retinal sparks.

And fear?

He couldn't do it in his lab, of course. That room had been designed without net access deliberately, to avoid any chance of accidents. Instead he would have to do it—where? All spaces on Tiananmen were equally unfamiliar. It generally took months for his *iru* soul to settle into a new environment, and here he had barely had an E-week. No place would be comfortable, it was as simple as that. There was simply the choice to be made between doing it around people or not, and nothing else mattered.

It was no choice at all, really.

He locked himself in his room, a small but well-appointed chamber on the main level of the station. As he shut the door, his wellseeker gently informed him that his hands were trembling. As if that were news.

For a while he just stood there, staring at the empty space before him. Then, methodically, deliberately, he sat down in front of the desk and looked up at the tiny node in the corner of the ceiling which would carry his signal to the galaxy at large. Such an unobtrusive thing, really. Hard to believe such a simple mechanism could give access to such an awesome creation.

He'd taken off his headset on the way from the lab, a planet-born habit; now he raised it up again and fitted it onto his head, over the contacts embedded in his skull. He felt a faint buzz as the magnetic clips took hold, fixing it in place so that it wouldn't move while he worked. He imagined he felt the subtle heat of the contacts coming online, but of course that was nonsense; the brain had no internal sense organs. He pushed a lock of hair out of his eyes, where the metal band had disarrayed it.

Then: no more steps left. No more avoidance possible. *Do it now, or do it never.*

Shutting his eyes, he envisioned the icon that would prepare his brain for interface. He imagined he could hear a faint hum in the headset's wiring as it began to process the signals necessary to log him onto the outernet for the first time. He found his palms were sweating, and wiped them off on the sides of his shirt. There was nothing to be afraid of, really. It was just a larger version of the system that every civilized planet used, which he worked with every day. So what if it had the history and idiosyncrasies of a thousand alien cultures jacked into it. So what if it was peppered with full-second delays, where a signal had to be skipped off the ainniq to a neighboring node . . . or even full-minute delays, if several such skips had to be made. So what if its signals crossed open space, to be intercepted by data pirates, altered by them, precious data corrupted in transit or simply stolen, the ultimate coin of the realm for this technological age. So what if the result of all that made for a system so dynamic and unpredictable that it might as well be alive, and therefore must be *courted* rather than *controlled*. He knew how it worked. He had written the book on it. The galaxy looked to him for guidance in how to understand this thing.

ONLINE, the headset informed him.

Trembling only slightly, he eased his way into the system. Gateway icons appeared one after the other, Guild-signs that had to be neutralized before he could contact the outernet directly. He gave them the codes they needed. The system tried to tie him into some virtual control system, which would allow him to visualize his options as doorways and his progress as physical movement, but he shut that down as soon as it started up. Such tricks were for those whose minds couldn't deal with pure code, not for him.

At last the outernet icon filled his field of vision, confirming his connection. He drew in a deep breath, scanned his collection of real-time investigative programs to make sure they were all ready to go, and requested a link to Aires Station.

There was a disconcerting pause, seconds in length, that made his heart lurch in his chest. *It's nothing. Just the skip. Ignore it.* You could hardly expect to make contact with a station halfway across the galaxy in the same time that you could send something across a planet. Nevertheless, that time was enough for his fearful imagination to go to work, and at last he ordered his wellseeker to release a few drops of sedative into his bloodstream, just to rein in his pounding heart. *Try not to think about what's out there.* The pressure in his chest eased a tiny bit as the Aires gateway icon took form before him. *It's just a vast network, that connects to systems all over the galaxy. No different in theory than the one back home, on which you do your research.*

But that wasn't true, and he knew it. That one was a quiet and underused library, the other a madhouse of human activity. On Guera one might search for a given resource, find it, and withdraw; in the outerworlds one was likely to be jostled by a thousand competing programs, swept away by sheer mass of data searches, drowned in games and advertisements and semilegal entertainments, and in general disconcerted until research was all but impossible. Most people could use enhanced interface programs to wend their way through the madness, but that didn't help when you had to study the code itself. Or when you preferred code, as he did.

He brushed aside two offers of a virtual menu for Aires points of interest, a display of popular station wares, and one particularly aggressive advertisement for a new viddie, that followed him around for several annoying minutes before he managed to trick it into going elsewhere. Such things were forbidden on Guera, whose innernet was strictly controlled. They were forbidden on every civilized planet, as far as he knew, as well as the ships and habitats that circled them. Only here, in the outworlds, had dataspace been made such a free-for-all.

He had a headache from it already.

He found a relatively quiet connection to Northstar's main processor, and slipped inside with the help of a codecracker stored in his headset. Once there, the datastream was somewhat quieter, calmer, and easier to navigate. Of course. No business could afford the kind of distraction that took place on the public wavelengths.

He took the time to get the lay of the land, dodging a few security programs that came sniffing his way. Nothing sophisticated, just your basic virus and intruder detectors. He knew what kinds of code to feed them so that they went away, satisfied he was nothing out of the ordinary. So far so good.

No wonder hackers thrived in the outerworlds. If this was the kind of security that was typical out here, he was surprised the problem wasn't worse. He was used to Guild security, complex megaliths of defensive programming that were updated on a regular basis. These basic sniffers . . . they were easy to dodge, and he could even have entrapped one and reprogrammed it to do his will, had that been his need. Oh, they'd keep the system clear of most viruses well enough, and nab a high percentage of intruders as well, particularly those who had no background in net security . . . but that wouldn't stop a real hacker. The kind of people who regularly attacked the Guild files could break into this system without pausing for breath.

Which was maybe why they went after the Guild files, he realized. Where was the challenge out here?

Strangely, as he headed toward Reservations, he began running across fragmented files. Oddly fragmented, as if pieces of them had been torn away somehow. He stopped to take a closer look at several, and downloaded copies for study at a later time, but it didn't appear that the damage was in any predictable pattern. Very strange. The programs running in this section seemed injured, too, for they were running much slower than what Masada had seen elsewhere. He caught sight of one that was doing the equivalent of limping in circles, spewing out the same set of garbled data over and over. That was very strange. Had the copies of Lucifer which disappeared in this place somehow damaged Northstar's programming? He'd never seen anything quite like this before.

It was then, for the first time, that he felt his own guidance programs picking up speed. Instinctively he adjusted them. He knew about this phenomenon, of course—the riptides of the outernet were infamous among programmers—and was prepared with a set of programs designed to stabilize his signal. Nevertheless he felt a cold rush of fear, as the full immensity of the creature that enveloped him hit home. His programs settled down a bit, but he found himself nearer to Reservations than he had intended. He tried to back out—

And his signal jammed. Menus opened like flowering buds before him, one after the other, welcoming him into the Reservations center. But he didn't want to go there yet. He flashed up an anchor program and quickly reviewed his code. Nowhere had he given any order which should send him into Reservations. How bizarre. The anchor searched out a string of stable code and locked him onto it; forward motion ceased. The welcome menu for New Reservations flickered in his field of vision, frozen in the instant of its appearance.

What the hell was going on?

He took a long and careful look at the data around him. It should be mostly stable, strings of numbers that had to do with hotel accounting, coordinates for data routing, general book-keeping. But oddly, some of that seemed to be edging toward the gateway to Reservations as well. There was no way to tell in the midst of all this just what was causing it, but he copied a few samples quickly, for study later. It was possible this was just some quirk of outernet behavior that the locals were used to, but he found it totally alien. He took a look around for data coming out of Reservations, to see if that was progressing as it should.

There wasn't any.

None at all.

With a thrill he realized that he was not balanced at the edge of some normal anomaly, but something deliberately crafted, and probably not by Northstar. No doubt this was what had trapped his virus, as it was now entrapping every other program that wandered too close. A dead zone, into which data entered, from which it could not emerge.

He had used such zones in his own research, though they had been on university machines, far away from vital consumer systems. He was willing to bet whomever had done it on this machine didn't belong here.

On the one hand the thought was discouraging, for it meant that the disappearance of his virus might have been pure coinci-dence, unrelated to the purpose of this illicit construction. On the other hand he was curious now, and since the odds were at least two to one that the perpetrator was a hacker of some kind, he sent out a program that he knew would draw response from that type.

A short program, that he simply released. Sure enough, the tides of shifting data caught it up and moved it toward the Reservations gateway. Soon after it passed through it was swallowed by the dead zone, and Masada could no longer track it.

One second. Two.

*Curiosity is the lifeblood of the hacker*, he had once written, *and curiosity is what you must use to manipulate them. What they will not do out of respect for authority, or even to safeguard their own well-being, they will do if you spark their hunger to know. New data, new techniques, exploration of the incomprehensible, these are the coins that can be used to buy them, the lures that can be used to trap them, the chains that can be used to bind them.*

Three seconds.

He would have no way of knowing when his message would make contact. It contained only one word, which would overcome all other images for less than a second. *Hello.* Just that. The word was simple, but it implied a host of other messages. *I'm out here. I'm watching you. I know what you're doing. Want to know who I am?*

If that was a hacker inside the dead zone, he was willing to bet he'd come take a look.

Four seconds. Five.

The anchor program indicated that parameters were shifting. The flow of data toward Reservations slowed, then ceased.

Six.

Something probed him, a tentative touch, subtle and quick. Not quick enough. The minute direct contact was made a real-time trace was possible, and he locked onto the signal and began to race toward its source. The time delay from the skip wasn't enough to impede his chase, but it made the effort disorienting; thank God his quarry wasn't on his home station either, so that they were on equal footing.

He followed the signal back through the node, into the skip, and onto another station. Code was strewn across his path like boulders across a road; he managed to work his way around the obstacles without pausing for breath. Another node, another skip, another hailstorm of obstacles. His quarry was trying to lose him with simple speed, and that just wasn't going to work. He followed him into the main processor of a waystation—

And hundreds of paths splayed out before him. Thousands,

in fact, each identical, each offering a gateway to somewhere else.

*Damn.*

This had been prepared long in advance, no doubt about that. This was the reason his quarry had taken the risk of probing him in the first place; because he knew that the way home was masked by so many forks in the road, no man could hope to follow him.

In the annals of hacking, Masada had just lost the chase. He could no longer follow the signal in real-time; by the time he explored half a dozen of these gateways the hacker would be offline and far from his connection point. No doubt he imagined himself safe already, and was congratulating himself on a neat escape.

Only it wasn't that. Not yet.

With the same meticulous care that Masada had once used to regress Lucifer, he now set up programs that would analyze all those gateways. He was willing to bet that they were designed to impede the flow of data, slowing down any programs that might try to get through during pursuit. All but one, of course; that way would be wide open, the mousehole through which his quarry meant to slip. In time he would know which gateway that was, and his sniffers would search for the hacker's trail on the other side. In time, by virtue of meticulous effort, not speed and ingenuity, those sniffers would work their way to the end of the trail, and discover what system the original signal had been launched from.

He couldn't get the hacker's name this way, nor any other specific information about him. But he could find out what station he worked from, and where on that station he went for outernet access. That was a start.

Setting his sniffers in motion, he retraced his own signal back to Aires Station, to the place where the dead zone had been. It was no longer there. A wealth of trapped data was stranded in Reservations, wounded programs limping home, new input rushing through the troubled area, searching for connection . . . and there was his virus. Lucifer-X. It didn't take him long to find it; the virus was motionless, and situated at what would have been the center of the dead zone. He called up its homing sequence just to make sure that this was the spore he had indeed lost, a simple act of confirmation. Or so he thought.

It wasn't there.

Across the light-years of inspace and outspace, across the vast synapses of the human brain, he stared at the code he knew all too well. This wasn't Lucifer-X, his own safe creation. This was another spore. The real thing. And from the way it was held still in the heart of what had been the dead zone, he was willing to bet this was what his quarry had been working with, hidden inside Northstar's system.

Heart pounding, he gathered up the deadly spore in a network of code so tightly woven that not even *it* could slip through. He'd never been this close to the thing before without a protective interface between them. But he could hardly go away and leave it here. Any minute now Northstar's security would be storming through the place, repairing crucial pathways, clearing out debris.

Slowly, carefully, cradling the killer to him, he backed out the way he had come. Through the sickening chaos of the outernet, which these people called home. Across the vistas of his own fear, cold sweat-drenched body sitting rigid behind its desk, headset and the hair beneath made clammy by the exudates of physical tension.

Carefully, as one might handle a bomb, he outloaded the spore that he had rescued and quickly sealed it up in a sterile chip. His wellseeker told him to go get food and drink, and to take a bath. Instead he picked up the chip and headed out to his special lab, where he might study it in safety.

Five hours later, he knew that the spore had been altered, and not by the Guild.

Six hours later, one of his sniffers returned to tell him where it had come from.

PARADISE.

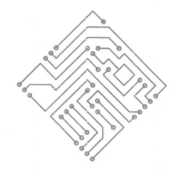

How ironic, that one of the most terrible conditions man can suffer should become linked to our conquest of the stars. How unfortunate, that in man's struggle to take control of his own destiny, he nearly eradicated the very genetic pattern which promised to set him free. How awesome a validation of our culture it is, that only here on Guera was such potential noted, nurtured, and finally made to serve us as it should.

GUILDMASTER ARIANNE BERLIN
"Guardians of Destiny": Keynote address to
the 421ˢ Guildmaster's Conference, Guera
Node, Tiananmen Station

# PROSPERITY NODE
# PROSPERITY STATION

**C**ALM WAS the outward world of Guildmaster Ian Kent. So calm. A world rendered in shades of gray upon gray, a tranquilized universe of ordered shapes and emotions. Peaceful gray halls with soft-edge shadows. Skylights of pearl and mist. Human flesh rendered in tones of clay and ash, with no hint of living blush, noxious sallow, or any other hue of life. And behind this bleached world, always, the gentle flow of chemicals into his bloodstream. He could hear it if he listened closely enough, sedatives seeping out into his veins with the measured precision of nuclear decay. Chemicals that diluted his despair until it was, like the rest of his world, muted and colorless.

The entrance to his home was impressive in its size, and doubtless it was pleasing in its design. He wouldn't know. His staff hadn't told him what colors they had used, and he would never ask. The words would mean nothing to him. Though the rods and cones of his eyes functioned perfectly, though the optic nerves transmitted signals without flaw, that portion of his brain which would interpret such concepts was gone. One moment was all it had taken. One moment of equipment malfunction, one second of feedback into his neural circuits, a flash of heat and unbearable light and then the slow awakening . . . into hell.

You are lucky, they told him. Damage confined to optical processing, and only a small part of that. You are so lucky, so very lucky. You could have lost motor control, and been crippled. Or intellect. You could have lost that. You could have lived life as a vegetable, not even knowing who you were. This is better, they told him, much better. You'll see.

Fools!

*Be wary of dragons breathing red*, his own notes warned him. Ainniq memories, recorded in happier days. Now he couldn't even read the simple message without a tightening in his gut, a sharp pain in his heart . . . and a twinge in his arm as the outpilot's mechanism within squeezed forth another precious drop of tranquilizer. What was red? He could recite its definition, he could list its associations—heat, anger, lust, violence—but it was book-learning only; the words might be in a foreign language for all he understood them.

Color.

You could survive without color, in the outworlds. You could maneuver without it, you could identify dangers, you could make your way from one day to the other without being devoured by monsters. You could live gray, and work gray, and die at the end of a gray life, a natural death.

Not so in the ainniq.

"Sir?"

He looked up from the work he was doing to acknowledge his secretary's appearance. Chezare Arbela was a man who had long since become accustomed to Kent's tranquil nature and adapted to it. Accordingly he never looked hurried, even when he was, and never, ever seemed anxious. It was as if he had established some osmotic link to the Guildmaster which allowed Kent's pharmacopoeia to flow directly into his bloodstream. Others found the relationship disturbing, and Kent knew they gossiped nervously about it when he wasn't listening. He found it calming to have a man so in sync with his moods, even if the moods were artificially induced. Even his Syndrome found this man acceptable company, which was saying a lot; without the flood of chemicals to rein it in, his Syndrome tended to regard every living creature as an enemy.

And yet, there was a pleasure in that. An honesty, in facing the darkness in your soul head-on, without mask or artifice. He used to say that piloting was his safety valve, for only then could he let the monster inside himself run free. The memory of those times was terrifying, but also exhilarating. To let this drugged tranquillity fade into the background, and slip off the yoke of conformity which brainware imposed upon his soul . . . and there was a thrill in that. There was *life* in that, as vital and as dangerous as the primeval experience. Man as prey, fleeing hunters. Man as victor, emerging unscathed. The unbelievable rush of triumph as your outship broke through the surface of the ainniq, dragons snapping at your very heels. . . .

What did he have now to take the place of that? Paperwork. Administrative duties. Occasionally diplomatic assignments, in deference to his drugged and adaptable nature. It wasn't what his soul wanted. It wasn't what it *craved.*

"What is it, Che?"

"The latest report on the League, sir." The secretary put a chip down in front of him.

With a sigh he picked it up and loaded it into his headset. Data scrolled before his eyes, and he glanced over it once just to see that everything was in order. It was. A little less data than usual, perhaps, but nothing to trigger alarms. At least not on the surface.

"Nothing unusual?"

"No, sir."

This was such a waste of effort. Having him scrutinize the Hausman League in the hopes that he would catch the Guild's saboteur was just . . . well, ridiculous. Granted, their station technically had Isolationist status and therefore fell into the Prima's *most suspect* category, but how could one even imagine that they were involved with Lucifer? The League venerated all the children of Hausman and believed the outworlds should belong to them alone. Their Isolationist status reflected the fact that no Terran, Earthborn or otherwise, was allowed in their station space. The disruption of ainniq-based transportation would hurt the Variant races much more than it would hurt the Terrans, so why would they ever launch something like Lucifer? Yes, they were extremists, but not stupid extremists.

"All right. Thank you, Che. Keep watching."

The secretary bowed and withdrew.

All right now. It was time to remember that there were other enemies, very real, whom he had to watch. Not aliens, nor saboteurs, but men and women who wore the same Guild sigil that he did. They were his allies in name, but no Guildmaster was foolish enough to believe that alliance was anything more than a token gesture. At least not anyone who had climbed as far up the ladder of Guild hierarchy as he had.

This E-month the competition was even more intense than usual, thanks to Lucifer. The Prima had chosen her five most trusted Guildmasters, and in doing so, defined the field of battle for them all. Kent had no doubt that any one of them would go after him in a minute if he gave them the opening to do so. Even Ra. Gentle, accommodating, hedonistic Ra. He trusted her least of all, for he knew from his own experience what kind of monster could lie coiled behind such a pleasant façade. Those who seemed most above suspicion were the ones you had to suspect the most.

Like all the Guildmasters, he had a cadre of communications experts who kept watch over his rivals' encrypted transmissions. His had been working double time since the day the Prima met with them, not only searching for Lucifer's source, but keeping a close eye on the others who were searching. He knew Delhi well enough to know that she thrived on situations like this, for a snake strikes best when its prey is distracted. He had spies in her node, of course, and mechanical spycams, and even a few data pirates whom he paid under the table, just to back up his more legal efforts. It was more effort than he had expended with any other Guildmaster, but she was truly dangerous, and only a fool would underestimate her. Varsav was devious but not as openly malicious, and Hsing's focus had all been internal since the day he returned from Guera. Nevertheless Kent went over their records as well, looking for some change in the pattern of data transmission which would indicate that something unusual was happening. A peak in communications activity, for instance, much like that which had drawn his attention to Delhi's node about an E-month ago. Some big project was underway in that woman's house, and the laws of political survival demanded that he figure out what it was.

He was halfway through the report on Delhi's activity when something began to bother him.

He shut down the data feed for a moment, so that his eyes saw nothing but the real world again, and tried to put his finger on just what manner of unease was stirring in the back of his brain, begging for definition. Something about the pattern of his search, the significance of a sudden peak in communications activity—

Or maybe . . . the lack thereof?

Very slowly, very calmly, he loaded the League chip into his headset again. And scanned the figures which his people had provided. No peak of activity there . . . but maybe just the opposite. Was that significant? He flashed an icon that would connect him to the house computer, gave instructions for isolating the information he needed, and waited several seconds while it digested the project. Then fresh new data began to scroll across his field of vision—a record of communications activity for the League during the past few E-months—and the numbers were remarkably uniform, profiling an active station with pretty much regular business in the outworlds.

Until now.

With a frown he flashed an icon to call his secretary back in. Arbela must have been close by, for the knock came almost immediately.

"Come in."

The secretary looked puzzled. As well he should, given that Kent was a creature of ritual and habit, and this behavior fell into neither category. "Sir?"

"Those files you gave me on the League. The com report." He paused. "Was it complete?"

Arbela's brow furrowed. "It's the same report you've gotten each day, sir."

"You're sure? Nothing's been left off? This is complete, absolutely complete as is?"

"Yes, sir. But I can check, if you like."

"Please do."

Arbela hesitated. "May I ask . . . sir . . ."

He stood, banishing the strange data from his head with a thought. "Let's say for now the League is . . . unusually quiet. Remarkably so. I don't know yet what that means, but I have no doubt it's significant." Damn it all, he could think of a hundred reasons why a station would suddenly become more active—a thousand, easily—but the opposite? How did you explain something like that?

*It might not be Lucifer,* he thought, *but something unusual is going on there.* "Confirm the data for me," he ordered Arbela. "Then let's start a more detailed sampling of the League's transmissions. I want to know why they're suddenly going quiet. Any ideas you have are welcome. This is most unusual." He shook his head in frustration. "Do we have informants on their station?"

Arbela hesitated. "Yes, sir. Two, as I recall. Do you want me to get in touch with them?"

"Not yet. Too risky. Let's see where the data analysis takes us first, so we know what questions to ask." He scowled, then flinched slightly as a twitch in his arm told him that yet more sedative was being released. "This may all be innocent as hell, but if that's the case I want it confirmed. You understand?"

"Yes, sir. Of course, sir."

He waved the secretary out with a short gesture. Che was a good man, he'd find the data if it was there. And of course Kent had his spies in the League, who could help him when it came time for a real investigation. He had spies everywhere that it mattered, even in Delhi's own household. How else did you keep control of your enemies, and make sure that friends were what they claimed to be?

With a sigh he called up the League's data once more, and began to scrutinize it closely.

Chezare Arbela walked quickly through the Guildmaster's house, flashing orders as he went. Instructions went out to Kent's programmers, to his analysts, to the people who designed and maintained his spy-eyes, everyone. They all had their part to play in this, and Arbela's job was to orchestrate the overall effort so that each part was not only perfect, but perfectly intermeshed with all others.

He would do that, of course. It was his job. It was what he excelled at, and the reason Kent had hired him.

SEND ME A COURIER, he instructed.

How the Guildmaster must value Arbela, who had served him faithfully for so many years. How content Kent must be to know that he had such a capable and intelligent man to rely upon, one who could serve as a true extension of his will in all things.

The courier met him in his outer office. He looked like a mere boy, whose bland countenance seemed devoid of any profound emotion. The age was the result of surgical art, of course, and the expression a sign of his professional competence. Live couriers had no value if they stood out from the crowd. This one would go unnoticed, he was willing to bet, even from Delhi's hawk-eyed crew.

Arbela took out of his pocket a chip he'd had ready for weeks, and watched while the boy uploaded it into his brainware. Data pirates might intercept the transmissions from a station, but they were hard pressed to pick out which traveler among millions had a vital letter tucked in between his brain cells. A simple enough program allowed the courier to store his message without giving him access to it, so that he might carry it in safety. And even if the message were hijacked somehow, Arbela knew that no one could break through its encryption, save the one person it was meant for.

He imagined the words as they would appear before that person's eyes, blood red letters against a background as black as space itself.

THE STILL WATERS STIR. ACTION IS REQUIRED.

"Go," he commanded. The courier obeyed. Arbela's program would give him further instructions on the way.

*Now*, Arbela thought, *the game begins in earnest.*

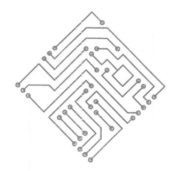

Until you understand how the enemy thinks—so well that you can pass for one of his own—you have no hope of ever controlling him.

DR. KIO MASADA,
*"The Enemy Among Us"*

# PARADISE NODE
# PARADISE STATION

**I**T SPOOKED Phoenix, what had happened in Northstar.

It wasn't like he'd never gotten caught before. It was just . . . a weird move that guy pulled on him. Too clever to be security, they just didn't think like that. And yet . . . a hacker?

Some of his diversionary programs had reported back to him. He had them do that sometimes, just to see who was following him and how far they got. It was risky, since anything coming back to him could be traced, but he had them do it way after the fact, long after security had stopped watching for him. And of course, he'd put in safeguards there, too . . . though he wondered now if this guy couldn't get through them. Damn, he'd been fast!

Anyway, he checked those programs out and then just sat back in amazement, not quite believing what he saw. And then he took a chance and actually hacked back into Northstar himself—they'd increased the security since his last visit, so it took nearly five minutes—to see what was left of the gateways he had set up. And to check who'd tried to go through them.

Every one had been tested. Every single one.

By the same program.

Now, if you'd told him that twenty or thirty had been breached, he'd have said that he expected it. Most guys would try that many before they realized that sheer numerical odds were against them. If you told Phoenix that some guy had waded through a hundred or so to find the one most likely to lead to him . . . well, maybe if he was determined enough he might, though most guys just gave up when they realized they could no longer catch him in realtime. *But every single one?* Statistically speaking, that meant that once his pursuer had figured out which way Phoenix had gone, he hadn't come right after him, but had inspected all the other gateways first. What a bizarre move. What kind of security worked like that, long after they knew the trail was cold?

Unless he wasn't smart enough to figure out which way Phoenix had gone.

*Yeah, right.*

So that made him nervous. Enough that he beefed up his own in-house security and sent out a few sniffers looking for the guy's equipment signature. He'd picked that up from one of the gateways—a refinement he'd only added recently—and it was hard to say how he felt when he saw the results. Pleased, that he'd gotten away from someone using an experimental Sonroya prototype? Or doubly spooked, that someone with access to state-of-the-art equipment was so obviously interested in him?

All right, so the sniffers would look for this guy. In the meantime, it really bothered Phoenix that he'd had to leave a copy of the virus behind. He hadn't dared go right back to search for it, for fear his pursuer was watching for such a move, but he'd come back a day later to scoop it up. No luck. It was gone from the cyber horizon, and all his cursing about the hours he'd put into making sure it couldn't wander off on its own was wasted. He, Phoenix, key man in one of the sleekest hacking cadres in outspace, had loosed another copy of the damned thing into the outernet. If his fellow moddies found out about that, they'd have him flayed alive and brain-fried. And he wouldn't try to argue them out of it.

"Hello?"

The unexpected noise broke his concentration, and the code which had been hanging in midair disappeared in favor of a shimmering hourglass. That wasn't like Chaos, to say something to him while he was so clearly working. He turned to the source of the voice . . . and then realized it wasn't Chaos. Of course not. Chaos was dead, fried by the same virus he had just let loose. This was someone else.

"I'm sorry, I didn't mean to bother you."

It was the girl from Nuke's.

How *soft* she seemed, compared to yesterday. All of her self-assurance must have slipped away while she was sleeping. He pulled out a chair for her and pushed it over. She was wearing a shirt he'd given her the night before, a big knit thing from Chaos' stuff. Only he realized now that it hadn't belonged to Chaos, really, but was one of his own that she'd commandeered months ago. On this girl it was really oversized, and those hesitant blue eyes combined with the loose folds of somebody else's shirt made her look just too waiflike for words.

In a strange way that was even more attractive than how she'd looked the day before. He found he had to clear his throat before saying anything. "Um, you want some breakfast?"

She looked around dubiously at the cluttered apartment, where the containers of at least five previous breakfasts were still to be seen. Her spiky hair had flattened down overnight, he noticed, and now you could see just how bad the cut was. Unless some planet thought that ragged mess was fashionable. Jesus, it looked like someone had just taken scissors and lopped it all off.

*Use your brain, Phoenix. She's in hiding. Wants to look different. Did it herself, maybe?*

Well, on a station like Hellsgate no one cared, but on Paradise people were fashionable enough that mistakes tended to get noticed. And he was willing to bet that the last thing she wanted to be, was noticed. He'd have to get her to a real stylist soon, or at least someone who could fake it better than that.

Speaking of which. The sniffers should be back soon.

She wrapped her arms around herself in a hesitant, vulnerable kind of way that shouldn't have gotten to him, but it did. "Yeah. That would be nice." There was hunger in her voice, pretty obvious once he listened for it. Strange that she hadn't asked for anything before . . . or maybe not so strange, if she didn't want to stress this unexpected hospitality which had come to her out of nowhere.

"What would you like?"

A hesitation. "What do you have?"

He got up from where he was working and maneuvered through the narrow path that wound between equipment benches, to where the keeper was. Opening it, he read off the labels of ingredients to her, shelf by shelf. Most of it was juice and fizz and stuff, but there were actually a few things that might have nutrients in them. Mostly stuff that Chaos had left behind. He read those labels off slowly, hoping she'd catch the hint. She looked like she needed some real food in her.

She chose a package of faux eggs and he decided to try the same. Thirty seconds to nuke them while he searched for clean plates. Usually he just ate stuff out of the packages, but this was different; she was *company*. In the end he could only find one plate that didn't have something old and dry stuck to it, so he put his in the cleaner and gave it a few seconds to vibrate the hardened crap off. That and the eggs finished up about the same time. He served them with a flourish, then chilled her a box of juice while she settled down into Chaos' old chair to eat.

God, she was pretty. More now than before. That had been a kind of obvious sex thing that went straight to your groin, circumventing the brain. This, this waif look, plucked at your heart strings. You wanted to help her, protect her, and feed her lots of nourishing things until the hollows under her eyes filled in and the color was back in her cheeks. He found himself almost blushing again, and turned quickly back to his work. A couple of sniffers had reported in, he saw, but he didn't want to go online long enough to see what they'd picked up. That would be rude with company in the house.

Like that would ever have bothered him before. Jesus.

He picked at his own faux eggs in silence as she ate hers with considerably more gusto. When she was done, he offered her more. She hesitated, and it took no expert to read that she was trying to balance her obvious hunger against a desire not to impose too heavily on his hospitality . . . so he just went ahead and cooked them up and gave them to her. These were chocolate chip. She looked at them pretty strangely, but ate them all the same. The way she handled her fork implied she had come from somewhere where pretty table manners mattered. For a moment he felt embarrassed about the cluttered state of his abode . . . then thought, *fuck it, she's a fugitive and I gave her safe haven, so she'd better have no problem with this.*

"So, like, Jamisia." He coughed a couple of times to loosen up the words that were catching in his throat. "I take it you've got a problem here that goes beyond money."

The blue eyes fixed on him, round and wide and . . . what?

Not quite scared. There was something else in those depths that wasn't just a lost waif, but someone very carefully dissecting his every word for hidden meaning. Spooky. Of course, she'd noticed his use of her real first name; he'd gotten that off the finance chip the other day. He'd thrown it at her to see her reaction, but she didn't seem surprised. It was almost as if the name she was called was irrelevant to her.

"Maybe," she said softly.

"The security bug on your accounts yesterday, that wasn't just looking for you, it was looking for anyone wanting information on you." He paused, drinking in those blue eyes for a moment. "Now, if this is drug stuff, or something else really black market, I'll be happy to feed you and get you on your feet, but then you've got to go."

"And if not?"

If not . . . would she stay? He felt strangely unwilling to meet that thought head on. "This is Paradise Station, and you probably don't know this, but there's a pretty strong popular movement against . . . certain things." *Like, Mama Ra lets us fuck around pretty freely, provided we don't fuck with her.* "So . . . it's not like I really think you would be into that . . ."

"I'm not," she said. She set the empty plate aside—she'd scraped up every last tidbit of egg, leaving it almost perfectly clean—and then straightened up in her chair. The softness in her eyes gave way to something that seemed almost . . . harder, somehow. More crisp. She seemed to consider for a moment, her eyes strangely unfocused, as if she were 'netting with someone. But of course she wasn't, not without a headset. You couldn't do that. Right?

"It's espionage," she said quietly. "Corporate. Terran corporate." She paused. "My father . . . did research. He died before that was finished. Some of his rivals think I know what it was about."

He had to ask it, of course. "Do you?"

She hesitated, then at last said, "No." But it sounded like she wasn't all that sure herself.

Corporate espionage. Jesus. Well, that would explain the level of security he'd run into on the Terran station. It also meant they were going to search for her and search for her and search for her again. Doubtless by now there were hundreds of programs scouring the outernet for any sign of her, and simple methods like cutting her hair or changing her name sure as hell weren't going to stop them. The Terran corporations were notorious in the outworlds, both for their Earth-based power structure and their utter lack of concern for local law. He'd recently heard of one case where a corporation blew up its rival's station, with people on it and everything. If that had happened in the outworlds there would have been swift retaliation, both from the Guild and from every station within shooting range. You didn't tolerate stuff like that, not ever. But Earth seemed to take things like that in its stride. Scary.

So . . . possibly the whole might of a Terran corporation was now focused on finding this girl. They'd have sniffers roaming all the stations, ID linked, and a host of other stuff. Dangerous, really dangerous, and not the kind of programs she'd be able to dodge on her own. He might well get himself killed for helping her. You shouldn't get involved in that kind of thing, he told himself, not when the stuff in your own head could get you locked up for life.

But . . .

Jesus, it would be a challenge. The kind of thing you probably couldn't brag about for a while, but if someday you could . . . yeah, that would be worth it. Bragging rights were a valuable commodity in his universe. Worth taking risks for.

And the girl. Hard to turn away a girl like that.

*You're getting soft in your old age, Phoenix.*

He brushed that thought away like a dust spot on a monitor. Didn't belong here. "Look, ah, I can help you. I've got some stuff on the outernet now, checking things out. We can take a look at that pretty soon, see what's come onto the station."

"I can pay—" she began. Then she flushed a bright red and looked down at her lap. "I'm sorry, that was habit, of course I can't—"

"Well, not without money I steal for you, but that's okay." He managed a grin and got up and took the plate from her. "Frisia's national debt was a little high anyway, nobody'll notice a few extra numbers added to it. Don't worry about it."

There: that sparkle in her eye, that told him he had pleased her and amused her and a dozen other good things. It was hard to get that from women. Most of them didn't much care what he could do with the circuits in his head . . . or with his brain, for that matter.

Something flashed red in his field of vision. Incoming. He stood still for a minute, accepting the icon, studying it.

"What is it?" she asked.

"One of the sniffers found something. Big time." He waved her to silence and shut his eyes, in order to see it better. Yeah, it was one of his, all right, and what it dragged behind it was longer than its own code. High security shit, right off the station cams. He found the chair by touch and sat down into it, heavily, ready to give the alien program his whole attention.

It was clean, and it was polished, and it reeked of the kind of programming you learned in school, or down the rungs of the corporate ladder. He recognized instantly what it was, of course; it was one of the things he'd expected to find, if someone big really was following her.

"Facial recognition program," he told her, his eyes still shut. "Looking for . . ." He scanned the codes, translating bits into features in his head, and finally said . . . "You."

"What does that mean?" She sounded nervous. Damn well should, too. This was no amateur maneuver.

"It means this little program is wandering around to all the security cams on the station and tapping into their feed. Then it's scanning for the most obvious features of your appearance— height, sex, Variation—" He waited for her to protest the last being included, but she didn't. Most Terrans in his experience would have. "Anyway, that done, it narrows down the field with other criteria, and so on and so forth, until eventually it matches the face recorded on the cam with its own files . . . look-ing mostly for bone structure and such, things that can't be changed easily."

"And it would . . . find me? Out of a whole station?"

"Only if you pass by the public cams. And even then it could take a good while. The program's only fast enough to sample a percentage of what it sees, if there are a lot of Terran women around on a given day who'll require attention. This isn't the kind of thing that gives immediate results," he warned. "Somebody's willing to put in the time it'll take to track you down. I think the pols actually run about eighty percent success on this kind of stuff, assuming their quarry isn't holed up in a private space somewhere. Or . . ." He couldn't help but grin; it was purely showing off. "Assuming no one's fucking with their programs."

"You can do that?" She was leaning closer to him, he could feel it. "I mean . . ."

"Fuck with their programs? Damn straight." He was already redesigning the sniffer, snipping off bits of its code and replacing it with segments of his own creation. "When I'm done with this thing, it wouldn't notice you if you walked up to the cam and smiled right into it." For a moment he was silent, as he wrestled with a particularly difficult bit of code. "Then . . . if it works right . . . it'll sail around the station finding nothing, appearing perfectly normal, so that its maker thinks it's working all right, you just aren't here."

She said nothing more, but he knew she was watching him. Too bad it didn't *look* more impressive, he thought. Like, something to do with his hands or his body, where each motion meant he had accomplished something. It would make programming a kind of dance that she wouldn't understand, but at least she could watch it happening. This way he was just slumped in his work chair, and could have been asleep for all she knew.

Far from it.

Sniffers like this were laden with security routines that you had to pry open carefully to slip your code inside. One wrong move and the thing would start sending warning signals back home. He'd already isolated it so that all such warnings would do was bounce around his home system, but it was still something to watch out for; you never knew when one might infect your machine and make its escape later. Surprisingly, this sniffer wasn't all that hard to work with. Good security, but nothing original or particularly dangerous. For someone who had cut his teeth on state-of-the-art security processors, it was hardly a challenge.

At last he had it done. He checked it over once more, just to make sure everything looked right, and then opened up his system and set the wounded bird loose. It would flop around enough to make people think it was doing its job, but the truth was it wasn't going to report anything to anyone. Unless you took a really good look at it, though, it would appear totally normal. *Good work*, he told himself. He called up his own sniffers again and checked them over, making sure that all was as it should be—

—only it wasn't.

"Phoenix?"

It was on the end of one of his sniffers, a small enough program that he had hardly even noticed it. Neat, clean, efficient . . . and linked to his own machine code.

Someone was trying to track him. They had found his program and followed it home. *Shit.*

"Are you okay?"

He sealed the thing up, wrapping it up in strings of security code so tight it couldn't move without his say-so, and then wrapping it up again. "Fine," he muttered. "Just fine." Someone was trying to trace him, and they had almost managed it. He'd been so busy showing off for the girl that he'd almost missed it. Jesus. That wasn't like him. He shook his head and then shut down his brainware, flashing it the icons that would put all his work on hold. He'd been careless, and that invited trouble. Hackers couldn't afford carelessness. Especially hackers whose own heads were so crammed with blackware that the first time the pol took a good look inside their skulls, they'd get locked up for life.

Like him.

"Phoenix?"

She was scared now, he could hear it. "Just a programming glitch," he assured her. It was clear from her expression that she knew it was something more. Damn it, he never was good at lying. "Look, there's just some work I have to do . . . but not from here. I'm going to have to go out for a while."

She reached for him and then withdrew her hand, clearly sensing that she could neither convince him not to go, nor come up with a good reason for accompanying him. "Look," he said, "you're safe here. As long as you don't go online nothing should be able to find you. And I won't be gone long, I promise." He hesitated, then took up a scrap piece of paper and scribbled down a com number. "Here's Nuke's number, okay? If I don't come back right away and you get nervous, you can call him. But I will. Really."

She looked unconvinced, but took the paper from him and folded it into her hand.

"It's okay. Really."

He knew she didn't believe it. He didn't believe it himself. But what else could he say?

He hurried out of the small apartment, flashing up maps of Paradise Station as he went.

*You don't hide a grain of sand by locking it away, you put it out on the beach and dare people to go looking for it.* Someone had said that in an old Earth viddie which he'd seen as a kid, and the line had stuck with him. He wasn't really clear on what sand was, of course, but a quick visit to a research site had given him enough information to make the context clear. He liked it.

He thought of that now as he took a tube to a distant mall, fighting his desire to fiddle with the programs stored in his headset. *Later. Later.* He couldn't afford to go shooting off thoughts to the outernet while he was still this close to home.

At last he got to his chosen "beach," a shopping mall on one of the interior rings. It wasn't on a level where tourists congregated, which meant that the locals flocked there to escape the press of alien crowds. A good thousand or more people were there in the section he chose, walking and talking and eating and shopping . . . or just hanging out, the favorite pastime of the young.

Of course there were the *loops*, and the *virts*, and infinite variations and combinations of the two. You saw those in any public place you went to, these days. He could see one woman sitting propped up against a storefront, her eyes glazed with contentment as some short bit of neural happiness-programming ran over and over through her head. There was a couple strolling hand in hand whose giggles and flushes were a good sign of some porn loop running through their heads. And of course there were the fantasy buffs with their state-of-the-art virt programs, translating everything into the context of their choice. One went flying past him on skates, swinging an imaginary sword at some imaginary enemy who just happened to occupy the body of a middle-aged Frisian. Another leered at every woman passing, as the program in his head substituted idealized naked features for clothing. Or maybe it put smiley faces on their butts; it was hard to tell what kids were into, these days. When Phoenix had been young—really young—the big thing had been Earth-virts, programs that substituted old Earth viddie settings for a more prosaic reality. He'd liked the science fiction settings best, bizarre alien landscapes with creatures so far removed from the human norm that not even the Hausman Effect could have explained them. You could buy a sandwich at a local vendor and turn the experience into some deliciously revolting piece of alien diplomacy, with live things squiggling beneath your tongue and some fish-finned snake-creature watching to see if you would *dare* spit it out. Of course, the other customers never quite understood why you made the face you did as you tasted the stuff . . . or maybe they did. It wasn't like virts were a secret thing, though they'd originally been designed for private entertainment. Adults were happy to use them that way, but kids were another thing. Was there ever a generation that didn't enjoy shocking its elders in public? Was there ever a world where adults didn't shake their heads in frustration, annoyed by the antics of the young, but unable to stop them?

At last he came to a place where consumer traffic was low, and a larger than usual number of virts seemed to have collected as a result. A handful of them seemed to be involved in some group fantasy down at the end of the corridor, which would eventually draw official attention; in theory such games were prohibited from the public walkways, though in fact they popped up any time the pol were absent. He bought himself a drink and walked slowly with it, sipping its frothy green contents as he sought out the pace of the local traffic. You could walk and work at the same time if you were good. He was good. All it took was a place where no one cared if he looked zoned out while he did so, and this was definitely such a place.

Slowing his step, brushing his hand against a nearby storefront to guide him, he gave his attention over to his brainware, and called up the program which had so disturbed him back at the apartment, to take a look at it. Slowly, carefully, he unwrapped it. It was a nasty little thing, a sniffer program keyed to the brand and model of his brainware. Not his headset, he noted; that would have been the normal search procedure, much easier information to access. Anyone with half an ounce of talent could trace a headset. But this sucker went for the brainware itself, the thing you couldn't change by buying a new interface. And it had found his codes attached to his program, and dug in its little data claws, and ridden the thing all the way back to his head.

*Not good.*

Thus far it didn't seem to be doing much damage, but that didn't mean it wouldn't start soon. Basically it seemed to exist only to locate him, and then send a signal back to someone once it had found him . . . which thus far he had kept it from doing. Now he needed to see if he could figure out where it had come from, and who the hell had his brainware specs in the first place. . . .

He took a table outside a local eatery, suitably crowded, and leaned back in the narrow chair, drink box in hand. Here in this public place the sheer number of users would help mask him from the enemy, if anyone tried to trace his signal.

. . . . *the enemy.* Jesus. Listen to him. It sounded like he was back in one of those virts right now, substituting aliens for shopkeepers and exciting spy plots for the angst of teenage existence.

But the girl was real. The people who were after her were real. Maybe this time, for once, life had caught up with the virts.

He lidded his eyes halfway, enough to darken his field of vision but not enough to look like that's why he did it. *Just a lazy guy, out for a drink and a snooze.* Meanwhile, inside his head, he began to unwind the nasty little sniffer, taking apart its code piece by piece, seeing what made it tick. It tried to send out a signal almost immediately, but that was okay; he had taken precautions, and its messages weren't going anywhere. Carefully he picked at it, searching for the one line of code that would tell its signal where to go. That's what he wanted to know. That's what he *had* to know, if he was going to come out on top of this crazy little cat-and-mouse game.

Suddenly the code faded from his field of vision. He stiffened, expecting trouble—but it seemed he had triggered some kind of graphics program, embedded in the homing sequence. Glittering stars suddenly filled his field of vision, then gathered at the edges in a luminous border. Part of his brain was aware that this could be a trap of some kind, meant to distract him, but he was so damned curious that he couldn't lock away. Slowly an image took form in the center of the darkness: faint outline of a way-station, encircled by half a dozen vast rings. Paradise. What the hell was this anyway, some kind of ad? That would be just great, all this work and fear and some stupid travelogue program had invaded his brainware—

And then an eddress resolved in front of his eyes. Just that. White letters against a black background: simple, plain, easy to read. Then it was gone. The after-image shivered in his sight for a moment, and then it too faded. The station and stars quickly followed, leaving him with only darkness.

*What the fuck . . . ?*

The sniffer had self-destructed, code strings unraveling into meaningless data before he could stop it. Apparently it had done its job, delivering that little scene, and now it wasn't going to give him a chance to analyze it further. Phoenix opened his eyes and blinked heavily, took a sip of his drink—now warm—and tried to make sense of what he had just seen. This guy had made up a sniffer program to find Phoenix, right? And it had found him, and tried to send out a message saying where he was. But all that was just window dressing for a three-second vid designed to play out inside his head? Which had been its purpose all along?

Shit. This was getting stranger and stranger.

He knew he shouldn't go check out that eddress. Doing so was about as reckless as a guy could get. On the other hand, how could he resist? The programmer who had sent this was good, damn good, and he knew that Phoenix was good, too, and respected it. He'd figured the hacker could spot his program, neutralize it, and then take it apart to see what was tucked away inside. There was almost an inherent challenge in the process: *if you aren't good enough to find this note, you aren't worth my time.*

How could any moddie resist that?

He had to take better precautions, though. He shut down his

hacking programs for a few minutes, letting ads run mindlessly through his upper visual field as he walked to the nearest tube. In better times he might have altered them, just for the fun of it, stripping models of their clothes or adding mustachios and sending them back to their maker. Now he was too preoccupied for such efforts.

This guy who had sent the sniffer . . . was he a hacker himself? The very nature of the invitation said he was, but other facets of his behavior argued against it. For now, Phoenix was reserving judgment. But whoever he was, he sure as hell was worth a hacker's attention.

He boarded an express tube bound for the upper levels. There were plenty of seats and he stretched out on three, body language making it quite clear that no one should ask him to move. He glanced up at the nodes in the ceiling, which would shunt his headset signal to the nearest outernet processor. At the speeds the tube would be traveling, that meant he'd be changing processors once every few minutes. If anyone was tracking him, they'd lose a lot of time adjusting, and time was everything in this game.

Content at last that he was as safe as he could ever get, he leaned back and shut his eyes and called up the eddress he'd been given.

He didn't head straight to it, of course. That would be too easy a trap to fall into, and not worthy of the invitation's maker. He rode the skip to Tiananmen Station, but then took a back door in through the shipping department of a local construction company. From there he hopped over to an educational processor, compliments of Rajastar University, and masked his presence with a torrent of undergraduate writing exercises, while he checked out the available routes to the data neighborhood he wanted.

So far so good.

He wondered if the guy was watching him. Probably he had sniffers lining every path to his place, and Phoenix had triggered all of them. If so, he hadn't seen any of them yet. Damn, this person was good. Who the hell was he?

He was all set up to move forward, and maybe launch a message into the guy's chosen site to stir up some response, when something hit him.

His field of vision suddenly went blank. He must have been pretty keyed up, because his heart almost stopped when it happened. Before he could respond in any way, an image appeared before him. Bright wings, red flames, a powerful bird flying headlong into a pyre of scarlet and gold. His namesake, the phoenix.

This was just too spooky. He tried to call up one of his own programs to break the thing down, to take control again, but every time he tried to bring up code, he just got another copy of the picture. It was as if he was surrounded by birds, and every time he tried to move, one got in the way.

For a moment he just sat there, breathless. Then he sent out an image of his own.

WHO THE FUCK ARE YOU?

The birds faded. Words took their place.

ONE WHO SEARCHES.

He didn't ask for what. That would have been too obvious. Only an amateur asked obvious questions. Only a amateur would answer them.

He thought about it for a moment, then flashed: MAYBE I CAN HELP.

And held his breath, waiting.

A data capsule appeared before him. He hesitated, knowing he shouldn't be taking chances . . . but curiosity won out. Just like this guy probably knew it would. He called up an antiviral program just in case, and cracked open the enclosing code on the thing. . . .

And saw what it was.

And closed it up again, really quickly.

Now his heart was pounding. Really pounding. There was nothing quite as scary as having *that* virus stare you in the face, and not know if it was a neutralized version or the real, very hot thing. Shit. He slapped a few extra security programs on the now-closed packet, just to make sure it would stay closed up tight, and then, for a lack of a more inspired response, flashed, NORTHSTAR

YES.

Shit. Shit.

WHY? appeared before him.

Shit.

*Okay, think this out. If he's the one who designed the damn thing, then he wants to know why you were fucking with it. There's no safe answer to that one. On the other hand, if he really was its designer, then he could have sent you a copy that would be in your head already, searching out the data he wants. Right? That damned thing was designed to snitch data, so why not just use it?* Suddenly he realized how utterly reckless he had been, opening the data packet up like that. But nothing bad had happened, right? So that told him something about the guy who sent it. *Okay, so let's say the odds are he's probably not responsible for it existing in the first place . . . and both of you know that. Right? So what does he want with it? And me?*

You didn't get that kind of data without offering something.

He thought about it for a few seconds, weighing his various options. Finally in his mind's eyes he formed the words, IT KILLED A FRIEND. And sent them.

There was no response.

Finally he added, YOU?

A long wait. Then: IT KILLED.

For the first time in several minutes, he found he could actually draw in a full breath.

YOU SEARCH FOR IT? he asked.

Again the answer was long in coming. It took no great genius to figure out why. If the guy was legit, and was really hunting the thing, he had to be sure that Phoenix was too before he committed himself. He'd be reviewing everything they'd said now, and everything he'd seen in Northstar, and assessing him with a hacker's eye. Because oh yeah, the guy had to be a hacker himself. There was no way around that. You could teach a good programmer how to track viruses and such, but you could never give them the cultural language that went with it. The minute Phoenix had seen the birds surrounding them, he knew this was one of his own.

I SEARCH FOR ITS MAKER.

He drew in a deep breath and sent back, DITTO. And he added, SO DO OTHERS.

YOU KNOW THEIR WORK?

Was it a trap? WHAT THEY'VE DONE. NOT WHO THEY ARE. That was true enough. Half of the people he talked to he only knew by their hacking nomen. It also was a clear signal to this guy that if he wanted information on others who were following the virus, he wouldn't get it from him.

WE SHOULD COMPARE NOTES, THEN.

MAYBE. He was taking a risk here, but shit, if this guy had more information on the virus than Phoenix's crowd had been able to dig up, that was a risk worth taking. He could see Chaos standing before him, bright as life, begging him with her eyes to find her killer, punish him, and see that no more moddies fell prey to his creation. NOT HERE. TOO INSECURE.

AGREED. LIVE ONLY.

He stared at the words in shock, not quite believing them. Was this guy crazy? Suddenly he was reassessing the whole conversation, and wondering just who and what it was on the other end. No hacker would have sent that suggestion to him. Hackers sometimes went their whole lives without meeting each other, outside of electronic forums. Did this guy really think he was going to put his *body* at risk for this? It was bad enough letting a stranger connect to his signal, he sure as *hell* wasn't going to walk into the office of some unknown person and just see what came of it.

NO FUCKING WAY, he sent. And he prepared to terminate the contact, just in case something nasty was to follow.

YOU WILL, the other assured him. BY YOUR OWN CHOICE. YOU WILL KNOW WHEN. And he signed it below, like a letter: MASADA

*What the fuck—*

The signal was gone. He tried to trace it, but realized pretty quickly that that wasn't going to happen. So he called back up that final image, that infuriating signature that promised too much and delivered too little.

Masada?

*The* Masada? As in Kio Masada, who had written the only handbook on computer security that any moddie respected? Who was a pain in the ass to Phoenix and his friends precisely because he understood them so well? Who had designed the

Guild defenses so well that testing them was almost a hacker rite-of-passage these days? *That* Masada?

Couldn't be. Shit. That would be like . . . that would be like meeting God online, and having Him drop you his eddress. Not damn likely.

So who the hell was using his name online?

He scoured around the data neighborhood for a brief while more, hoping to find some sign of the guy, some more information on him. But whoever he was, he hacked clean; every trail Phoenix could find dead-ended in a loop, sending him back where he started.

At last it was clear he wasn't going to find anything useful, and he gave up in frustration. He flashed an icon that cleared his field of vision so that he saw nothing but the real world again. The dead world, as some of his friends called it. People. Packages. The tube's interior. Blurred images outside, local stations not worth the time involved in stopping.

*Masada. Yeah. Right.*

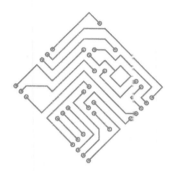

Sex isn't about sex. Sex is about power.

The pleasure of the body is mere window dressing to one who truly understands the game

SHARON GREER,
*The Human Dynamic*

# PARADISE NODE
# PARADISE STATION

SHE WAS WAITING for Phoenix when he came back. Of course. Where else did she have to go? She wasn't nearly as confident as he was that the station was safe for her, now that the facial recognition program had been neutralized, and besides, what business was there for her to attend to, that she had to go anywhere? For now it seemed safest to remain sheltered here, in the apartment of this man who so obviously found her mysterious and attractive. If only that could be manipulated into some more lasting feeling! What would happen when all her mysteries were solved, or other mysteries beckoned more loudly to him? She'd be on her own again, and that wasn't good. No, if Phoenix had taught her anything in their few hours together, it was that she needed a hacker to survive. The data jungle that was the outernet simply could not be navigated safely, not when so many predators were at large in it, creatures with her scent in their nostrils and blood on their claws.

She dreaded the day he would ask her more questions. She dreaded the moment he found out that she really, *really* didn't know the answers herself, and couldn't give him more information than she already had. Would he leave her then? Decide the intriguing mystery of her presence was not worth the risk of harboring a fugitive? Grow frustrated with her refusal to share her secrets with him, not really believing that she herself didn't know who was after her, or even why?

That could be dealt with. He was a man, and men could be manipulated. Men could be bound in a web of emotions so delicate that they never felt its touch, yet tangled so tightly they could never break free. It was hard to do such a thing quickly, of course . . . but then, that only made it more of a challenge. All of the Others could appreciate such a challenge, though they might argue for hours about how to meet it.

In the end it was Katlyn who told them what had to be done. Katlyn who made the preparations, and waited with bated breath to see what his response would be. The Others crowded around the edges of her consciousness like children at a viddie, vying for the best view. Even Derik was there, which surprised her. Normally when she took control of their body, he just sank down into the darkness and sulked.

*It's not that easy*, he told her.

Isn't it? She smiled. *Just watch me.*

Then the door slid open, and the hacker was home at last. Tall and a bit gangly, with a shock of blond hair haphazardly brushed across his forehead and a faraway look in his eyes. Not bad-looking, she assessed, though it was clear from the plain cut of his clothes and the rather careless way they had been assembled that he was unconcerned with his own appearance. She could have done worse.

He seemed not to notice her at first, lost in some hacker's reverie. She suspected that was pretty much his normal state. "Jamisia, I'm sorry it took so long, I had to—"

He stopped in mid-sentence. He had seen the apartment's interior. Clearly for all his sophisticated brainware, he had no way of processing such a vision.

Katlyn looked about the small space with what she hoped was an expression of charming innocence. "I just wanted to help out a bit, for all you've done." There: add a slight tremor at the end, expressed in voice and the trembling of a lower lip, to imply she was afraid she had displeased him. Because her fate was now in his hands, and she could not afford his displeasure.

*I'm going to gag*, Derik warned.

*Do it on your own time*, she thought back.

Phoenix entered the apartment and walked around, as if in a daze. In truth the transformation was hardly spectacular, but apparently it was unexpected enough to render him speechless. He went to the table where old dirty plates had been piled—now cleaned and stored away, and the other items on its surface neatened—and touched a finger to it as if suddenly remembering that yes, the tabletop *was* that color, how long since he had seen it?

It wasn't clean. Oh, no. Katlyn wasn't foolish. Katlyn knew what game she was playing, and she played it with finesse. Katlyn had been abandoned for a half a day on a strange and hostile station, and had realized that she needed more assurance of this man's protection than she currently had.

*He's mad at us,* Zusu crooned.

*Shhhh.*

Phoenix looked like a man in shock as he wandered around the apartment. He stopped at one or two places where items of special value were scattered—like his worktable, with all its electronic paraphernalia—and she could see him open his mouth as if to voice some criticism of her cleaning. But those things which he treasured had not been touched at all. Every piece of wire, every chip, every headset fragment, was exactly where he had left it. She had cleaned around those things, avoiding the sacred sites of his manhood, sweeping away the mess which surrounded with enough discernment and sensitivity that he could find no cause for protest.

He knew, of course. Deep inside his soul, where men rarely looked, he knew exactly what had taken place. She could see the concept struggling toward his lips, trying to shape itself into words. But men didn't have those words. Men were creatures of confrontation and certainty, who didn't deal well with the subtle gray realm of hints and intuition. And she could see it in his face when he finally decided to ignore those internal warnings, the hints of a game that was beyond his understanding.

"You . . . cleaned up."

She bit her lower lip in what should look like uncertainty. He responded well to her vulnerability, so she was trying to play up that role. "I hope you don't mind. I was here for so long, and the place . . ." She managed to blush, as if from embarrassment. "It kind of needed it."

*You were gone for a long time and I marked your territory, not so blatantly that you would reject it, not so subtly that you could ignore it. Can you feel my presence around you now? Everywhere you look, everywhere you move.*

When he said nothing she offered, "I tried not to move any-thing important—"

"No. You didn't. You didn't at all." He shook his head as if to clear stray thoughts from it, and at last, the male processing done, a grin spread slowly across his face. "It's great. Thanks."

She beamed at him, warmed by the light of his praise. It was an expression she'd been practicing all afternoon, and it had its intended effect.

*This is no challenge at all,* she mourned to the Others.

*Stop complaining,* Raven told her. And Derik smirked, *They can't all be Variants.*

He sat down in the chair by his desk in what was obviously a state of utter exhaustion. She could not have asked for a better opportunity if she had scripted it herself. Slowly she came up behind him as he rubbed at a kink in the back of his neck. Physical tension. Good. "Did you do what you needed to?"

He began to curse, then stopped himself, as if embarrassed at giving her offense. That was pretty amusing, as she'd heard far worse inside her own head than he could ever manage. Derik had inured them all to such language long ago.

"Sort of. I—" He jumped slightly as her hands touched his shoulders—gently, so gently—and then began to stroke the points of tension along the crest of his muscle. "Ah. I . . . ah, found the person I was looking for. Don't know who he is yet, not really. Gave me a name." Eyes shut, he relaxed into the gentle kneading, surrendering his tension to her caress. "Not his real name, of course."

"How do you know?"

"Said he was Masada." He laughed shortly.

"Masada?"

"Famous outernet theorist. You wouldn't know . . . oh, that feels good there." She saw him sink down into his chair about two inches as she stroked the muscles of his upper back. "Scary son of a bitch, whoever this guy is. But not damn likely to be Masada."

There was silence then, a few minutes stretched out long and smooth by the contact of fingers upon flesh. The thin material of his shirt slid easily over his pale skin, and it was some minutes before she slipped her hands under it, touching his skin directly. He jumped as she did so. *Easy. Easy.* . . .

He had to talk, of course. The silence was too intimate. "It was really nice, what you did with the place. That you did it, I mean."

Her fingers slid down over his chest as she leaned forward, the warmth of her body close enough to be felt now along his back. She felt him shiver slightly, and knew that he was aware to the inch of just how close she was. "You've done so much for me," she said softly. Hands stroking gently over his lean torso, feeling him stir slightly, clearly both aroused and disconcerted by her attentions. That was good. Men were easiest to control when they were off balance. This one was working out just fine.

At last he moved, rising from the seat, taking two steps forward to get out of her reach. *Not unexpected*, she assured the others. All part of the game. She could sense Jamisia watching in awe, which was good; the girl had to learn this someday.

"I . . . um . . . it's all right, I was glad to help . . ." He fumbled with some piece of machinery on his workbench, turning it this way and that and tapping it against the table, as if trying to think of something suitably urgent to do with it. She didn't move toward him, but let the moment play itself out. If the prey got too nervous, he would bolt for cover, and then the chase must begin all over again. Not a bad prospect under normal circumstances, but right now she didn't have the time for that kind of prolonged game.

Finally he looked up at her. That was her cue. Holding his gaze, she moved forward again—slowly, softly, and most importantly, wordlessly. He started to say something. She reached out and touched a finger to his lips, warning him to silence. *No, my sweet, this isn't something you can put into words, so don't even try. What are you going to say? That you don't know what's happening here, or why? That part of you knows you should protest, but the far larger part of you has no desire to? That you're used to cold data, which can be categorized, analyzed—controlled—but the chemistry of human interaction is something else again?*

*My sweet little hacker, it's all just a fantasy. Pretty young girl wrapped in mystery winds up in your arms, and I know you want her. I saw that clearly yesterday. You don't know her name and you don't know her story, but there just might be something in her head that's worth finding out about, and that's sexier to you than half the showgirls in Paradise, isn't it? Warm and willing flesh wrapped about dark tech secrets, the ultimate elixir of seduction for your kind. Can you resist it? Do you have a reason to?*

Apparently not, for as she came to him he made no attempt to escape her. She did not need to draw his arms around her, or make more than a token effort to invite his embrace. He tried once more to say something, and once more she stopped him, this time with a lingering kiss. *It's a fantasy. Just a fantasy. Words will make it real. Shhh.*

There were probably men who could resist such a lure, she mused. Not that she'd ever met one. Her men had all been delightfully predictable, from start to finish.

This one was no exception.

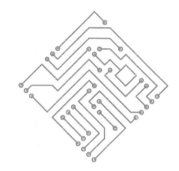

People of Earth.

We have come back to you.

Across alien vistas unimagined by your science, past dangers more terrifying than you can guess, through three years of slow-space travel to reach Terra from the nearest transit point. We have come to tell you that man has claimed the stars once more. And we are offering you a share in his triumph.

Do not mistake my message, or my nature. My race is one of very few who still wear the outward form of our ancestors. All those Hausman mutations which you so feared, they have all come to exist. The galaxy is filled with creatures you would not recognize, all of whom call themselves human. My people, the Guerans, have committed themselves to finding them all, every lost and lonely colony, and bringing them back into the human fold. And we make the same offer to you now. Throw off your Isolation and embrace the stars; we will take you there, and show you how you can share the galaxy with us.

But if you choose to remain here in solitude, know that this offer will never be repeated. My crew and I have all given six years of our lives to come here to say these words; if you turn us down, there will be no second chance.

As for Hausman's children, should you join us, you will attempt to accept them for what they are.

They, in turn, will attempt to forgive you.

Choose.

> SEARCH COMMANDER HARIMAN
> ALEXANDRIA,
> in his televised address to Earth.
> (Historical Archives, Hellsgate Station.)

# GUERA NODE
# TIANANMEN STATION

THE DOOR chimed to let Dr. Masada know he had a visitor. It wasn't a particularly welcome interruption, but when you weren't in your own home you had to deal with such things. Back on Guera the portal mechanism would have made it quite clear that he was busy, and would rather not be interrupted.

"Who is it?" he demanded.

The voice that responded was unknown to him, but its owner claimed to be a Guild messenger. Very well. He flashed for the lock to disengage and it did; the heavy panel slid aside to reveal a man with the Guild sigil brightly embroidered on his uniform.

"I'm here to inform you that you have a visitor," the man said stiffly. "Guildmaster Anton Varsav."

Varsav? A Guildmaster? Why would such a man come here to him? He could think of no reason . . . unless Varsav had discovered something that couldn't be entrusted to the normal lines of communication.

If so, *that* would be worth hearing about.

He put his work on hold with a quickly flashed icon and stood. After so many hours staring at nothing but computer code in his head, the sudden motion made him dizzy. "Tell him to meet me in the forward reception room."

The servant bowed a crisp acknowledgment and left. Despite his excitement, Masada took the time to shut down all his programs and double-check his security guards. Was he reading this visit right? He was all too capable of mistaking alien protocol, and the Guild's customs here in the outworlds were foreign to him. Nevertheless, the signs seemed unmistakable. Guildmasters didn't make trips like this for casual reasons.

The walk to the reception room was short, the more so since he walked it quickly. Varsav was already there. He was a darkly impressive man, whose long Gueran traveling robes were split open to reveal a tighter, more polished layer beneath. His dark eyes roamed about the room quickly, restlessly, absorbing all, and his hands moved likewise to the nearest furniture, as if to assure himself that it was solid. His kaja was primarily *natsiq*, with traces of the restless *shru* woven in. He stared at Masada's own face for a minute, taking in its painted message, then said curtly, and without offering his hand, "Anton Varsav, Guild-master of Adamantine Node."

Masada likewise offered no physical contact. The involuntary movements of the *shru* were hard enough on his *iru* nerves; putting his hand in the grasp of such a man was out of the question. "Kio Masada, Specialist in Data Security . . . currently in service to the Guild."

Varsav looked about, noted several chairs grouped around a table, and gestured toward them. They took up positions opposite each other, Varsav's hand roaming the edges of the nearer chairs as he spoke. In deference to Masada's kaja—and perhaps his own as well—he jumped right into the business at hand.

"I have a communication my people collected from one of the stations in my node. An Isolationist station, Terran extremists. . . ." He exhaled noisily in what was obviously disgust, and pulled a thin plastic sheet out from his inner tunic. "This was going out to the Terran waystation."

Masada took the sheet from him, unfolded it, and skipped over the codes of interstellar communication to read the brief message beneath.

TROUBLE COMING. THE ENEMY SEEKS CHILDREN. SEND ALL HOME ASAP. LUX AETERNA.

Masada's brow furrowed as he read the words once, twice, and then again. There were almost too many questions to ask; it was hard to pick which to start with.

Restless with his extended silence, Varsav offered, "We had to sort through every fucking piece of mail in my node to get hold of that. My programmers must be cursing my name by now . . . as I'm cursing this whole damned project." He gestured impatiently toward the letter. "Well? What do you think?"

"I think . . ." He drew in a deep breath. "It could be part of this. Hard to say, with so little text." He studied the text again. "Lux aeterna?"

"Eternal light. Lucifer was the angel of light, in Terran mythology. That was one of my search clusters."

*The enemy seeks children. . . .*

"This could refer to the data I'm now seeking," he said quietly. "If so . . ." He shook his head, his mood dark. "Then someone is leaking very confidential information." He looked up at Varsav. "You say this was going to Earth."

"No. The Terran waystation. I checked the routing string, it leads to a mail drop for Earth." His dark eyes fixed on Masada; their sudden stillness was disconcerting. "The station that sent it might well be conspiring with Earth. don't you think? First to steal our secrets, then to strike out at our pilots. They hate us enough to do that. Shit, they've got an outernet site that all but tells 'true humans' to go out and kill us. Practically gives them instructions on how to do it."

Masada nodded. That made sense. Process and motive all wrapped up in one neat little package. The letter was a slim lead at best, but in a game like this that was likely to be all they'd get. He'd work with it and see if Varsav's hypothesis could be verified.

He smoothed the letter down on the table and said, "We'll start by investigating the mail drop—"

Varsav reached out suddenly and put his hand on Masada's own; the unexpected physical contact was jarring.

"There's more," he said sharply.

Masada withdrew his hand, said nothing.

Varsav took out a second piece of paper from his tunic pocket and spread that out for the professor to look at. Masada did so, and recognized immediately the audit trail for the message. Long strings of code which would track where it had been written, what kind of machine it had been written on, and how and where and on what it had been transmitted. He glanced at the header to see if the serial code matched that of the letter. It did. So did the counter which was hidden in mid-string, meant to reveal if the code had been tampered with. It hadn't been.

Finally he looked up at Varsav, waiting for further information on exactly what he was supposed to be looking at.

"Don't you see it?" It took no great *nantana* skill to hear the hostility in his tone. "I thought this was your specialty."

"It traces this message from its origin on the New Terran Front Station—I assume that's what this part refers to—to wherever you intercepted it." He looked up at Varsav again. "These things can't be faked, Guildmaster. The eddress on a letter, yes. The visible signs of where it came from. You can even alter the codes used to confirm such things, if you have the skill, so that it's all internally consistent. But these audit codes, which are normally invisible to the sender . . . if you knew enough to seek them out, then you know they can't be changed. They've tracked every phase and movement of this message, from the moment it originated until the moment you intercepted it. Those facts can't be altered."

Varsav rubbed the table with both his fists, a frenzied movement. "The machine, man. The thing that sent it out. Look at *that*."

He did so. "Sonroya model XSE 200 + ." He paused, all too aware that he was failing to see whatever Varsav was driving at. "That's one of the best portable computers made. I would assume anyone doing work with Lucifer would have at least something of that quality, if not—"

"Don't you see!" He snatched the paper back in frustration and shook it in Masada's face. "*Sonroya*. That's a Frisian-owned company, start to finish. A *Variant* company." He paused, drawing in a long, noisy breath. "*Now* do you understand? These are Terran extremists on that station! They hate to breathe the same *air* as Variants. It bothers them to be within ten million miles of anything *touched* by a Variant. Now, you're telling me they're sending out their most secret data on a Variant-made machine? *I don't think so*."

For a moment there was silence. A long and heavy silence, with those words hanging in the air between them, daring either one to speak.

At last Masada dared, "You're saying this letter didn't really come from the Front."

"Damn right." He settled back into his chair with an expression that might have been satisfaction. "Now you see it."

"But . . ." He looked over the audit codes again. "All right. It had to be sent from the station. That doesn't mean the signal couldn't have originated on foreign machinery, if it was routed through—"

"We've got all that," Varsav said impatiently, cutting him off. "A mecho-pod buzzed the system several hours before this went out. Ten to one it bounced a signal off the station to get that initial ID. We tried to track it down to get confirmation and maybe some info on its source, but the damn thing apparently went right for the harvester station and smashed itself to pieces on a chunk of ore. Pretty clearly deliberate. We collected all the debris we could, but none of it showed any sign of manufacture."

"Frisia?"

He shook his head. "Like you said, Sonroya makes the best in portables. Anyone could have bought that equipment and shipped it over to us. *Anyone*." His hands rubbed against one another as he spoke, restlessly, frustrated. "So how do we find out who it was? And why they wanted the Front to answer for it?"

Masada wasn't a master of human motivation, but it seemed in this case that the path to enlightenment was rather clear. "I suggest," he said quietly, "that we start by looking at the Earth station."

"And see who this was being sent to?"

"Among other things."

*The enemy seeks children. Send all home ASAP.*

In his mind it was all coming together now, vague goals and suspicions coalescing into concrete patterns of potential action. Human motivation was not his forte, and the guildmasters knew that. They had hired him, knowing it. He needed to follow trails of data, not roads of emotional speculation. And this letter gave him a trail to start with.

"I'll take this back to my room and see what's out there, waiting for us to find it. . . ." *And then you can weave it all into some grand conspiracy theory, and use that to entrap the guilty parties.*

God, he was glad he wasn't responsible for that part of the search.

He started to get up, but once more Varsav reached out and grabbed his arm. His expression was dark, and even Masada could read the anger in it, raw and undisguised. "They designed it for me, you know that. They knew how much I hated that station and would jump at a chance to take it down. They figured if they gave me what I wanted I wouldn't look too closely at it, but would just send you all searching in the right direction, ready to blame everything you found on the Front . . . serving their purpose."

Gently but firmly, Masada disengaged his arm. "Then we're fortunate you're a logical man, not ruled by his emotions."

For a moment it seemed that Varsav stared at him with what seemed like it might be hatred. Then, unexpectedly, the Guild-master laughed.

"Yeah," he said. "Very lucky." He stood. "Come on, I want to be there when you check this out."

It was hard to work with Varsav in the room. At last he found an angle of view and an internal sensory adjustment that cut out all awareness of the fidgety, high-strung Guildmaster. Thank God for those sensory programs. Let Varsav watch him if he wanted to; all he was going to see was Masada sitting back in a molded chair, staring at the monitor he had brought with him, perhaps grunting now and then as a particularly frustrating piece of code slowed his search.

Connecting to the outernet was less of a shock this time, as the monitor gave him a sense of distance from it, but it was still annoying. How did these people live with such a system, stalked by advertisements and "free" offers and icons that would take you to another site, unasked-for, the moment you gave them your attention? It was like wending your way through an obstacle course. Perhaps after a while you just learned to tune it all out . . . or perhaps you could buy programs that did it for you. He would have to design himself one of those before he did any more real work on the outernet, though he suspected that the consumer programs which were stalking him were capable of adapting to anything he could turn out quickly. *Advertising: the ultimate predator.*

He longed for the simplicity of the Gueran network, which simply did what it was supposed to and no more. When had these people lost touch with the fact that the purpose of a network was to facilitate communication, not impede it?

With care he rode the skip out to the waystation that served Earth. It wasn't a large one, and its datasphere was rather prosaic. Earth didn't encourage tourists, and most of those who used the waystation as a transfer point got onto the first ship that would take them where they wanted to go. As a result, the station was lacking in the kind of frenetic activity which existed elsewhere, in which entrepreneurs and industrial spies and brain-modified hackers waged a secret war over every bit of code, and junk bits of dead viral matter trailed in the wake of every legitimate program.

This was almost peaceful, by outernet standards. Too bad he couldn't relax and enjoy it. But if this trail did lead to Lucifer's maker, or was connected to him in any way, relaxing was the last thing he should be doing. God alone knew what was waiting for him up ahead.

He had no problem working his way through the main gateways of the system, though it took inordinately long to manage it. How long had it been since Earth had last updated its master programs? They ran so slowly he could almost picture an ancient programmer with pad and pencil and slide rule, entering his data by hand. On the other hand, security was fairly easy to circumvent. Of course, it helped that the planet was too far away from its waystation to maintain a real-time connection. Most communication from the outernet wound up bundled into neat little packets on the waystation, waiting for one of the periodic transmissions to the homeworld. That minimized the need for live security, and what there was seemed to be no match for Masada's skills. Not here, anyway. It occurred to him as he dodged his third or fourth security sniffer that perhaps it was just a little too easy getting in. Like perhaps, someone wanted him there?

Aware that he might be heading into a trap, but seeing no other way to get the answers he needed, he pressed onward.

The mail drop was a closed system, which normally accepted messages and then closed up tight behind them. Under normal circumstances you couldn't go in and rummage around inside, because the return signal which would tell you what you were seeing couldn't get out. He had to dismantle a portion of the gateway program itself, and that took a while. The security there was tighter than it had been elsewhere, which befit a transfer point for sensitive data. He took it as a hopeful sign that he was going in the right direction.

He could hear Varsav pacing as he worked on the gateway. A programmer would have known there was no point in rushing this part, but the Guildmaster clearly had no appreciation of such fine points. Masada could hear him muttering angrily to himself, and for a moment he nearly lost concentration and let the gateway close up again. Damn corrective programs; he flashed an icon to shut down his hearing so the man wouldn't distract him, then went back to what he was doing. It was like cutting into a body, peeling back layer after layer of tissue to get to the organs inside. The only problem was that this body kept trying to heal itself, and security sensors imbedded in the skin threatened to sound an alarm every time he cut into it again.

Then at last he was through. He waited a few seconds for something to respond to his intrusion, but nothing did. He had already shut down the input receptors in his brainware, and now he double-checked them to make sure they were closed up tight. He had no intention of wandering into an area that was possibly controlled by Lucifer's designer with his brain wide open.

A counter told him there were nearly a million data packets inside the mail drop, waiting to be gathered up and sent to Earth. Doubtless they would have been sent already if the message from the New Terran Front had gotten through. Even so, the time for regular shipment was coming up soon; he'd better get any data he needed this trip, as there might not be time for another one.

But where to start, with so much data? He did a scan of the packets, a general survey of message length, encryption type, and origin. It was as good a starting point as any other, to see if there were patterns here worth exploring.

He found out that the messages came from all over, a random sampling of major and minor stations throughout the out-worlds. No help there.

None were encrypted. That was curious.

And . . . they were all the same length.

He could feel his pulse speed up as he read the last figures. In his gut he thought he knew what these data packets were, but he wouldn't allow himself to react. Not yet. He checked again to see that his analytic programs were working properly (they were) and that the results were indeed what they seemed to be (all segments of code were long and nearly exactly the same length, the difference between them so slight that it might almost be discounted) and then he cracked one message open carefully, oh so carefully, almost as if he expected that something might jump out at him from inside.

Which it might, he thought. Literally.

Evidently something in his posture warned Varsav that he had found something; he sensed the man coming up behind him, not quite touching him but close enough to make his presence known. Maybe he was saying something, but Masada couldn't hear it. He couldn't waste his time making small talk, when he was handling the most deadly piece of code ever loosed in the civilized worlds.

Lucifer.

He resealed the first data packet and went on to another. And another. They were here, all the missing spores, enough of them to explain why his numbers had fallen short. Versions of Lucifer from each generation, quiescent now as they waited to be shipped to Earth. To meet their maker? The thought was chilling. He wanted copies, but didn't dare make them yet; the self-destruction sequences on these spores were too finely tuned, and each one would be different. He remembered the hours it had taken him to copy Lucifer the first time, and how many copies he had ruined in doing so. He didn't want to leave his mark here, not even by the loss of one single spore. Whoever had set this virus up damn well knew what he was doing, and he'd be watching for signs of such interference.

It took an act of pure willpower for him force himself to withdraw from the mail drop. The gateway programs closed up as soon as he released them, and he stayed there just long enough to make sure that no sign of his interference was visible. Though his wellseeker told him that his blood pressure was dangerously high, and distantly he could feel his forgotten hands trembling, this was no time to be careless.

Lucifer.

He retraced his steps to the next node out, far from Earth's waystation, and then finally shut down. His thoughts were confined to his head again with a suddenness that was numbing. His throat was dry, as if from hours of thirst. Maybe it had been hours. It had felt like years.

"Well?"

It was hard for him to find his voice again. "It's Lucifer. All the information I'd predicted its designer would want, packaged to be shipped to Earth. All its 'children.' "

"To Earth." He could hear Varsav hiss softly.

"Yes."

"That means . . ." The man's dark eyes were fixed on him, shadowed beneath scowling brows. "This thing is from Earth?"

He said it quietly. "So it would appear."

Varsav exhaled noisily. "That means . . ."

He didn't finish the thought. The words didn't have to be said. The ramifications were . . . stunning.

"It could be just one company," Masada offered. "One of Earth's Corporations, acting on its own recognizance."

"Perhaps." Varsav's expression was dark. "Or perhaps a few of them in concert. With Earth's compliance. It's happened before. Or perhaps . . . some official branch of Earth itself."

No one had to say what would come of that. Not even Varsav, who seemed to like stating the obvious. Putting it into words would be too, too terrible.

At last the Guildmaster said, "You going to tell Gaza, or should I?"

"It's my job," Masada said quietly. "I'll take care of it."

He had to get more data first. He had to be sure, absolutely sure, before he told anyone.

*Sure of what? That the spores are being sent to Earth? That they are exactly what you predicted, samples being collected by Lucifer's maker, because he can't be here in the outworlds to watch the virus' progress himself?*

The fate of the universe seemed to be on his shoulders at that moment. Its weight was crushing.

"I'll tell him," he whispered.

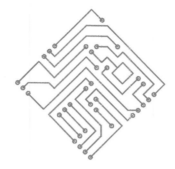

All data leaves a trail.
The search for data leaves a trail.
The erasure of data leaves a trail.
The absence of data, under the right circumstances, can leave
the clearest trail of all.

DR. KIO MASADA
*The Enemy Among Us*

# REIJIK NODE
# TRIDAC STATION

THE BOARDROOM was strewn with the trappings of a recent meeting: silvered boxes of gourmet coffee, now crushed and empty; data printouts sorted carefully into piles, now discarded; a single stylus left behind, its laser tip glowing scarlet against the table's dark surface.

She stood at the end of the table, her attention fixed upon some inner vision. He entered silently and waited for her to notice him. When some time passed and she did not, he coughed softly and took a step forward, taking up a position behind one of the molded chairs.

For a moment longer her eyes remained unfocused, as she shut down whatever internal programs she'd been processing, and then her attention turned outward again.

"Miklas."

He bowed slightly, acknowledging the greeting.

"I didn't expect you so early. You have news of our . . . search?"

He nodded and began to speak, but she waved him to silence. "Shut the door."

He did so.

She turned up to face the security node and for a few seconds stared at it, soundless. No doubt she was feeding it the codes which would shut down the cams normally present in such a room. The thought made a cold thrill go up his spine. If this matter was so secret even here, in her own domain, what rewards might there be for the man who brought it to successful conclusion?

At last she turned to him again, and nodded. "Report, then."

"We know where the girl is."

Her eyes flared, the only life in a stone-like expression.

"You're sure."

He nodded.

"Tell me."

"I designed a facial recognition program to search her out, and sent it out to the major waystations. It managed to infiltrate the station security system in all but three, and is tapping the public cams for images."

"And it found her?" Her tone was frankly incredulous. "So quickly? Such luck is . . . unusual."

Much as he had told himself he wouldn't preen in front of her, he could not help but stiffen proudly as he said, "No luck at all. I wasn't hoping for it to succeed."

She said nothing, waiting.

"I sent out thirty-four copies of the program. Yesterday I checked on all of them. Thirty-three are unchanged."

"And the last?"

"Altered, and by a skilled programmer. Though it looked much the same at first glance, a key section of the recognition code had been altered." He paused. "So that if it found this girl, it would no longer be able to identify her."

"This girl's not stupid. She dodged Earth security on Reijik, and we know the Guild is after her as well. So far they haven't caught her. So she knows what she's doing, and has made the right contacts. That's the real clue."

"No one can truly disappear in outworld society, not by purely physical means. There's too much of a data trail left behind in day-to-day business. The fact that we haven't been able to locate such a trail means that she has help. *Skilled* help." He paused. "It stood to reason they'd interfere with any program searching for her. That's why I sent it out. The chance that it would actually find her was a long shot at best . . . but the chance that *she* would find *it*, and alter it, was another thing altogether. With the results that you see."

Her thin lips pursed as she considered that. Then, very slowly, she nodded. "Yes. You did well."

He could feel himself stiffen at the unexpected praise.

"Where is she?"

"On Paradise Station. And we'll know if she leaves it, because the same thing will happen elsewhere."

"It's a large station."

He smiled tightly. "But we know what we're looking for now. Not a girl, but a hacker. Someone who is going to erase every trail she would normally leave behind . . . and leave us signposts by doing so." He paused. "Each time she dodges one of our data traps, I'll know how to refine the next. Each one will demand a different response . . . and that response will be traceable." He paused. "We'll find her."

She stared at him for a long, long moment in silence. Despite his self-confidence the moment was tense.

"All right," she said at last. "Well done." She paused. "Do remember, Miklas. The goal is not only to get hold of her, but to do so before the Guild does."

"Of course." He bowed his head in acknowledgment, deeply enough to hide the glow of triumph on his face. "I promise."

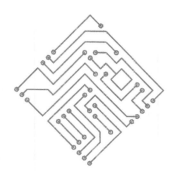

The ancients said that knowledge is power. How much more true that is in our state now, where the most minimal data can open the door to a treasurehouse of secrets.

SORTEY-6,
*On Human Power*

# GUERA NODE
# TIANANMEN STATION

IT WAS a somber Kio Masada who called for a meeting with Gaza and the Prima. Not that anyone else would notice that quality in him. The *iru* was inward-focused, and rarely offered other kaja the cues they needed to interpret its emotions. Yesterday he had been quiet and reserved and dressed in black. Today he was quiet and reserved and dressed in black. Yesterday he had been chasing a data phantom across a vast and fascinating universe. Today the crushing weight of that universe was on his shoulders, and he knew that the words he chose might condemn a guilty world to hell, or damn an innocent one. Who could tell the difference?

The Prima suggested a small meeting room on an inner ring of the station. That was fine with him. There was no place that was truly comfortable for him, outside of the workroom where he now spent so much of his time. Yet even these rooms were familiar compared to where he might have to go soon. At least this station was peopled mostly by Guerans, and most of them Guild; he was of their race and their culture, and theoretically knew how to deal with him. Other stations would be very different. Yet as much as he dreaded leaving Tiananmen, he knew it might soon be necessary. There were some meetings that simply could not be managed, except in the flesh.

The Prima was dressed formally, which told him that she had official business lined up right after this meeting. He wondered if she'd cancel her next event, after what he had to tell her. Devlin Gaza was more casually attired. It struck Masada suddenly that he hadn't seen the programmer as much in the past few days as he was accustomed to. Was that a sign of his trust in the professor, that he could manage his job now without being supervised? Ironically it had come at the time when Masada most would have liked another human being to share in his discoveries, someone to bounce ideas off as he tried to weave facts together into some meaningful whole. Human conspiracy wasn't his strong point.

They knew that, of course. It was possibly even why they had made an effort recently to see that he was left alone. Objectivity.

Gaza called up the room's security system and gave it instructions verbally, so that they might all know what he was doing. He engaged the soundproofing, ordered a data filter, and called up recording cams they could turn on at will. He glanced at the Prima, who shook her head ever so slightly; no. The cams remained off, tiny glass eyes staring down at the table, cold and blind.

"Well, Dr. Masada." The Prima folded her gloved hands on the table; the sigil of the Guild, embroidered on each cuff, was turned back neatly at each wrist. "I take it you have something to report?"

He drew in a deep breath and for a minute he didn't look at them, but turned inward, composing himself. The intensity of their gaze was hard to meet, so he didn't even try. He just said quietly, "I may have discovered Lucifer's source."

He could hear her indrawn breath, and he saw out of the corner of his eye that Gaza stiffened.

"*May* have," he stressed.

"Of course," she said softly, and Gaza urged, "Please, tell us."

"As the Director knows," he still didn't look directly at him, "it's been my theory since the beginning that whomever created this virus would want to watch it, and possibly fine-tune it as it evolved. That implied there would be some kind of collection system, or perhaps a homing pattern within the virus itself. When I arrived in the outworlds to discover that a large percentage of Lucifer's spores were unaccounted for, this seemed to confirm that theory. Either spores had been removed from the outernet, or they were being collected at one point, where they could be studied."

"The Professor's figures on this were most impressive," Gaza said quietly. There was an odd tension in his voice. Jealousy, perhaps? This should have been his speech to give, not an outsider's.

Masada forced himself to look up at them again, knowing his direct gaze would give his words more power. "I found that collection point."

"Where?" the Prima demanded.

*Now. Say the words. Commit that errant world to its fate.*

"Earth Node. The waystation." As always his words were voiced without emotion, but clearly none was needed. The name itself, in this context, had all the power of a scream. He could see them both stiffen in response, and cursed his own lack of skill at reading human expression. Were they more surprised, horrified . . . or pleased? Many Guerans considered Earth to be an enemy, and would be all too happy to have evidence of Terra's guilt in something like this. It was his job to be objective, but it wasn't theirs. "They were being gathered at a mail drop, for delivery to the motherworld. Over a million of them." He paused. "Deactivated."

"Earth!" Gaza muttered. "We should have known—"

The Prima held up a gloved hand, silencing him. "*Deactivated*, you say?"

"Yes."

"Then we know how to do this now. How to shut the virus down. Yes?"

"Not yet, Prima. But we will. I managed to visit the mail drop several times before the dump, and collected several copies of what should have been the most dangerous spores. If we compare those to our 'hot' copies of the same generation, we should be able to figure out what was done to turn it off."

"That's our priority," she commanded him. "The hunt for its maker can wait. Lucifer is still killing."

"With all due respect," Gaza said quietly, "if we let the trail get too cold, we may lose sight of it entirely—"

"The two goals are not exclusive," Masada told them. Why couldn't people stay with the natural flow of a conversation, and not stray? There was information to impart, and he knew how to do it; he wished they would trust him to lead this, and not interrupt. "Director Gaza has copies of nearly every variation on file. The comparison work shouldn't require my attention; a

good program will do the first steps automatically. In the meantime, I've been working on identifying the data trail from both
ends." He paused. "I don't yet know where Lucifer came from,
but I know exactly where it was going."

The Prima said, "You know where the deactiviated spores
were being sent."

It seemed to him a question that didn't need to be asked, but
in deference to her rank he answered it anyway. "Yes." *And
therein lies the weight of the universe which chokes my very
breath. . . .*

"To Earth?" Gaza demanded.

He nodded. "To Earth." And then came the words which
would echo in history for eons to come. They were the most
powerful words he had ever uttered, and he could taste their
power as they left his lips. "ECS."

The Prima exhaled a sharp breath. "Earth Central Security?"

"Are you sure?" Gaza demanded. "Absolutely sure?"

Masada nodded.

The Prima sat back heavily in her chair. Gaza muttered something under his breath that might have been a profanity.

This was no corporate effort, one move in a vast war between
Terran industries. It was no experimental gambit either,
launched by an independent researcher who hoped to make his
name at the expense of Gueran secrets. This virus was from
Earth, from the center of Earth authority itself, launched by
those very people who were responsible for seeing that the
motherworld acted like a responsible member of the galactic
community.

Earth had betrayed Guera. *Earth.*

She had betrayed her Guild treaty.

She had put all of humanity at risk. All of her children.

"You are *sure*," the Prima pressed. Her tone was icy. "There
can be no doubt, if we take action on this."

Masada pulled a chip out of his headset and slid it across the
table to Gaza. "Look for yourselves. The data is all here. Transfer
codes for the mail drop, standard ECS encryption. I even watched
the transfer take place, just to make sure as they were sent out
according to those codes, to confirm where they were going.
There's no doubt, none at all. One million plus spores of Lucifer,

shipped via official channels to ECS, on Earth. Now, as for who is in charge of it once it gets there . . . I regret there's no way to know that.''

Her brow furrowed. "You can't . . .'' She glanced toward Gaza as she sought the proper word. "Can't follow the trail back? See where it goes?''

Gaza shook his head. "Two-month signal delay. No way to work in real-time. Earth is just too far away.'' He tapped the chip sharply; his mouth was a hard, thin line. "This is enough though. This . . . this will be enough.'' Masada could well imagine what he was feeling. Here was the enemy who had infected his most advanced programs, spied on his greatest secrets, and killed the outpilots he was sworn to protect. Now, for the first time, he had a name for it, and even Masada could hear the hate in his voice. And of course there would be vengeance. The most terrible vengeance imaginable. An echo of the horror Earth had once let loose on all of them, from which Variant society had never fully recovered.

Interstellar isolation. And this time there would be no Gueran search mission to come rescue them.

Masada couldn't think about that now. There were still too many other things to do. And besides, if he ever really connected emotionally with what this evidence would lead to . . . he couldn't. He just couldn't.

So instead he folded his hands before him and moved to the next subject at hand. "That's only one end of the trail, of course.''

Gaza said between gritted teeth, "Lucifer's going home to Earth. That implies it came from Earth in the first place. Yes?''

"Maybe.'' He was uncomfortable with such speculation, and knew that insightful kaja such as these two could read it clearly in his face. "There's no proof of that yet. And even if it's true, there may be others involved. We found this mail drop because of a signal Guildmaster Varsav intercepted in his node. It was supposedly sent from one of the Earth extremist stations, I believe called the New Terran Front.''

"Bastards!'' Gaza muttered, but the Prima put a warning hand on his arm.

"*Supposedly?*'' she asked.

"The signal did come from that station. Which hints that the New Terran Front is in league with Earth, part of a larger conspiracy. The only trouble is . . . Guildmaster Varsav believes the signal didn't originate with them."

Gaza was stunned for a moment. It seemed to take him some effort to speak. "I assume you checked the point of origin. The audit codes. Yes? Did it come from the station or didn't it?"

"It came from the station. But Varsav insists it wasn't originally transmitted from there. He seems to know these people well enough to judge such a thing."

"Based on what kind of proof?" Gaza demanded.

The Prima overrode him with a short gesture. "So what are you saying? Someone set that station up? Wanted them to get caught?"

"That is Varsav's suggestion."

Gaza asked sharply, "And you? What do you believe?"

"I'm a creature of data, Director. You knew that when you hired me. I need more data now before I can evaluate this. We know where the trail is meant to end, and a probable point of origination for Lucifer, but that isn't enough. That still leaves someone inside the Guild who is involved in this, remember?"

"You're still convinced of that?" the Prima pressed.

"There's no question in my mind. The virus simply couldn't have been designed without a core of Guild code. Maybe the designer had hoped to disguise it well enough that no one would figure it out . . . but he failed at that. Punishing Earth without finding that person still leaves the Guild vulnerable. Especially if Lucifer's designer isn't on Earth when punishment is meted out."

"He'd wind up in outspace, trapped here with us. Frustrated, furious, cut off from his homeworld. He'd have a whole planet to avenge, and a whole lifetime to do it in."

"Precisely. And if there is still someone in the Guild willing to feed him code—for whatever reason—he could design something far worse than Lucifer. Something not programmed to sneak around and spy on us, but simply to destroy."

"All right." She nodded. "You've done well, Dr. Masada. I thank you. The Guild thanks you. What more do you need from us now?"

He shook his head. "Nothing more than you've already given me. I may travel. There are others who've been tracing Lucifer, it seems. They may have access to data I don't. Different types of data."

"Guild?" Gaza demanded.

Masada met his eyes directly. It was a thing he did rarely, and he knew for that reason it had power. "No. Not Guild."

The Prima hissed softly. "Dr. Masada . . ."

"I know the security risk." He met her eyes now. "You know I'll be careful."

"Who is it?" Gaza asked.

He shook his head. "No. No names yet. I don't want you watching them. I don't want them scared away."

Despite herself, the Prima smiled. "You make this sound like some kind of wild animal. Bolting for cover at the first sign of danger."

Masada's normally impassive face brightened. "Yes. That's it. Just so." He nodded graciously to her. "I thank you for the metaphor, Prima Cairo. I'll remember it when I write my next book. Most appropriate."

"I hope you find your trail soon," Gaza said darkly. "Before the one you search for realizes you're looking for him, and destroys the evidence you need."

The half-smile faded from Masada's face as quickly as it had come. "Yes, of course. You're quite right, Director. It's a race now, isn't it?" And he nodded to Gaza, but his expression was grim, and it had a different meaning. "I will try to be . . . efficient."

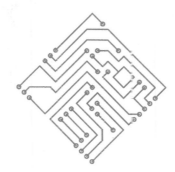

Even in this world of instant communication and precise data flow, the ancient modes of social intercourse still have power.

SORTEY-6
*On Human Power*

# PARADISE NODE
# PARADISE STATION

THE CASINO ROYALE was busy tonight.

Wealthy humans of all Variations gathered around gaming tables, dressed in their most elegant finery. Precious jewelry glittered about throats, on arms, on tentacles. Waiters moved effortlessly through the crowds, offering drinks and drugs to the patrons. Red velvet curtains framed windows that looked out into the majesty of space, and two false moons hung perennially in view, replete with their own illumination.

In this setting even a presence like that of Sonondra Ra might go unnoticed for a time. If not for the delicate kaja painted on her face she might even be mistaken for a Terran, for her minimal formalwear showed far more of her body than most Guerans ever revealed. But that was a first impression only. Closer examination would discover the network of jeweled receivers embedded in her copper skin, with lines connecting them so fine that they were sensed rather than seen. And, of course, the eyes. Once her jeweled eyes turned in your direction, there was no mistaking who she was, or what. No one ever forgot those eyes.

She made a quiet entrance through the grand front doors of the casino and nodded to the servants there with regal grace. A few of the nearer gamblers saw her enter, and paused to favor her with a nod or a bow or some Variant-specific gesture that acknowledged her presence. A smile was all she offered in return, but that was enough. Dice rattled in their metal cages. Plastic cards riffled at one table, then another. Holographic homunculi evolved through a series of random mutations, while gamblers bet on the results.

She crossed the main foyer quickly, her diamond-and-black

silk formal gown fluttering as she walked. Three quarters of the way across she paused at a shimini table, where gyroscopic gaming pieces danced across the board in seemingly random display. There was a man, of Terran stock, and he was just putting his thumb seal on his recent winnings when a gentle touch on his shoulder informed him that she was there. Just that. She waited until he glanced back to see who it was, then went on her way as if nothing had occurred. Past a Yin who was playing the machines, while guards watched to make sure he stayed away from any game involving human thought. Past a Saurin whose gleaming scales had been studded with precious stones, a most extravagant display. Past a sextet of Belial twins, who for some unfathomable reason were playing poker against each other.

Up the stairs at the end of the foyer she went, and into a lush room situated beyond. A one-way mirror in the shadowed chamber would let her watch the games below if she so desired. She didn't, and turned it off.

A moment later the Terran followed. In a gesture as old as time itself—or the civilized portions of time, which were the only centuries that really mattered—he took her hand in his and raised it gently to his lips, brushing the receptors on the back of her fingers with a kiss that hinted at intimacy yet to come. She squeezed his hand gently in return and murmured, "You're winning, I take it?"

"My casino. My option."

Her smile betrayed pearl white teeth, surfaced with the shimmer of abalone dust. "You are evil, Sergey."

"And you, Madame Ra, are the mistress of evil incarnate." He stepped back from her with a smile and folded his arms across his chest. "And how may I serve you this evening? Or have you merely brought your beauty here to humble us all, a reminder that Earth no longer possesses all that is precious in the universe?"

"Your tongue is golden, as always."

"It is my business. As always."

"I daresay you could talk your way out of a federated prison with skill like that."

"And in fact I have done so. As you know." He bowed, a faintly mocking smile adding spice to his refined features. "How fortunate that I found a patroness willing to let such a soiled creature set up business on her station."

"How fortunate that your business is clean." Then she smiled. "Mostly."

He laughed, a clear and clearly practiced sound. "So how may I serve you, Guildmistress of my heart? Besides with my own personal attentions, which are better called worship than service?"

"I think perhaps you overstate your skills," she mused.

"I think not." He smiled. "Maybe you undervalue them."

She laughed softly. "Today I need something sweeter than love, my dear. And harder to find."

"And that is?"

"Information."

"Ah. I see. About what?"

"Let us say . . . Terran matters?"

He shook his head sadly. "My queen, you would blind us with your beauty until we would even betray our race for you. How cruel."

"Nonsense. I give you choice commercial sites, keep the pol from reminding you of legal appointments you have . . . forgotten . . . and shower you with political favors." She flicked his chin with a long dark finger, capped with a sterling nail. "That's worth more than beauty, I think."

"A hard choice," he mused.

"And besides, you're not Terran. Not as Earth uses the word. Born in the outworlds and raised in the outworlds, with nary a desire to tread the sacred soil of the motherworld."

"I do hear the air there is very unclean."

"And I hear you do commerce with those who breathe it."

"If I did, I would certainly keep that a secret."

"Ah, Sergey, but secrets are so . . . boring." She blinked; thick lashes swept downward over the faceted surfaces, leaving them clean to glitter in the room's dim light. "Don't you think?"

"Nothing bores me that interests you, my goddess." He took a step closer. Her receptors translated the colors of his clothing into a caress along her skin, and the warmth of his body into color within her brain. "What is it you want? You know I can deny you nothing."

She held up a hand, keeping him at arm's length. For the moment. "Corporations," she said softly. "They're here, and they're invading my security. I'm plucking their annoying little programs out of my cam system right and left, and Customs has a ship full of bits and pieces of things that look like they might become weapons, if properly assembled. And strangely enough, they all seem to come from Earth." The jeweled eyes fixed on him. "I thought you might know why."

The change in his expression was almost imperceptible; a scaling down of the warmth of his smile by one degree, or maybe as much as two. He did not step back, but he did stop pressing forward.

"That's quite an answer," she assessed. "Elaborate."

"I don't know much."

"I'm not quite sure I believe that yet . . . but do go on."

"The company behind it's called Tridac. It's an Earth corporation, and one of the more competitive ones."

"A shark among sharks, as they say."

He nodded.

"Did you know that sharks kill other sharks even while they're still in the womb?" Her jeweled eyes glittered. "I always wondered if we shouldn't use that as a symbol for the Guild, rather than the *natsiq*. But perhaps it applies to Earth politics even better than it does to us." She nodded. "Please go on."

"Rumor has it now they were after something Shido Corporation had. Shido is now dead and gone, and I do mean that in the literal sense; Earth Corporate law isn't a gentle thing. And that *something* they had is now free in the outworlds."

"Indeed? That *something* would not have happened to wander aboard my station, would it?"

"So Tridac seems to think."

"Perhaps in the form of a young Terran woman? I ask only because there are a few identity sniffers roaming about looking for such a person. In fact, more than a few."

"I wouldn't know, Madame Ra." His dark eyes sparkled. "Your sources are much better than mine."

"Oh, I don't know about that." She smiled. "But they are . . . different. For instance, my sources indicate that the Guild lost track of such a person several weeks back in Reijik Node. That's an interesting coincidence, isn't it? One young girl, with all these important people chasing after her. You wouldn't have any idea what that was about, would you?"

"Alas, I fear you overestimate the quality of my contacts. Would they have access to Guild secrets? I think not."

"But do tell me what the Terran grapevine is chattering about, won't you? I do know they don't say a word that you don't hear. And record. And use for profit."

He spread his hands in mock humility. "You flatter me."

"Nonsense. I am merely . . ." She tapped a slender finger to the side of one diamondine eye. ". . . observant."

"Of course." He bowed his head, acknowledging the point. "It's said that Shido was experimenting with something that would give them access to the ainniq. True access. Something that would permit the Terrans to have outpilots of their own, and break Guera's monopoly."

She hissed softly between glittering teeth. "Ah, that would be . . . bad."

"Depending on where your investments lie, Madame. I hear stock in Tridac is doing quite well, right now. I picked up a few shares on Monday."

"There are things more important than money, Sergey."

"No, my queen, there you are wrong. There is nothing more valuable than money . . . because everything can be bought. The only question is price."

"And what is your price?" she said softly. "What coinage buys your loyalty?"

He took a step forward then and took her in his arms. His fingers brushed over the hard nubs of receptors as he ran his hands along her bare back, drawing her to him.

The kiss was long and deep and not at all innocent, and when it was done, he held her close to him, his hands resting on her waist through the cut-out sections of her gown.

"My price was met," he told her. "I'm no longer for sale."

"How fortunate," she purred. "For me." She ran a hand up through his hair, long dark hair, fine and silky; her receptors translated the sensations of it into nameless flavors within her brain. "I want more information, Sergey. You have the contacts.

You be my ears. I want to know who she is, and what she is, and who is coming after her, and with what, and why."

"I can't answer for the Guild," he warned.

"Leave the Guild to me. Petty little Guildmasters, seeking to play chess with the fates on my station! I'll make them sorry they ever turned their eyes in my direction. You just tell me what the Terrans are doing, and leave the rest to me." She kissed him softly. "Yes?" And then again, more deeply—much more deeply—a kiss warm and wet with hints of pleasure to come. "Yes?"

He answered her. But not in words.

Sometimes silence is a far more binding promise.

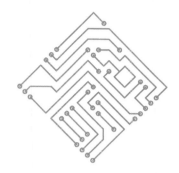

Take an almost infinite database. Plug a hundred trillion human brains directly into it, young and old alike, trained and untrained, Terran and Variant. Give them access to everything, let the net interact with them, let it absorb their living motives and their excesses and their human hungers and even their madness.

You think you can predict what the result will be? You think you can control it?

I think not.

DR. KIO MASADA
*The Pygmalion Factor*

# PARADISE NODE
# PARADISE STATION

**T**HE LAST person Phoenix ever expected to get a real vid call from was Nuke. He'd have sworn the guy didn't even know where his vid software was, much less how to use it. But there it was, a pretty clear holo with reasonable sound, just the kind of image you might send home to mom. If you ever talked to mom.

He said, "Shit, man, you'll never guess what's happening."

Phoenix banished the lines of code he'd been working on, that ran across Nuke's face like some weird kaja pattern. "I guess it's a pretty big deal if I get to see your face. And a lovely face it is, too." He gave it demon horns and little smiley faces for eyes; somewhere behind him he could hear the girl stifle soft laughter.

"Seriously, man." Nuke squinted for a minute as if looking at something, then shook his head. The alterations disappeared, and in their place for the briefest moment was a fisted hand, middle finger upraised. "No jokes, man, I'm serious. Guess who's on the fucking station?"

Normally he enjoyed talking to Nuke, but right now he wasn't in the mood for games. He'd gotten some new leads on the virus which were sending him in all kinds of different directions, and then there was the girl and . . . well . . . there was the girl. Amazing how hard it was to think of programming, sometimes.

"Just tell me, Nuke, okay?"

The figure drew itself up melodramatically, paused just long enough to build the irritation level to a peak, and then said, "Kio Masada."

Phoenix could feel his mouth drop open. It was the kind of

expression he thought only appeared in books. But there it was, on his own face. He couldn't close his mouth either.

"Phoenix?"

The girl had heard enough to come up beside him, not close enough to the vidcam for Nuke to see her, but close enough for Phoenix to be aware of her physical presence. Finally he managed, "You're kidding me."

"No, man, I swear it. Came in today on a public transport, under—get this—fake ID. If I hadn't been trolling for data, I'd never have caught the scam. As it is right now, I think you and I are the only ones who know he's here, but it ain't gonna stay that way. Jesus Christ, what do you think he's here for? And in secret? I figured I'd tell the whole crew, but I'm a little worried they'd mob him. Not sure whether they'd fall down and worship him, or tear him to pieces to get a look at his wiring, but definitely they'd do something."

*I know why he's here*, Phoenix thought. He couldn't quite believe it, but he knew.

"Probably the latter," he said. He managed to smile. "Rumors have it he's mod, you know."

"Yeah, like I believe that. Guerans don't fuck with their own heads, remember? I thought this guy never left his planet, didn't I see that on the news once? What do you suppose he's doing here?"

"Can't say," Phoenix managed. "What do you think?"

*LIVE ONLY*, the hacker had flashed. *BY YOUR OWN CHOICE. YOU WILL KNOW WHEN.*

He'd traveled here incognito. False ID, imperfectly protected. Only moddies would know he was here. And moddies *would* know he was here.

Shit. *Shit!*

Somewhere in his brain he realized he had missed Nuke's last statement. He wasn't really sure that a repeat would help, either, given the weight of data he had just inloaded. "Um, Nuke . . . listen, thanks for this . . . I've got something I have to do. . . ."

The holo cocked its head to one side, studying him. "You gonna head out there?"

It took him a second to decide if he was going to lie about it. It didn't really matter much, since Nuke could always tell when he was lying, but there were things it would communicate. Like how much of this he was willing to discuss at this time. "No."

The figure stared at him for a minute, then nodded. One thing about Nuke, he knew when to back off. "Okay. That's good. 'Cause if you were going to do something stupid like bother him, you'd have a long trip. He's staying at the Waterfall in red sector, room 1214. Not under his own name. But of course you're not going there."

"No, of course not. I . . . that would be bad." He wiped his forehead, amazed to find that he was sweating. "Thanks, Nuke. I, um . . . I owe you."

"Big time, my boy. And I'll take it in data, as always."

The holo winked out. The vidcam hummed for a moment longer, then returned to its usual quiescent state.

Masada. Here.

*Jesus . . .*

"Michal?"

LIVE ONLY

He shook his head and managed to glance at Jamisia. She had clothes of her own but had chosen to wear one of his shirts.

"What is it?" she asked him.

LIVE ONLY

"The guy I contacted the other night. The one I said it couldn't be." He shook his head, as if trying to loosen up the tangle of thoughts inside. "It's him, all right. And he wants to meet me. Live."

There was a flicker of fear in her eyes at that word, and he reached out instinctively to comfort her. "Hey, shh, it's okay, nothing to do with you." How did she manage it, going from self-assurance to pure vulnerability to . . . well, to what happened last night . . . all in the blink of an eye, as if a different woman was suddenly standing there? She was a weird one, that was for sure.

Not that he was complaining. She was cute, she liked him, and there were all kinds of high tech secrets tucked inside her head. It was hard to say which part of that made her the most appealing.

Nah. Not hard at all.

He put a comforting arm around her waist and said, "You'll be all right here. I won't be long."

The blue eyes were fixed on him, a flicker of accusation in their depths. "He said it was a long trip."

*Oops. Damn. He did at that.*

She said, "I don't want to be left here alone."

"I think it's a bad idea for you to go out."

"Why? You said you got the sniffers."

"I got the ones I *found*," he told her. "God alone knows how many more are out there."

"And I would rather be out there with you taking that risk than sitting here alone hoping something nasty doesn't find me while you're gone. Think about that, Michal. What it's like. Hours and hours of sitting with nothing to do, because if I go online to do *anything*, even order fast food, something can trace my signal back to here. Don't you think I'm safer with you, so that if, God forbid, something happens, at least you know how to do something? And just because . . . you know this place better than I do." Her passionate tone had become exchanged for something softer, that plucked at his heartstrings against all defensive masculine instinct. Damn, she was good at it. He could see it happening and still couldn't put up a good defense. "I just don't want to be alone here. What happens if something goes wrong? You wouldn't even know. You'd just come back and I'd be . . . gone."

She was going to win. He pretty much knew that. He wasn't too strong with women at the best of times, and this one definitely had his number. Jesus, when had it happened? He'd only known her for a couple of days. He'd like to think that not *all* of his brain cells were located below the waist.

"All right," he said quietly. "But this meeting is really sensitive stuff, you need to—"

She kissed him. His train of thought got lost somewhere.

*Ah, what the hell. . . .*

**S**he didn't know why she wanted to go with him.

Yes, she was safer in his apartment. Any sane person would

know that. And she wasn't yet so senseless that she'd go running out of a safe place just out of fear of being left alone. That was the stuff of which bad viddies were made, not real life. Not *her* real life, anyway.

*Which is all a kind of bad viddie now, isn't it?*

Maybe it was the dreams she'd been having lately. Not dreamscapes really, nothing so precise or preprogrammed. But in some indefinable way they had the flavor of her tutor's old programs, and each time she woke up from one, she had the distinct feeling that she needed to figure it out somehow, that its meaning would really matter in the coming days.

The problem was that they were mostly chaotic, and defied all her attempts at waking analysis. One was just a random pastiche of natural images from some planet, ice and water and strange swimming creatures that looked somewhat like fish but were covered with fur. The animals were vaguely familiar, as if she had seen them in a book or a vid at some point, but she couldn't come up with a name for them, or any reason why they would be significant to her life. Then there were several dreams filled with images of Guerans: face-painted, black-robed, fearsome in their power. Strangely they didn't frighten her in her dreams, but rather she felt drawn to them, as if they had something she wanted. In one dream a man with fierce black facepainting tried to tell her something, but she couldn't make out the words. In another everything looked normal, but there was a high-pitched screaming in the background, as if someone were keening in terror over and over and over again. She ran to one of the Guerans—his uniform proclaimed him to be a Guild officer of some kind—and begged him to make it stop. "It never stops," he said, and then added, "we don't want it to stop. Do we?"

And then there were the dreams of the crying one. Always the same image, of a naked and forlorn figure curled up in terror on the ground, surrounded by the figures she now recognized as her Others. The most frightening part of that dream was that each time it recurred she began it by hurrying to the spot where she knew he would be lying, terrified that he might not be there. Why did she want him there? What would it mean, if he *was* gone? Try as she might, she couldn't weave the images into anything akin to a meaningful message. Maybe they weren't.

Maybe the fear was just starting to get to her, and her brain was being flooded with random data bits, hopes and fears and distorted memories jostling for space in her processing center.

God. Processing center. She sounded like Michal now. What was his hacking nomen, Phoenix? How ironic, that she should wind up in the care of a man with two identities. How completely appropriate.

He had tried to draw her out about herself, there as she lay in his arms that night, and she had ached to have some facts to give him, or even a wild theory he might dissect. She suspected he might be the one person who could actually help her understand what was in her head. But she had been keeping secrets for too long and the habit was too strongly ingrained. Even the little she did know—what her tutor had told her about her brainware's capacity—froze on her lips as the words were formed, and she could not force them out.

Poor, poor little hacker. He lay there curled up next to the woman of his dreams and didn't even know it. What was her processing capacity, ten times that of the next best brainware model, a hundred, a thousand? She could no longer remember exactly what her tutor had told her. But she understood the cause of it now. Oh, yes. Your average run-of-the-mill brainware couldn't service a dozen independent personalities with simultaneous and often conflicting agendas. They had wired her for her condition. They had *intended* it.

If only she knew why.

*At least we're safe now*, Zusu crooned. Even Derik seemed much pacified, which was nothing short of amazing when you consider what Katlyn had been doing with their body. And Verina, always practical, said, *Look, at least we have a few days to collect ourselves, and someone to help us cover our tracks, and a little while to think. That's all we can ask at this point.*

Was it? Would her life never be more than this, a few stolen hours of safety?

There had to be more. There had to be a reason for all this. The dreams were the key. Dreams full of Guild symbols, peopled with Guerans.

Of course she had to go with Michal. Not until she met a Gueran face-to-face was she going to be able to confront the secrets that were tucked inside her . . . and this was as safe a chance as she was ever going to get.

She just wished, as they left the cluttered apartment, that she didn't have the gut feeling she was never coming back to it.

**R**ed sector was far, far away, but they took a flyway across the inside of the ring for much of the trip and had a spectacular view to distract them. Phoenix watched as Jamisia drank in each new sight as though hungry for the sensation of it all. Golden rings swept overhead, lit by docking lights in a variety of surreal patterns, all against a backdrop of stars that was richer here than in most other nodes. She'd never seen anything like it on Earth, of course; the motherworld was much farther out in the galaxy than most of the populated nodes, and its sky was sparse and dreary compared to this display. And of course, the sheer artificiality of it must disturb her. Here there was no planet. There was no sun. There were a lot of artificial things that orbited or swooped or just hung in the darkness, but except for a few fake moons that orbited the tourist ring, none of it looked even remotely like anything from a natural environment. That was the price of the ainniq, which had offered humankind the freedom of the stars at the cost of its native soil.

He wondered if Jamisia would miss the feel of a planet beneath her feet, and the pull of gravity coming from pure mass, instead of a generator. The sensation was said to be quite different, though the degree to which it kept your feet on the ground was pretty much the same. He knew that in the early generations of the second stellar age humans had gotten terribly homesick for the dirtworlds, which seemed to him nothing short of incredible. Even if you figured that 99% of the popular viddies that focused on dirtworld disasters were exaggerated, that still left an awful lot of nasty stuff going on. Floods, earthquakes, volcanoes, hurricanes, droughts, dust storms . . . shit, how did humans have any time to get any work done, in the midst of all that? And of course you couldn't adjust the atmosphere at all, or control oxygen content, or do much of anything that civilized life required. It was amazing humankind had developed the technology needed to get to the stars, in such an environment.

Red sector was a posh stretch on the inner tourist ring, and the Waterfall was a state-of-the-art hotel awash in gimmicks. The main entrance was through a vast tube of spinning water, kept aloft by air flow and a grav net and God alone knew what else. It looked rather like pictures he'd seen of the inside of a hurricane's eye, walls of water spinning about him in a frothing cylinder. In another time and place he might have been impressed by it, but here and now he could think of nothing but Masada and the virus. Jamisia seemed taken by it, and he offered to let her stay in the lobby and look around while he had his meeting . . . but that clearly wasn't going to fly with her. "You're going to be lost in this," he warned her. "It's all tech stuff." She insisted she'd be okay. She just wanted to be there with him, she said.

He wished something better than fear was the motivator.

When they got to the room at last, he hesitated. He felt strangely nervous about putting his hand to the door, as though somehow it might decide that his prints were unworthy. *Ah, come on, Phoenix, don't be an ass. He's just a human being, you know that.* He touched the lock plate and a mechanical voice chirped for him to give his name. He hesitated, then said, very quietly, "Phoenix." And it opened.

Inside was a spacious suite already filled with stacks of paper, racks of chips, and what looked to be the most expensive portable computer setup he'd ever seen. Jealousy nipped at his heart for a moment, then was forgotten as a figure at the back of the room stood up and approached.

*Masada.*

He was like and unlike his pictures. Darker skinned than Phoenix had pictured, and not quite as tall. The kaja pattern on his face was fierce, made up mostly of angular lines that gave his visage a markedly threatening quality. He sensed rather than saw Jamisia step back a few inches as he approached; no doubt this was the first time she'd been up close with a Gueran. The faces took some getting used to, that was for sure.

"Dr. Masada?" He hesitated, then offered his hand. The man

was close enough to take it but he didn't, which resulted in a remarkably uncomfortable moment. "I, um . . . that is, I . . ."

"I've been expecting you," the professor said. His eyes alighted on Jamisia then and Phoenix quickly said, "She's with me. It's okay."

Dark eyes glanced at him, assessed him, and judged. "It's not 'okay,' given our business, but for the moment I'll accept it. You speak for her security?"

He wasn't quite sure exactly what that meant, but he nodded.

"Very well, then. For now."

He gestured for them to come over to the conference table that was across the room. Jamisia shot a questioning look at Phoenix which he didn't know how to interpret, but she came up with an answer on her own and went off in another direction, to settle on a small couch by the bedroom door. Still present but discreetly out of immediate sensory range; it was a good move, and for the first time since Nuke had dropped his bombshell, Phoenix found himself relaxing a bit.

He took a seat opposite Masada, studying the man, drinking him in. It was not a move that was reciprocated; the professor's eyes rarely fixed on him, or on Jamisia either. The lack of eye contact was disconcerting.

"I'm glad you could come," Masada said, without warmth or smile. "I'll make this short and as productive as I can. I'm hunting Lucifer. Those who employ me mean for its creator—"

"Lucifer?"

Masada blinked heavily, as though having trouble processing the interruption. At last he said, "The name of the virus is Lucifer."

"Ah. I see." He smiled somewhat sheepishly. "I'm sorry. I didn't know it had a real name. In my crowd it's just *that evil son of a bitch.* Or maybe sometimes *motherfucker,* just for short."

A flicker of a smile ghosted across Masada's face. It was a reassuringly human expression. "Apt names, I agree. At any rate, let me continue." He paused for a second, as if consulting some internal log. "I hunt for Lucifer. Those who employ me mean for its creator to be discovered, arrested, and punished on a scale suitable for internodal terrorism." He looked directly at Phoenix. "Do you have a problem with that?"

Was he asking him as a hacker? Shit, the thing was killing hackers. "Sounds good to me." *Real good.*

"I've had several incidents lately in which I've been tracking one data trail or another, only to discover your signature along the line. Very dangerous, Phoenix. Another man might mistake it for a sign that you were involved with Lucifer yourself."

He could feel the anger rise up in him like bile, could taste it in his voice. "Look, this thing has killed my friends. If you think I'm involved with it somehow, then you can just—" And then something else hit him, stopping him cold. "You found my signature? Where? I erased every trail except for that one time at Northstar."

"Yes," Masada said. "I know you think that."

That's when it hit him just who he was talking to. That's when he remembered that this man wasn't just some net theorist with a PhD, but a guy whose brain was running on a whole different standard than the rest of the outworlds. A guy most moddies would kill to be sitting across the table from, and never mind that they were discussing the most advanced piece of viral programming ever seen in the outworlds.

Anger gave way to awe, and to speechlessness.

"It is my impression," Masada said quietly, "Or perhaps simply my guess, that you and your people have been tracking this thing as well."

"Been trying to," he managed to get out.

"It is my guess that, given the nature of your investigative network, you may well have uncovered information my lone efforts would not."

A smile spread slowly across his face. "You're saying . . . you want my data."

Masada said nothing.

"And for me?"

"Name your price."

"You know my price."

Masada stared at him. Just that, for an awfully long time. God alone knew what was going on inside that Variant head of his, but Phoenix could bet it involved issues of confidentiality and trust. Moddies weren't known for keeping secrets from one another. He wanted to start to say something like, *to get back at this bastard I'd hold to any conditions,* but it sounded lame, like something out of a bad spy viddie. And he wasn't all that sure that Masada would believe him.

Masada looked at the girl. She took the hint without a word and moved into the bedroom; the door hissed shut between them. Then the Professor looked at him and said, "The Guild wants this done."

Phoenix felt his heart skip a beat. Between those five words there was a whole contract assumed, and his name was already on the dotted line. "Why?" he dared.

Masada shook his head. "No. That can't be shared."

"Ever?"

The dark eyes fixed on him. "No. Not that."

Bottom line. Take it or leave it.

He offered, "I'm part of this now."

The dark eyes fixed on him for a moment, then moved quickly away. "As much as any outsider can be."

From another man he wouldn't have accepted such a condition. But from Kio Masada . . . he felt a rush of elation as the full scope of that agreement hit home, the fact that he was going to *work* with this man, not to mention handle sensitive data— maybe—and get his revenge for the deaths of Chaos and Torch. "Okay, then. All right. What do you want to know?"

"Where you've found this thing. Who else is working with it. I don't need your code analysis—I've done my own—but I want all the rest. The things that come through the moddie network."

"That's a lot of data."

Masada said nothing.

"Okay. Okay. I can give that to you."

"For now the high points will do. Where has it been active the longest?"

"That one's easy. Prosperity Node. Moddies there found something almost four years back, didn't know what it was then, but now they're saying it looks a lot like this—like Lucifer. Just a fragment of replication programming, apparently sent out on a test run. They forgot all about it until I started sending samples around."

"Does it have the same programming chart?"

Phoenix blinked. "Huh?"

For a moment Masada just stared at him. At last he said, "You've never charted it."

He felt somehow like he had just been discovered doing something dirty. "Well, I . . . no."

Masada reached to the sideboard behind him for the nearest stack of papers. The one he wanted was at the bottom; he withdrew it from the pile and slid it across the table. Phoenix picked it up and looked at it.

"Holy shit. This is its programming chart?"

"That's right."

"This is . . . wow."

A double helix. The symbol of life.

He shook his head. "Man, this guy is crazy."

A faint smile touched the professor's lips. "Not a word we use often on Guera. But perhaps it would apply here."

He wanted to ask why the guy had done it, what he'd hoped to accomplish with this virus. He knew it was searching for information, but information on what? But those were all forbidden questions. For now. He had no doubt that he could win Masada over in time and be privy to all his secrets, but it wasn't going to happen fast and it wasn't going to happen easy.

He couldn't brag about it either. That was going to be a *real* bitch.

Masada had questions, many of them. Phoenix did his best to answer them. They weren't programming questions, more like things that the moddies had gossiped about. He couldn't begin to judge what data would be useful to him, so he just told him everything he could. Masada was particularly interested in the moddie deaths; they seemed to really surprise him. "Lucifer wasn't designed to kill outsiders," he mused aloud. *Outsiders?* Phoenix started to ask what he meant, but Masada's expression warned him that he was once more treading on ground where no one could be trusted, not even him. But what could that mean, other than the Guild? This thing was designed to kill Guild people? He stared at Masada in astonishment, but didn't even attempt to voice the words. There was no way in hell Masada was going to confirm something like that, even if it was utterly true.

"Possibly it could not predict how late-life brainware modifications would affect the basic program," Masada said. "Maybe something triggered it into thinking . . ." he subsided into silence then, thoughtful and deep. You could almost hear the data churning in his head. But no more secrets were forthcoming.

"Very well," he said at last. "You have been most helpful . . . as I suspected you would be. I would like to speak to your colleagues in Prosperity. Is that possible?"

He bit his lower lip, considering. "Maybe." *For you, anything is possible.* "They're pretty paranoid. You'd have to go there."

"That goes without saying. None of this is ever to be 'netted, by Guild orders." A faint smile touched the corners of his mouth. "I seem to be traveling a lot recently."

"I'm surprised you left Guera," he dared.

"No more than I." He stood, an official end to their meeting. "I'll be in touch. In the meantime, if you need to reach me again, it will be through Guild headquarters on this station."

Awkwardly Phoenix rose to his feet. It was hard to know exactly how to say good-bye. It was a good bet Masada still wouldn't shake hands, and the weird way he never quite met your eyes made you feel like some part of him had already left the meeting. "It's been . . . an honor." Stilted words, but what did you say to the one man all moddies idolized? "I really mean it."

Again the faint smile. "Thank you." He glanced to the door of the bedroom, still closed. "I hope your friend wasn't too frustrated with the waiting."

"She'll be okay."

The dark eyes met his, fixed them in a powerful gaze. "When this is done, I'll give you the deactivation codes for Lucifer. You can spread them across the outernet as easily as I can . . . and I think you will enjoy it more."

Deactivation . . . ? He'd have the codes? He, *Phoenix*, was going to shut down Lucifer? That was the stuff that legends were made of, in his turf. More than payment enough for keeping his mouth shut about other things.

Which was exactly what it was, of course. Payment in kind. This guy knew him inside and out.

He went to the bedroom door to get Jamisia. He hoped she

wasn't too upset with being shut out of things, but then, he'd warned her that might happen. Would she have understood any of what they'd talked about, if she had listened? He'd have to think of something to tell her about the meeting, because he knew she'd ask about it and he couldn't brush her off with total lies . . . not anymore . . . but that wasn't the real problem. There was something far worse than that coming, and he didn't know how he was going to deal with it.

What the hell was he going to tell Nuke?

*Green fields. Clear water. Blue sky with a single crescent moon.*

*She knows this place. She remembers.*

*She walks quickly past the trees whose names she once recited for her tutor, trying to find the field where she once met her Others. She has to find it soon, before he has a chance to leave.*

*Can he leave?*

*She looks around quickly, searching for landmarks. There. There.*

*She breaks into a run and the landscape becomes more and more familiar; her footfalls make soft squishy sounds on the wet grass. Earth, Earth, this is Earth. He should be here. She searches around, and as she cannot find him, begins to feel a rising tide of panic. What if he's gone? What will she do then? Her heart begins to pound from fear, and she thinks, he must be here. . . .*

*And then she sees the huddled mass lying on the ground some yards ahead of her. Her breath catches in her throat in pure relief. She walks toward him, and it seems as she does so that the blue sky grows darker, and a wind begins to blow across the open field, spiced with the cold bite of winter. But that's all right. He's still here, and still whole, and that's all that matters right now.*

*His naked body is shivering, and covered in sweat. She can sense the fear pouring out of him in waves, a terror so intense that it seems no human mind could sustain it. Yet sustain it he does. He is strong, so very strong, not with Derik's obvious strength but with raw endurance. No one else sees that in him, but she does.*

*She kneels down by the side of the crying one and gently holds out her hand toward him. She doesn't touch him, not this time; she's learned from before that he fears her touch more than all his internal terrors combined, and the last time she made contact it kicked off some kind of seizure in him. So she just waits, the offer made, wet grass cool against her knees.*

*And he moves.*

*His hand edges forward, gripping grass as it moves, tearing the green stalks loose with its spastic, clutching motion. She holds her breath, afraid to move either forward or back, sensing how fragile this moment is. Still the hand moves even closer to where her own hand lies, and the fingers slowly open, knobby knuckles bending with painful effort—*

*And he touches her. Flesh on flesh. Electrifying contact.*

*And he looks at her.*

*Dark eyes, as empty as space itself.*

*Tears like blood coursing redly down his cheeks.*

*Black lines swirling across his face, primitive pattern reminiscent of—*

"Jamie?"

Startled, she lost hold of the image. It took her a minute to remember where she was, and who the face belonged to that was staring at her with such obvious concern.

"Are you okay?"

"Sure." She managed a smile. "Just fell asleep while waiting for you, is all."

Except she hadn't really been asleep, not in the usual sense of the word. She had been awake, just . . . elsewhere.

Dazed, she let Phoenix help her up. The dream had come as if in response to her summons. Could she do that again? Was there perhaps another dreamscape from her tutor waiting in the wings of her brain, struggling to get through? Damn, she had been so close to learning something. With a sigh she let Phoenix lead her through the motions of departure, and nodded a polite farewell to the strange and somewhat disturbing man they had come to visit. Phoenix was obviously elated about their meeting, which was good; it would keep him from noticing her own distraction on the way home.

*Guerans are the key,* she thought. *But what is it I'm supposed to know about them?*

It was late when they finally got back to Phoenix's apartment, and both of them were tired. Jamie had been having internal conversations all the way home, and frustrating ones at that. Most of the Others didn't seem to know much more than she did, although a few were conspicuously silent. Was it possible that one of them knew what was going on, and just wasn't telling her? If so, she would be pretty angry about it if she ever found out. What was that like, to be furious with someone who was in your own head? The Others did it all the time with each other, but she had never been a part of it.

The dream itself both frightened and elated her. If she could bring on such images and explore them at will, that was great. But if they were going to start showing up of their own accord in her waking life, that was going to be a real problem. It was hard enough to navigate through life already with a dozen different identities sharing her head; if she now had to fight her way through dream-images to perceive reality, the whole thing might finally prove to be more than she could handle.

Finally they were in the narrow corridor leading to Phoenix's apartment, and she desperately hoped that Katlyn wouldn't feel the need to cement their relationship further when they got inside, because she was dead tired. She waited while Phoenix opened the door and then smiled wanly while he ushered her inside. Maybe they could go to sleep soon, and more useful dreams would come.

She walked into the cluttered space, past piles of chips and wires and bits and pieces of electronic equipment she had so carefully cleaned around what seemed like an eternity ago.

*No,* a voice warned. *That's wrong.*

Startled, she asked, *Raven?*

*The table. It's wrong.*

She looked at it closely, and at the pile of electronic clutter in its center. It was hard to dredge up the memory of what it had looked like before, but not impossible; she had studied his mess long and hard when she was cleaning, trying to determine what parts of it did and didn't matter to him. And yes, hadn't there been a pile of chips round about there, and a couple by the forward edge of the table. . . .

She said nothing, but reached out for Phoenix. He was close

enough that she got his arm. She warned him with a glance to keep quiet and then nodded toward the table. Would he notice? Apparently so, for she saw him stiffen immediately, suddenly wary. He looked about at other things in the room and she could see from his expression that some of them were wrong also. Someone had been here, gone through his things, and maybe even taken a few bits and pieces. Which meant they wanted something he had. Or something she had.

Which meant they might come back, if they hadn't found it yet.

The bedroom door was closed. She didn't remember closing it.

She felt her heart skip a beat in sudden fear. She glanced at Phoenix, toward the door, and back at him. He was managing somehow not to look perturbed, but it was clear to her that it was just a mask for her benefit; the color was all gone from his face, and he gripped her arm and squeezed it tightly as a warning of his own.

He smiled then, a forced expression, and said, "You know? We forgot to get food. I don't have anything in the apartment. You want to go pick something up? There's a decent food court a few corridors over. We could bring it back and eat here."

"Sounds good," she managed.

They moved quickly toward the door. Maybe too quickly. Or maybe whoever was waiting in the apartment didn't have enough patience to wait for them to come back.

The bedroom door hissed open.

Something small came flying toward her, and it grazed her upper arm as she jerked away. ALERT! her wellseeker warned in bright red letters. FOREIGN SUBSTANCE IN EPIDERMAL LAYER. There wasn't any time to respond to it. Phoenix pulled her back out the door with enough force to jerk her off her feet. Someone was coming at them, but the door hissed shut too quickly for her to see who or what it was. Then Phoenix stared at the door for a few seconds, his brow furrowed as if in concentration; she guessed that he was accessing the locking mechanism and jamming it somehow.

"That'll hold for a few seconds," he muttered at last. Even as he grabbed her arm to pull her away from the door, she could hear some kind of weapon or tool being used inside, presumably to break it open.

They ran. Down one corridor and then another, taking turns that seemed random. Once, in the distance, Jamisia heard someone cursing, and guessed that their pursuers had finally broken out. Hopefully Phoenix's trick with the lock had bought them enough time to help them.

"This way!" Phoenix whispered sharply, and he grabbed her arm and pulled her to the left with a force that almost knocked her off her feet. Couldn't he see that she was none too steady right now? Whatever had been shot into her arm was seeping into her head now, and she could scarcely think. Were those hurried footsteps ahead of them to match the ones behind? Of course, she thought. You didn't set up an ambush like that without closing off the avenues of escape. Which meant that there was no way out. They would have all the corridors covered.

Visions came back to her of another flight three years ago, and the substance of Shido Habitat vibrating beneath her feet as explosions rocked the corporate center. She stumbled and Phoenix had to help her back to her feet. She could barely feel his hand on her arm. The sounds of pursuit were getting closer. Oh God, this was it—

And then he faced the wall and was still again, just for a second. And a hidden maintenance panel slid open. "Inside!" he commanded, but she didn't need to be told. She fell through the narrow hatchway, hitting the floor hard on the other side. He moved in after her and ordered the door shut once more. Then they both held their breath while the muffled sound of footsteps on the other side came from the way they had come and continued without pause beyond the door.

"That won't hold them long," she managed to whisper. Words tasted strange, and her tongue was oddly swollen.

"Isn't meant to. But every little bit helps."

He waited for her to get to her feet and she tried, she really tried, but her body would no longer respond to her orders like it should. Finally he pulled her up and draped her arm over his shoulder—far from a comfortable fit, as he was much taller than she was—and with a hand around her waist he tried to help her forward. She stumbled but managed to make some progress.

Not fast enough. The drug they'd hit her with was taking effect fast and hard, and she didn't know how much longer she could fight it.

How long would it be before their pursuers realized that the quarry had escaped them, and figured out where they'd gone?

Phoenix froze then, and she could see that his concentration was elsewhere. Just for a moment, and then he was back to her. "Nuke is going to try to close down the access systems so they can't come in this way. If he pulls that off, we might be okay." He looked down at her. "You all right?"

She smiled weakly and lied. "Sure."

He helped her move along the narrow maintenance passage, through a labyrinth of pipes and wires and things whose purpose she couldn't even begin to guess at. He seemed to know his way, but of course he probably had maps in his head for that kind of thing. She couldn't even walk straight, much less think clearly. The numbness from the drug had spread into her shoulder, and her lungs tingled ominously each time she moved. Was it meant to kill in higher doses, or just incapacitate? Her wellseeker kept flashing her warnings and asking for instructions, but she couldn't think clearly enough to deal with it.

Then Phoenix muttered, "Shit!"

"What . . ."

"Nuke says they've hacked into the system and are doing a heat scan to track us. Damn! Well, at least we know they aren't Ra's people, or they wouldn't have to break into the system like that. She'd have the access codes." He smiled grimly. "I'd rather it was her, truth be told."

"Can you do anything?"

"Nuke is trying to block it. But he says it looks like a team effort, and it's going to be hard for him to handle alone."

"Can you help him?"

He looked down at her with something akin to amusement. "Not while I'm running from those guys. Even I have my limits." He hoisted her arm to a more secure position across his shoulders. "Let's just hope he remembers everything I taught him." The emergency lights, dull orange spots set at intervals along the wall, blinked off suddenly. Then on again. Off. On. Then they held.

"Michal—"

"System's confused, that's all. Too many people fucking with it." His words were casual, but the tone behind them was anything but. "Come on."

He was trying to get her to run, but the best she could manage was a stumble. She could feel nothing on her right side now other than the pounding of her heart, which reverberated with the force of thunder in her flesh. She was going to pass out soon, or maybe die from this poison, and what would he do then? Maybe if he just left her behind, he would be safe. She was pretty sure she was the one they were after, and not him. If he left her behind, would she wake up in some operating theater, being dissected for her wiring? Would she wake up at all?

Phoenix stiffened suddenly. She looked up, alert for danger, but saw nothing in the passageway which could threaten anyone. Was it some kind of message he was getting? Or had someone hacked into his brain, to attack him directly? She'd read that could happen.

Then he looked looked down at her and said, "Ra's people are moving in."

"Good or bad?" she managed

"Good. I *think*."

He hesitated, consulting his inner maps, then chose a new direction for them. "Her people caught the hacking, and they're tracing it. They know someone is in the tunnels. Nuke thinks they don't know who we are. She's just guessing that something is up and getting people into place." Jamisia stumbled, and he had to shift position to hold her more firmly. "She's got some of the best hackers in the business on her staff, you know, the elite of the elite . . . anyway . . . she won't take kindly to a hit squad coming into her city, regardless of who and what they're going after." He looked down at her. "We might be safe with her people. Unless you have something to hide from them, too."

She could feel the tears coming to her eyes, and couldn't even control her body enough to blink them free. "Don't know," she whispered. The words had no volume. "Don't know why anyone . . ." It was all she could say. Her legs gave out from under her for the last time, and she sagged against his side. The little orange lights were swimming in her field of vision like little glowing fish, shimmering in the water.

"Okay, girl. Here we go." There was a thudding impact in her stomach and she bent over his shoulder; her feet were lifted off the floor and for a moment she thought the resulting vertigo was going to make her sick. Then she just lay limp where he held her, arms and torso hanging down his back, and hoped he had the strength to carry her as far as they needed to go.

Which was where?

She could feel him stumbling beneath her weight as he tried to keep up some kind of speed. She wasn't heavy, but he wasn't exactly an athlete. Maybe he'd have the intelligence to go down to the lo-G levels, where the burden would be less. Of course their pursuers would expect that, and they'd be waiting down there. She found herself fading in and out of unconsciousness as he ran, her body bouncing rythmically against his back. They'd be waiting for them everywhere. . . .

And then Phoenix stopped. He put her down gently. She saw through blurry eyes another hatchway, larger than the one they had first come through. A complicated looking control box of some sort was next to it, which Phoenix opened. Poor boy, he was covered with sweat from the strain of carrying her, and his hands were shaking as he worked the controls. "Nuke says they're here, in this sector. If I can get us to them, maybe we can ask for sanctuary." It seemed to her that there were footsteps resounding in the hallway behind them. Muffled voices, an occasional clanging. "We'll be safe then."

Safe? But the Guild itself was after her. He didn't know that. She hadn't told him about the trace in her arm. She tried to get the words out now, but they just wouldn't come.

"If it's really Nuke telling me this," he muttered. "Of course, there's always the chance they hacked that connection, too, and our friends are right out here waiting for us." He glanced back the way they had come; clearly he could hear the voices as well. "Not like we have much of a choice."

The door slid open. He picked her up in his arms and carried her through the hatchway, into a public corridor. Someone came running, apparently alerted by the sound of the door opening, or possibly some distant alarm. Uniformed people. A lot of them.

She couldn't make out the details of their uniforms, but she could see that they all held weapons. And all the weapons were pointed at her and Phoenix.

*This is safe?* She wanted to ask. But all that came out of her mouth was a moan.

She heard Phoenix say something to them, but couldn't make out his words. No sounds could get past the ringing in her ears, or the poisoned fog inside her brain.

The weapons weren't lowered. A harsh command was voiced from somewhere, and they were moving again. . . .

Fading into darkness. The lights, the sounds, everything. She tried to hold on, to cling to the last bit of light she could see, but the drug was just too strong for her.

*Make us safe, Phoenix. Please.*

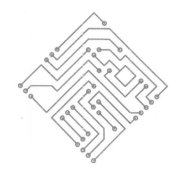

How can you speak of the human soul, you who abandoned it long ago? Do you think that when you tweak a gene here or there, or adjust some chemical oh so slightly, you don't change the sum total of who and what a man is?

We of Guera relish the soul in its natural state. We draw strength from its weaknesses, wisdom from its faults, and joy from its idiosyncracies. Where you look at us and see only illness, a curse to be corrected, we see the untapped potential of humanity.

And we revel in our natural state, and make no apologies for it.

DR. ALEX ROME,
*The Sacred Soul*

# PROSPERITY NODE
# PROSPERITY STATION

IT HAD BEEN a long day. Ian Kent could feel the weight of it on his shoulders as he reached the main portal of his home. He hated the days when he had to play Governor for his node; it made him feel like a petty bureaucrat, and that in turn reminded him of what he had been before, and how much he had lost.

Security programs greeted him, scanning his body, his head-set, his brain. Apparently he was himself, for the portal opened to admit him.

He wished he felt as sure.

With wearied step he walked through the entrance foyer, loosening the clasp at the neck of his long robe. The load of tran-quilizers in his bloodstream had become oppressive by midday, dulling his wits, and at last he'd had to adjust the flow so that he could get some work done. He had done it hours ago . . . and now the pain was seeping through. So much pain. He tightened his hand on the banister as he climbed, trying to focus on the physical sensation instead of his own thoughts. Maybe if he got a neural implant instead . . . but no, the mere thought of letting anyone work on his brain, even for such simple surgery, was more than he could bear. Enough damage had been done. He would risk no more. The drugs in his arm were good enough, it was the system all outpilots relied upon. If it wasn't enough to calm him, then he wouldn't be calm.

He would go to his studio tonight.

He slipped off the long outer robe that was his sign of rank and chuted it for cleaning. Beneath it he had on another layer, close-fitting, not unlike the uniforms that outpilots wore when they were working. Some days it hurt unbearably to wear such garments, but he couldn't bring himself to do otherwise; it was as much a part of him as his skin, a crucial part of his identity. He stopped in the kitchen to pick up some food—gray dough wrapped around colorless meat, he didn't even care what it was—and ate mechanically as he walked to the portal of his studio, flashing it his entry icon.

Beyond . . . he entered the room and heard the door whisk shut behind him. In the center of the studio was an artist's console, a semicircular desk with embedded controls and a chair with full headset attached. Surrounding it were pictures. Abstract pictures, all worked in shades of gray. Some were jarring, jagged compositions, broken planes and shattered edges and lines whose beginnings and ends could not be traced. Some were sinuous creations, subtly threatening, coils and loops that seemed to throb against a foggy backdrop. Most were combinations of those elements, shapes and textures mixed with seemingly random purpose, to produce artwork that was strangely ominous, dissasociative . . . dare one say insane? Wasn't that the ancient Earth word for it, a state in which the mind could no longer connect to the reality of one's fellows? Was he, Ian Alexander Kent, insane?

With a sigh he regarded the disturbing pictures, shaking his head in frustration. They were failures, every single one of them. That which he sought to express could never be captured in artform. That inner vision which he had lost, which no longer even had a name in his injured brain . . . he hungered for the ainniq, he burned to create one little corner of the outpilot's universe in this world, wherein he might escape for a moment. But it evaded him. Other outpilots had tried, and even with color available to them they failed to capture the terrible, terrifying beauty of the ainniq; how could he succeed, who had only this crippled brain and shades of gray to work with?

For a moment he thought about killing himself. Only a moment. Words flashed in the corner of his vision, a warning from his wellseeker: *SEROTONIN LEVELS DROPPING. CORRECT?* He hesitated. Default was *yes*; if he did nothing, nothing at all, within ten seconds appropriate medication would be released into his bloodstream, to work its healing magic. It was all part of the complex machinery used to keep an outpilot functioning outside of the ainniq.

*We are aliens*, he thought. The words had a dark taste, ominous but not unpleasing. *We wear human bodies, but it takes drugs and software to make us truly human. Only in the ainniq can we let all that go, and be ourselves.*

He wanted to be himself tonight. Just for a moment.

Drawing in a deep breath, he visualized his negative icon. *NO.* The wellseeker subsided; its message faded into blackness. Let his brain do what nature intended, for once. A twinge of fear accompanied that decision, but even that was not unwelcome. Fear was part of the outpilot's world, a fear so intense that no other men could endure it . . . but without that fear, no travel between the stars would be possible, and so it was valued.

*Beware of dragons breathing red.*

He sat down in the smooth sculptured chair before the console, letting his hands rest on the controls before him. In his mind's eye he flashed the icons that would let him access his medical programs, and at last settled on a chart profiling his medication. There it was: Outpilot's Syndrome, reduced to a series of prescriptions. Feed this drug into the bloodstream, and the fear would be quelled; stimulate these neurons, and the parts of the brain that might otherwise shut down would be sustained at their normal levels. He scrolled through over a hundred instructions, drugs and programs and monitors and controls, the software and hardware and brainware of sanity.

There was one procedure that would shut it all down, initiated by an icon never used in safespace. One secret symbol, used only prior to transition. He shut his eyes so that there was only blackness before him, and visualized it in glowing amber.

A pause, then. ARE YOU SURE? his brainware questioned. Amber words, bright, like his icon.

He hesitated only an instant. *YES*, he flashed back. *I'M SURE.*

For a few seconds, he knew, he would feel nothing. His long fingers played over the controls of the console, preparing a sheet of plastex for a new composition. His hands, he saw, were trembling. Was it starting now? Could he feel it? The controls under his fingers were like the switches of a transport ship—he had designed them that way, deliberately—and for a moment he forgot just where he was. He looked up and imagined the vast reaches of safespace before him, and the slender fault that was an ainniq . . . out here it did not matter if he had no color sense, for the sky surrounding him was black as jet, the stars a shimmering silver, the ainniq a pale strand almost too faint to see; he would have to get closer before its appearance changed, much closer. He would have to maneuver the ship into the crack of light just so, slipping into a wound that was made back when the universe was born, waves of compression from that vast explosion ripping flaws into the very substance of space. . . .

He gasped, his hands clutching the controls. Random patterns of black and gray splattered across the plastex sheet before him, responding to the emotions welling up in his brain, expressing his fevered grip in patterns of light and dark. He wasn't controlling the artform program the way he should, he knew that, but his hands seemed strangely divorced from him now, and it was hard for him to control them. In his chest his heart was pounding a feverish rhythm, and his wellseeker was scrolling up warnings in the corner of his vision. The words were gibberish, a language he had never learned; what were they doing in his head? Who had put them there? All that mattered was the ainniq, he had to get to the ainniq . . . only there could he be safe.

Passing his hands across controls that he could sense but not see, he maneuvered his vessel into position. Terror was building inside his head, but it was still confined by the outpilot programs embedded in his brain; not until he passed into the ainniq itself would the full force of his Syndrome be unleashed.

He hungered for it. He feared it. He knew it for what it was in truth, a disease so devastating that even Gueran society, normally tolerant of any mental variance, beat it down with drugs and programs until it crouched in the brain like a wild beast, subdued but never tamed. And only subdued for a while. There would come a moment when the ainniq gaped wide before him, the vast worldwound that shimmered with unnatural light . . . and he would see that secret universe in all its glory, and in response the transition programs would kick in—the Syndrome would roar to life within his brain, swallowing his sanity, filling his veins with its hot red terror. . . .

He gasped, leaning back in his chair for support. What could they know of that moment, the fools who ran the Guild? What could they know of that primal instant when the Syndrome took hold, when civilized thought gave way to raw survival instinct—when the universe roared with a thousand voices and cymbal-clashes of light, as he slipped into the ainniq itself, like a surgeon slipping laser-scalpel into flesh. . . .

*I need it,* he thought. Sweat had broken out on his brow, hot beads that trickled down his face as he trembled.

*I need it so badly.*

It had been years since his last transition . . . or had it? Suddenly he wasn't so sure. Wasn't there a freight convoy just last E-week that he had outpiloted to safety? The memory was a strange thing, oddly distant; he couldn't pin it down. And then a string of passenger pods the E-month before that. . . . Why were his hands shaking? Why did he feel such a terrible need to immerse himself in the Syndrome now, quickly, lest someone or something stop him?

A roaring had filled his ears, like a thousand voices all screaming at once. He knew the sound well, knew the change that it presaged. Where was the ainniq? He scanned space with a wary eye, anxious to catch sight of the precious conduit. In the distance the artform program caught up his emotions, translated them into digital format, and splattered them across his chosen canvas. Hot gray, ice gray, the gray of flowing blood. . . .

EMERGENCY—his wellseeker scrolled—*SAFESPACE MAINTENANCE PROGRAM COMPROMISED—EMERGENCY—SAFESPACE MAINTENANCE PROGRAM COMPROMISED—*

There it was. Like a flaw in crystal, shattered planes of space meeting with luminous friction. You couldn't really see it until you were right on top of it, but then suddenly it was spread out before you, a veil of light only visible from one special angle—

*—EMERGENCY—SAFESPACE MAINTENANCE PROGRAM COMPROMISED—*

Suddenly it was hard to breathe. He gasped as his small ship swung into position for entrance into the ainniq. There was a band about his chest, squeezing. Spots before his eyes. . . .

And safespace cracked open before him. Monsters poured forth with a roar that shook the stars, dragons of the ainniq universe now set free in this world, bellowing their fury and their hunger in colors no human eye could see. He could feel their hunger as the sana raced toward him, as frigid and consuming as space itself. Thousands upon thousands of them, pouring out of the worldwound like demons from hell, their bodies mutating even as they flew toward him, different each moment than the last—

Suddenly there were no controls under his fingers. There was no headset on his head. He was naked in the darkness, with no air to breathe, and the ice-cold vacuum of space scouring his lungs. In terror he struggled to comprehend what was happening, but his thoughts would not gather into coherent patterns. Crystals were forming on his lips, in his hair, and the moisture of his breath was a rain of stars as it froze. And the sana were gathering about him. Not merely hungry now, but malevolent beyond any human measure; they circled him, taunting him, exacting their vengeance for the years in which he had defied them. *Where's your ship, little human? Go flee to your pods, why don't you.* Flee? How could you flee something you couldn't see? Without vision one was helpless.

Then the first one touched him and he felt it tearing into his flesh as he fought to breathe—no, not his flesh, the creature had hold of his very soul—crushing, rending, tearing open the boundaries of his being until the very life within him bled out into the darkness. And they began to feed—

*EMERGENCY*
*EMERGENCY*
*WELLSEEKER MALFUNCTION*
*BIOSYSTEMS DOWN*
On his soul—
*You knew we would win, Kent, didn't you?*
*Didn't you?*

*OTTA*

Others work so that they can survive. The *otta* works so that it can play.

Others eat because they hunger. The *otta* eats for the pleasure of taste.

Others love to dispel loneliness. The *otta* loves to share joy.

Some disdain it, others envy it, but one thing is true of all other kaja: Those who do not share in the otta's nature and join in its games can never truly understand it.

KAJA
An Outworlder's Guide to the Gueran Social
Contract, Volume 2: Signs of the Soul

# PARADISE NODE
# PARADISE STATION

JAMISIA AWOKE in a laboratory. Gleaming dials overhead, scrolling holos, painted faces . . . it took her a moment to gain real control of her body, and for a moment she thought one of the Others would claim it. But this wasn't the time to be changing souls, and she told them so. Not when the faces blurring in and out of her field of vision were wearing Guild markings.

Guild markings? Startled by her own thought, she turned inward for a moment. *How did I know that?*

*You don't,* Raven told her. *I do. Found a tutorial on kaja that must have been inloaded on Earth. I'll go over it with you when you're up to it.*

Thank God parts of her were still functioning anyway. God knows the *Jamisia Shido* part wasn't.

"Kandra?" It was one of the painted faces, a woman's. "Kandra, we need you to talk to us. Let us know you're okay."

For a moment she thought the woman was talking to someone else. Then she remembered the false name she had adopted back on Paradise, the name that hadn't fooled Phoenix for a minute. Apparently he had given it to them instead of her real one. Smart boy.

"I . . ." The act of speech made her suddenly dizzy; for a moment it was all she could do not to throw up. "I'm okay," she gasped.

It was hard to read the expression on that painted face, but she thought she saw relief. "All right, the speech center is functional." She felt something mechanical let go of her arms, her feet, her torso. A large half-cylinder hummed as it withdrew from over her body, to rest on its tracks somewhere below her feet. "Looking good so far. I think we have a no-damage situation."

She saw Phoenix's face swimming in fog and managed to get out, "What?"

"Neural poison." His expression was grim. "Meant to take you out permanently, leaving only enough gray matter to question and enough working flesh to keep that alive. That's the guess, anyway."

"They might have fine-tuned it," the Gueran woman corrected him. "It's impossible to tell from what's in your bloodstream whether they intended permanent paralysis or just some temporary stasis." The reassurance rang false, and she guessed that Phoenix's version was much closer to the truth. The concept of it made her even sicker than she already was. What better way to get at the secrets in someone's head, than when it had no working body to run away with? The only thought worse than being caught by your enemies, was being caught by your enemies and stuck in a box somewhere, fed by tubes, until they wanted to talk to you.

"Here, girl." Strong hands grasped her by the shoulders; an arm slipped behind her from the other side. "Try to sit up. We'll help you."

She did so, and the room swam dizzily around her. She lowered her face into her hands, ready to vomit; seconds later a bag was there, which she grabbed and quickly filled.

"Okay, okay, there. It's only to be expected. You should be all right now." Another hand offered her a damp towel and she used it to wipe off her face. She did feel marginally better now, as if somehow emptying out her stomach had drawn the poison from her soul as well. "You really lucked out. Another fraction of an inch deeper into your flesh and it would have dumped more poison than your system could handle."

"Thanks," she managed. And then added, with a somewhat dry smile, "I guess I'm . . . lucky." There were at least half a dozen Guerans in the room, she saw, which seemed to be some kind of medical station. The bed she'd been lying on was overhung with an array of equipment like—

—*screaming, screaming, and the pain never ends, the fear, the*

*abandonment, here! I'm over here! Come back to me, I can hear you,
come back!*

"What is it?" It was Phoenix. "What's wrong?"

*—memories, memories, dry hot pain dying abandoned lost lost
lost. . . . Come over here! Can't you hear me! Don't leave me here!*

She managed to gasp something incoherent. The medic came
back to her and put something cold over her head. Sparks began
to play in her field of vision, all the more frightening for the
ghostlike images behind them.

*I need the memories—I need the fear—Try it again—*

*NOOOOOO*

"Kandra? Kandra?" It was the woman again. Whose name
was she calling? Nobody in here by that name. Many, many
names, but not that one. "Kandra, I need you to look at the light.
It's right in front of your eyes. Focus on the light."

"I'm reading a seizure," a man's voice said. "Right mne-
monic complex—"

*NEED THE FEAR NEED THE FEAR NEED THE FEAR*

Something hissed at the side of her neck. She felt another
wave of dizziness and then a sharp pain coursed through her
neck and head; light filled her eyes and blinded her.

"Oh, God." The screaming voices faded from her head, but
she could still hear them faintly, a whispered echo of pain.
"What was that?"

"Stable now," a man's voice said.

The woman told her, "You need to stay here for a while.
Make sure there's no recurrence."

"No." She looked up at the medical equipment. That's what
triggered it, some deep-seated memory with an image like that
in it, front and center. She had to get out of here or it would
happen again. "No. I can't stay here."

In her ears she could hear wailing. She knew whose it was.
The pain had woken *him* up.

Phoenix helped her get down from the table. The meds were
still arguing with her to get her to stay, but she shut them out
of her brain. Zusu was crying, saying something about how bad
men were going to come and get them now. Mental admonitions
to please be quiet accomplished nothing. Finally she just whispered "Stop it!" loud enough that everyone in the room looked

at her in surprise. Even Phoenix. Tears started to come to her eyes, of fear and frustration and horrible isolation. There was no one she could trust with the truth, not even him. There never would be. She was alone forever in the real world, and never, never alone in her head. The combination was getting to be more than she could handle. She just wasn't that strong. . . .

She recognized where that thought was leading, and who had probably originated it, and thought sharply, *Zusu! Out of my head, now! You don't belong here in this.*

There was the sense of someone shuffling away from her, sulking. The weight of depression lifted slightly, and she found herself able to think again.

"Where are we?" she whispered to Phoenix.

"Paradise Station. Guild headquarters." His expression betrayed his excitement and also nervousness about what that might mean. "Ra's people took us in. You were out of it. The medics said you had to be dealt with right away, so she's going to meet with us later. When you're up to it."

"Ra?"

"Yes."

Oh, that was bad, very bad. If the Guildmistress was going to meet with them personally, that meant she thought they were very important, which implied in turn that she knew something about them. Jamisia sighed heavily. How many people were there who knew vital things about her, when she knew so little herself?

She was tired of running. And besides, it wasn't getting her anywhere. Her pursuers weren't giving up, they weren't going home, and they weren't being fooled by her various tricks. Not for long enough, anyway. How long was she going to last in outspace, with no home and no family and no station to protect her? Despair welled up in her with numbing force.

*Go away, Zusu,* she thought. But the girl was already tucked away in a corner of her brain, shivering. This depression was Jamisia's own.

"Okay," she managed. She slid off the table onto her feet, and though they were unsteady, they held. "Okay. Just get me out of here, all right? We need to wait somewhere else. Anywhere else."

She could still hear the screaming in her brain, as a med led her out.

⌞⌟

**"M**y guests," the Guildmistress said, "usually arrive with less . . . melodrama."

She was a striking woman to start with, and the alien gems embedded in her skin added further impact to a strange and compelling beauty. Yet there was a quality in her far beyond mere beauty, which made one's breath catch in one's throat as she entered. Tall and well-shaped, with deep copper skin, she wore a slender garment which was no more than two long strips of fabric, one in front and one behind, linked side to side with delicate chains. Had she stood still, men would have desired her. When she walked, the languid sexuality of the motion was so thick about her you could taste it. And of course there was the kaja. Sinuous and strangely appealing, the thin black lines on her face hinted at primitive cultures long since dead, alien customs, and mystery.

She had seen that food and drink were brought to them before she would allow either of them to speak a word. Jamisia and Phoenix eagerly accepted the offering. They'd been too long without a meal, and the stress of the chase had burned up what little reserves they'd had.

Finally it came time to answer questions. It was a moment Jamisia dreaded. She wanted so badly to trust this woman . . . but was that because she sensed Ra was worthy of trust, or because she was just desperate at this time to trust anyone?

*You know that our secrets are connected to the Guild,* Raven said. *Without them we'll never find out what's going on.*

"Tell me about those chasing you," the Guildmistress urged.

*Better not to know,* Zusu moaned.

Jamisia sighed. "I wish I could." She hoped Ra could hear the sincerity in her voice. "All I know is what Michal already told your people. We came back to his apartment and they fired at us. We ran. We found your guards."

Ra *tsked-tsked,* but her tone was more amused than offended. "My dear, I know more than that just from looking at my power grid. Your friend here," a nod toward Phoenix, "has many associates, and they were quite free with my maintenance controls for a while." She glanced at Phoenix. "Did you think I wouldn't know that? The best hackers work for the Guild, you know."

"The best *Gueran* hackers," he corrected her.

She laughed softly. "Not always. Occasionally we find . . . a gem in the raw. Yes? Competition's quite fierce, you know. You can't rise in the Guild these days without a virtual army of data savants behind you, and if someone else's army is better than yours, then you don't rise at all. Now, where would we be if we all limited ourselves to those of Gueran blood? That gene pool is so small. Hardly enough hackers to go around."

"You trust outsiders to work for you?" Phoenix's tone was frankly incredulous.

She smiled; her smooth teeth glittered with rainbow highlights. "Some of them," she said sweetly. "Others . . . sometimes. But enough about that." She turned to Jamisia again. "There are a lot of people chasing after you, my dear. Surely you know by now that you can't evade them on your own. Now, you're free to leave my house if you wish, but I don't imagine you'll get very far before your trail is picked up again. And then who will you run to?

"I, on the other hand, might offer you sanctuary, but I won't do that without knowing who it is I shelter, or why she needs shelter in the first place."

Jamisia glanced at Phoenix for guidance, but he clearly had none to give her. Was it time to trust someone? Did she dare trust anyone? She had run away for so long she had forgotten what it was like to do otherwise. Or so it seemed.

At last it was sheer exhaustion that won her over, the certain knowledge that if she left this shelter she would just become a fugitive once more. She couldn't do that forever, not with no hope of it ever ending. Run, run, run, until they catch you; what then?

*There is no other choice*, Verina agreed. And Raven prompted, *You know you need the Guild to unlock your secrets. What better chance are you going to get than this?* Even Zusu, frozen with fear, managed to mutter, *She seems nice. Maybe she'd really help us.*

Maybe or maybe not . . . but at any rate, there were few options left.

"My name is Jamisia Capra—" she began.

"Oh, no, my dear." There was laughter in Ra's voice, but it was a gentle chiding. "Your name is Jamisia *Shido* and you fled from Earth a little over three years ago when Tridac Enterprises blew up your habitat. You've traveled under false ID ever since, and dodged more enemies than you know about. Tridac believes you harbor secrets that will give Earth power over the ainniq, and allow them to unseat the Guild." The diamond eyes sparkled. "Why don't we start with that much, and save us all some time?"

She was speechless. Her mouth opened to form words . . . and then shut again, numbed.

"Did you not know that?" Ra asked. She seemed genuinely surprised.

"About the ainniq?" She looked at Phoenix. His expression mirrored her own. "I . . . no. I didn't. No one ever told me."

"How extraordinary. They chase after you with enough weapons to wage a nodal war, and you don't even know why." She reached over for a glass of deep red wine, which she sipped before speaking again. "Why don't you tell me what you *do* know, Jamisia Shido, and let's take it from there. Shall we?"

She looked again at Phoenix; he hesitated, then said quietly, "Your choice. I don't know what the hell is going on."

*But Ra seems to,* Verina noted.

*Trust her?* Katlyn asked.

*We're beyond issues of trust now,* Derek pointed out. *Unless you want to go out there alone again.*

Zusu moaned in dread.

"All right," Jamisia said at last. "I warn you, I don't really know a lot. But here it is." And she told them of that terrible night when her tutor had awakened her, of what he had said then—as near as she could remember it now, years later—and fingered the icon necklace around her neck as she did so. She didn't tell them about the voices, of course, who had turned out to be the Others. That was too personal. And . . . they would surely think her crazy. Because she was, in the old Earth sense.

She knew that. She was crazy. And she was afraid of what would happen if anyone else ever figured that out.

Phoenix stared at her in amazement through all of it. She didn't dare meet his eyes, but she could feel the intensity of his gaze on her.

When she was done at last, there was silence, as the strange bejeweled woman before them took time to digest all she had said. "So," she said, "this secret they're all after. You don't know what it is."

Jamisia hesitated. There was that last hurdle of fear to overcome. How much could she trust this woman? She was all too aware that Ra's casual air might be a façade, and with the right piece of information delivered the compassion might slip away, removing the illusion of a savior, leaving an enemy in its place.

*But as you have noted*, Verina thought quietly, *there is nowhere left to run.*

*Let it end here*, Raven urged. *One way or another. Force the game.*

Most of the Others seemed to agree with that. Derik raged at the concept of helplessness and Zusu was whimpering with fear in the darkness, but for the most part there seemed to be consensus. For once.

At last she took a deep breath and forced the words out. "He said to me, 'They want your brain and all that's in it.' " Out of the corner of her eye she could see Phoenix surprised at that—or perhaps just surprised that she had said it—but she didn't dare look directly at him. It was too important for her to watch Ra's face, and to try to read it.

But if Ra had suddenly decided to imprison her, or dissect her, or whatever, it didn't show. Calm as always, she simply asked, "That's all you know?"

"That's it." She could feel tears coming to her eyes, and blinked hard to try to keep them away. "I swear it."

"And do you want to find out what this is all about?"

The question startled her. "Well . . . yes. Of course. But I mean . . . how?"

"We start with your brain, my dear. Simple enough." She must have seen Jamisia flinch, for she laughed. It was a silken sound. "Don't be afraid. As it turns out, I have one of the leading experts in computer programming as a guest right now. Let's see what we can turn up with some superficial tests, before I have you quivering in fear behind a surgeon's laser."

"Dr. Masada?" Phoenix asked.

"Yes." She cocked her head and studied him intently, as if his words had sparked new interest in him. "Kio Masada. He's coming here on Guild business, but I'm sure he can be convinced to spare a few moments for this. Particularly if you are as important to the Guild as rumor would have us believe, Jamisia."

She hesitated. "What if it's not a brainware thing?"

"There is always that possibility," she agreed. "But if that were true, why would Shido go to such efforts to disguise what you have? No, there's at least one secret inside your head, my dear. Let's see what we can figure out without having to open it up, shall we?"

They met Masada in the med lab. He hardly seemed surprised to see them, though of course it was doubly impossible to read emotion on that impassive, painted face. The only response he offered was to look at Phoenix with something that almost amounted to a smile, and to say, "I should have known that if you brought a woman to that meeting, she would turn out to be more than she appeared."

Even just walking into the lab again was stressful for Jamisia, and it took the combined willpower of all her Others to tune the place out and just get through it. There was no doubt about it, the place awakened memories and they weren't good ones. Shadows of forgotten fear coursed through her head as she followed Ra and Phoenix through the lab, and she could hear the screams of the Others echoing through her brain, protesting against . . . what?

They had a machine they wanted to hook her up to, something to scan her brain. The mere sight of it started her whole body shaking, and it took all her self-control not to turn and run away right then. To her conscious self the equipment was strange and unfamiliar, but deep inside there was another part of her that knew it all too well, and the memory was clearly a traumatic one. The urge to just turn and flee this place was strong, but what would happen if she did? She'd lose these people's sympathy, and then what? What if there was just no other way to get answers?

She looked at Ra and the strange doctor and Phoenix and thought, *When will I ever trust people more than this?* And she let them affix her to the strange machine and adjust the strap that would keep her head stationary. When they turned it on, a wave of fear surged into her gut, and she reached out in sudden panic and caught someone's hand, which she squeezed so hard it felt like she was crushing bone. Phoenix accepted the pain and stayed by her, clearly sensing how hard this was for her. Little did he know! Screams filled her head and she could do nothing to escape them. God, how long could she take this? She should have asked earlier if this procedure was a thing of minutes or of hours; she sure as hell couldn't form the words now.

*. . . need the centers of pain—stimulate directly—need control!— fine-tune—try again . . .*

"Are you all right?" someone asked. She managed to nod, a necessary lie.

*No! Don't leave me here! Come back, come back . . .*

Finally they let her free. "Thank God," she whispered, and she sagged into Phoenix's arms, grateful for the support. She could sense the eyes of Ra and Masada on her, filled with questions, but she knew she didn't dare address them. How could she explain to someone that their "superficial" examination might be enough to push her fragile and unbalanced psyche over the edge for good?

Then the display came on, and fear gave way to wonder.

Her brain turned slowly in holo before them, reproduced in all its complex glory. The outline of her face was a mere shadow surrounding it, and as she watched, it peeled back and vanished. The skull did the same. The brain itself was a construct of shadows, whose transparency shifted a few times before Masada, controlling it, was satisfied. "All right now," he muttered, "let's see what we've got." The fine lines of electronic connection suddenly turned vivid scarlet, allowing them to see the pattern of her brainware—

And she heard Ra's sharp intake of breath. And Phoenix muttered something like, "Holy shit." And even Masada, impassive Masada, seemed frankly astonished.

There was almost more bioware than brain, or so it seemed. Not merely a processor tucked into the ventricular space, with a network of contacts fanning out from it, but half a dozen clusters of bioware tucked into an assortment of spaces. There was one like a spider that fanned out just beneath her skull. There was one tucked deep into a fold of her cortex, and another nestled up against her limbic system, and much, much more. Anywhere a spare millimeter could be found, it seemed, bioware had been added. Connecting it all was a webwork of contact lines so complex that it looked like the brain was being forced through a sieve. Seeing it, Jamisia was amazed she could think at all.

At last Masada turned to her. "How long have you been modified?"

"What?" Phoenix turned away from the image and looked at her. "You're mod?"

"I . . . I don't know." She was terribly confused. Late-life modifications were dangerous, illegal, and almost unheard of in the Terran system. "I don't remember. . . ." She couldn't even finish the sentence. It was all too incredible to absorb. "Are you sure?"

Finally Masada turned back to the display. "The ventricular processor's a standard birth implant. The rest looks like anything but. I'd say this system's been added to at least twice, possibly three times. In childhood, most likely. That would explain the positioning." He looked at Jamisia again. "You're damn lucky your brain is in working order," he said. No criticism there, only statement of fact. "Whoever did this . . . they took a great chance with you."

Shido. Beloved Shido, her family by adoption. They had done this to her. Why? Was it all just to give her personalities processing space of their own? She could see how that would be necessary if she was to function at peak efficiency. But the time involved with it, the expense, the secrecy . . . she could barely absorb it. Finally she took a step forward and put her hand to the display, as if she could touch it. Red spider-shapes of bioware spread out upon the back of her hand like splatters of blood.

"So, then." Jamisia wondered if she sounded as shaken as she was. "Then . . . this is it? This is what they're after?"

"Oh, no." Masada folded his arms, regarding the holo; it turned slowly before him, cerebral layers parting like the petals of a flower to reveal first one brainware cluster, then another. "This is just a series of bioware implants, I'm afraid. A high-risk combination that might well have cost you some brain functioning had it been done badly, but no more than that. And the bioware itself would be worthless without you attached. No, the questions here is, what did they think you needed all this for?"

She couldn't tell them the truth, of course. Which was that it could just be the demands of her unique condition, having twelve or more souls all hooked up to the same brainware. But why would Shido bother with something like that? Why go to such extremes to indulge the Others, if they didn't serve some purpose?

She now knew more than she ever had before, but felt emptier than ever. Where was the key she was missing to all this, the one thing that would cause it all to make sense?

She began to speak, but Ra held up a warning hand. The Guildmistress was still for a minute, accepting some input into her own system. A message?

Then she breathed in sharply, and a moment later whispered, "Oh, my God. When? How?"

More silence.

Finally the communication ended. She let her hand down slowly and drew in a deep, long breath.

Masada said, "Mistress Ra?"

She turned to him and just stared for a minute. The artificial eyes and the painted face were impossible to read. It seemed to take her a minute to find her voice.

"Ian Kent is dead," she announced.

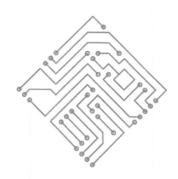

For as long as there are Terrans among us, for as long as we have to waste time and energy dealing with their ignorance, their condescension, and their convoluted legal system, we will never be more than second-class citizens in their galaxy. And they will never be more than unwelcome intruders in ours.

Would it not be best for all involved if we went our separate ways?

(Excerpt from a Hausman League propaganda page, author unknown.)

# PROSPERITY NODE
# PROSPERITY STATION

MASADA TOOK one of Ra's outships to the ainniq, and from there to Prosperity Node. The hacker came along with him, to collect data from his contacts while Masada dealt with this new investigation. Phoenix was less than happy about having to sleep through the dive—apparently he'd been hoping that being on a private Guild ship would exempt him from that requirement—but the outpilot insisted. He was the kind of pilot who tamed his Syndrome by invoking elaborate protective rituals, and apparently his particular formula required that all non-Guerans on board be unconscious through transition. Masada didn't argue with him, of course. No one ever argued with an outpilot. If they told you that the ship had to be painted purple and that all its passengers had to be stripped naked and wear live birds on their heads . . . you didn't complain, and you certainly didn't argue, you just did it. Because in the end it was the outpilot who had to face his Syndrome alone, and dodge the most vicious predators in the known galaxy, and if it helped him to have those conditions met, that was a small price to pay for safety.

The Guild didn't lose many ships anymore, but every now and then it still happened. A ship would return with the bodies of its passengers all intact, but emptied of all human spirit. Or sometimes a ship would just disappear, and no one would ever know whether its outpilot had failed to manage his Syndrome, or simply failed to outrun the hunters.

And now Kent. A pilot once, accustomed to the deadly Syndrome and the surreal universe to which it granted access. A pilot robbed of his livelihood in an instant, and left embittered and crippled to live out his years in safespace. Kent didn't have the skill to design Lucifer, but he might have aided others who did. Did he hate outpilots enough to strike out at them like that, resenting the power and the freedom they possessed, which he had lost forever? Devlin Gaza thought so. Gaza had said that Kent was one of the most likely suspects in Guild circles. The Prima said only that she couldn't imagine Kent hurting his own people . . . but she didn't deny that he had the profile for it. Outpilot's Syndrome by definition was an unstable condition, and though drugs and bioware could rein it in, they could never fully eradicate it. The Syndrome required enemies, or it fed upon itself, that was a known fact. In a world with no more monsters to flee from, had Kent created monsters of his own?

All of those were questions for others to answer, not him.

And then there was the girl.

Phoenix had insisted on bringing her along. Ra had insisted that she must stay on Guild property if he did, and a contingent of Ra's own personal guards would travel with Jamisia to assure her safety. Masada knew that the Guildmistress was willing to indulge the pair in the hopes that their actions would reveal something of the girl's true nature, but he had his doubts. Fortunately, she wasn't his project. He had promised Ra he would observe her and report all that he saw, but he doubted that his *iru* nature was going to provide any great insight into what was obviously an unstable psyche.

Maybe the girl had just a touch of the Syndrome in her. Maybe an echo of that dread disease had somehow survived all the years of eugenics. If so, she was hardly going to prove a threat to the Guild. If she was walking around and talking like a normal Terran without a battery of drugs and med programs to boost her sanity, then she wasn't affected enough to be an outpilot, now or ever. And the drugs weren't there, though the programs might be. Ra had checked.

It was too much for him to think about now. He had been so absorbed with Lucifer these past E-months, and now was so elated by the new wealth of information that Phoenix promised to make available, he could muster no interest in the twisted plottings of Earth. For hundreds of years the motherworld had dreamed of having outpilots of its own. For hundreds of years it had failed to create them. It might have come close if Lucifer had succeeded, but Lucifer had been discovered and would soon be neutralized. Now Earth must start all over again in searching for the Guild's secrets.

Except of course that it wouldn't be able to. When the connection between Earth and Lucifer was proven to everyone's satisfaction, the waystation at that node would be dismantled and the motherworld abandoned. Let them stew in their own overpopulated juices and reflect upon the fact that this time they had brought their misery upon themselves. Masada knew there were trillions in the outworlds who would applaud Earth's downfall, and commemorate the day of her isolation as a holiday for centuries to come. He suspected Gaza would be among them.

And he would go down in the history books as the detective who had made it happen. A strange kind of glory, that. He wasn't all that sure he liked it.

The body lay on the floor of the studio . . . or rather, the holo that replicated the body did so. It was a truly gruesome sight even without solid flesh behind it. Whatever had killed Kent had been agonizing, that was clear. His eyes were wide open and staring, bulging out from his head as though his very flesh had tried to squeeze them out. His hands had dug into the floor where he had fallen, so that shards of it were driven up under his fingernails, splitting them into a bloody mess. And his face . . . his face was a mask of fear, wide gaping eyes the centerpiece of a countenance consumed by horror.

Masada knelt by the body for a long time, studying it in detail. He was no forensics specialist, nor was he an expert in reading human expression. But he was going to have to go through the mort log in detail, and everything he could observe about the body now might help him interpret that later.

The wide open eyes seemed to stare at him. Eyes of a tortured man, gone to peace at last. How did Kent fit into all this? What about the report that Phoenix had given him, that Lucifer might have been tested first in this node? Was he connected to that somehow?

"What do you think?" Gaza asked.

"He died a tortured death." Masada looked around at the art surrounding him, strange canvases worked in shades of gray. Twisted and tortured shapes that seemed to shift form as you watched them. One piece had a violent splash of red across it, and he couldn't help but wonder what had gone through the man's mind as he had applied it. Unable to see the color, judge its tint, or even comprehend its nature, he had nonetheless added it to his storehouse of personal visions. Why? "After a tortured life. What killed him?"

"Coronary arrest, preceded by wellseeker malfunction. I'm still working on deciphering the mort log, but right now it looks like the safeguards on his Syndrome shut down."

"Is it possible he did that himself?"

"The mort log says he did, in fact. But the system should have come back online at the first sign of trouble. It didn't." He nodded toward the holo. "There was enough adrenaline in his bloodstream to have triggered the safeguards ten times over."

Masada looked up at him sharply. "That's a very familiar pattern."

"You mean Lucifer."

"Yes."

"I scanned for it. No sign of it in the outpilot programs. I'm having the wellseeker programs scanned now for any signs of a virus. If one turns up, even if it's not Lucifer . . ."

"Then the same people who launched Lucifer may have killed Kent."

"Exactly."

"For information, you think?"

"No. Not this time. This time I think we're looking at simple murder."

"How can you know that?"

"Timing, Dr. Masada." Gaza's expression was grim. "Think about it. We just discovered Lucifer's source and a possible conspiracy with the Terran isolationists. As we were meant to, no doubt. Whoever launched that message from the Front's station probably thought it would all end there. But it didn't. The gambit was discovered, and the search continues. So now the key evidence has been destroyed, the record in Kent's own brain. As I predicted it would be.

"That said, I can see one of two possible reasons for this murder. Let's begin by assuming that Kent leaked a fragment of outpilot's code to a Terran conspirator, an action motivated by festering bitterness over his own condition. He never thought he'd get caught. But then you came to the outworlds and told us there had to be a leak among our ranks, which you began to search for. The investigation seemed to be hitting closer and closer to home, and might eventually have uncovered his treachery. Kent had no feelings of loyalty for Earth; quite the opposite. It had simply served his purpose at the time. Now, in order to save himself, he launched a message from the Terran Front to alert us to the Earth connection and give us someone to blame. That drew our attention away from him. If he'd succeeded in making the Front look guilty, the whole search would have ended there.

"That's what I postulate about the overall situation. From there I see two possibilities. Either Earth learned it had been betrayed and simply had its revenge." He indicated the faux body. "Or Lucifer's creator realized we were getting too close to the truth, and decided to cover his tracks. Better to kill Kent now than run the risk of his talking too much later."

"You're assuming Kent's guilt."

"I think that's pretty clear. Of course, we have the mort log now, and whatever else could be salvaged from his brainware. We can study them at our leisure and search for proof. But I have no doubt about what we're going to find."

A figure appeared in the doorway. "Director." It was Chezare Arbela, Kent's personal secretary. "That scan you wanted is finished. Also the mort log has been recorded for you. I've set up a vid link for you in the Guildmaster's office."

"Good. Thank you." Gaza smoothed his clothing with careful gestures, first the right side, then the left. Perfectly even. "Come on, let's take a look at this now and see if we can't find some substantiation for my theories." He waited until Masada took one last look at the body, then led him toward the office. "I hear you have company, by the way."

It took him a few seconds to realize who Gaza meant. "A

moddie from Paradise Station and his girlfriend. He has friends in the node who may have valuable data for us. Arbela arranged transportation for him. In the meantime, she's waiting in Kent's gallery, where guards will see that she stays out of the way. Nothing to worry about."

"What kind of valuable data?"

Masada hesitated. He hated to present data in bits and pieces like this, would much rather wait until Phoenix returned and then give a full report. But the question was too direct to be refused. "He and his friends have apparently been tracking Lucifer for some time . . . though they didn't know what it was, of course. He said that fragments of the virus have been found in this node, as far back as four or five years ago. Which may imply that its designer is located here, or at least was at that time. Or had contacts here who would run the thing for him when it needed to be tested."

Gaza looked at him sharply. "If Kent was guilty, might he not have done that?"

Masada shook his head. "Kent lacked the skill. He might be a traitor to the Guild, but he wasn't a programmer. And whoever handled these fragments would have had to know what they were doing. No, there's someone else involved here, and this hacker may be able to prove that. And possibly even turn up some clues as to who it was."

For a moment there was silence. Gaza gestured toward a doorway; Kent's office. "You're determined to find them all, aren't you? Every single person ever connected to that virus."

"Isn't that my job?"

The office was dark, and despite its dimensions felt somewhat claustrophobic. Dark bookcases and darker furniture underscored the mood of the man who had lived here. It was an interior room with neither window nor viewscreen. No view of space to taunt Ian Kent. No hints of the ainniq to torture him.

Arbela was waiting for them. He indicated a monitor that had been set up on the desk. "The scan found something," he said. "I've had it isolated for you. And here's the mort log." He held out a chip. Masada reached for it, but Gaza was ahead of him and claimed it first. The professor was somewhat startled by the move; prior to this, Gaza had preferred to let him handle data collection.

*The tension must be getting to him,* he mused.

They pulled up chairs in front of the monitor and Gaza took control of the display. Slowly he scrolled through the lengthy code, occasionally stopping when Masada asked to take a longer look at something.

It was a virus.

"Shades of Lucifer," Masada mused aloud.

"What do you mean?"

"It's the same style. I'd put money on it being the same programmer."

Gaza looked at him sharply. "How sure can you be of that?"

"Programming style is like a fingerprint. Sometimes the mark may be unclear, but it's always there. Little quirks of code that are unique to each programmer. Go on to the next section." He waited while the monitor display complied with his instructions. "I studied Lucifer every day for six months, Director. I know it like I know my own work. And my own particular strength is in abstract visualization; a gift of my kaja. Trust me, this virus is from the same designer. And . . . there." The code froze on the screen. "That's it." He read for a moment, then cursed softly under his breath. "That's your killer, Director. It went straight for his safeguard programs and disabled them. The first time the Syndrome became active in Kent the whole system shut down. He might have had enough medication in his arm to control the Syndrome safely, but if his wellseeker didn't tell the delivery mechanism it was needed, nothing would have made it to his bloodstream."

"So it was murder."

Masada said nothing.

"My theories seem rather sound, then," Gaza mused.

"They do."

"Well." He sat back in his chair and tapped a restless hand on the table. His expression was grim. "At least we don't have to worry about a leak in the Guild anymore. That question's been answered." He reached out and straightened the monitor screen so that its edge was parallel to that of the table. "We should return and report this to the Prima. I'm sure she'll want to hear it."

"You go ahead. I still have the boy to hear from."

"Does it matter so much now? We have our leak, we know the virus' source."

"Maybe. I'd rather be sure. There are still a few unanswered questions, you know. I'd rather see that there's no doubt left anywhere before I present my findings to the Prima."

Gaza stared at him. "You are persistent, aren't you?"

Masada smiled faintly. "Of course, Director. You knew that when you hired me."

"No, Dr. Masada. No, I underestimated you." He crossed his arms and leaned back in his chair. His posture might have seemed relaxed, but his gaze was still intense. "That's not a mistake I'll make again, I promise you."

They had left Jamisia in a vast room filled with pictures and told her to wait there until the guards returned. Apparently the Guildmaster had been an artist in his spare time, for nearly all the paintings were his. Or so the guards told her before they left her alone there.

She shuddered to think of what kind of man might have painted those pictures. They weren't merely abstract images, nothing so mundane as that; they were surreal landscapes, vividly unnerving, and they hinted at an inner landscape more warped than any reality. They repelled her, but they also fascinated her, and she found it impossible to turn away from them. One in particular drew her attention, a jarring collection of jagged shapes that seemed to move as she stared at them. Were they pictures of something in particular, or just the random outpourings of a tormented brain?

She felt something cold and dark stir in the back of her mind and wondered if it was one of the Others. But none of them had ever felt like that, even back when she feared them the most. This was a markedly ominous sensation, and the more she tried to tell the unwelcome presence to go back to where it came from, the more insistent it became. What was happening? Why weren't any of the Others helping her with this?

Nervously she tried to step back from the painting, thinking that somehow the bizarre art was connected to all this. But she couldn't. Her feet wouldn't move. It was a sickening sensation, not merely that her feet were frozen in place, more as if . . . as if they weren't really hers anymore. Her entire body felt disconnected, the flesh a mere shell that her soul was using, not *hers* in any real sense, not subject to her control. She was aware of the Others now as if at a distance. Their voices fluttered around her head like insects, but they no longer seemed to be a part of her. She tried to talk to them, but the words wouldn't come.

What was happening to her?

Maybe it was the body, she thought. Maybe the Others wanted it for themselves. Maybe that was what this was all about. Suddenly it all came together in her head, a truly terrifying conclusion. This was what they'd been waiting for all these months. That's why they'd befriended her and helped her all this time. They wanted her to *trust* them. They wanted her to grow accustomed to their presence, and to letting others control the body, so that when the time came to finally make their play, she wouldn't see it coming.

She could see it all now, everything they'd done, all part of a larger plan. That's why they'd never made contact with her on the habitat, all those years. They'd hoped to just do away with her and take her place before anybody noticed. But of course that wasn't possible in the outworlds, where they all had to help her survive in order to keep this flesh alive. They didn't care about her welfare, only the safety of the body they coveted; she saw that now with perfect clarity. If not for her fleeing Earth, she might never have known the truth. . . .

How did you fight enemies who lived in your own head? She remembered how Verina had taught her to sink down into the darkness within, shutting out all input from the body's senses. Now, now she understood what that was all about! They were *training* her. Teaching her to submit. So that when at last she was locked away in that place, where no light ever shone and no thought ever stirred, she wouldn't be able to break free. She could scream all she wanted in that place, and no one from the outside world would ever hear her.

She needed Phoenix. Where was Phoenix? She started to turn and run to the door, to seek him out, but then she remembered. Phoenix was *hers*. Katlyn had seduced him and Katlyn pulled his strings, and Jamisia realized now that this, too, had all been part of their plan. She had no one to turn to, no ally she could trust. They had isolated her from the world, and when she disappeared and they took over her body no one would notice or care.

Fear came crushing down on her, not just an emotion but a physical weight, black and suffocating. She felt herself sucked into it, drowning, her lungs drawing in thick cold terror instead of air. She could feel the Others hovering about her, waiting for her to break free, ready to shove her back into the choking blackness. This was the time they had all been hoping for. Years and years of waiting, of plotting, of preparing for this day. She tried to scream, but of course her body made no sound; *they* had control of her flesh now, and they were never giving it back to her.

*No!* she screamed silently, defying them. *I won't go back there! I won't let you have it!* Inside her head she beat at the darkness, but the body she was trapped in wouldn't move. *I won't let you kill me—*

*That's it!* Derik thought. *I'm pulling the fucking plug NOW.*
Blackness.

**"M**ichal Andres, this is Devlin Gaza, Director of Programming for the Ainniq Guild. Mr. Andres is . . . freelance." It was clear to Phoenix from Gaza's expression that he knew exactly what the phrase meant, and he didn't approve.

"Dr. Masada tells me you have information for us."

Phoenix cleared his throat nervously. He'd been comfortable enough with Masada, because in a way he already knew the man, but this was different. This scene he didn't quite know how to play. Devlin Gaza was one of the two or three most powerful people in the outworlds, and as much as Phoenix might play at disdain for administrative types, he couldn't help but be aware of that power. Besides, the guy was good at what he did. Not as good as Masada, God knows; no one could lay claim to that. But good in a clean, conservative, formal-education kind of way. And since the only way to win respect in Phoenix' eyes was with programming skill, that said a lot.

"Yeah. I went to see some of my friends here, who work on this station." It was awkward trying to explain this without the moddie vocabulary to fall back on; he found himself fishing for the right words to use. "First of all, they said that yes, they remembered the viral fragments from way back. Trash—that is, a friend of mine—he had a copy of some of them." He pulled a small chip out of his jacket pocket. "This is all his stuff and also a few things caught by other people. There are notes on when and where everything was found."

He held it out to Masada, but Devlin took it first. Phoenix couldn't be sure of Masada's reaction—it was so hard to read that painted face—but he thought the professor looked surprised.

"It goes back almost five years," Phoenix continued. "Apparently someone did some test runs with parts of Lucifer, not the parts that fuck with anyone's brain—sorry about the language, I mean, like, affecting the brainware—but just to test, you know, the replication module, that kind of thing." Damn it, why did Gaza's mere presence make him feel so self-conscious? Masada hadn't done that to him.

"Five years is about right," Masada mused aloud.

"You think someone worked on it that long?" Gaza asked.

"Oh, yes. Lucifer's a masterpiece. It could have been launched in half the time if its designer hadn't been such a perfectionist . . . but since he clearly was, that much time would have been required to test and polish it. And to do it carefully enough that he wouldn't be caught." He favored Phoenix with a dry smile. "Only apparently he didn't count on being discovered by . . . hobbyists."

Phoenix said, "I've got a friend who does a lot of . . . um . . . communication work with the Hausman League." He saw Gaza's expression darken. Shit, was there going to be trouble if he admitted he hung out with hackers? He'd thought from Masada's description of the project that Gaza would catch on and accept the situation, but now the professor seemed to be avoiding the "H" word like the plague, and Gaza looked like he'd rather shove him out an air lock than listen to his "amateur" attempts at sleuthing.

You never knew when someone in administrative circles was going to be closed-minded like that. You also never knew when they were going to butter you up to learn what they wanted, and then throw you into some pol cell to cool your butt for an E-year or ten. If Masada wasn't involved in this Phoenix sure as hell wouldn't be talking to the likes of Gaza, much less letting him know what the Preservation moddies were doing. He wasn't all that sure he should be doing it now.

*You've got to take Lucifer down,* he told himself, *or moddies will die. You can trust Masada. Only Masada. He won't let you go down for this.*

"My friend says there's been a lot of com activity between the League and this station. Encrypted shit. Super secret. He thinks it went straight to the Guildmaster's office."

Gaza drew in a sharp breath but said nothing. For a moment there was silence. Doubtless, both men were trying to figure out how to continue the conversation without giving Phoenix some juicy fact he shouldn't know.

"The Hausman Guild hates Earth," Masada said at last. "They want Earth to be cut out of the ainniq system. They've lobbied for it for years now."

Gaza said nothing.

"Maybe they got tired of waiting. Maybe they decided to take things into their own hands and force the issue."

Again, the silence. So many things weren't being said, Phoenix could just taste it. Man, he wished he was in on all those secrets. Even his limited contact with the Guild had made it clear they were playing a game far beyond anything he had ever been a part of. It awakened a hunger in him like he hadn't felt since the Pol on Hellsgate announced they were coming up with a system to keep hackers out. He wanted in.

"I think," Gaza said slowly, "we have much to discuss. Back on Tiananmen, where security is tighter. Yes, Dr. Masada?"

Maybe Phoenix was reading the professor wrong, but it seemed to him that he was startled by that decision. "As you wish."

"You take Ra's ship back to Paradise and drop this young man off back home." He glanced at Phoenix; it was hard to tell if the look was one of grudging respect or just irritation. Phoenix was used to both, and simply smiled back. "I'll meet you on Tiananmen. We'll brief the Prima together."

"If the Hausman League is involved—"

Gaza held up a hand, warning him to silence. "Later. Not here. Kent was clearly allied to enemies of the Guild; I think we should say no more while we're in his house. Who knows what it's wired for?"

Masada bowed his head, acknowledging the point.

"In the meantime . . . let me see if I can't get some kind of com record from the house computers. Something more . . . *complete* than what we've been looking at." His expression was dark. "If what Mr. Andres says is true . . . then we have a whole new situation here. Far more complex. It would be unwise to judge it prematurely," he warned.

"Of course."

Gaza nodded to Phoenix. "Thank you for your help in this. Dr. Masada will see that you get home all right."

"Sure." *Like I was some fucking pet who had to be delivered to his owner.* "I'm glad I could help." He managed to stick a smile on his face and keep it there until Gaza left, but that was as long as it lasted. "Shit!"

Masada came up behind him. There was a moment's pause, and then a hand gripped his shoulder. Just for a second. "If the Prima doesn't see you rewarded for this, I will."

"Reward? Shit, that's not what this is about. You know that."

"I'll tell you all I can when it's over. You know that." And then, to his amazement, Masada chuckled softly. "Of course he's not going to trust you, Phoenix. Would *you* trust you?"

He snorted, then grinned. "*Hell* no."

"All right, then. Go get your friend. I'll see to the outship."

**S**he was sitting on the floor of the gallery. She looked really bad, eyes bloodshot and face pale and looking like all the life had just been squeezed out of her. He didn't know what to say. It twisted his heart to see her like that, but he didn't know how to start to make it better.

She got to her feet with effort and came to him. And then, without a word, she came into his arms and . . . well, not wept exactly. There weren't any tears, or the kind of noises he'd expect when someone was crying. But he held her as her whole body shook for a long, long time. Silent weeping.

"It'll be all right," he whispered. "I promise. It'll be all right."

He wished he knew how to make it true.

Devlin Gaza saw them off from the dock. It was a courtesy, he said, to make sure that Sonondra Ra's guests were safe until they left his care.

He exchanged some last words with Masada, but the need for privacy kept them from discussing anything important. "We'll meet later," he promised.

The outpilot boarded, and the inpilot, and then the young couple, flanked by Ra's guards. He nodded a farewell to the hacker, a gesture of courtesy with no real warmth behind it. Annoying young man.

The outship was sealed and its engines engaged, and with a low throbbing roar it backed out of the dock. Arbela came up to Gaza and stood by his side as it slowly pulled away; they both watched the ponderous ballet of ship and station on the viewscreen as it maneuvered into the proper position. Facing the ainniq. Heading home.

Gaza looked at Arbela, then back at the image. His expression was grim.

"This game has gotten too complex," he said quietly. "It's time to remove some pieces from the board."

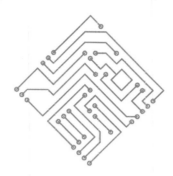

The only thing more frustrating than failing to achieve an objective is failing, and having a rival succeed.

> SORTEY-6,
> *On Human Power*

# GUERA NODE
# TIANANMEN STATION

THE HOLOCAST took on color and form slowly, as Guild computers untangled the encryption codes used in sending it. Not for a full minute did it manifest in detail, which gave the Prima time to put aside the reports she'd been reading and prepare herself for what promised to be a formal call.

Light and color resolved itself into the form of a woman in a plasteel carapace, dressed in formal Guild clothes. A few seconds after the image stabilized, the woman bowed ever so slightly, a position her mechanical exoskeleton clearly did not assume easily.

The Prima bowed her head in response, welcoming her. "Chandras Delhi."

There was a delay as the signal was encrypted, skipped past five nodes, and decrypted at the other end. Several seconds.

"My Prima. I hope I don't catch you at a bad time."

"Not at all. You're always welcome. How are things in your node?"

"Busy, as always. My search team has found another system to mine, not three month's travel from here. They're outfitting the harvesters now. It should cut our building costs considerably."

"You're still expanding?"

"I've had two settlement requests from Frisia and one from Belial. Both are reasonable. If we can find another system to harvest ore from, we should be able to accommodate them both." She paused. "And I had one request from a Terran corporation, but I'll be turning that down."

Her tone warned Alya that the last comment wasn't merely small talk, but touched on the reason she had called.

"Be careful," the Prima warned. "They have a right to settle in outspace. If you deny them station rights, you'd better have a very good reason."

"Only the best," Delhi assured her. "You see, these corporates came into the outworlds to find someone. A young girl. Perhaps you've heard of her. Jamisia Capra."

The Prima's expression revealed nothing.

"It seems she left Earth with some great secret in her possession. Something destined to unseat the Guild and give control of the stars to Earth."

"Indeed. I've been hearing stories like that for years. Forgive me if I'm skeptical."

Delhi scowled. Clearly she knew that Alya's people had been following the girl, but if the Prima wouldn't admit to it then it couldn't be discussed openly.

"If a person like that existed," Delhi said finally, "she might be a real danger to the Guild."

"If I believed anyone to be a danger to the Guild," Alya assured her, "that person would be dead."

"Perhaps you would believe it worth the risk. To follow her, maybe, and see who else was interested in her."

"Perhaps," she said quietly. "And why would that be a concern of yours?"

"It wouldn't, for as long as she was in the outworlds. But if she fell into the hands of someone who might use her for personal gain. . . ."

There was a long pause. Longer even than the time required for the transmission to get from one office to the other.

"Such as?" Alya prompted.

Delhi seemed to consider the question before answering. "A Guildmaster, perhaps."

"Someone other than yourself."

"Of course."

"Because you would be no threat at all to anyone. The girl would be quite safe in your hands."

"Of course."

"But in someone else's . . . you're saying that's a different matter."

Delhi's expression darkened. "Someone with less commitment to the Guild, perhaps. Someone whose penchant for playing dangerous games could put us all at risk."

"One of my Guildmasters? Surely I can trust them all."

"Their loyalty, Prima. Not their judgment."

"Ah. I see."

"I speak only of some of them, of course. A rare few."

"And you think that if one of those got hold of this girl, it would be bad for the Guild."

"Her very existence is a threat to us. Something we might be willing to tolerate for a while, to see who comes after her, but not for too long. And once she's in the hands of a Guildmaster, her usefulness is at an end, for no Terran corporate is going to raid Guild property to gain access to her."

"A valid point," the Prima allowed. "So what you're saying is, if a girl like that fell into the hands of a Guildmaster—one without your own appreciation for the subtleties of the situation—she should be killed immediately, to keep her from becoming a threat to us in the future."

"Yes, my Prima. That's what I was thinking, exactly."

"Indeed." She made sure her expression revealed nothing of what she was thinking, and kept her tone carefully neutral. "How fortunate that no situation like that has arisen. But I'll keep your words in mind, just in case it ever does."

"You do me honor."

"Your counsel is always welcome, Guildmistress. Always."

*Even when you do not say what you mean.*

They went through the ritual of ending their conversation with polite trivialities, a process drawn out to tedious length by the transmission delay. Then the holocast switched off, leaving the Prima alone once more.

*Do you think I don't know what you want, Chandras Delhi?*

She took up the report again and put it before her. It was the most recent of several hundred documents analyzing the path of Jamisia Shido, or her history, or her potential threat to the Guild.

*You were after her yourself for reasons of your own, and it irks you no end that now someone else has control of her. So, rather than leave her in Ra's hands, or give her into mine, you would simply have her destroyed. Remove the piece from the game board so that no one else can use it. That's your style, isn't it? Take control of what you can and destroy all the rest.*

She gazed down at the report, which chronicled Jamisia's arrival at Ra's house on Paradise, and the desperate efforts of a Terran corporation to get hold of her.

*Of course,* she mused, *that doesn't mean that in this case you aren't right about the girl, does it?*

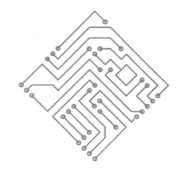

If you want a truly alien creature, look deeply at your own Terran self. Probe into that layer of being which evolved before we had speech or walked erect, and see if it seems at all familiar to your modern, civilized self. Study the parts of the soul that hide from daylight, the quirks and terrors of our insecurities, the inner conflicts that are the very foundation of our human identity. There you will find a creature truly alien, nearly incomprehensible, and as awesome in its potential as it is terrifying in its capacity for self-destruction.

TYE CHIVAL,
*On Being Human*

# OUTSHIP: DIONYSUS

JAMISIA FELT as if her mind had been scraped raw.

She tried to act normal as Phoenix helped her into her sleep chair on the outship, but it was impossible. Something had been inside her brain that didn't belong there, and now that it was gone, it had left a gaping wound. And the worst part was that she felt driven to prod it with her thoughts, forcing it open, testing the pain.

What had happened in the gallery?

"You all right?" It was Phoenix. In his eyes she could see just how much he wanted to help her, and how he didn't know where to start. She didn't know what to tell him either. *Just be here for me. I don't want to be alone.* But she sensed that when the episode had happened in the gallery, it wouldn't have mattered if ten thousand people were with her, or if they all loved her to distraction. She had been alone then, utterly alone, and even her Others couldn't help her. The ultimate Isolation, inside one's own head.

"I'll be fine," she assured him, and she managed a strained smile.

He tightened the straps one last time, securing her into the chair, and then went to strap himself into his own. Once more the outpilot was insisting that they sleep through the journey. The first time she had been disappointed, for she had wanted to see the ainniq from the inside. Now she was merely exhausted, and welcomed the theta-sleep which would be imposed upon her. At least she didn't have to be in some coffinlike shell this trip, as she had on her first outspace journey. This would be a lighter sleep, more easily managed, a state *suggested* rather than *mandated* by the programs being fed into her headset.

With a sigh she shut her eyes and leaned back. She could feel the ship's engines rumbling, a soothing vibration through the padded chair. An icon appeared before her and she confirmed it, and almost immediately felt the comfortable disassociation of light sleep take hold of her brain, as the outship's theta-program started to cycle her down into the deepest phase of slumber.

DREAMSCAPE 99.0000 LOADING

    . . . .

*The field is darker now than ever before, and storm clouds are drawing in. The light is harsh and low-angled, casting knife-edged shadows across the grass.*

*Something's wrong. But what?*

*The Others are all there with her, and now that she looks at their faces, she can see the resemblance to her own. Even in Derik's male face, even in Raven's dark one. It's not a quality of color or shape, but something much more subtle. As if she can sense the soul within each of them and recognize it as cousin to her own.*

*Her tutor approaches the group. She can see the tension in his eyes.*

*He tells her, "I hoped this day would never come."*

*"What is it?" His demeanor frightens her. "What's happening?"*

*He shakes his head. "Ah, Jamie. I've done everything I can to protect you. You don't know how much. You don't know how many programs are in your head that I put there, trying to stave off this day." He sighs. "But you are what they made you to be. And now the worst is manifesting. Very well."*

*Dark clouds are moving in. The farthest trees are fading into a misty grayness, veiled by distant rain.*

*"I'll tell you what I know," he says. "And mind you, it's all I know. I wasn't part of the team that designed your psyche, nor was I one of those who did the work. I helped cover up their tracks now and then. I wrote up reports on you so that they could see if their efforts were bearing fruit. I knew some of the details of what was going on because doing my job required that I know. But they didn't*

tell me anything they didn't have to. And they were right in that, weren't they? Because in the end I betrayed their purpose."

She says softly, "You saved my life."

He is only a program, of course. A recording of the man who once cared for her, with a finite store of variations on file. He can't have real feelings. He probably can't even pretend to have feelings, because that wouldn't have seemed important when he was being made, so the proper facial expressions wouldn't be in his program set.

Nevertheless, she thinks he looks moved.

"The ainniq are the key to interstellar commerce," he tells her. "Yet we of Earth know very little about them. Guera has kept it that way on purpose, so that all the human worlds would be dependent upon the Guild for interstellar travel. The most perfect monopoly humankind has ever known.

"My employers—your creators—meant to break that monopoly.

"We do know that any pilot can navigate the ainniq, that isn't a problem. Occasionally Terran thrillseekers still attempt it, and rarely—very rarely—one survives. From them we know that the ainniq gives access to a universe so alien that no human mind can truly comprehend it. The brain will apply colors to it, form and movement and sometimes other sensations as well, but it's clear from the few reports we have that each experience is individual, and each is utterly chaotic."

She knows most of this, of course; it was covered in her basic education. But there is more coming that she may not know, and so she says nothing to stop him.

"In that universe are predators. The Guerans named them sana, monsters of the deep. In outpilot slang they're called dragons. We don't know what they are, or how they move, or even how they feed. The Guild may have learned some of those things by now, but they're not about to tell outsiders. The point is . . . we appear to be food to them. The only pilots who can make it through the ainniq safely are the ones who can avoid them; the rest are devoured in transit.

"Which would all be a very simple problem if their world was like our own. But it isn't. Our machines can make no sense of it. The best of our sensors can't pick the sana out from their landscape, and apparently the normal human mind can't either. They're all but invisible to us, Jamisia." *He puts his hand under her chin gently, sadly.* "And that's where you come in."

*The wind is growing colder. She feels it distinctly, as she senses the coming darkness. She needs no scholarly discourse to tell her that the dreamscape is reflecting her mood; that much is all too clear. The sky is the color of fear.*

I don't want to hear this, *she thinks.*

*An inner voice whispers:* You must.

"You see, there's a condition which allows human beings to see things in the ainniq . . . but it destroys their souls otherwise. You know what it feels like, don't you? I know that you do, because that experience was the trigger for this dreamscape. You carry the seeds of that sickness inside you, and I'd hoped they would never come to the surface . . . but if you're running this program, then the process has started."

"You mean—" *She can't finish. The words are all caught up in her throat, and she can't force them out.* What happened in the gallery, was that—? *She remembers her dreams, the recurring image of the lost one crying in terror, of running to find him . . . was he . . . oh, my God . . .*

"I see you understand."

*The sky has grown dark now, and she can feel the icy bite of the wind on her skin. Droplets of water have begun to fall from the sky and they splatter down on her hair and shoulders, a jarring and unfamiliar sensation. In her heart is a growing certainty that she knows what he is going to say and doesn't ever, ever want to hear it. But it's a dreamscape; she has no control over it, or over him.*

"The price of the stars is insanity, Jamisia. Earth has known that for years. What they didn't know was how to control the madness, so that it would only surface in the ainniq. That's why they did what they did to you. Divided you up into separate souls, using the only method known to them. The mind is still a mystery to us; there are no easy switches to throw. I'm sorry, Jamie. Sorry about the pain. It was the only trigger they knew how to use."

*Fragments of memories come back to her now. A lost and frightened child, buried under tons of debris. Abandoned. Pain and terror, day after day, inescapable. By the time they pulled her free, the damage was done, patterns of fledgling insanity etched into her young and malleable brain. They tested her for it as soon as she was* rescued, and knew the risk. They should have seen to it that she was treated and healed. Instead Shido bartered for her, body and soul, and nurtured the darkness within her. Until her young spirit made what adaptation it could, and divided, and divided, and divided again.

"They thought it would give them control," her tutor says. "They thought if they could cordon off the madness into a separate persona, let it surface only when it was needed, they would have a functional outpilot. That's why you . . . that's why Raven was taught how to fly a ship, so she could provide the technical expertise needed. There was no way to teach the sick one anything."

She thinks of the crying one and shudders. Was that what came into her head in the gallery? That injured soul, trapped in eternal nightmare? "So what happened?" she demands. She can hear the edge of hysteria coming into her voice and wonders if the tutor-program will even understand what it is. Did he program it to recognize such things? "You said it didn't work. What went wrong? Tell me!"

"You know the answer to that one, Jamisia. The separation isn't strong enough. The sickness is bleeding out from his mind into yours. You've felt it already, yes?"

She whispers it: "Yes."

"He's stronger than they expected him to be, and your defenses are weaker. Which means you can't afford to complete the experiment. Thus far you've remained the dominant personality because the others are content with that arrangement, but he knows nothing of such agreements. If you let him take control now, he may never let go."

She lowers her face into her hands, trembling. She's remembering what happened in the gallery, how terrified she was then that the Others would take control of her body, how she fought to keep it from happening . . . if that was just a reflection of the crying one's madness, what would happen if it were fully unleashed? She remembers the struggle she had with Derik over the simple destruction of a headset, how hard it had been to regain control of her flesh when another had it, even with all the Others helping her. What would happen if he took control?

"I'd hoped it would never go this far," her tutor says.

The sky is nearly black now, and flickers of light flash ominously

*across the heavens. She tries to find her voice, tries to force words
out past the lump of fear that's formed in her throat—*

*—And a scream splits the darkness. A sharp, shrill sound that
cuts through the night, making the very substance of the dreamscape shiver. For a split second the image of her tutor disappears,
then it returns. What—?*

*Another scream follows the first. A sound born of pain and fear,
horrible to hear. She trembles as the Others begin to shimmer and
lose substance, as her tutor splits apart into a field of binary chaos.
His image reforms again, but this time his features are scrambled,
and they began to twitch across his face as she watches, seeking
their rightful position. What the hell is going on?*

*A sudden panic wells up inside her. She needs to know where he
is. The one this is all about, the one whose madness may well over-
whelm her if he's ever set free.*

*Running. She's running. Under the lightning-filled sky, across a
landscape drenched in screams. Where is he? She has to know. He
looked at her once, and his eyes were almost sane, she touched his
hand! The ground rumbles and the grass begins to dissolve into code.
No! No! Not yet! Not yet! She has to find him—*

DREAMSCAPE ABORT

WELLSEEKER OVERRIDE

THETA SEQUENCE ABORT

WELLSEEKER OVERRIDE

ESTABLISHING BETA STAGE CONSCIOUSNESS

Awake.
She was awake.
It took her a moment to get her bearings. It took her another
moment to realize that although she was still in the passenger
chamber of the outship, she was now the only one there. Phoenix was gone, and the straps he had worn now hung limply
down by the sides of his chair where he had apparently dropped
them.

Before she could move—or even think—there was another scream, a sharp and tortured sound that ended abruptly.

It was real.

With shaking hands she unhooked her own restraining straps and got up quickly. Was the ship in the ainniq yet? There were no windows in the passenger compartment, no way to tell. She hesitated for a second and then started heading toward the direction the scream had come from. She could hear voices coming from there, but she couldn't make out the words. Was Phoenix there, were the Guerans? What was wrong?

The door of the bridge was open, and as she came up, she could see people inside. Masada was seated at the pilot's console, staring at it with an intensity which hinted at volumes of data being processed though his headset. Phoenix had just knelt down on the floor beside what looked like a Gueran body, with two guards behind him. On the other side of the body was the inpilot, and he was running some sort of scanning device over it. The skin beneath the kaja paint of the fallen man was a chalky gray.

"I can try to take control of his wellseekers," Phoenix was saying. "That might work."

"Too late." The pilot shook his head grimly. "He's gone."

Overhead on the main viewscreen a slender vein of light flickered against an ebony starscape. It looked like the ainniq she had seen near Earth, but much closer and much brighter. From here she could see that light flickered up and down the length of the fault in spurts, like the lightning in her dreamscape. Colors sputtered along its length in seemingly random patterns, sparkling as they collided with one another. It was strange and very beautiful . . . and under the circumstances, not a little threatening.

Finally she dared to ask, "What's going on?"

As soon as he realized she was there, Phoenix rose up and went to her. His expression was strained. "Outpilot's dead," he said. He put an arm around her shoulders and squeezed, as much for his own reassurance, it seemed, as for anything she needed. She could feel him trembling slightly. "So we are in very deep shit right now."

"I'd call that an understatement." The inpilot grunted. "It's sabotage, and a damn good job, too. We were hit hard and clean, no warning. The outpilot went down as soon as he hooked up. Navigation's locked out, I can't access a single control. Dr. Masada's trying to reroute the signal so that we can at least maneuver."

Masada reached out to the control panel before him and pressed something. A moment later he cursed softly. "No. That's locked up, too."

Jamisia could see the fear in the pilot's eyes. "You *have* to get the helm back before we hit the ainniq."

She could see that the ainniq was closer now; it was possible to see veils of light shimmering about its edges, bleeding out into the black of space. They were heading straight toward it.

Masada muttered. "Every pathway is blocked."

"Keep trying," the inpilot ordered. He sat down before the controls and tried a few, then cursed as they failed to respond properly. "Less than a minute left."

"To what?" Jamisia whispered.

Phoenix nodded upward toward the viewscreen, where the ainniq was rapidly growing larger. "Course was set already. If Dr. Masada can't bypass the damaged navigational programs, we're going in."

"Without an outpilot," one of the guards added. She could hear the fear in his voice.

It was said to be the worst death imaginable, to be eaten by the sana.

THIRTY SECONDS TO IMMERSION, the bridge announced.

"All right," Masada muttered. His attention was now wholly fixed on the crippled programs feeding into his head, and he was clearly making comments to himself, not to them. "There's the problem."

Sabotage. To kill her, or Masada, or Phoenix? Or all three? What a clean death it would seem from the outside, with no evidence that anything had gone wrong. A ship had gone into the ainniq. It never came out. Such things happened.

TWENTY SECONDS TO IMMERSION.

Computer sabotage. Neat and clean. They had probably shut down communications as well. The ship would go down without so much as a ripple in the outernet. No one would ever know what had happened.

"Dr. Masada." The pilot's voice was strained. "I need helm control *before* immersion."

"If you keep interrupting my concentration," came the answer, "you will have nothing."

The viewscreen was blazing with light now, the darkness of surrounding space withdrawn to the farthest edges of the display. In the midst of that brightness shadows shimmered and swayed, hinting at forms unseen, dangers unnamed.

"Can I help?" Phoenix offered.

Masada shook his head sharply. "It's Guild code. I can't let you have access to that."

"Even if that means we all die?"

TEN SECONDS TO IMMERSION

"Don't be foolish. Not even you can hack a foreign system in ten seconds." He shook his head in frustration. "Whoever did this knew his stuff. He also anticipated everything I would try to do to reestablish control. Damn . . ."

The viewscreen was filled with writhing colors, shapes and streamers and twisting shadows that moved too quickly to follow. Closer, it was coming closer—

"I need the helm!" the inpilot cried. Jamisia could hear the raw panic in his voice as the ainniq moved forward to swallow them whole.

IMMERSION, the bridge announced.

A full set of viewscreens blazed to sudden life around them, circling the bridge with its display, 360 degrees of blazing light, surrounding them with the nightmare vision. Was it Jamisia's imagination, or could she sense something out there, bright and hungry and winging its way toward the crippled ship? She was reminded of the queasy feeling she'd had while staring at Kent's paintings; looking at the ainniq was like that, but a thousand times worse. Was this what he'd been trying to paint?

It was beautiful. It was horrible. It was chaos, utter chaos, and the mind couldn't even focus on it without feeling the boundaries of sanity give way. She turned and looked at the rear viewscreens, the space that was presumably behind them. There was no sign of the way they had come, or anything that might mark the way out. What landmarks could exist in such a place, where everything was in constant flux? They were lost, truly lost. And it was only a question of time, she knew, before one of the predators of this realm spotted them. Maybe only seconds.

*You could find the way out*, an inner voice whispered.

A looming shadow began to move toward the ship. The inpilot saw it and cringed back in his seat. "Oh, Jesus." Phoenix's arm tightened around Jamisia as the thing drew closer, and she could feel her own heart pounding in fear. Her wellseeker posted several warnings, and she finally just shut it down. What did it matter how fast her heart was beating, when her soul was about to be ripped from her body?

The darkness enveloped the ship and for a moment all the screens were flooded with blood-red light . . . then it passed over them, or through them, and was absorbed into the mad skyscape beyond.

Not a dragon. Not a real one. Not anything.

*You can see the real dragons, Jamisia. If you want to.*

*No*, she thought back, *I can't. Only* he *can*. The thought of the sick one taking control of her body, even for a moment, was terrifying. She couldn't consider it. She just couldn't.

"All right." It was Masada. "I've got the auxiliary systems freed up. That's a start."

"So what? We dodge things we can't see?" The inpilot gestured toward the display. His forehead was beaded with sweat, and it dripped down the lines of his kaja, obscuring the design. "Do *you* know how to fly us out of this?"

*I could do it*, Raven thought. *We could fly it together.*

*Yes*, Jamisia answered her, *and then I would die. This body would live, but I would be gone forever. No!*

She could feel something coming up behind the ship again and she whirled around to look at the viewscreen. Colors boiled over one another with shadows swirling between them, a visual maelstrom in which it was impossible to focus on any one point for more than a second. Yet something was out there, she could feel it even if she couldn't see it. Something very hungry, very powerful, and very swift. She could feel it bearing down on them, licking at the human souls within the ship, tasting their substance—

"I can pilot," she whispered.

Only Phoenix heard her, and he didn't know enough about

what was going on to understand. "That isn't what they need." There was fear in his voice now, cold and shaking and not at all like the Phoenix she knew. He was used to dangers that came at him through a network of delicate circuits and threatened at most a handful of neurons, not invisible demons who hungered to rip his very soul from his flesh.

It was said to be the most horrible death a human being could know. Did she fear that more than she feared what was inside her? She drew in a deep breath and tried to not to let the fear resonate in her voice as she said it again, more loudly. "I can pilot." Still no one responded to her, so she added, almost angrily, "I can *see* them, damn it!"

"You're a Terran," the inpilot snapped.

Masada said, "You don't even know what that means." Then he shut his eyes for a minute to concentrate on something internally. "Almost there. . . ."

"*I know what it means*," she said. When no one responded, she persisted with single-minded stubbornness, "It's a sickness. It lets you see the sana, but it destroys everything else in the mind. Right?"

The pilot turned and stared at her.

So did Masada.

The hunter was close, so close. She could feel it. There was no time left. Why couldn't these people understand? "*I have it*," she told them. It infuriated her that now that she had finally decided to risk her very existence for them, they were too stupid to take her up on it. "*I have the disease. I can see them.*"

Finally Masada seemed to get the message. "Go," he said, nodding dismissal to the guards. He pointed to Phoenix. "And take him with you."

The hacker started to protest, but the guard who grabbed his arm would hear none of it. "You're not Guild," Masada said as they dragged him out. "It's for your own protection."

When the last guard had passed through the door, it hissed shut, leaving Jamisia, Masada and the inpilot alone.

*God, what am I doing, this is crazy. . . .*

*There is no other way,* Raven whispered, and Verina agreed, *it's that or die.*

*We're with you,* Katlyn promised.

*All of us*, Derik agreed.

All but one. . . .

"How?" the inpilot demanded. "How can you do this?"

She met his eyes with a fierce but frightened gaze. "Does it matter? If I say I can see them, do you really care how?"

"This isn't the time to argue." Masada's voice was cool and even, a perfect counterpoint to the inpilot's fear and her own incipient panic. "If what she says is true, then we stand a chance. If not, we die. And if we don't try anything . . . we die." The dark eyes focused on her. "There'll be time later to ask questions."

"Of course," she whispered.

*Oh, God, help me, please. . . .*

Down, down into her soul she reached, down to that dark place where the youngest Others huddled, into those secret recesses where Others went to escape each other. Down past there, to places so secret she barely knew they existed.

*Jamisia.* An icon appeared before her. *Use this.*

She flashed a confirmation and saw data begin to scroll in her field of vision. Line after line after line of unknown code swam before her eyes, without a single icon for identification. "I don't know what this is—" she began to protest, but Raven's calm voice sounded in her brain. *I do. Pilot's code. Trust me.* Someone started to speak to her again, but she waved them to silence. "It's all right." Raven was trained for this. Raven knew.

With a sick feeling in the pit of her stomach she focused inwardly once more. She was vaguely aware that Raven was feeding instructions to the outship, allowing it to tie her into the helm control programs, but that seemed like it was a universe away. Another world, peopled by souls unconnected to her own.

*She runs across the rain-soaked grass, crying out for him. Does he have a name? Would he answer if she called it? The rain is so heavy she can hardly see. She has to find him!*

*The sky is black with storm clouds, and icy water beats down upon her. The wind is so powerful that it knocks her off her feet, and she lands heavily on the muddy earth. No! No, she has to keep going! She struggles to her feet again, mud dripping from her hands and knees. He's always been here, every time she came to this place. He must be here now!*

*She screams out for him, but her voice is drowned out by the rising wind. "Take it!" she yells. "Take it! It's all yours! They need you more than they need me. . . !"*

*Tears run down her face and are immediately washed away by rain. Tears of fear, or of remembered pain? She staggers forward, heading toward a nearby rise where the faint glimmer of stars has broken through, revealing something huddled on the ground. As she gets closer, she can see him there, lying on his side, curled up in terror. She stumbles to him and drops to her knees by his side, weeping in terror. "Come on," she urges. Voice lost in the wind. "Come on, we need you." She hesitates, then chokes out, "I need you."*

*The pale head lifts, the hollow eyes meet her own. Such pain in those eyes, such terrible pain! She has to fight the urge to look away, to save herself. "Come on," she whispers. "Come back with me." She can feel herself being drawn toward him, sucked in by the emptiness within his soul. It takes all her strength not to fight it. Did she ever think she was alone? She didn't know what loneliness was!*

*Her tutor is standing over her. She can hear him trying to warn her. No good, no good. The sana are coming, don't you know that? The dragons feast on human souls, and I have so many souls to give them. . . .*

*Didn't they know that to bring her on this ship would draw the dragons? Didn't they understand that the sheer wealth of souls in her flesh would be a delicacy too rare to resist?*

"They've come for me!" he burst out. He could see them now surrounding him, hiding behind the bursts of color, hunger burning red along their bodies, and one was moving in, gold light blazing along its path, sparks of shadowy hatred disguising its length—

"It's there!" he screamed. It was coming at them fast, so fast, why couldn't they see it? He could see all the colors drawing together in front of it, scattering in its wake, could feel the pressure of its mind on his own. More and more of the creature was becoming visible now, as his sight picked it out from the roiling background. Those blue shapes there, that was all part of it, and the gold part beneath was what gave it the power to move, and now there were more coming in from behind, each with its own color and form—

"Now! he screamed. "Go!"

—and all of it was alive, he saw, everything out there had its own consciousness, its own hunger. The vista that had seemed bizarre only moments before was now revealed for what it truly was, a jungle teeming with life, vicious and hungry life. How could anything human survive here? It was alien, too alien; human beings didn't belong in such a place.

He saw the navigational menu appear before him and then disappear. *She* was taking control of the ship now, the dark one. Translating his visions into motion. What if she got it wrong? What if she chose to feed him to the sana, to sate their hunger so they would leave her alone? There were two men on the bridge, what if they chose to throw him out the air lock to save themselves? He saw one taking a step toward him and backed away hurriedly; his back slammed into the emergency door. "Stay away!" he screamed. "Stay away from me!"

*Where are they?* a voice in his head prompted. *Look!*

The outship's programs fed the viewscreen images right into his head. He could see the dragons all around him now, layers upon layers of them, colors shifting and shapes evolving and hunger a red tongue that lashed out between clouds of hate. Beneath his feet the ship moved suddenly and he fell to his knees; the vision was jarred out of his head for an instant. Lost, lost, they were all lost! Did they think they could run from such creatures? The sana were everywhere, all but invisible, always hungry . . . with a gasp he let the viewscreen's images fill his brain again so that he could seek them out. There, there was one, winding its way slowly toward the ship, shifting its colors as it went! Move away from it, quickly! And that one there—that could sense the grav web, so shut it down, shut it down!

They were gathering in a pack now, and he knew that they were intelligent, and they were aware of him, and they were focused on his destruction. The ship didn't even matter to them anymore; he, he was their enemy, the focus of all their malevolence. A pack of them came together off the rear of the outship and started to move in; he cried out a warning and felt the ship lurch in response. He could hear the dragon's laughter as they chased him, creatures of color and shadow placing bets on how long it would take them to catch him, exchanging plans of what they would do with his soul when they did. Speed, he needed more speed! Clouds of silver and scarlet parted to reveal creatures of silver and scarlet. One came toward the ship with a chromatic roar, the gold of pure hunger blazing from its surface as it lunged toward them. He ordered the ship into an evasive maneuver that left it lost in a boiling cloud of orange mist.

There, up ahead. What was that? A thin black line, almost hidden behind clouds of fire. What was it? Someone was saying something to him, but he could no longer understand their language. He had become something without speech, a creature of speed and fear and silent vision. Moments later words were placed in his head by her, the pilot, and because she was inside him he understood. *That's the ainniq. Follow it. You can't exit safely until we find a node.*

Follow it? Didn't the dark one understand that the dragons knew where he wanted to go, that they were gathering at the ainniq, waiting for the outship to come to them? She must not be an ally of his after all, but some kind servant of theirs. He'd been tricked, they'd all been tricked. . . .

A cold tongue licked at his brain. Alien, malevolent. Hungry. With a gasp he fed instructions to the ship, trying to get away from it. The sana followed, its substance spread out across the miles, across a thousand hues of light. He could feel it in his head as he directed the ship, sharp teeth ripping at the substance of his mind, trying to yank it loose from his flesh.

Then: there it was. Straight ahead. A place where two of the ainniq converged, providing a sure landmark in this chaotic realm. He could feel the ship surge forward suddenly and he had to scream that no, no, there were sana waiting there, they couldn't come in straight! The sudden burst of speed threw off the one that had been following them. There, see that pack of hunters? Go around them. More speed. Put the grav web back on, it'll confuse them. Come around, straight into the intersection of space-black lines, the node—

He could hear the dragons screaming as they broke through into safespace. Rage, hot rage, followed them out through the fault, licking at their heels as they dove into the black night of safety. He had escaped them. This time. But they'd be waiting. They'd learn.

Now he had to escape the others.

The two men were watching him. They wore human bodies,

but they were no less alien to him than the sana were. And no less dangerous. They'd want him to go back into the darkness again, the suffocating darkness where fears lurked hidden and unseen monsters crawled through his veins. He wasn't going back. He wasn't ever going back. . . .

One of the men began to approach him. He screamed for him to get back. Two other men were coming into the chamber now with weapons drawn, so you see, he'd been right, he'd been right! They'd just used him to get past the dragons, and now they were going to get rid of him . . . and they came at him and he struggled and fought for his life, gouging and clawing and struggling to get free . . . but a medgun hissed against his neck and suddenly his strength was failing. "Bastards!" he screamed. "Bastards! I saved you! Bastards . . ."

Then the anger faded into darkness, and the fear into sleep. A drugged sleep, but it was a kind of peace. More than he had ever known before.

Masada stared down at the girl's body, now spotted with blood and foaming spittle from her wild struggle against her Gueran guards. The men backed off when they were sure she was out cold, leaving her as she had fallen.

Slowly, carefully, he reached down and gathered her up. She was slender, and so very light. How could anyone so frail-looking put up the kind of fight she did? The terror must have been great in her, to have lent her such unexpected strength.

"Where are we?" he asked the pilot.

"Harmony Node. I'm making contact with the waystation now." He wiped the sweat from his forehead with a shaking hand. "Jesus, that was some ride."

"Not one I would like to repeat," he agreed.

He'd make sure the girl stayed asleep until Gueran meds could deal with her. They knew the science of the Syndrome and could keep it from swallowing her alive. Until then . . . sleep would be a mercy.

He wondered if the Guild would kill her. Probably so. Whatever Earth had done to give her an outpilot's capacity, it was a secret that had to be buried forever. Poor girl. To come through the ainniq intact and then be destroyed for doing so . . . it wasn't justice, but it was political necessity, and he was a wise enough man to know that sometimes one had to give way for the other.

When he was sure that the girl was safely asleep and resting peacefully, he gave her into the arms of one of the guards. "Put her in the pilot's cabin," he ordered. If the inpilot had any protest to voice he didn't want to hear it. She had saved all their lives, and until her own life was terminated by the Guild, she had a right to be treated well. "Clean her up." The guard started to say something—probably that it wasn't his job to do so—but a scowl from Masada quieted him. The professor didn't want to hear that either.

The truth was that his own nerves were hanging by a thread. If the problem with the navigational programs hadn't been so engrossing, he might have actually paid attention to what was going on in the ainniq, and that would have been disastrous. His *iru* nature had a hard enough time dealing with mundane environments that were new to him; he knew he had no coping mechanism whatsoever for a trip through hell.

*I'll be very glad to go home*, he thought. *I'll write a book or two about the ainniq and the outworlds, and be happy to never set eyes on either of them again.*

He felt exhausted and wanted to lie down and rest, but he knew that first he should check the ship and just make sure everything was all right. The sabotage which had taken out their pilot and their navigational system had been a hellishly efficient piece of work, and he just didn't want to discover there were any more surprises waiting for him. His nerves couldn't take another ride like that last one.

But the ship looked sound enough, and Ra's guards were restless but uninjured. The inpilot told him that all the programs he'd cleaned up were checking out okay. He went last to the pilot's cabin to see how the girl was doing. Just to check. She wasn't awake to answer his questions, of course. But it reassured him to see her with the blood cleaned off her face, and her torn clothes arranged in some semblance of decency.

Phoenix was with her, but not by her side. He was sitting at the pilot's auxiliary console controls, deeply engrossed in some bit of programming. Masada took that in stride for a moment—and then realized just what it meant. They had shut him out of the bridge for security reasons, and he had used the time to hack into the ship's system.

The words exploded out of him in anger, venting all the tension of the past few hours. "You fool!"

Phoenix looked up. His expression was strange, not at all the defiance Masada would have expected. Not apology either. You would think that upon being caught breaking into the outship's databank he would evince one response or the other, either defensive hostility or a humbling attempt at self-preservation. Masada walked angrily over to the console, flashing it an override message that would keep Phoenix from shutting it down before he could see what he'd been working on. But the hacker didn't even try. He seemed more stunned than anything; perhaps this was the first time he'd given thought to what the consequences would be if he were caught.

Death, if the offense was great enough. Or at the very least a brainwipe. The Guild wouldn't stand for a hacker having seen their code, least of all one who was already involved in Guild business. Masada could protect him for minor offenses, but this . . . this might be beyond any fixing.

He looked down at the screen and saw a segment of the outship's security code. Bad, very bad. Stupid boy. There were times you didn't play games with the Guild, and this was one of them.

Then Phoenix looked up at him and said, very quietly, "Who wrote this code?"

The question took him aback. "What?"

"Who wrote the code?" He pointed to the segment on the screen, then fed it some mental command that made it scroll upward. There was a strange intensity to his manner, that Masada couldn't read. "Who designed it?"

He took a closer look. It was a familiar program, one he'd helped edit in his more active days. He tried to remember who had designed it. "Why?"

For a moment Phoenix said nothing. He stared at the bed where Jamisia lay. Then he said: "It's the same guy."

"Who?"

"Lucifer. The same programmer."

He said sharply: "Are you sure?"

"It's the same use of memory. The same . . . I don't know, I guess rhythm is the best word. The way it's arranged. Trust me, I've spent so long staring at Lucifer's code I'd recognize it anywhere." He laughed shortly, a sound without humor. "I'll bet if you chart this fucker out, it even makes a pretty picture."

Masada stared at Phoenix for a few seconds in silence. Then he leaned over to enter the commands which would copy the program for him. Phoenix stopped him and handed him a small black chip. "Already did. Thought you'd want it."

He started to say something—and then he remembered whose program that was. And he could no longer get the words out. Or any words.

Something of that revelation must have showed, for Phoenix said quietly, "You know him."

"I know his code. I'd have to see more than one sample of it to be sure."

*Devlin Gaza.*

And yes, the Director fit the parameters. Right down to the one condition Masada had always insisted upon . . . that Lucifer's designer would have made arrangements to collect and study the virus. What better collection facility than the whole of the Guild's security network? What better way to study the virus than to be ordered to do so by the Prima?

*If he is to be questioned, it will have to be done most carefully. He's very good . . . and the Prima won't want to believe that he's guilty. The proof must be undeniable.*

"But you think you know who it is," Phoenix pressed.

Masada said nothing. Thoughts were a storm in his brain, and he was struggling to sort them out.

"Hey, if I helped in this, I want to know what happens."

He put up a finger in front of Phoenix's mouth, a warning to silence. "You will, in time. You can be the one who announces to the moddie world that Lucifer's maker went down in flames. You can even take credit for it, if you like. But not now. Now . . . I need your silence. Not a quality you're accustomed to, but consider it a challenge."

Had Devlin Gaza been the one to sabotage the ship? He'd have had the access . . . and the motivation.

If so, he would think they were dead now.

Masada had to stop the inpilot from informing anyone otherwise.

He reached out suddenly and grabbed hold of Phoenix's headset. The motion was so unexpected that the hacker actually
yelped as he pulled it off.

"You're offline for the duration," he said. "Consider it the
price of fame." Phoenix started to protest angrily, but he hushed
him. "You want to be part of this? Then you have to be dead to
the world for a few days. Your choice."

It took a few seconds. There was no choice, really. Masada
knew it.

That taken care of, he went off to talk to the inpilot.

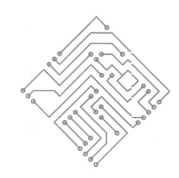

The manner in which a man lies can sometimes reveal more of his nature than the truth.

C. J. AMBERLEIGH,
*The Art of Inquisition*

# GUERA NODE
# TIANANMEN STATION

"**A**H, DEVLIN, come in."

He entered the interview room, saw no one else was about, came over to the Prima, and kissed her on the cheek. Did she seem cold? She hoped not. As yet, she had no reason to be cold to him. One did not damn one's lovers without proof.

On the other hand, when proof was promised . . . one had to be prepared.

"Business?" he asked.

"Yes. A few questions. Please, have a seat."

He took a position precisely opposite her across the conference-sized table and poured a glass of water from the pitcher before him. He offered it gallantly to her, and when she turned it down, set it down in front of himself, perfectly centered.

"Devlin, I . . . need to ask you some things about your work."

"Ask away."

"I need it to be on the record." She paused. "Verified."

His expression darkened. Was that guilt? Or only the valid concern of a man whose mistress had just asked him to submit to a proof of his honesty?

*If he is innocent, truly innocent, I may be wounding our relationship in a way that will never heal.*

She had no choice. It was her duty.

She hoped he was innocent. She prayed he would forgive her.

"May I ask what this is about?" he said.

She hesitated. "I would rather that be under verification. Please, Dev." She smiled, and hoped it looked genuine. "Indulge me."

He looked as if he might protest, but then spread his hands

wide in a gesture of acceptance. "You are my Prima. Your word is law."

She flashed an icon to call in the technician. He was a quiet and efficient man who quickly set up the equipment needed to establish a verification link and record the results. Devlin seemed to be cooperating . . . though she had been warned this would be the case. If he were innocent, she'd been told, this process would prove it. If he were guilty, then he was skilled enough to manipulate the verification process so that it still proved him innocent.

*The process is all*, Masada had told her.

*I'm sorry, Dev. So sorry.*

Within a few minutes the link had been established, and the feed from Devlin's wellseeker was visible on the technician's screen. Theoretically it was a direct link, with data being outloaded before the subject had access to it. Theoretically.

She began by asking him simple questions to which she already knew the answers. He understood the process and showed no impatience. It was a procedure they used often with Guild personnel, whenever security was in question. Devlin was used to being on the other side of the monitor, true, but at least he knew what it was about.

He didn't know that all the data was being shunted to Masada, who was watching the proceedings through the room's cams. He didn't know that the Paradise hacker was there helping him, because, in Masada's words, "Gaza knows my style and how to guard against it." He didn't know that the Prima was connected to them both, and that she flashed Masada ARE YOU READY? and waited for confirmation before moving on to more serious questions.

"Baseline established," the technician said. No doubt it was being compared to previous readings as well, to provide a biological portrait of Devlin Gaza that was as close to *normal* as possible.

They also knew what his stress patterns looked like, of course. All Guild employees had to test for that when they were first hired, and Devlin Gaza was no exception.

Finally she said, "I have some questions to ask you about Lucifer."

LIGHT STRESS, the technician sent. Well, Devlin was surprised by the question. That was reasonable.

"Had you ever seen the virus prior to when it was reported to me?"

"No," he said. There was a pause, and then VERIFIED appeared in her field of vision.

As expected.

"Do you have any knowledge of Lucifer that you haven't reported to me?"

He hesitated, then smiled faintly. "Probably a few tidbits of data theory I didn't bother you with, but if you mean, am I hiding anything, then the answer is no."

VERIFIED.

He said, "May I ask what this is about now?"

She held up a hand to ward off the question. "Later. When we're done." She looked into his eyes and felt a sudden clenching in her heart. *Is this the last time I will ever look at you as a lover? Will you be a criminal to me after today?*

*Please be innocent. Please.*

"Tell me about your thoughts, when Lucifer was first described to you."

He was silent for a moment, trying to remember. That was fine. The purpose of the question was to give Masada time, so that he and his protégé could use the verification gateway to hack into Devlin's own internal programs. Searching for something which, if found, would be an all but certain statement of guilt.

She asked other questions, similarly intended. The minutes passed. She watched his face as he spoke, tracing with her eyes the features she had grown to love.

Then those features were suddenly overlaid with words.

WE'RE IN.

How strange, to talk to a man while others rummaged around inside his head. How . . . violating.

She waited until he had finished answering her last question, then drew in a breath as she gathered herself for the true test. "Devlin . . . do you have connections to anyone in the Hausman League?"

He looked her straight in the eye and said: "No."

The technician flashed to her: VERIFIED.

And a second later Masada's message followed: HE'S OVER-RIDING IT.

She felt her own heart miss a beat at that news. Thank God she wasn't hooked up to that thing herself. Evidence of stress in any form was as good as damnation in her position.

And he showed no stress, none at all. Of course. Masada had said it would be so.

*No man who designed such a virus would ever trust himself to a verification program,* he had said. *There'll be an override somewhere, a special program that makes sure the readings are exactly what he wants them to be. Question him long enough, and I can search for it.*

Implied guilt, in a neat little data package. Not enough to convict him—that would take more—but enough to call for a trial. Enough to tell her that the time had come to remove this man from her life, this man who had won her heart and then betrayed her most sacred trust.

*Why?* she wanted to beg him. *Why have you done this to me—to your Guild—to your people? I thought you believed in the same things that I did. I thought that you shared my dreams.*

"Have you ever deliberately taken action to put Earth's status at risk?"

She thought she saw a flicker in his eye then. A hint of recognition. Had the pattern of her questioning given away the game? If so, it was intended to.

"No," he said firmly.

VERIFIED, the technician sent.

*Oh, my love, my love, you slip farther through my fingers with each word, each thought. . . .*

NO QUESTION ABOUT IT, Masada sent. I DOUBT THE VERI-FICATION PROGRAM IS EVEN CONNECTED WITH HIS REAL WELLSEEKER. HE'S FEEDING YOUR TECHNICIAN PREPACK-AGED RESPONSES. I'M COPYING THE EVIDENCE OF IT NOW.

She asked a few more questions, these more innocent than the last. She was biding her time now, waiting for Masada's next signal. When Devlin paused to take a drink of water, she graciously didn't rush him. There was one test left, which would absolutely reveal whether or not Devlin was running programs to fool the verification process. A simple test, traditional in form, one might even say primitive. Sometimes she liked those the best.

Then the signal came. DONE, Masada sent. Devlin's defensive programs had been copied. They could be gone over later at leisure in the search for evidence of wrongdoing.

She waited a few minutes more, then said, "I have someone else who would like to ask you a few questions."

The door behind her opened, admitting Masada. She watched Devlin's face.

It paled.

No change in expression, beyond the twitching of a brow. No real sign of tension, save the tensing of the muscles at the corner of his mouth. But Devlin was *nantana* through and through, and understood social interaction well enough to hide his emotions.

She was *nantana*, too, and knew how to read them despite that.

*You son of a bitch*, she thought. *You thought that he was dead. Only one man would think that.*

She looked to the technician. "What were the readings as Masada came in?"

He showed her the screen. Level, absolutely level. Not a tremor in his whole biosystem to match that response of shock on his face. Even a nonprogrammer like herself could see how damning that was, how clearly he had done something to feed the verification program lies. All that agitation, and not a single peaked reading to show for it.

*My poor, stupid, traitorous love.*

She nodded to Masada, who left the door open. There were four armed guards outside. "No more questions for now," she said quietly. She could feel the weight in the corner of her eye, and hoped that no tears would come in public. She was the Prima of the Ainniq Guild, and a certain strength of demeanor was expected. No matter what.

"No more questions until trial."

She left before Devlin could respond.

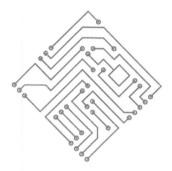

Sometimes the only way to preserve a life is to destroy it.

J. XAVIER MONROY,
*What Price Destiny?*

# PARADISE NODE
# PARADISE STATION

**M**IKLAS TRIDAC was not in a good mood.

It had been nearly an E-week now since the girl had evaded his people. A humiliating failure, that. Two teams of trained operatives and half a million to cover costs, and still she had gotten away. One girl, unarmed, a stranger to the outworlds, versus two dozen of his best.

Not good. Not good at all.

It was Ra's fault, of course. She had proven to be a major irritant from day one of this project. First she had confiscated his weapon shipments, then she'd had her customs people harass his operatives, and now . . . now she had the girl. Tridac's power was vast and its resources almost unlimited, but even the Corporation wasn't about to raid the household of a Guild official.

None of which would matter to them when he reported his failure. The Corporation didn't care much for excuses.

He was about to call up the day's intelligence report—it came to him in hourly increments, a breakdown of every operational statistic that might possibly impact the girl's behavior—when there came a knock on his door. "Come in," he called out, and he thought, *It had better be good news.*

It was Dhera, one of his lieutenants, and although her face was impassive as always, her step seemed confident as she came to him where he sat and laid a piece of plastic on the desk before him. He noted the heading which revealed it to be a communiqué from the Guildmistress' office, one of the thousands that his people were scanning through various illegal means. This one seemed to come from the office of Sonondra Ra herself.

MIA PRIMA,

IN ACCORDANCE WITH YOUR INSTRUCTIONS I AM RELEASING THE GIRL. SHE HAS ASKED FOR TRANSPORTATION, AND I HAVE ASSIGNED HER AN INSHIP, TERM OF USE INDEFINITE.

PLEASE NOTE THAT I DO NOT CONSIDER THIS A WISE COURSE OF ACTION. I AM NOT AT ALL CERTAIN THAT THE PARTIES WHO PURSUED HER HAVE ABANDONED THE CHASE. THERE IS EVIDENCE OF THEIR CONTINUED PRESENCE ON MY STATION. I URGE YOU TO RECONSIDER, AND IF YOU DO NOT WISH HER TO REMAIN IN MY DOMAIN, THEN GIVE HER SHELTER IN SOME OTHER NODE.

A BILL FOR THE USE OF THE INSHIP WILL BE FORWARDED TO YOUR OFFICE.

SONONDRA RA

PARADISE NODE

He read it over three times before he responded. Making sure. Savoring the moment. "Is it possible she knows we intercepted this?"

"No, sir."

He looked up at her. "You're sure?"

"Quite sure, sir. We've taken all possible precautions. Ra's security hasn't responded with so much as a cursory probe."

He allowed himself a smile. A small one, not of triumph— that would be premature at this point—but anticipation. "All right. You've done well. Now I want to know what ship she's taking, and the time and place of departure. And I want you doubly certain that Ra knows *nothing* of your inquiries. One hint of any security response, and you warn me immediately."

"I understand, sir."

The girl was leaving Paradise Station. Even better, she was leaving alone, and Tridac would know where and when. With news like that he could call in another team of operatives, specialists in safespace interception. Within hours of the girl leaving Ra's station, Tridac would have her in his possession.

He allowed himself the indulgence of a real smile then, and hurried to give the proper orders.

The ship was a small one, and it left from a public dock, presumably because Ra expected her private facilities to be under surveillance. Half a dozen guards in civilian disguise had escorted Jamisia Shido safely there, seen her aboard, and stood by while she received her transit instructions and backed out of the ring and into the blackness of space.

So Miklas' men had reported. They had also reported that there was no one on board with her, which meant that the girl could pilot her own ship. Good enough. It also meant that even if the ship had armaments, she'd be hard pressed to use them; mustering a sound defense while in flight usually required one mind devoted to nothing else. If they kept her running fast and hard, she wouldn't have time to take action against them.

Miklas drew in a deep breath as his own ship launched and tried not to feel too exultant. The girl wasn't exactly in his hands yet . . . but she would be soon, and when he delivered her safely to the Board of Directors, they'd reward him as his action deserved. Perhaps someday he might even earn a seat in that august body himself.

"I've got her on screen," his pilot informed him.

The skies were crowded, transports and shippers and yachts and pods all maneuvering for the proper alignment to enter or leave station space. There was no way to reach the girl now, and certainly no way to chase her down safely. Traffic Control would have the Pol on him faster than he could give the orders.

"Follow at a distance," he ordered. "Vary the approach path."

She was heading away from the ainniq, toward a less densely populated sector. That was perfect, Miklas thought. The last thing he wanted to be doing was tripping over tourists as he chased the girl.

Hopefully it wouldn't come to that. Hopefully the Fed ID on his own ship would reassure her that everything was on the up-and-up, and she would submit without a fight. But this chase had thrown him too many surprises already, and he wasn't going to bet on anything going right. Tridac Corporation didn't want to hear about another failure.

He sent out a signal to his waiting ships, telling them where to meet up with him. There was an industrial station in that sector they could use for cover and a harvester compound right next to it. His people could tuck a good dozen ships in behind there and be ready to come to his aid as soon as he called for them.

She was well out of Paradise Station's space now and past the tourist sector. The last garish casino station passed behind them, and then a few hotel rings, and finally only open space and the stars lay ahead. Thus far she didn't seem to have noticed him. Or maybe she simply thought that a ship from Federated Safespace Security was nothing to worry about.

He gave the orders that would bring them in closer and thought, *So sorry to disappoint you.*

She didn't appear to notice him at first. Or she noticed, but didn't worry. He told his pilot to keep to a direct approach and slowly come in closer. Half the distance between them was slowly taken up. Closer, closer . . .

"She's pulling ahead," the pilot told him.

"Stay with her."

It would be clear to her now that a fed ship was pursuing her. Would she try to get away from it, or just establish a safe distance and wait to see what happened?

"Picking up speed now," his pilot warned him.

So much for that question. He nodded for the pilot to keep pace and then sent out a direct signal to her. It started with an ID code that verified his FSS identity. It ended with a command to slow down and prepare for boarding, allegedly for a routine security search. Such procedures were not uncommon in this stretch of space, where smugglers and their patrons were known to congregate, and hopefully she would reason to herself that if she truly had nothing to hide, the easiest thing was to simply submit to a cursory search and let the fed see that for themselves. Dozens of tourists and business folk made the same choice every day.

He waited in silence, wondering what her answer would be.

"Picking up speed," his pilot said again. Miklas didn't need to be told this time; he could see quite clearly on the screen that the ship was pulling away from them. *All right*, he thought, *so it won't be easy.*

"Get us into combat range," he ordered. He had two gunners on board, crack men from Tridac headquarters, and he signaled for them to get ready. "I want the engines, and only the engines," he told them firmly. "Disable the ship, don't destroy her."

So close and yet so far. . . .

He could feel the pressure shove him back into his chair as the ship accelerated suddenly; he felt the thrill of the hunt heat his blood. She was running now, and both of them knew it. There was no question of what the outcome would be. He knew from his spies that he was better equipped than she was for either battle or extended flight. At this speed she couldn't even dock somewhere for safety, but would soon have to head out into truly empty space, where he could run her down at his leisure. Yet she was running. Human instinct, the eternal dance of predator and prey.

"Stay with her," he muttered.

Closer and closer they came, his pilot maneuvering to get them a clear shot at the girl's engine housing. As they finally drew into position, he saw his gunner stiffen in anticipation, ready to fire . . . and then suddenly the other ship swerved, and he cursed as he aborted the shot.

"We'll get her," Miklas promised.

She was fleeing them now at full speed, her flight pattern erratic. No doubt that was deliberate, Miklas mused, to keep them from being able to fix her in their target field. Not a bad move, for a habitat girl. He doubted that before this journey she had ever flown anything more complicated than a pleasure yacht.

"Station coming up to port," his pilot told him.

It was the harvester station, surrounded by a field of massive ore samples, some nearly as large as the station itself. Did she mean to try to take shelter behind one of them? She was going too fast for such a maneuver. And if she thought she would thread her way through that field to throw him off her tail, then she was stupider than he thought. His outworld pilot could handle a ship far better than any habitat fugitive. Besides, he had three ships hidden behind that station that would join in the chase as soon as she came around it. The chase was all but over.

*You were a good opponent,* he thought to her. *But the chase is only truly enjoyable when it ends in victory.*

She was heading for the far side of the station now, skirting the ore in a zigzag path meant to throw off pursuit. His own ship was larger and not quite as maneuverable, but his pilot was good and managed to keep pace. His gunner couldn't land a shot on her, though he tried several times; one slammed into a vast piece of ore with enough force to split it in two, sending sparks showering into the blackness.

But that didn't matter. They were coming within range of the other ships now, and as soon as those moved into position, the chase would be over. Barely a minute more . . .

"Get ready," he warned them over the com.

She was picking up speed again. Making for open space. Did she hope to outrun them?

"Now!" he ordered.

They moved out from behind the station and took up position ahead of her. In unison they fired warning shots across her bow, a gesture replete with warnings: *We're out here. There are three of us. Give up the chase now and save yourself the trouble of being shot down.*

He hoped she would slow down. Any sane pilot would.

"She's accelerating," the pilot said.

He gritted his teeth. *All right, if that's the way she wants to play it.*

She turned. Toward the ore field.

*What the hell—?*

Maybe she meant to take shelter behind one of the captured meteors. Maybe she meant to try to dodge between them, slipping through spaces where the larger ships could not follow. Maybe she just meant the move to confuse them, or to dodge their fire, or . . . who knew what was going through her head?

She couldn't make the turn fast enough. No pilot could. Perhaps if she'd been born in the outworlds, she would have known that and adjusted her course accordingly. But she wasn't. And she didn't.

She hit the meteor head-on with a force that sent huge chunks of ore spinning off into space. The explosion was a burst of light that filled the viewscreen, all the more blinding to his eyes because it was unexpected. A second later, warnings began to sound from the pilot's console as bits and pieces of the shattered ship went flying across their flight path. Her ship. Her engines. Her body.

He just stood there and stared. There were no words for such a moment. Not even curses had power enough.

"Sir—"

He waved all questions to silence. His hand, he noticed, was shaking.

"Check for biosigns," he said at last. "Get me confirmation."

The pilot's tone was almost apologetic as he said, "They're there, sir. Just pieces. I'm sorry."

*Sorry isn't going to save my neck when the Board finds out.*

Amazing, how fast your career could disappear. All in an instant, like a ship exploding into a vast wall of rock. One moment there, and the next . . . debris.

He drew in a long breath, shut his eyes for a minute, and at last growled, "Take us home."

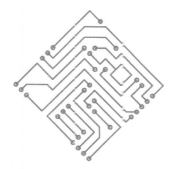

Those who hope to lead with strength cannot afford to let others see in them any sign of personal weakness.

What they hold in their hearts, of course, is another matter.

SORTEY-6,
*On Human Power*

# GUERA NODE
# MOSKVA PRISON STATION

**"I**T'S TIME."

Devlin Gaza looked up at the guards in the doorway, drew in a deep breath, and nodded. His eyes had been bloodshot for lack of sleep, but he'd had his wellseeker correct that. The moisture content of his skin had been corrected also, so that its dull, dry state wouldn't reveal his exhaustion. His fear.

Now, as they gestured for him to leave his cell, he wondered if those had all been good choices. Would she be more moved by seeing him thus, without visible sign of fear, or would he gain more sympathy by appearing to be a mere shell of a man, tormented by guilt and anxiety? Such signs meant much to a *simba*, and making the right choice could well make the difference between life and death for him.

But it was too late to change things now. He rose to his feet and left the cell as ordered, falling into place in the center of a squadron of a dozen armed guards. A dozen! Good God, what did they think him capable of, that such force was deemed necessary? He was a programmer, not a warrior!

*They think you are a terrorist,* an inner voice intoned. *And they know you work with terrorists. So is all this really such a surprise?*

Terrorist. What a joke. An ancient word, applied blindly to anyone the Guild would like to blame for their troubles. Didn't they understand what the League was all about? Couldn't they open their minds enough to grasp that the destiny of mankind was something you sculpted with care and precision, not something you left to chance? It had been centuries since the League had last been accused of true terrorism, that blind, random violence which all civilized stations abhorred. Couldn't they under-

**551**

stand that this was about much more than that? This was about the very future of humankind.

*Look,* he had begged her after the trial, *you know and I know how much we need to be free of Earth. All I did was provide the excuse. It is such a terrible thing to leave them to make their own fate, without our technology, without our aid? It's barely a shadow of what they did to us!*

And then: *We need to be free of them, Alya, you know that as well as I do. Can you honestly condemn me for trying to make that freedom possible? Take what I've given you and use it! My God, there are Guildmasters who would sell their souls for something like this—*

She had said nothing. Nothing.

Ten years his mate, his lover, his partner. He thought he knew her.

Nothing.

They were taking him to the dock of the prison station, he saw. Thus far they had told him nothing of where they were going, or why. When he asked them, the guards did not even turn their heads to acknowledge his speech. He tried to access the prison's innernet, hoping to route the query elsewhere, but though his headset made the connection his queries were shunted to a dead end and extinguished. Of course. They had given him a headset to facilitate communication and biological observation—they had locked it down onto his head in the manner common with prisoners—but they were hardly going to allow the galaxy's most notorious programmer free access to their system.

He could have been free in a day if he'd tried hard enough, despite that. He could have reprogrammed his interface and sprung the locks and reassigned the guards and prepped a ship and gotten out of there, with enough time to spare to compose a farewell speech and post it to the outernet for all to see. In any system run by computers he was master, and all their precautions could not stop him from doing what he wanted. Not even Masada could stop him.

But that way he would have lived his life in hiding, the most notorious fugitive ever known to the outworlds. Where would he run to? What friend would protect him? Any station that took him in would be assuring its own Isolation, the most dreaded of all Guild punishments. And the Hausman League was certainly under close observation now; running to them would be the same as running right into the arms of the Guild. No, it was better this way. Tell Alya the facts of the case, plain and simple, and trust that in time she would understand what he had done, and pardon him.

She was Gueran, after all. She hated Earth as much as he did.

In the dock was a small outship, Guild symbols bright on its hull. That was a good sign, he told himself. As long as only the Guild was involved in this, as long as the outworld press had no real idea what was going on, he still had a chance. They could keep this a secret as they kept so many other things a secret, and take advantage of his virus—or not—as they chose. Yes, the outship was an excellent sign.

They brought him to a small launch lounge and had him sit in one of the padded chairs. Mere minutes later he felt the ship shudder, and knew it to be leaving the prison station. "Where are we going?" he asked. He didn't really expect an answer, and he didn't receive one. All right; if silence was what they wanted, he could play that game, too. Sooner or later someone must tell him something; his rank demanded it.

After the ship was well clear of the station, and its gravity stabilized at a comfortable, if somewhat hi-G level, they indicated he should get to his feet once more and follow them. He obeyed. He knew this style of ship, so he wasn't surprised when they indicated that he should turn to the right—that would bring them to the main passenger chamber, where any manner of interview or interrogation might take place. Two guards entered first, with him behind, and the remainder of the small troop either following or spreading out in the hallway he'd just left, presumably to discourage flight.

As if there was anywhere to run to.

The door slid open and he stepped inside. Harsh lights glared in his face, blinding, unexpected. He raised a hand to shield his eyes. There were people in the room, rank upon rank of Guild uniforms . . . and civilians as well. He saw to his horror that some of the latter weren't even Guerans—unthinkable!—then looked to the source of the lights and saw vidcams whizzing about, vying for the best possible view of him.

*Oh, my God. The press.* He felt a cold clenching in the pit of his stomach as he recognized the sigils of major news industries adorning the headsets of some of the spectators. If the press was here . . . He shuddered. That was bad, very bad. Once news got out of exactly what he had done, all the rules of the game would change. Had she done that already? Surely Alya wouldn't, Alya who loved him, Alya who understood.

And then she was before him. He didn't even recognize her at first. Her face was unpainted, a blatant defiance of all Gueran custom. He had seen her thus in their private chambers, of course, but that was different; here, where her authority was absolute, the lack of *kaja* seemed almost primitive, too bizarre to absorb. Her every expression could be read now, by strangers who would attach whatever meaning they chose to each subtle movement. While he . . . he was given no hint as to her purpose or mood, such as the *kaja* would have provided. The lack of paint made her vulnerable in fact, but as she stood before him thus, it was he who felt most naked because of it.

"Alya—" he began.

She glared at him, and rightfully so. Even when he was in favor, he had never been permitted to use her common name in public. It was the lights—they were making him crazy—and all those vidcams buzzing around his head, hungry for the most dramatic angle, dizzying him until he couldn't think straight. He needed his surroundings to be ordered and regular, measured, precise. Not this chaos of wildly flying vidcams, with a hundred strangers standing behind them.

"Quiet," she ordered. Her voice was like ice. Heart pounding, he obeyed. The sight of her face, naked in such company, was so bizarre he could scarcely begin to interpret it. But she was *nantana* as well as *simba*, and such kaja never did anything without purpose.

She turned her back to him then, to face the crowd gathered about them. He felt a guard's hand on his shoulder, warning him to be still. How could he be otherwise? They'd run an inhibitor through his wellseeker that slowed all the long muscle response in his body. He'd learned to walk despite the awkwardness, but he sure as hell couldn't run. Or fight. Or do . . . anything else they might expect of him.

*Alya! You know me, you know my values, surely you understand why I did this! It may be a crime on the books, but surely you know why it was necessary! You can still save me, Alya!*

She began to speak then, her voice without emotion, her body unusually still, bereft of its usual lexicon of gestures. Clearly she meant for no human to have insight into what she was feeling at this moment.

"Citizens of the outworlds." The vidcams ceased buzzing about his head and turned to her. "Men and women of the press. Representatives of Terra proper, and of all the Terran stations. I thank you for coming to Tiananmen Node, to stand as witnesses to my judgment.

"Today's announcement follows on a two-year investigation of the virus known as Lucifer, and lengthy interrogation of all those responsible. Today the people responsible for that virus will meet justice."

Was there a hesitation in her voice, a faint break between words in which emotion might be glimpsed? He prayed that it was so, even as his heart went cold with dread. She loved him, didn't she? Loved him still? If so, she could hardly condemn him. Could she?

"Even as we speak here, conspirators in a dozen nodes are being arrested. Their fate will be that which they intended for Earth: to be Isolated from the galactic community, denied all congress with the outworlds, until the end of time." She paused, letting the enormity of that sentence hit home. "It was what they tried to manipulate us into doing to all Terrans, so I consider it a suitable judgment."

She glanced at Devlin, then quickly away. He could read nothing in her eyes.

"We of the Guild are not a political entity, using our power to facilitate the dominance of one world over another. And we will not be used as such. The Guild's purpose has always been to contact the descendants of Earth and bring them safely through the ainniq, so that they can share in what we have built here. This we have done, for centuries. Some of the Hausman worlds which our scouts rediscovered had only the most primitive settlements, with Variants that were barely human, who had no knowledge of their heritage. We rescued our lost cousins, we educated them, and we made them part of our society. We forced others to accept them as well, and fought wars when necessary to guarantee that acceptance. That is what the Guild exists for: to find *all* of Earth's lost colonies, so that *all* the children of the human race might be reunited at last.

"We knew where Earth was from the start, of course, for we had the ancient maps. We *chose* to go find her. We *chose* to bring the unaltered children of Terra into our society, because it is their birthright. So did the founders of the Guild believe, and so do I believe as well."

Now she looked again at Gaza, and her gaze was frigid. He felt his heart stop beating for a moment, and a band of steel seemed to contract about his ribs, so that he could hardly breathe.

"*This man,*" she pronounced—and there was no emotion in her voice, absolutely none, as if that whole part of her had suddenly gone dead—"This man, Devlin Gaza, intended to destroy all that we have built. This man intended to use our ancient hatreds to split the human race asunder—again—so that the sons and daughters of Earth would live and grow in ignorance of each other. Such action would be criminal for any man, but for a *Guildsman* . . . it is unforgivable. It is an insult to everything we stand for. Everything we believe in. Everything we *are.*"

He started to move, to voice some protest—if he couldn't save himself, at least he could speak for his cause—but the guard at his side snapped, "Silence!" Something in his headset buzzed something in his brainware, which jarred some vital neural connection out of alignment. And he no longer remembered how to speak.

IT'S OVER, DEVLIN. The words that appeared before him were hers, though he couldn't say how he knew that for sure. PROVE YOURSELF A MAN AT THE END, AND GO WITH DIGNITY.

His headset would not let him respond.

"Variants, Terrans, members of the press." Her tone was utterly formal, the pitch and cadence of an empress addressing her court. "I have called you here today to see how such a crime is punished. I want no rumors of leniency for those who wear the

Guild's sigil. What is unacceptable in other humans is ten times more unacceptable in us, and will be punished accordingly." She nodded toward Gaza, a sign for the guards who flanked him. "Take him."

He couldn't fight them. He couldn't protest. With his speech centers shut down, he couldn't even cry out her name. When he tried to move, he discovered that they'd increased the inhibitors on his motor control, making every motion an agony of effort. Numbly he managed to force each foot to move, so that he would not fall on his face as the black-clad guards dragged him forward.

The press followed, vidcams buzzing overhead, with other guests behind. God, how he hated them! Hated them all. How could they not understand what he had done for them? They should be crowning him with their glory and gratitude, not forcing him into exile.

They brought him back to the dock. There was a small pod there now, which hadn't been present before. Suddenly he saw where this was heading. Terror gripped his heart, and in panic he tried to pull from the guards. The defiance lasted but a second, and then a command from someone's headset shut down several more muscle sets. By the time they got him to the pod, he could barely walk, and his arms were all but useless.

*NO!* He screamed it in the silence of his own head. *NO!!!!*

They put him inside the pod. They strapped him in. They let him see the navigational chart before they shut the door, so that he would understand exactly where the pod was going. Vidcams buzzed about the edge of the door until it finally shut, fighting to get that last shot of his horrified expression.

The last thing he saw was her eyes. Cold, so cold. Had his lover ever had eyes like that?

GO QUICKLY, the words came in his head. And then, after a pause: I DID LOVE YOU, DEV.

*Alya!*

The pod began to move. Slowly at first, as the massive braces of the transport pulled it into position. Then there was that momentary sickness which accompanied all launches, as real grav and faux grav and a dozen other forces, inertial and otherwise, warred for dominance in his gut. But it meant nothing to him. His eyes were fixed on the screen before him, a tiny portal through which he might view his fate. He watched as the pod hurtled through space, toward the ainniq nearest the station. Slowly it took form before him, searing in its beauty, closer and larger with every passing moment. There was no more he could do; the controls were all locked until immersion, and his prison headset lacked the programs he would have needed to free them up in time.

*Prove yourself a man.*

He could sense the great predators stirring even as his tiny pod dove into the ainniq. Hunger and hatred in perfect unity, and perhaps intelligence also. Did they have a territorial sense, these sana, did they understand enough of the human worlds to hate the men who had invaded their homeland? Was this rare conquest not only dinner for them, but vengeance as well?

He tried to flee from them. He couldn't steer the pod more than a few degrees but he managed to take control of its acceleration, and he ran for all he was worth. It was a futile act, he knew, but no man could do otherwise. The patterns of predator and prey were hardwired into his human brain, and once one of the monsters caught his mental scent his hindbrain took over, prolonging the hunt as long as it could.

Not long enough, however. Never long enough.

He didn't scream until the end.

**A**lya Cairo watched the screen until the pod was gone, swallowed by the ainniq. And then she watched it yet longer, waiting. Silent. The guards by her side dared not stir, not knowing how to read her. The press was restless but respectful. They did not need access to her emotional circuits to know the pain she was going through. Her unpainted face would be splayed across news files within the hour, the ultimate story of human anguish. It was a perfect counterpoint to the death of Gaza, the imprisonment of so many League members, and the data purge which had been going on since Lucifer's origin was known.

Slowly she turned, silently facing her audience. There were no tears in her eyes, or any other sign that others might read. She nodded to someone in the crowd, who brought a small bowl to her, filled with black fluid. She did not look at it, but found it by feel, dipping her fingers into the paint within. One touch to gather up paint, then a stroke to smear it across her face. Gueran mourning custom; the vidcams buzzed with activity, preparing for the articles on Gueran social habits that would appear in newscasts later that day.

When her face was thus marked in a primitive pattern of sorrow, obscuring any natural expression as it might have obscured her kaja, she walked slowly through the crowd. Questions were tossed at her from both sides; she ignored them. Guards flanked her uneasily; she didn't seem to notice their presence. One man stood in her path long enough that a guard had to grab him by the arm and pull him out of her way; she would probably have walked right into him.

Unseeing, unfeeling, the Guildmistress Prima of the Gueran outworlds walked past guards and press, guests and advisors, into the narrow hallway that would take her to her chamber. No one followed her there. No one dared. A few vidcams flitted behind her head for a yard or two, until a signal sent by one of her people scrambled the navigator programs and they dropped to the floor with a sharp thud.

She walked on, alone.

Into her chambers. Standing there alone, silent. Seeing the icons that would enable all the systems she'd shut down an hour before, preparing for the press. RELEASE CONTROL OF TEAR DUCT FLUID PRODUCTION, she instructed her wellseeker. Tears began to seep out of her eyes. RELEASE METABOLIC INHIBITORS. Her heart began to pound heavily, flushing her cheeks with hot blood, and her measured breathing became deeper, and strained, and faster than was normal. RELEASE EMOTIVE INHIBITORS. She shut her eyes in dread as synapses opened and shut, neurotransmitters stirred, dendrites sparkled with fresh activity.

And grief, like a vast tsunami, rolled over her brain, and flooded her body, and disrupted every natural system within her, until the warnings of her wellseeker drowned out her vision in a field of bright red letters, and the real world could not even be sensed through her sorrow.

Alone in her chamber, the Guild's Prima wept.

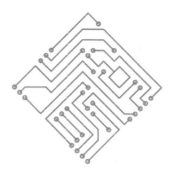

## RUSA

The forest is deep and green, its air warm and thick with moisture. Through it the hunter moves, silently, carefully, hand-carved weapon tucked against his side, poisoned darts fitted into a pouch at his hip.

There, there, the trail ends. He pauses, testing the air with his nose. A faint scent of animal musk drifts toward him on the warm breeze, assuring him that prey is near, assuring him that it cannot smell him.

He fits a dart into the long tube, lifts it to his lips, and moves forward slowly. Step by step, pressing the leaves so slowly beneath his feet that they barely make a whisper of sound.

Now he can see a clearing before him. Now, through a curtain of leaves and branches and twisted vines, he sees the deer.

*Rusa.*

The hunter feels his breath catch in his throat. Perhaps he moves. Perhaps he makes a noise. The deer looks up at him, startled, and the deep brown eyes meet his.

*Rusa,* the keeper of spirits. *Rusa,* the sacred deer, whose flesh is a house for the souls of lost humans.

He lowers the weapon from his lips. His heart is pounding. The deer does not move. What spirit wears this flesh now, whose ancestor, whose lover, whose lost child? What soul looks out from those lambent eyes, which personality chooses to make the deer step away, shift its ears, prepare to run?

He does not shoot it, of course. How can you kill a living thing, without knowing what manner of soul is inside it? How can you judge it in any one moment, when the next may require a new and different judgment?

He watches as it walks away: slowly, majestically, sensing its own invulnerability. And then, when the awe in his heart gives way to hunger once more, he turns to other trails, to hunt for simpler prey.

*KAJA: An Outworlder's Guide to the Gueran*
*Social Contract, Volume 2: Signs of the Soul*

# PARADISE NODE
# PARADISE STATION

THE OBSERVATION LOUNGE was nearly deserted when Sonondra Ra came into it. The lush padded seats surrounding glass tables were empty. The bar was shuttered, and the illumination had been turned down, allowing the distant station lights to cast gleaming lines across the floor.

Phoenix stood by the vast window looking out at the rings of Paradise. Though he had lived here for much of his life, he had rarely been in a place where such a view was possible. From here, inside the Guild complex, one could see all the rings of the station sweeping across the glittering sky, and the stately dance of pods and transports as they wove in and out of them, seeking sanctuary.

She came up beside him and just stood there for a while. Sharing the view, and the silence of the moment.

Then she said, very quietly, "You miss her a lot."

"Yeah. Pretty stupid, huh?" He brushed a lock of hair out of his eyes, then lodged both hands deeply in his pockets. "I only knew her a few days. Never figured anyone could get to me that fast."

She said it gently: "You know it had to be done."

"Yeah. I know." He sighed. "Earth aggression and all that bullshit. Had to be dealt with."

An outship was disengaging from the inner ring; its docking lights swept across the darkened room. "Tell me again how she's happier where she is."

"Her nature is Gueran. She belongs among us. Maybe not by birth, but after what Shido did to her, she has no place among Terrans. Guera will accept her for what she is. And now that Tridac's been fooled into thinking she's dead, there'll be no one coming after her. She'll have time to come to terms with what she's become. And in time she'll realize that on Guera she has no need to hide her nature."

"I would think she'd have it hard there," he said. "Your kaja system seems rather static. I mean, she's not going to change her face paint each time she . . . each time she . . . well, shifts. Is she?"

She chuckled softly. "My dear boy, there's no condition of the human soul that Guera hasn't dealt with. There are kaja even for the changing ones. Special customs, even for them."

He turned to look at her. Guidelights from the main docking ring reflected highlights across his face. "Why did you spare her life? It would have been so much easier to kill her. I'm sure the others would rather have had it that way."

Sonondra Ra smiled. "You do understand so little of us, don't you?" She gazed out at the starscape with rapt attention. "There were other Guildmasters who wanted her dead. Therefore I saved her life." She chuckled softly. "It will all make perfect sense to you once you understand our ways. As you will someday." She paused, and for a moment merely observed it all: the stars, the station, him. Then she asked, "Have you thought about my offer?"

He drew in a deep breath, and felt like a swimmer about to immerse himself in measureless depths. "You sure you want to do this?"

"I hire non-Guerans occasionally. You must know that." She paused, and it seemed to him that the strange diamond eyes glittered with amusement. "Of course, if you don't think you're up to the challenge of hacking Guild systems—"

"Like hell I'm not!" That brought a grin to his face. "Look, I really want to do this, I'm just surprised you . . . you know, trust me. Being an outsider and all."

"Trust you, my dear boy?" she smiled. "Perhaps not. But know you? Yes. Yes, I think I do." She placed a hand on his shoulder and squeezed it gently. "Come. I need you. Delhi just brought in a team of encryption specialists, and I think she's up to something. Pays us to find out what it is, don't you think?"

Phoenix nodded, and with one last look at the starscape, followed her back into the station.

About the Author to come